Bennett
MAFIA

TIJAN

Edited by Jessica Royer Ocken
Proofread by Paige Smith, Kara Hildebrand, Chris O'Neil Parece, and Amy English
Formatted by Elaine York, Allusion Graphics, LLC
www.allusiongraphics.com

Bennett
MAFIA

TO MY READERS!

A NOTE TO THE READER

To my knowledge, there is no Lakeshore Wharf.
I needed to fictionalize this area for the purposes of this book.

PROLOGUE

Fourteen years earlier

My boarding school roommate was a mafia princess.
Although I didn't learn that at first. Our beginning six months went by without a hiccup.

When I first walked into our room, I took in her bedding, which looked like a cloud with crystal lights surrounding it, the massive amount of photographs she'd taped to her wall in the shape of a heart, and the framed canvas with a quote in glittering font that read, *Fairytales Happen.*

That'd been the only pause for me, because I was not this type of girl.

I'd been shipped to Hillcrest Academy slightly against my wishes—but also not. The fighting between my parents was at an all-time high, and even though we lived in a mansion and they kept to their wing, I could still hear them. It was hard not to when I snuck up to sleep in the hallway adjacent to theirs. I was an only child, and lonely. Maybe not all twelve year olds have that insight, but I did.

I also had the insight that while I loved my mother, I loathed the battlefront that was in our home, and my shoulders sagged in relief at the quiet in Hillcrest Academy.

On the day I moved in, there'd been some shrieks, some giggling, music playing, and a mom who'd shouted at a little boy who darted under my legs and took off down the hallway, but none of that was really noise. It would never match the shouts, the

1

yelling, the sound of walls being hit, and especially not that last thing I'd heard two nights ago: a bloodcurdling scream.

I hadn't even been in my parents' hallway when I heard it. I'd been over in my wing, having given up on trying to be near them, but I'd bolted upright in my bed.

I'd laid back down after a few moments when no other sound followed, feeling and hearing my heart pounding in my chest. I wasn't altogether shocked when my dad's secretary told me the next day to start packing. I was going to boarding school.

My dad was gone the next day.

My mom cried in her room. The whole day.

I was told by Claude, our butler, when to be ready to leave. And it was only when I stood in the doorway, feeling all sorts of weird and sick butterflies in my stomach, that my mom came to the entryway. She seemed so frail.

I knew she was thin, but I would have the image of her that day seared into my brain forever.

She shuffled forward, as if walking was painful, wearing a sheer robe with a white nightgown beneath. Her feet barely peeped out from the robe, but when they did, I saw she wore her usual fuzzy-slipper thongs. They were her favorite. She wore them when she got pedicures, but today she also had a wrap around her hair, half shielding her face. The part I could see was perfectly made up, with pink crystal lipstick over her mouth and her skin caked over with complexion smoother. Sunglasses hid her eyes.

I stepped into Claude's side when I saw them. I hadn't meant to. The sight of my mom wearing sunglasses wasn't unusual, and it wasn't even unusual for her to wear them inside, but this was my day to leave.

I wanted to see my mom's eyes before I went.

She never took them off.

She knelt in front of me, where I was half hiding behind Claude now, and she opened her arms.

I ran to her, throwing my arms around her neck. I didn't care how skinny she was. I wound my legs around her waist, and still kneeling, she caught and held me. She ran a soothing hand down my back, bending to kiss my shoulder.

"I love you, my little ray of sunshine," she whispered. "Have fun at this new school. Make new friends." She squeezed me tight.

Claude cleared his throat, opening the door behind us.

I pulled back reluctantly as she let me go.

Claude already had my bags in the car. He wasn't going with me to the new school. My assigned car ride was with Janine, the secretary who'd told me I was leaving the day before. I had no doubt she'd made all the preparations for me.

As I walked out the door, I looked over my shoulder.

A single tear streaked down my mother's cheek.

That was one of the last times I saw her.

CHAPTER ONE

"Die, you fly!"

I locked eyes with a black fly, or maybe our eyes weren't locked, but he was perched on the rock next to me. He was going down. He had been harassing me for the last hour. I was outside, trying to clean up the yard, but I was going nuts with this damn thing buzzing all around me.

He was teasing me, taunting me. He flew out of the way every time I swung at him. He was too fast, and as he paused on my shoulder, I swung at the same time the screen door opened. I heard its creak across the yard right before a numbing pain exploded in my shoulder.

"Ry—did you just clock yourself?"

Fuck. Fuck. Fuck.

I groaned, my knees buckling.

I had.

I'd swung with the rock in my hands, and now I felt blood trickling down my shoulder and arm. My shirtsleeve was rapidly turning red.

The fly fucker was trying to kill me, by outsmarting me.

"Shit."

The door slammed shut, and I heard Blade's feet scuffling down the stairs as he ran to me. The gravel crunched under his weight, and then he slid in behind me. His pants would be ripped up, but knowing Blade, he wouldn't care.

4

He rarely cared about clothes. We were just happy he wore them, most of the time.

"Fuck." He swore under his breath, his very tanned and slightly oily fingers gentle as he looked at my wound. His dark eyes seemed to penetrate my shoulder before he sat back on his heels, raking a hand through his dreadlocks. "What were you doing?"

I wasn't going to admit a fly had outwitted me.

When I was doing yard work, Blade made himself scarce. For the years he'd been living with us, he'd been content to clean the inside. He did most of the cooking, cleaning, and dishes, and it wasn't uncommon for us to come home from shopping and find him wearing a maid's apron and duster—and nothing else.

So for him to come looking for me outside like this wasn't normal.

"What is it?" I jerked my head toward the house, hearing the television blaring.

His concerned eyes lifted to mine, and a whole different look slid over him.

My alarm level went up three notches.

Of the three of us living in this little cabin outside of Calgary, or Cowtown as we called it sometimes, Blade wasn't the one who got concerned about things. He enjoyed indulging in marijuana, kept his hair in tight dreadlocks, and dressed like a child from the sixties in a brown vest, no shirt, and a tie-dyed bandana over his hair. Only instead of bell-bottoms, he wore tight, frayed jeans over regular runners. He handled all our computer stuff, and when we walked inside, I wasn't surprised to find he had switched over the news he'd caught on his computer to the main television screen.

I also wasn't surprised to be watching a report from New York City.

"—ennett mafia princess has been missing for forty-nine hours now."

Ice lined my insides.

A picture of my old boarding school roommate, Brooke Bennett, flashed on the screen, along with numbers to call if she was found.

Found...

As in, she was lost?

I felt punched in the chest.

Brooke was missing.

Dazed, I reached out for a chair to sit in. Blade moved to my side.

"That's your old roommate, right?" The chair protested. Blade's hand left my arm, and his voice came from my side. "The one you had at that rich school."

I almost snorted at his wording, but I was still in a daze. I nodded instead.

Brooke. *Man.*

The news was showing pictures from her social media accounts, and she was gorgeous. Fourteen years. I don't know why that number popped into my head, but it felt right. It'd been so long since I last saw her, or was it fourteen years since we first met? One of those.

"She was always so girly," I murmured, almost to myself. She'd been so full of life.

Not me. I'd been a numbed-down, post-traumatized zombie when I walked into that room.

"Oh my gosh! You must be my roommate!" She had launched herself at me from behind the moment I entered the room, wrapping her arms around me. Her face had pressed into my shoulder.

Janine had squawked. *"Oh my."*

I'd ignored my dad's secretary and had taken one second before the girl let me go and hurried around in front of me. Her hands went to my arms, just underneath my shoulders and she'd looked me up and down.

I did the same: black oval eyes, stunning jet-black hair, a pert nose, small mouth—but lips formed just like the ones that had been a stamp on my last Valentine's Day party invitation, full and plump.

I was slightly envious, or as envious as I could get since I wasn't usually the jealous type. She had a small chin to end her perfect heart-shaped face, and her eyes were glittering and alive.

That had been the one moment when I truly was jealous of her. Life. She had what I didn't. I wasn't jealous of her looks, though if I'd had a different upbringing maybe I might've been? In a way, that was something I was thankful for. Life meant more to me than looks or things. It meant yearning for safety, smiles, the feeling of being loved.

The other girls had been jealous of her money. For a "rich kids" school, everyone seemed to be pissed about how much money they had. They always wanted more, and they seemed to know who had the most. I was toward the lower end of the wealthy crowd, but Brooke—as it had been whispered around school—was at the top.

There'd been other whispers, other looks, but we were twelve in our first year there. I didn't understand what the word *mafia* actually meant. But it was used often as a taunt by our second semester at Hillcrest. The first semester there hadn't been that kind of bullying. Some girls liked us. Some girls didn't. A few hung out with us, and our room became known as the "hot guy" room. Not because we had guys there. Far from it. I would've died if a cute guy even looked my way. No, no. Our room had the name because of all the posters and photographs Brooke plastered all over our room. All gorgeous males.

It never made sense that some of her pictures didn't look professionally taken, but the posters were real, and who wouldn't drool over a full-length shot of Aaron Jonahson, the best football player in the United States—or the celebrity actor from everyone's favorite television show, or the so-hot model that'd been a convict first. Brooke seemed to have all the guys covered, but some pictures seemed more like snapshots. Which was the truth.

I found out around the holidays: they were her family.

They weren't celebrities—not in the sense that I understood back then—they were her brothers, all four of them.

Cord was the oldest at eighteen.

Kai was fifteen.

Tanner was fourteen.

Brooke was twelve.

And Jonah brought up the rear at nine years old.

Brooke was quiet about her family, *really* quiet. But when I found out those boys were her brothers, and their names, I was fascinated. I couldn't lie about that. I just hadn't known who I was becoming obsessed about.

Cord kept his hair short, almost a crew cut above his more angular face. Brooke told me he was usually the reserved one, and artsy. She almost hissed when she used that word, as if it was a curse, but then she shrugged. "It's the truth. He wants to be a painter one day."

Next in line hadn't been Kai. She'd skipped over him and chewed on her lip, pausing before pointing to Tanner. As she did, her eyes lit up and a bright smile took over her face.

"Tanner has this shaggy hair that he bleaches blond, and sometimes it's dark when I see him. He's funny, Ry. He's *so* funny, but he also has an attitude. All the girls here would die over him, literally just die."

I still remembered all the emails she got from a tannerinyour-mama—almost her entire inbox was emails from him.

When she'd gotten to Jonah's picture, she'd quieted, but a fondness had shone through her. She'd spoken almost as if he were in the room and words could break him.

"Jonah's the baby," she said gently. "He worships Kai..." She'd paused and scratched at her forehead before continuing. "But he doesn't look like the rest of us." That's all she'd said about him.

I'd inspected the picture of her and him together. She had pulled Jonah onto her lap, her arms around him, and his still-baby cheek pressed against hers as he smiled. His skin had a darker tone than the others, but they all had the most luscious facial features. All dark eyes.

Cord and Kai had black hair in their pictures. Tanner's was lighter, and Brooke's a lovely shade of dark copper. Jonah's hair matched hers, with a twinge of curl in it too. Tanner's was long and shaggy, sticking up all over. Kai's was short, where a hand could run through it easily and it'd fall back in place—just a touch longer than Cord's barely-there hair.

I returned my attention to the television now, coming back to the present.

In the photos on the screen, Brooke's hair was still the length it'd been in school. She'd kept it trimmed just above her waist and had been adamant that no one would cut it. She'd whispered one night about a fight with her dad, that her father went after her with a pair of scissors. But her hair was still long when she told me, so whatever the fight, he hadn't been successful. And like all the other times she talked about her family, she didn't go into detail. She always said just enough so I knew what she was talking about, and then she would close up. Her shoulders would shudder before a wall slammed down, and that night had been the same.

A soft sigh left me as I continued to watch the images on the news.

Brooke had her chin up, proud, as her braided hair curved around her neck. In another she struck a sultry pose in a bikini. She could've been a model, except maybe she didn't have the height—not like me. She'd been an inch shorter than me in school, though now I had shot up even taller to five ten.

They teased us about being sisters at school.

I had loved it, though I never said a word. I didn't know if Brooke enjoyed it. She never spoke for or against it, but I could see now why people thought that way. We both had dark black hair. Okay. Maybe I couldn't see why now. That was the end of our similarities. Brooke had a rounder face. I was fairer in skin. My eyes were more narrow. My face a little longer. And taller. I was always taller.

Brooke used to sigh that I could be a model, but she was wrong. She was the future model. I saw the proof now.

She looked like she'd gotten a tad bit taller too, maybe another inch, but that was it. It didn't matter. Brooke could've been a model just because she had turned into a celebrity—which was also why the story about her being missing had been picked up by a news channel from New York City, where I didn't think she lived.

"That's her, right?" Blade prompted again. He shoved back his chair to stand as I heard the sounds of an approaching car outside.

We lived near Cowtown, but we kept to the forest for a reason. The cabin we were renting belonged to a friend of a friend of a friend of another friend, and there were probably three other sets of friends before we actually got to the owner. There was a reason for that, just like there was a reason Blade hurried to his computer, turning off the news as he brought up the feed from the electronic sensors outside.

A second later, he relaxed and flipped the screen back.

All was clear. It was our third roommate, Carol. But I wasn't paying attention to her or to the sound I heard when the screen door opened and something dropped with a thud on the floor. Carol cursed.

My eyes returned to the screen, glued there because an image of Kai Bennett appeared now.

Just like the last time I saw my friend, the bile of loathing pooled in my mouth. Kai stared right at the camera, offering whoever had taken his picture the same look he'd given me before taking my roommate away so many years ago.

While I couldn't remember the last look on Brooke's face, I couldn't get *his* out of my mind.

Death.

His eyes were dead, just like they'd been back then.

A shiver went up my spine. I'd only seen Kai Bennett in person once, but it was enough.

I hated him.

CHAPTER TWO

Thirteen years ago

"Riley, dear?"

I liked Mrs. Patricia. Most of our other instructors were mean, always snapping when they talked to us. Not Mrs. Patricia. She was nice, kind. She spoke in a soft voice, and maybe that's why it took a few minutes before I realized she was calling my name.

We were taking a test. I was focused. Question sixteen was going to fail me. I knew it, but when I felt a tap on my shoulder from the student behind me, I jerked my head up.

Mrs. Patricia was standing at the door. The headmistress was beside her, and she was not wearing the same smile as my instructor. Wait. I sat up taller in my seat. The headmistress never came for me...and her forehead seemed pinched together, her always-disapproving mouth turned even farther downward now.

That's when I took in Mrs. Patricia, really took her in. She wasn't smiling at me. Well, she was, but it was lined with sadness and something else.

She motioned for me. "Can you come here, Riley?"

I started to feel the same numbness it had taken almost a year to shed as I stood from my desk.

Sympathy. I named her missing emotion then. She pitied me. *My mother...*

I felt a ball in my throat, and it grew as I started toward her.

"Bring your test, Riley."

The headmistress barked, "Bring everything! You're not coming back."

That got everyone's attention. Their heads snapped up like mine had—those who hadn't already been watching.

Mrs. Patricia stepped away, her lips pressing together as she shot the headmistress a look before approaching my desk. She bent to pick up my books.

Collecting everything for me, she nodded. "I'll hold your things for you, Riley."

I was in trouble? Was it my mom?

I tried to ask her with my eyes, but she wasn't looking at me. In fact, as I walked next to her down the aisle and toward the door, she swallowed and looked away. She was now actively avoiding my gaze.

That wasn't good. Not at all.

"Come, Riley." There was that same curt tone from the headmistress. She flicked her hand to me, motioning toward the hallway. "You're needed."

I was needed? No one needed me.

But the headmistress was already striding away in brisk steps, and I hurried to catch up. I lowered my head, even though the hallways were empty. This was how I walked at Hillcrest. Brooke was the opposite. She held her head high, and her hands were always waving in the air. When she spoke, everyone listened, even if you didn't want to.

That had started to grate on the nerves of some of the upperclassmen girls. I'd caught the envy and bitterness coming from them, but when I mentioned it to Brooke, she'd laughed and said, "What are they going to do? Take me out?" She'd been mocking as she added the last bit, but there was a roughness in her tone.

I never brought it up again. That wasn't the normal Brooke I knew, but there were times I heard that side of her come out on the phone—when she was talking to her family. Always her family.

She was so secretive about them.

As I followed the headmistress down the hall, I'd assumed we would be going to her office, or even my room, but when she veered to the front entrance, I slowed down.

Going to the door, she turned and flicked her hand toward it, the same quick, sharp movement as before. "Your presence is needed outside." Her hand smoothed down her pencil skirt and straightened her collar before she raised her chin and began to leave.

"Oh."

I looked back at her.

A fierce frown clouded her face. Distaste flashed in her eyes. "You are not to speak a word of this to anyone. Do you understand?"

I nodded slowly.

She sniffed, rotating back around as if she were a soldier. "You are dismissed from all classes until Miss Bennett no longer needs your presence."

And with that, she walked away, her heels clipping out a sharp staccato on the floor.

CHAPTER THREE

Present day

K ai Bennett still looked the same as he had on that day: smoldering black eyes, prominent cheekbones, the same luscious features as all of his siblings.

I remembered that day, and I hated it, but the same shiver curled around my spine. It was writhing around me, because this was bad. This was so bad.

"Who wants to try Eggwhite Chips and throw up with me?" Carol tossed the bags of snacks on the counter. "Anyone? Anyone?" Her voice dropped to imitate the "Bueller? Bueller?" line from *Ferris Bueller's Day Off*. Rustling through the bags, she continued, "By the way, I got that new job, so after you give me a round of applause, I was thinking we could all get wasted tonight. The job pays better. More money for the bills, right?"

The rustling stopped.

Her voice grew clearer. "Anyone? Wasted? Bueller?"

Silence.

Absolute silence.

I had to look away, but I couldn't.

Blade had hit the pause button when Carol came in, so I was staring at those dark eyes and feeling my insides shrivel into a puddle.

I was lost in my memories again. I'd returned to that day.

I hadn't been prepared *that* day. I'd thought I was, considering the status of Kai and his family. But that day had been the first real eye opener for me as to how powerful the Bennett family was—and by Bennett family, I really mean *The* Bennett Family.

They were mafia, and they were ruthless.

Brooke had gotten word that her father and brother were coming to visit her.

We had visitor days at Hillcrest, but for Brooke to be pulled out of class and be waiting for them on the front steps of the school wasn't normal. If a family called ahead, they *would* have the student waiting for them, but usually in her *room*, not the front steps. And not with her roommate/best friend acting as a source of support.

Brooke had been pale when I pushed open those doors, hunched over with her arms wrapped around her knees. She'd lifted her head to look at me, and I saw tears streaks on her face. They were fresh.

Even as I sat beside her, she couldn't stop crying to talk. A gurgling sound had come out of her throat when she tried, so eventually I'd just told her it'd be fine.

I'd had no idea *what* would be fine, but I didn't know what else to say.

I'd pulled her into my arms, cleaned off the streaked mascara and tears, and stroked her hair and back. We sat there for forty-five minutes. The bell rang, and I tensed, knowing some of the girls would come out to see what was going on. A few of the classrooms had windows facing where we were so I had no doubt they'd seen us.

When no one came out, I glanced back.

The headmistress and three other instructors were there, their arms wide, blocking people from coming to us. I saw them shoo the others away until the next class started, and even then, the headmistress had stayed.

She looked at me, and I saw her fear.

It was brief and gone so quickly, but it stuck deep in me.

Thinking back on it now, I realized that'd been the first time I felt afraid of Kai Bennett. There'd been an uneasiness when Brooke talked about him, or because she *wouldn't* talk about him.

She talked about Cord. She was proud of him. She gushed about Tanner, and she adored Jonah. But Kai? There was a tension. She'd been scared of him.

Before, I had only thought she—I didn't know what I'd thought. I hadn't, I guess. I'd just known there was an air of mystery around him, and though I'd tried not to be, in a reverse kind of way, I had been the most fascinated with him.

Out of their whole family, Kai Bennett was the most.

He was the best looking.

He had their dark and hypnotic eyes, but they were *more* with him. More smoldering. More hypnotic. More powerful.

More alluring.

He had the same facial features as the others—a perfect, lush mouth, as if formed just for kissing. And he had the body of a professional soccer player or surfer. There wasn't an inch of softness in his pictures, and I felt my face flushing even now as I remembered how often his picture had captivated me. It had been his face that I studied the most, dreamed about the most, and fantasized about the most.

But that day he had killed it.

When their cars pulled into the school's two-mile driveway, Brooke had stood. Moments later, she'd buckled.

I'd caught her, an arm around her to hold her upright, and she'd begun to shake.

She kept hiccupping as she sobbed, but she faced forward the whole time. She never turned away. Her hand gripped mine until it went numb.

A black SUV pulled up to the school and rolled forward.

A second SUV stopped right in front of us.

A third SUV parked behind it.

A fourth lingered in the driveway, partially blocking anyone else from pulling up if they had tried.

I wasn't prepared for the spectacle that came after that.

All of the doors had opened at once.

The drivers of all four cars got out and stood guard.

Then the passenger doors opened, and more guards emerged, taking point.

The only two doors that had remained closed were the back two on the SUV right in front of us. The second SUV.

Two guards approached. They went to each side of the second vehicle, and as one, as if they'd rehearsed (and they might've), they opened the doors.

An older man wearing a suit stepped out of the door closest to us. He wasn't tall; he was average height—maybe around five eight?—and he had a full head of graying dark hair. I saw the same eyes, the same chin that Brooke had, the same face as hers and her brothers'.

This was her father.

She barely ever talked about him.

She'd never talked about her mom, either.

It was only Cord, Tanner, and Jonah.

No father, no mother, and hardly any Kai.

I'd looked over to the other side of the SUV, and *he'd* been standing there.

I'd sucked in my breath.

Everything had paused for a second—it was like the world felt a full glitch.

I had not been prepared for Kai Bennett.

Then again, how could I? It's not normal. *He's* not normal.

In photos, his pull was excessive, but in person? It was astronomical.

He'd looked up and sought his sister first. Brooke had stilled, as if feeling his gaze, and then his eyes had moved to me.

I'd felt a punch in the sternum, along with a full blast of ice.

He was cold. He was calculating. And he was ruthless. I felt it all at once.

The air had sizzled around him, power coming off of him in waves as he'd rounded the car to stand beside their father.

I'd felt a tug in my gut toward the elder Bennett. He was dangerous too. I couldn't have explained how I knew, but I felt it. I could taste it. Brooke's father wasn't the more dangerous of the two. Kai was. I couldn't take my eyes from his face. And he knew it—and how I felt that too, I had no idea.

He'd known the effect he had on me, and it wasn't normal, but he didn't care. A wave of embarrassment washed over me, heating my neck and cheeks, and it was only then that I tore my gaze away to bring Brooke closer to me. I wasn't sure if I was comforting her or myself.

"Papa," she'd rasped out, her body stiff in my arms.

"My daughter."

My skin had crawled when I heard his voice.

I'd tried to check my reaction, but when I looked away, my gaze skimmed over Kai, and his nostrils flared. He knew what I felt in response to their father; I couldn't hide it. Instead, I lowered my head and held still. I was a statue, the way I'd been when my father paced the house, in the moments his anger left their bedroom.

"Dude!" A hand waved in front of my face.

I crashed back to reality. It left a sour taste in my mouth.

I was here in the cabin, not at the school. Not on those steps. Here, Cowtown. Calgary. I wasn't there anymore, but man, I felt trapped in the past.

"Riley." Carol's head turned as she spoke to someone. "She's out, like *out* out. It's weird."

Carol stepped backward as Blade came forward.

I pulled myself out of my memories and gazed at them, standing together as they regarded me, their arms crossed over their chests.

"I'm fine. Sorry." My insides trembled. I coughed and tried to steady my voice. "I mean it. I just got...shaken for a bit."

Blade grunted. "I'll say." He went back to his computer and turned off the news a second later.

They stared at me.

"You know the Bennett mafia family?" Carol asked, speaking almost as gently as Mrs. Patricia had all those years ago.

That was the crux of it all. Even all those years ago, I'd known who they were.

There'd been another time, one I didn't piece together until later when I'd heard my father speak of them, and he'd been scared. He'd been on the phone in his study, and I'd been passing by the door. I'd heard him and stopped.

I'd never heard my father scared, and he was terrified that day.

I'd pressed my ear to the door, and I hadn't moved until he'd ended his phone call. I didn't know who the Bennett mafia were at that point. I just knew the name *Bennett* made my dad nervous, and I'd figured that was a good thing to know. A very good thing to know.

Maybe I should've put two and two together the first day I met Brooke, but it hadn't been like that.

Brooke was bubbly. She was one of those girls who could've had anything or anyone, even at that age, and she was still nice. That amount of power corrupted a person, but not her.

Even though she was an extrovert and lively and opinionated and loud, she was warm and mostly down-to-earth. Okay, maybe not down-to-earth, but she was kind. That overrode everything.

She was humble. She was *extra*, but she was humble.

That had said so much to me, even back then, and as I looked at the black screen where her brother's image had been not long ago, I wondered if she had remained true to herself until she went missing.

I felt Carol and Blade waiting for me to talk. Lowering my head, like I'd done all those years ago, I started to explain. "For a year and a half of my life, before everything went to shit, Brooke was my best friend."

• • •

It was two-fifteen in the morning, and I stared at my roommates.

They were curled up in blankets, sleeping in the living room. Blade had taken the chair, his long legs resting on the coffee table. Carol was twisted in her blanket on the couch across from me. A dribble of drool glistened on her chin, and her hair had fallen over her face.

They'd sat and listened to me as I told them everything.

What I'd said wasn't a total revelation. Blade knew I knew Brooke Bennett. They just hadn't known how much I cared for her or how much I loathed her brother. I'd told them about the day her brother and father came to see her.

I'd told them how Brooke's father took her into the park, how she didn't want to go with him.

How they'd talked.

How Kai Bennett had stared at me as we both waited, his eyes lifeless and cold.

I told them how I'd been scared to move, to look at him, to make a sound. I'd felt the same fury and violence from him that I'd seen from my father, and it had almost made me piss myself.

And then I told them how as I stood there, I'd heard Brooke cry out.

She'd folded to the ground, sobbing, as her father stood over her.

He'd just watched—*watched* as his little girl, his only girl, fell apart in front of him, and he hadn't made a move to comfort her.

I'd moved to try to go to her, but Kai had blocked me.

"She's fine," he'd said, like I was trying to bat a mosquito.

I'd hated both him and his father with the same passion in that moment. Unable to hold my anger back, I'd glared at Kai.

He hadn't cared. He hadn't even batted an eye. He'd just stared back at me, unblinking, no reaction.

When his father came back, Kai had turned to follow him.

They were both silent as they returned to the car, and almost without a pause, both got back inside.

But there *had been* a small pause, because that was the only time I saw her brother hesitate.

The guard had opened their father's door, and Bennett Sr. got inside. The door shut right away, and that guard returned to the third SUV. But Kai stood there a second, just a split second.

His gaze went to his sister, who was still crumbled in a mess on the ground.

She rocked herself, her sobs shattering me. It was the sound of true agony, as if someone had torn her soul from her heart, and he'd stared at her. One blink. His face had shuddered. Then his father had called him from inside the car, and the emotion was gone. Anything he'd felt had vanished. His face was devoid of all emotion as he'd sat inside.

The door closed.

His guard returned to his seat in this third SUV, and at once, all of the remaining guards returned to their vehicles.

There was a second's pause before the caravan moved forward.

One by one, the four SUVs had left, and as soon as they were gone, I'd sprinted for Brooke. My heart was in my throat as I slid to my knees beside her, wrapped my arms around her.

Her hand had fisted my shirt as she spoke. "He said—he said. Ka—he killed my brother."

Kai had killed him.

21

CHAPTER FOUR

There was a creak from the floorboards outside my door, and I looked up.

It'd been two days, but Blade still had concern in his eyes. Not that I could blame him.

This wasn't me. Not usually. Not anymore.

I'd been in a stupor since the news broke about Brooke being missing. There'd been no new reports, just speculation that it had something to do with the Bennett family. I knew that family was big news, but they resided up in Vancouver—Canada, where we were. Still, when news broke about Brooke, Blade monitored the stations in the States, which had learned who exactly Brooke was related to. Images of Kai Bennett, along with Tanner and Jonah, flooded the networks. It was the biggest news story down there, though the local news channels around here were more subdued. They were aware of how the Bennett family worked. If they said anything too outlandish or hinted that one of the Bennetts had something to do with Brooke's disappearance, they would feel the full force of the Bennetts' power.

It had happened before.

A reporter produced a full-hour show about the Bennett family, and she was fired the day it aired. There was no word about where she went. There were pictures of her later on blogs, but all with her shielding her face and hiding from the camera.

I never heard a peep about that reporter after that, and she never worked as a journalist again—I knew that much because a

Google search of her name brought up nothing, not even from the channel that fired her.

"You going to work tomorrow?" Blade asked.

Shit. I jumped where I'd been sitting at my desk.

He leaned against my doorframe, his arms crossed over his chest. Today he wore a black tuxedo vest, still no shirt, and his dreadlocks were pulled back in a loose ponytail.

"Um..." I groaned. I'd had the last five days off for what the nursing home thought was a family vacation.

"You might want to get a spray tan, since, you know." He smiled.

Since they all thought I'd been in Florida visiting a grandma who didn't exist.

He was right. I had a tan from being outside and doing what yard work I could between our "errand" and my time watching the news, but it wasn't a Florida tan.

I sighed. "I should go now. It's my turn to cook tonight."

His eyes got big. "Spaghetti? Please spaghetti?"

Blade enjoyed the gluten-free vegetable meatball spaghetti with zucchini noodles I made, and so did I. We worked to keep our bodies in the best shape for work reasons, but Carol wasn't the same.

Carol was wild, adventurous, and a bit quirky.

She loved junk food and every new fad. Eggwhite Chips were the latest in a bunch of new creations she'd brought home. Her stomach was a block of cement. Put anything in it, and she'd crush it and ask for seconds. On the other hand, Blade's stomach rebelled against processed food. I wasn't as exciting; I just didn't like it.

I only liked a few things: bread, some form of protein, and anything the world naturally kicked up. I usually filled up on berries or things I grew in the garden. So no, I I had not consumed the Eggwhite Chips the other night.

"Oh, and hey..." His voice dropped to his serious tone.

"Yeah?" I straightened up.

"I got a call this morning." His eyes bore into mine. "You need to get off work this weekend. We have a pick up in the States."

My mouth dried.

I nodded. "I'm on because I was off last weekend, but it won't be a problem. I'll take a holiday."

Holidays were good bargaining chips, at least for me—for us. Normal people wanted their holidays off. They wanted to spend time with friends and family, but not us. It was the time immediately after a holiday or right before a holiday that we needed off.

People tended to have emergencies at those times, but not usually on the actual day.

He nodded as one of his alarms started beeping, and he headed for the living room to check it out.

I had to stop what was going on in my head.

I had to focus again.

Brooke Bennett was no longer my roommate. She wasn't my best friend anymore. That had ended thirteen years ago. A lot of other crap had gone down in my life, changing the direction of everything.

I was no longer Bruce Bello's daughter.

When my mom had died, so had his daughter. My death just took a different turn and a lot longer.

This was my life now.

I lived outside of Calgary, and yes, I was hiding. With Blade and Carol. We were doing a lot more than just hiding, though. And in light of that, I had things to do to help set up our next trip— or "errand" as Carol liked to call them—and one part of that was getting a spray tan.

I picked up my wallet and keys, and I headed for the door. Moments later I was pulling out of the driveway in our rusty '72 Chevy truck.

• • •

"Back again, Raven?"

Raven. Not Riley.

I made a mental note to remind Carol and Blade to use my cover name. We'd all slipped over the last nine months, starting to use our real names around the house. To them I was Riley. Carol had never learned my last name, though I knew Blade knew, but keeping these secrets was a point stressed during our training.

We were no longer our pasts, and last names were forbidden. We couldn't use them, say them, or even think them.

So to them I was Riley, because that's how we were introduced when we got our assignment, but to everyone in Cowtown I was Raven.

Raven Hastings.

Along with my fake name, I had a whole fake personality to put on, and I sent Holly a dazzling smile I rarely used. "Hey! Yes! You know me."

Raven Hastings was enthusiastic. She was happy most days, with a bright and cheery disposition. She enjoyed inspirational quotes, and she liked to dress beach casual, in Canada. When Raven went out with Blade, they complemented each other. She was boho chic, and he was blissful hippie.

Today I (or Raven) had dressed in a bohemian light pink skirt that fell to my feet with a slightly see-through white T-shirt knotted over my stomach. Thank God it was summer because I had committed to this look. Right now I was able to pull off sandals with straps running up my legs like ballet slippers.

I stuck my hip out and propped my hand there, striking a pose. "I have a date next weekend, and I have to look good."

Holly was the Sun-n-Fun's main evening worker, and she was an eternal romantic. This wasn't my first time here, and I'd noted she had a stack of at least three new books next to the till every time I came in for a tan. Holly also knew a few of the girls from the nursing home—another way to cement my excuse for next weekend. I knew one of those friends always wanted to trade for the closest holiday or big event, and the next one coming up was the Stampede.

Holly's eyes lit up, and she asked me all about my date.

I made it a weekend excursion.

Annie didn't waste any time.

Word had traveled fast to my coworker from Holly at the tanning salon the night before. She plopped down at my table during my first break at the nursing home where I worked as a nursing aide.

"Heard you need next weekend off?"

I smiled. "You wanted to go Stampeding?"

She didn't even blink, only leaned forward. "I want that whole weekend off."

"Done...if you take my Friday shift too."

Annie had started to rise, but now paused and hissed. "Are you serious?"

In some nursing homes, a full weekend was Friday through Sunday, but not this nursing home. If we traded a weekend with someone, it was just Saturday and Sunday. So I had to make it clear I wanted that Friday off too.

But I knew Annie. She loved partying, and Stampeding was a huge party. Ergo my sunny Raven disposition.

I couldn't mess around. "Take it or leave it..."

She growled under her breath, but nodded. "Fine. I'll write up the slips to put in for the trade."

And I was now free for whoever we were helping next weekend.

Bolstering a bright smile, I bounced in my seat. "Great! Thanks! I can't wait for my date now." And because Raven loved inspiring quotes, I added, "Be fearless. Be beautiful."

Annie's eyes flicked upward before she pushed away from the table. "Yeah, okay."

"Weirdo," she breathed as she left.

But Raven loved all, even meanies.

With Riley that girl might've been introduced to a door, but I was Raven today.

"Hey, Rave girl. Bee is taking her clothes off."

I checked the time. I had five minutes left.

"Okay. I'll head up in three."

Bee loved being naked, but she had dementia.

"By the elevators," he added.

And I was up and leaving. Bee had been in bed when I left for break.

CHAPTER FIVE

I called Blade as I was leaving work.

I'd parked close to the staff door, so I was just getting in when he picked up.

"You get off?" he asked.

Two retorts came to mind.

Raven's was, "Embrace your orgasm."

Mine was, "Last night. Thank you for your concern."

But Annie and another girl who worked on our floor were walking by, and I still hadn't closed my car door, so I went with Raven's comeback.

Blade snorted as the girls moved past my car, rounding my trunk, and I reached for my door.

"I'll take that as an affirmative, and I'll start making the arrangements."

I shut the door and replied, "Roger that. I'm going to the gym." So they shouldn't expect me for two more hours.

"Hey. Can you grab something from The Chopped Leaf on the way home?"

I heard Carol yell in the background, "And those chocolate-flavored Pringles."

"Ew. No." He immediately shut her down.

I laughed into the phone. "I'll see what I can do. See you two at home."

I was reaching for my seatbelt when Blade hung up, and that's when it happened. There was no warning. No sudden tingling to hint at something amiss. I hadn't been watching my perimeter as I usually would. I was distracted, talking to Blade on the phone, and I cursed myself as two of my car doors opened at once: the passenger front and the one behind.

My training kicked in, like a switch being flipped on.

I didn't wait to see who it was.

I bailed. Or I would've.

I had my door open even before they sat down, but they had someone outside my door. As I pushed it open to run, he shoved it back, and then I heard a gun cocking.

"Don't, Riley."

I stilled, knowing that voice.

He found me.

But no. My split-second panic flared to something else. Curiosity?

The guy next to me hadn't spoken. The voice was the guy behind me, and I'd heard that voice on the other end of numerous phone calls.

I looked. "Tanner?"

Brooke Bennett's brother stared back at me through the rearview mirror. His face was like a concrete slab, total lockdown.

"We won't hurt you," he said. "We just want to ask you a few questions."

The guy with the gun growled, "So drive."

Some of my fear diminished, but a firm knot remained stuck in my throat, along with my training, which was telling me: "*Run, bitch. Run fast.*"

The guy who'd been outside my door was heading to a car parked in the next row, and this was my only window.

My seatbelt had already snapped back since I hadn't clicked it in place.

One second. That's all I had. I had to make the decision NOW! So, I did.

I ran.

I went with the door as I shoved it open, and my feet hit the paved lot hard.

Oompf.

Something twisted, but I didn't stop.

Adrenaline raced through me, and I was three steps away before I heard them in pursuit.

Tanner barked out, "Grab her. *Don't* hurt her."

Fuck, fuck, fuck.

They were already on me. I saw the shadow as one grabbed my arm. I swung with a roundhouse at the same time I jumped in the air.

Tanner and the other guy were barreling after me.

I couldn't take on three guys, and seeing more co-workers coming down the stairs, I started screaming.

One of them grabbed me and yanked me back against his chest as Tanner bit out, "Shut her up!"

A hand covered my mouth.

I bit down as I kicked in the air. A roar came from behind me as my foot smacked against something, hard. I threw my body sideways, and the guy dropped me from the sudden movement.

"Godda—"

A shadow moved in from the side, and fast.

Everyone seemed to pause, and time slowed as Tanner fell back a step, and then the shadow was there.

An arm wrapped around my waist and lifted me as if I weighed nothing. I looked slender, but my body was all muscle. I knew how much I weighed, and that feat was impressive.

Then I stopped thinking as another arm wrapped around my neck, applying pressure. He was putting me out.

I couldn't fight. He immobilized me and then...

Darkness.

• • •

I came to in the back of a car and immediately felt my pockets. They were empty. My phone was gone.

Looking around, this was the back of a luxury car...no, SUV.

One guard sat next to me and another across from me. I knew what they were by how perfectly they were positioned: upright, shoulders back, one hand on their thighs next to their gun holsters, and the other checking in with their earpieces.

The other occupant sat diagonal to me, slouched down, his feet spread wide and his phone in front of him.

When I looked over, Tanner smirked. "Heya, ballbuster. I see you got more spunk than you did when you were a preteen."

He looked older, but he still had the shaggy blond hair Brooke's pictures had showed at school. And that same smirk too.

"Fuck off," I growled.

Looking around, I saw only forest moving by at a fast pace, probably over a hundred kilometers. There was an SUV in front of us, and looking back, I saw another trailing. *Shit.* No. There was a third behind that one. Four in all.

"All this for me?" I asked, though as I spoke, I knew the answer.

Tanner Bennett was in this vehicle. The convoy was for him, not me.

What time was it and where we were going? I needed those answers. I could formulate my escape plan then—*They found me!*

I hadn't taken that in.

If Tanner was here, that meant the whole Bennett family knew about me. They. Had. Found. Me.

Pure and genuine panic started to filter in.

They knew my father.

Did he send them for me?

Had he found out about me?

They were capable of murder. Were they going to ki— I had to wait and think. Be clear-headed.

After the oldest brother had died, it was ruled an accident, but I knew Brooke never agreed. After her father and Kai left that day, she'd broken down, saying Cord was murdered. That had been all she ever said. She'd never talked about *how* he died, just that he *was* dead.

Three months later, we'd found ourselves back on the front steps of Hillcrest again. This time Brooke hadn't been crying. She'd been pale and holding on to my hand as if it were a life preserver, but she'd known why they were coming again.

They were coming for her.

Her father, Anthony Bennett, the patriarch of their family, had died in his sleep.

Kai Bennett, the oldest remaining brother, was the new boss of the family, and he wanted Brooke back at home.

That was the last day I saw her, until the pictures on the news after her recent disappearance.

There were whispers around school after Brooke was gone that Kai had killed both his rivals. Brooke and I continued to talk on the phone and email for a few months after she left, but I never asked. I knew she'd never tell me anyway, even if she knew.

Fear trickled through me, expanding to my toes as I looked around the SUV again. Were her brothers behind Brooke's disappearance?

Or—ice lined my veins—was Brooke dead too?

"Don't do it, Ray ray."

I gritted my teeth. "*Don't* use that name. That was Brooke's, *not* yours."

Tanner laughed, raising his phone again. "All I'm saying is don't let your mind wander down to all the dark and twisted places you're going. Let us get where we need to go, then you can embrace all the accusations." He continued to chuckle as his attention went back to whatever was on his phone.

"Where are we going?"

He smiled, his gaze not leaving the screen. "You'll see."

I bit back a growl. "What time is it?"

I had two hours before Blade would start looking for me. They had a two-hour head start. That was it.

"You'll see," he said again. He still didn't look at me.

The lie fell from my lips so easily. "I'm diabetic, Tanner. I need to know the time to see if I need to check my blood sugar."

He looked up then. So did the guards.

His eyes narrowed. He didn't move his phone. "You're lying."

I rolled my eyes. "Right. Who'd lie about having diabetes?"

"Someone who wants to judge how far away we are from her hiding spot." He smirked again. "And speaking of, why Calgary?

You know we have holdings there, right?" His eyes slid up and down my body, lingering on my lips. "Though, I have to say, the woodsy, all-natural look you have going on works for you. Makes me think of embracing some wood too."

I felt a flush trailing up my neck.

What was this? Tanner was flirting? No, this was just his personality. Brooke had talked about how he was a player, even back then. It seemed that hadn't changed. In a way, it calmed me a little bit, finding something still the same. Something at least sort of familiar.

But I had to know. Feeling my throat growing raw, I rasped out, "Did you find me for him?"

Tanner lowered the phone to his lap. His head tilted to the side.

He didn't reply, just stared at me for a full minute. He wasn't going to answer, damn him.

"My father," I clarified.

His eyes widened a fraction of an inch. An emotion flared before he stomped it down. His phone came back up, and his gaze returned to it. "No. Now shut it and chill."

"My blood sugar—"

"You're not diabetic. You weren't when you were twelve, and there's no way you got type 2 since then. Stop insulting my intelligence."

Well then.

I could try the door, jump out of a moving car, and tear through the woods—but that would only work if I could run after I landed. We were moving so fast, it would be useless. They had four fucking vehicles here. Who knew how many guards were in each of them.

I sat back. I would wait to see who was at the end of this drive.

That was my only option.

CHAPTER
SIX

I slept for a while—not sure how long—but we drove for three hours after I woke up before we stopped. I'd been counting and looking around until we pulled into a gas station. There were no other businesses around it, just forest. I had to figure they'd picked this place for that specific reason.

Once our vehicle stopped, both the guards got out and opened our doors.

Tanner put his phone away and sighed. "Don't try anything, Gone Girl." He gestured outside. "See all those guys?"

I gulped.

Ten of them got out of the cars and took up positions around the gas station.

"They will surround the station so you can walk free in there, but if you try to make a run for it, they've been approved to shoot you."

My eyes flew back to his.

He seemed smug. "With that said, have fun peeing. Pick anything you want inside and put it on the counter. We'll foot the bill." He whistled as he got out on his side. His door closed, and the guard followed him as he went toward the building.

The guard on my side was still waiting. My stomach clenched, but I got out too.

I needed a camera—just one connected online would be enough for Blade to find me. It was past time now that my roommates would've realized something had happened to me. They probably looked for my car, which would've still been at work, and Blade would've sent all the alerts on full blast for me.

We were trained for situations like this. I just needed to leave a trail of some sort. As I crossed the parking lot (empty except for our vehicles), I spotted a camera at the corner of the building.

Thank God.

I raised my head so he could get a positive ID.

"It won't work," Tanner called from the door. He waved to the camera. "They're offline. It's why we come here."

But there'd be video, at least. Some proof that I'd been here. Blade would find it, eventually.

I stepped inside, and as if hearing my thoughts, Tanner added, "The whole system was shut off before we even pulled in. We called ahead."

He stopped to look over the magazine rack, pulling out an issue of something that had Brooke's face on the cover

His mouth tightened. "Go to the bathroom, Riley. I'll still be here when you're done."

He pulled out his phone, so I went ahead. I felt like collapsing on the toilet.

They'd taken my phone. I had no clue if they'd taken my bag too or left it behind in my car. I still didn't really know how far away we were, but they were driving back roads for a reason.

They were smart, damn smart.

I left the bathroom, and even though I knew they had guards outside, I poked my head around for any escape routes.

There were none. The door that led to the rear of the gas station was kitty-corner to the front desk, and three guards stood in front of it. The clerk was a gangly teenager, standing off to the side by the register. Tanner had placed some water bottles, food, and a few other things on the counter, but the kid wasn't ringing anything up.

A second later, the bell over the door jingled and an older man entered. He nodded to Tanner and walked around the counter, then did the same to the kid, who looked relieved as he slipped out the front door.

They'd called in the owner, or the manager. Whoever he was, he moved with purpose and familiarity as he began ringing everything up.

Tanner looked over as his phone began ringing. "Get whatever you want, Riley."

My neck was stiff as I moved toward the beverage aisle. I needed water, food, but I didn't move far so I could eavesdrop when he answered the phone.

"Yeah?" A pause. "We are." Another pause. "Will do."

Well, that was informative.

I shook my head and went to grab everything I needed. I bought a toothbrush, toothpaste, and deodorant, along with water and a couple pieces of fruit, up to the front.

Tanner moved aside as I put them on the counter. "We have all of that for you where we're going."

"You didn't tell me that." I still pushed them ahead.

It was small, but it was my only way to resist. I didn't think a toothbrush, toothpaste, and deodorant would break the Bennett bank. They were billionaires.

The owner/manager didn't meet my gaze as he rang my items up and bagged everything.

Tanner said something to one of the guards, gesturing to me. The guard nodded and moved toward me as Tanner went to the bathroom. I realized the guards were slipping into the bathroom through a back door I'd missed. They were coming in and out in pairs.

They had coordinated all of this to help them as well.

I went to the front door to wait. Two guys moved with me, and it was eerie how two other guys from outside came to stand near the door at the same time. I knew they were talking into mouthpieces, but it just showed how prepared and professional they were. A whole new level of helplessness washed through me, but a surge of anger came right after it too.

I didn't like this feeling.

My father was powerful too, dangerous, and he'd never had a setup like this. He couldn't have afforded it. He also didn't have the need for it. I hated him, but he didn't have the enemies the Bennett family did. Owning his trucking business wasn't profitable enough to put him at the billionaire level. Not even close.

"Okay." Tanner emerged from the bathroom, putting his phone away as he walked toward me. "We're ready to go."

I spied one of the men handing an envelope to the owner before picking up all the bags.

I had to admit, I was surprised they didn't just go in, take what they wanted, and leave. The owner wouldn't have done anything. No one went against the Bennett family, but he seemed happy as he skimmed through the envelope.

"Riley."

Tanner waited for me outside the vehicle, one of the guards holding the door for me.

I hurried my pace, then cursed myself for doing that. I could walk the speed I wanted to walk. There was a slight breeze in the air. It was usually in the twenties in June around here, but I shivered. The temperature had dipped lower as the sunlight began to wane.

SHIT!

I'd forgotten to look at the time inside.

I'd been so consumed with thinking of escape routes, then watching how the guards were operating, that I completely forgot. But, thinking back, I had taken a step toward the counter, and two guards had moved to intercept me.

They'd planned for that.

It wouldn't have made a difference.

There had been no clock in the gas station, or I know I would've noticed it.

My throat started burning.

They really were prepared for me.

"How many girls do you kidnap?" I yelled to Tanner.

He glanced to me before rounding the back of the SUV. I could see him through the windows.

I snorted as a guard opened the door for me. "Is it a regular thing? Monthly? Bimonthly? Every week? Every few days?"

I didn't expect a response as I got inside, but I *was* expecting Tanner to get in with me. I was going to keep taunting—another small point of resistance, the only thing I had going for me at this point.

But he didn't get in.

His door closed abruptly, and so did mine. My leg had barely cleared the door before it slammed shut, then locked.

I looked around in alarm. I was the only one in the SUV, but they'd locked me in.

"Hey!" I banged on the window. My voice was probably muffled, but they could hear me. Or so I assumed. "Hey!"

No one looked.

Tanner had disappeared from his side.

A complete wall of guards came around my SUV, blocking everything except the little I could see through the gaps between their necks and heads. I moved around, trying to get a better look at what was going on.

I could see Tanner walking toward an empty section of the parking lot. Four guards trailed him, but stood a respectable distance back.

Something was coming.

Some*one* was coming.

And we didn't have to wait long.

Three SUVs sped down the highway and turned into the parking lot, parking in front of Tanner with a swirl of dust.

I half expected all the doors to open and guards to emerge, since those looked like the same SUVs as we were traveling with. But they didn't. The only door that opened was the back door of the second SUV.

Kai Bennett had arrived.

CHAPTER SEVEN

I hissed to myself as my blood boiled and froze all at once.

He'd only become *more* since I last saw him.

Taller. More good looking. More riveting. More dangerous. More, more, more. And I hated it. That had become more too.

I loathed him now.

There was no comparison between Kai and Tanner. Tanner had been the womanizer, the flirt back then, and besides the smirking asshole he was for kidnapping me, there were plenty of hints that he was still those things now.

But as I looked at the brothers standing across from each other, power dripped from Kai Bennett. Authority emanated from him, even just standing there.

Every single guard stood an inch taller.

The tension in the air went up a notch, and I felt it even inside the vehicle. The hairs on the back of my neck stood up, and goosebumps ran down my arms.

Sunglasses blocked his eyes as he listened to what Tanner was saying, but his eyes flashed in my memory—how dead they'd looked when he told me to leave Brooke alone, right after their father had told her Cord was dead.

I felt sick to my stomach, and my hand moved there, as if to keep the contents in.

No one else made my skin crawl with disgust except my father. Kai Bennett and Bruce Bello were cut from the same cloth.

I should have looked away, if only just to keep from emptying my stomach, but I couldn't.

My heart picked up. I felt it pounding in my eardrums, and I tasted bile in my mouth. But still, I couldn't look away. Resting a hand on the window, I scooted even closer.

I needed to try to read their lips—beep.

No. They couldn't.

I heard another beep, coming from the front of the car.

Crawling forward, I heard a third beep. A phone had been left up there. There was a wall and a small window separating the front from the back, but I could get through that window. Feeling it, it moved an inch.

They hadn't locked it, but I could see why. It took all of my muscles to get it open that one inch. A fourth beep sent my blood rushing through my body. Adrenaline and excitement filled me with almost a frenzied need to get to that phone.

I used my entire body to get the window open farther.

One more inch.

Goddamn, a fifth beep.

The phone was in the console, right underneath my fingers.

I tried again, almost throwing myself backward to get it open a bit more. I didn't want to rock the vehicle, make them aware of what was I doing, but it worked.

Shit.

I felt the SUV tremble, and I paused, glancing over my shoulder.

The guards remained with their backs to the SUV. The two Bennetts were still talking, neither looking my way. I was safe, for now.

The window had opened another two inches, more than enough to get my arm inside. Snaking it through, with my face pressed against the window, I reached down to the console.

I grabbed the phone, my fingers just grazing it. I cupped it and pulled my arm back through the window.

My pulse jackhammered inside me.

I was shaking, almost uncontrollably, but as I opened the screen, I nearly wept. No passcode needed. I dialed in a safe number to call.

A second later, I heard, "411. What is your information?"

Tears wet my face. "This is Section 8, Hider 96. My location is at these coordinates."

There was silence on the other end. They were listening.

"I've been kidnapped by the Bennett family."

That was all I needed to say.

They knew what to do, and no matter where I went now, they would find me. That's what we did. As soon as I gave them my Hider number, Blade would receive an alert. He'd be listening within a second, and right now, I felt sure he was locating me.

A minute later, orders should've been dispatched to the nearest Hiders, and within five minutes of those notices, they would be in a vehicle, heading for me.

I only had to wait for them to arrive.

I knew Blade, and one phone wouldn't be enough for him. He would use this location to find other phones, and he would ping trackers on all of them. Unless the Bennett family had anti-trackers to mask their signals—which I had never heard of—Blade would track me even if we departed from this location before the Hiders found me.

"Four Hiders are en route," said the voice at the other end of the line. "Terminate this number. Erase your steps."

Gladly.

I erased the history of the phone call, put the phone back in the console exactly how I'd felt it placed, and went to work getting that window shut.

I had it shut minus a centimeter when the guards began moving.

They parted at my door, and I saw Tanner heading back to me, his head down and his jaw clenched.

I scrambled to my seat, sitting there as if I'd never moved. My head was down when his door opened and he got inside. I sniffled, wiping the tears away as the other two guards got in their seats.

I could feel Tanner's gaze on me.

No one said a word, and a second later, the SUV started to pull away.

We were leaving.

Looking over, I watched the other three SUVs go ahead of us, and as we returned to the road, our pace kicked up compared to the speed we'd been traveling before. The tension I'd sensed outside had come into the SUV with Tanner. He didn't lounge now, or take his phone out. He sat almost as a guard, except those guys seemed to sit even taller, even straighter, and with their heads back another inch.

Both guards kept their fingers on their earpieces.

We drove for a complete hour like that, until it got dark.

When we slowed, it was pitch-black outside, except for the headlights.

We turned onto a gravel road, forest still all around us. We went over a metal grid in the road, then through a gate after that. Moving at a snail's pace, it was as if we were waiting for something until suddenly, we began moving faster. We hurtled down this narrow gravel road, and I clocked it around two miles before we slowed again.

This time, we paused before another grand gate, and it opened to reveal a house. The word *mansion* couldn't describe it. It was more of a compound. The driveway circled in front of the main house, but there was another house just as big to the right and more buildings behind them.

My people were out there, but I had no idea how they'd get to me. A hopeless feeling filtered in until, no. I wouldn't have that. I'd just have to get to them.

Somehow.

Then the doors opened.

It was showtime.

CHAPTER EIGHT

I didn't see where the Master of the Bennett Universe went, but Tanner went up the stairs, surrounded by guards. Another two waited for me, and as I started up after him, two more moved in behind me.

They led me into a grand entryway with white marble flooring. Flecks of gold nestled within the rock, which matched a fountain off to one side. The underside of the fountain shimmered gold as well. A large, white-carpeted staircase circled around, curving upward, and that's where my guards seemed to be taking me.

Tanner ignored me, disappearing somewhere farther into the house.

My guards and I kept going, all the way to the fourth floor and down a long hallway, then up another set of stairs until I felt I was in a whole other wing. We passed through a glass-encased walkway that led us from the main home into the second building, and then up another set of stairs. I tried to keep track of where we were going, but it was getting harder the farther we went.

They led me into a back hallway that rounded the second home and up one last set of stairs. A granite wall stood in front of us, and a guard pressed his earpiece, saying, "Here."

An unlocking sound clicked, and a door opened for us. We went inside, and I knew this was my prison.

Though, for a prison, it was a nice one.

It was an entire apartment, really. Sleek and modern with black countertops in the kitchen and a dark oak dining table. The couches in the living room were black leather, sitting on a white rug, in front of a television that looked more like a small movie screen. The bathroom had an oval drop-in sink of black glass, with the same hints of gold from the entrance. A chandelier hung high over the kitchen table.

A doorway led into a room past the living room, and I could see the corner of a bed there. A sheepskin had been laid across the edge, creating a scene that could've been photographed for an interior design magazine.

Two of my guards stood to the side of the door, and the other two positioned themselves outside.

I didn't ask questions, and none of them said anything.

I felt it in my bones: I was waiting for Kai Bennett.

I knew I wouldn't be able to find an escape route from the apartment. But I still looked around to get my bearings.

Inside the bedroom was a king-sized bed, and a wrap-around deck beyond two sliding glass doors. As I stepped out onto it, my heart sank.

There was nothing for me to climb onto if I wanted to make my way down. The fall could've fit a thirty-eight-floor hotel, and I could see rocky terrain at the bottom. It was a rock-climber's dream, or challenge, but not mine.

"Gonna jump?"

I jerked, my hands clenching the railing as his smooth voice slid down my spine. It awakened all my nerve endings, and I gritted my teeth, hating how I reacted to him. Those were the first two words he'd spoken to me in fourteen years, making four in total now.

I didn't know this guy. Why did I react to him this way?

Turning around, I found Kai standing just inside the bedroom doorway, his head cocked to the side as if he found me a puzzle.

I'd seen it before, but his presence was like a punch to my sternum. He'd been devastatingly handsome at sixteen and he was even more so now, and that set my teeth on edge.

Dressed in a business suit, the shirt unbuttoned and the ends pulled loose from his pants, he had bare feet. He looked as if this trip to see me was the last thing he had to do before relaxing completely, as if I were an afterthought.

Then he shrugged off his suit jacket and shirt, catching the collars of both and tossing them on the bed. He turned to the closet behind him, which opened to showcase an array of men's clothes.

My mouth dried.

This was his bedroom.

Was it?

I glanced to a second closet, wondering if I'd find women's clothes in there or more of his.

He brought out a T-shirt and pulled it on. It molded to him, revealing broad shoulders and a lean waist that had been trimmed down to a core of solid muscle.

His hands dropped to his belt buckle, and I pulled my gaze away and turned around.

Reaching out to steady myself on the railing, I heard his pants drop to the ground. My fingers clutched the steel railing, my nails digging into it.

"So are you?"

I hadn't heard him move, but his voice was closer. I turned again to find him fully clothed, wearing a pair of dark gray sweatpants that molded to his bottom half the way his shirt did to the top.

He motioned to me. "Come on. I'm tired, and I don't want to have this talk worrying my little sister's dear friend might jump to her death." He snorted to himself. "She'd really be furious with me then."

There was a twinge in his voice. Exhaustion? I heard it now. I followed him, at a reluctant pace, as he went to the bedroom's far wall and pushed a button.

Two doors slid open, revealing an entire bar built into the wall. As he poured a glass of bourbon, I saw the slope in his shoulders. There were bags under his eyes, and a tired softness around the corners of his mouth.

I really was an afterthought for him. He'd been somewhere else, doing something else, and whatever it had been had tired him out.

The power and charisma he exuded was still there; it was just slightly diminished. Slightly.

He was dangerous. I felt zapped by his energy, and as I moved into the main room with him, that zap just grew. He sucked the air out of wherever he was—so much that my insides started to feel his same exhaustion.

"Are you going to speak, or do I need to test your vocal chords a different way?" he asked, swinging his heated eyes my way. His nostrils flared as his hand tightened on his glass. "Hmm?"

Make them underestimate you.

My Hider training kicked in, and I lowered my gaze.

I didn't like the storm inside of me. I was all over the place—feeling enraged, then heated, then other things, but rounding back to hate. I needed him to view me as submissive, timid, so even though my neck tightened so much I could barely move, I forced myself to look at the ground.

The goddamn ground.

This guy—he didn't deserve having me look down before him.

I knew he'd had thousands killed for the Bennett family. He'd murdered his older brother. And Brooke had never said anything, but I didn't believe for a millisecond that their father had died in his sleep. Kai had killed him too.

He was a murderer, and he was behind so many girls being trafficked, behind millions of dollars of drugs moving through his territories—he didn't deserve anything from me.

He *deserved* to be killed. And if he was the reason for Brooke's disappearance, I was going to be the one to do it.

I would cut him from dick to throat, in that direction too.

He snorted again, this time with a twinge of genuine amusement. "Don't kid yourself, and don't insult me, Riley Bello. You don't have a timid bone in your body. If you did..."

He started for me, and I couldn't help myself. I raised my head, and I couldn't look away.

"You wouldn't be a Hider for the 411 Network," he finished softly.

My worst nightmare.

He droned on, sounding almost bored, "You were recruited into their network when your father murdered your mother. Six months after I pulled Brooke from Hillcrest, they told you your mother was missing, but you knew. You knew what happened to her when you went home the next day."

I was frozen.

"You went to her funeral. You sat beside your father, but you knew the whole time he'd killed her, because that's what he did. He hurt her. It's why you were sent away, so he wouldn't hurt you too. Am I correct?"

I felt sick.

"Their recruiter agents approached you when you were shopping. It was the day after you'd buried your mother in an empty casket. You were at the mall with two of your friends, or two girls your father had deemed appropriate for you. You didn't even know them, but they were daughters of his colleagues, and you didn't like them. Am I correct?"

I couldn't look away. I couldn't stop listening. I couldn't do anything as he stripped my world right in front of me.

He knew everything.

How did he—*Brooke*. Brooke must've told him.

He tossed back the rest of his drink. "That was the day you decided to leave, not because he killed your mother, and not because you knew you'd be next, but because they told you the real truth." His eyes flashed at me, an unnamed emotion there. "Your mother was still alive."

I couldn't even swallow.

"How—" I managed to say. "How do you know this?"

"I'm not done, little girl." A glint of cruelty gleamed at me from his eyes. "Your father *did* beat your mother," he sneered. "He *did* believe he'd killed her. He *did* order her body to be disposed of, but it was a 411 agent he sent to do it. He believes your mother was thrown to the bottom of a cliff and her body swept out to sea, when instead, she was hidden by the 411 Network. And when they asked you to join them that day in the mall, you said yes so fast you never stopped to think what would happen to anyone you left behind."

My gut twisted.

A flame flickered to life.

"What are you talking about?" I demanded.

He yawned—he goddamn yawned—and went over to the cupboard to pour himself a second glass of bourbon.

He spoke with his back turned to me. "You haven't checked in with your father recently, have you?"

I narrowed my eyes. What was he talking about? Blade would've—

"Your friend Blade never told you..."

A knife plunged into my chest, hearing him say Blade's name.

Kai turned back around, holding his glass in front of him. He leaned back against the wall, his eyes locked on mine. "...because he didn't want you to leave your location, and he knew you would."

"What are you talking about?"

"Your mother had family."

My aunt. My cousin. I had an uncle too.

I shook my head. "But they—"

They hated my father. They blamed him for her death. I knew they did.

"You had a cousin. Do you remember her? She's your age, Brooke's age."

Tawnia. I didn't know her that well. My mother had kept us away from her family, more for their safety than ours.

"No. What are you saying? My aunt hated my father."

"She did. But she didn't convey that adequately to your cousin."

Was he...no. No.

I didn't want to think about what Kai might be inferring. There was no way.

"My aunt would never allow that," I hissed.

"Your aunt is dead."

He said that in the same tone he'd used when he told me to leave Brooke alone.

"She's fine." "Your aunt is dead." Both statements meant nothing to him.

"*Fuck* you."

He shrugged. "Maybe later." He drank from his glass. "I brought you here for two reasons. One, a trade. You tell me where my sister is, and I'll help with your cousin."

Fuck. Seriously. Fuck. He was serious.

"What exactly are you saying about my father and my cousin?" I eyed him warily.

He finished his drink and set the glass beside him on the counter. "Your cousin didn't believe your father murdered his wife. She believes your father lost his wife because she ran from him. She believes his daughter was so distraught at being abandoned that you got drunk and caused the car accident that supposedly burned your body to oblivion minus the few traces of DNA left behind. She believes your father is someone to feel pity for, and that he is loving, and kind, and softhearted, and rich. Your father preyed on your cousin, and I'm sure he enjoys the close resemblance she bears to his daughter and wife."

My father was a monster, but so was the man standing in front of me. He was just as much a monster as Bruce Bello.

"You're sick. You and him both."

He stared at me, not moving an inch. An uneasy feeling traced up my spine, making the hairs on the back of my neck stand up. I felt as if I had baited a cobra.

But Kai just nodded toward the door.

"Enough. We'll continue our talk tomorrow."

No one else was in the room. I hadn't noticed the absence of guards until now. But as he spoke, the door opened and Tanner walked in.

"Take her to her room," Kai told him. "She's to stay there until I come for her."

My lips parted.

The way he said that, I felt a bolt of fear slice through me, but then Tanner was next to me. He took my arm, leading me out as I stumbled over my feet, feeling numb.

I hadn't felt this emotion for a long time, not since my father.

"Wait." I had to know. Just as Tanner was about to walk me out of Kai's apartment, I turned back. "How?"

How is he going to help with my cousin?

A glimmer of a smile taunted me. "I'll have him killed."

CHAPTER NINE

They knew.

They knew it all.

They knew Blade, the Network. My father. My mother. They knew she was alive. Of course I'd known the Bennetts found me, but I hadn't thought about it. I hadn't wanted to.

Tanner pulled me down a flight of stairs, and I tripped again, almost falling, but he caught me and steadied me.

He wouldn't look at me, though. His jaw was clenched, and his hand dug into my arm. It'd leave a bruise there later.

"How long?" I rasped. It seemed the only way I could talk since they'd taken me. "How long have you known?"

He didn't answer, a vein bulging in his neck. We turned a corner, and there was another door in front of us. He banged on it, stepping back until it opened from the inside. More guards came out. There were always guards.

He motioned inside. "If you need food or anything, ask the guards. They'll get it for you. This is your room until Kai wants to see you again."

I stepped inside, but turned to him. "Tanner, how long?"

His eyes flicked up, and I saw remorse there.

"Since the beginning." His lips pressed together. He looked as if he had more to say, but thought better of it. He shook his head and barked out, "Lock her in."

The door slammed shut, and a whoosh of air hit me in the face. I barely blinked, everything in me going into shock.

They knew about the 411 Network, which wasn't good. In fact, it was really bad. The 411 Network was an organization that hid people who couldn't survive otherwise—those women and children, and sometimes men, who aren't protected by the legal system, by cops or whoever else, so we step in. We hide them, sometimes making it look like they're dead.

The "errands" we run are to pick up people who need transport somewhere else. We handle anyone needing to get into Canada—any survivor who needs help. We don't discriminate, and most of the time, we aren't told their names or situations.

We're given coordinates to go to, pictures of who we're looking for, and directions on where to take them. We pass along files and packets with their fake passports or ID or whatever else they need for the leg of our trip. That's all.

In the ten years since I'd been operational, only once did my team have to fight an abuser.

But I knew there were times it happened.

I was proud of this part of my life. I was proud of 411's mission, of what we stood for, and now the Network was being threatened. The Bennett family couldn't know about us. I'm certain they were the ones we hid people from sometimes.

My heart raced. My palms were sweaty.

My vision blurred.

I was panicking, like earlier, but this was on steroids. I couldn't breathe. The room was spinning.

I was feverish. I was cold.

I was falling.

The ground rushed up at me until arms caught me instead. I looked up, and though the room still rushed around me, I saw a firm jaw and corded neck muscles.

Tanner had come back for me...

He carried me out of the room, through a hallway, and up a flight of stairs.

Tanner was taking me to his room...until no. We went back through that same set of doors I'd entered earlier. Black and gold swirled around me as I tried to see where we were. We went into a back bedroom, and he laid me down on that shaggy sheepskin blanket. Recognizing the glass balcony doors behind him, my teeth started clattering.

Tanner hadn't come for me. Kai had.

As if hearing my thoughts, he looked down. Those dark and almost soulless eyes stared right into mine. He didn't blink. Nothing showed. No irritation. No concern. Not even surprise.

I grew warmer by the second, and began shivering.

He felt my forehead, pushing my hair out of the way. His eyebrows pulled together. Confusion showed for a second before he turned and said something to someone behind us. His voice droned in my head, vibrating in a deep baritone. It sounded like I was underwater and he was above, talking to someone on a boat near us. There was a buzzing sound, like an engine.

I wondered again what was going on... And then there was nothing.

CHAPTER TEN

I woke in a bed with the softest sheets I'd ever felt, and drool. So much drool.

It took a second for me to catch up, but once I did, I bolted upright with a gasp.

It was pitch-black outside.

Glass doors. The same modern bedroom with an entire apartment just beyond the doorway and the soft glow of a light on in the other room.

I was in Kai Bennett's room, in his bed.

Could I close my eyes, go back to sleep, and wake up in Oz? Was that an option? I'd take it in a second if so.

The sound of a page turning came from the next room. Then I heard a chair push back.

Soft footsteps came until he stood in the doorway.

The light was on behind him, casting him in full shadow, so I couldn't see any details except his very trim and toned silhouette.

Why'd someone so evil have to be that good looking?

"Why'd you take me?" I shifted to a sitting position, pulling the sheets around me and noting that I was in a different shirt and wore boxer briefs over my underwear. He'd changed my clothes.

That was low on the list of problems, but... "Where are my clothes?"

He let out a soft and tired-sounding sigh. "You stumbled going into your room and hit your head. My brother didn't notice the blood trickling down your back, but my guards did. They alerted me." He nodded. "Your clothes were bloody. They had to be changed."

Now that he mentioned it, my head was pounding.

I touched the back of my head and hissed, feeling a large bruise. The fact that I hadn't noticed that spoke volumes. I was too consumed by everything else.

And speaking of that, on to my second question. "What do you know about 411?"

He answered without hesitation, crossing his arms over his chest and propping one shoulder against the doorframe. "I know they helped hide you and your mother. I know they're relatively new, but they're effective. They have heavy funders backing them, and I know they set up one man for murder, who is now in prison. I know your employers might mean well right now, but they are dangerous."

I blinked a few times, taking that in.

I winced on the inside when he mentioned the frame job. That had been an operative who went rogue, but no one fought to defend the guy.

I scowled. "He tried to murder his wife."

"But he didn't."

I snorted. "You're sticking up for the one slightly innocent monster? You?"

Watch your tone, Riley. You forget who you're talking to.

I could hear my mother's voice admonishing me, and I bit my lip as soon as the words were out. It was too late, though. I waited, watching to see if this infamous murdering monster would come toward me now.

He didn't move, just murmured, "You are not a good enough fighter to speak like that to me."

That same shiver went up my back. There was a deadly warning in there too.

I swallowed over a lump. "I'm sorry."

But was I? Was I really?

He had murdered. Cord. His father. Brooke?

I frowned. "You're looking for Brooke? That's why you kidnapped me?"

"Among other reasons, yes." He lifted his head again, straightening from the doorframe and taking a step toward me. Just one step—enough to be imposing, slightly intimidating, but still giving me space to breathe so I didn't scare away.

He was so measured, so calculating.

"My sister contacted you the day before yesterday. I want to know where she is."

All the oxygen left the room, and my head started spinning again. "You think—what? No."

"Yes." His voice was hard now. Gone was the subtlety. "Brooke asked me to keep tabs on you. She cares about you. You work for a network that specializes in helping people disappear, and I know she was desperate. She went to you; I know this much."

He took another step toward me.

I sat up straighter, rolling to my knees and then to my heels, ready to spring if I needed to.

Another step.

He squatted next to the bed so he was level with me, and now I could see him. He'd shifted out of the shadows, and I saw how fierce his eyes were. They blazed with anger and determination.

His perfect lips barely moved as he grated out, "You *will* tell me where she is."

I swallowed again. The lump in my throat had doubled in size.

He wasn't going to take no, but I had to try. "Before I saw your sister on the news, I hadn't really heard much from her since you drove her away from Hillcrest. I swear to you that's the truth."

His eyes narrowed. "I know you know where she is, but don't worry. If you won't tell me, I know others who will." He stood abruptly and went back to the main room.

I scrambled out of bed and padded after him.

I wasn't prepared for what I saw. I don't think anyone could've been.

I thought he had been reading a book, maybe looking over files for his business. I'd been sleeping in his bed, and he was waiting with a glass of wine beside a fire. Something cozy like that.

I was so wrong.

As I got to the doorway, I saw them, and someone started screaming.

It was me. I knew it was me, but I didn't hear it that way. I heard someone else scream from far away, even though I was the only one who had her mouth hanging open, the only one who started vomiting right there on the floor.

I fell down, not feeling a thing, as I couldn't bear the scene in front of me.

He had four Hiders there.

I recognized them by the way they were dressed: all in black and all with the same pin we wore to signal who we were. It was the one thing survivors were told to look for, a penguin. As my senses came back to me, I knew these were the four Hiders dispatched to rescue me.

Their hands were bound behind them, and they lay on the floor, their feet crossed over each other, bound around the ankles. Rags had been stuffed in their mouths, and all of them looked bloodied and bruised.

That sick feeling slammed back into my chest again, and I bent over, emptying the little that remained in my stomach.

I wretched in a corner, and no one made a move.

There were three guards standing behind the four Hiders. Kai stood off to the side. They all waited for me to finish. No one had a look of disgust or irritation—just patience, and that sent my stomach hurling once again.

"Are you done?" Kai asked a few seconds after my last round.

I didn't trust what I would say, so I didn't look at him. I didn't respond.

"Riley."

That same softness as before. Damn him. I felt him pulling, chiding me for not paying attention, and feeling that power I hated come over me, I looked at him. I couldn't refuse. My body reacted without my permission.

His eyes were hooded. He gestured to my co-workers. "You know where my sister is. I know this. You know this. Perhaps even these four know, so I will give you an option. You tell me where she is, and I will let your friends go." His head tilted to the side. "I will let them live, if you tell me right now where she is."

He was delusional.

He was mad.

He was cruel.

"I'm not fucking lying!" I spat. "I don't know where she is!"

Let these people live. Let them go. Let them be free.

He stared at me a full thirty seconds before he nodded.

One of the guards jerked forward, grabbing the back of the nearest man's shoulder. He pulled him up. The Hider began kicking, trying to lift his bound hands, but he couldn't do a thing. He flapped around like a fish. He was wearing a cap, the penguin emblem sewed into it. He rolled, but that cap stayed on.

It stayed on. Like it was trying to tell me something.

Stay on. Stay true. Stay strong.

The other Hiders began rolling around, one female screaming around her rag.

I couldn't—I didn't—I screamed, "I DON'T KNOW WHERE SHE IS!"

The guard lifted his gun, placing the muzzle against the back of the guy's head, pressed right up to the cap. He waited, watching Kai for the order.

"Oh my God. I don't. I swear I don't know where she is," I sobbed.

I dry-heaved again. My vision was swimming. If I moved for him, the guard could pull the trigger. If I stayed still, he could pull the trigger.

His life was in my hands, and I had nothing to give up for him. Nothing.

He was going to die.

The Hider stilled, coming to the same realization, and his eyes found mine, a stark pleading there. I felt it deep inside of me. He was scared, so scared, but calm.

He shouldn't have been calm.

I swallowed the tears streaming down my face. "Please, Kai! Please. My God. Please! I don't know. I swear I don't know. Please don't kill him—"

Then, two soft words, "You're lying."

And the guard pulled the trigger.

All the time with the Network, I saw people near death, but I'd never seen someone die. Never.

Until now.

The Hider's body jerked forward. Blood splattered everywhere, and the guard stepped back, releasing his body. He fell limply to the floor. His eyes were closed. He was so still, and I fell to my knees, trying to hold everything in—my tears, my vomiting, my screams, but it wasn't working. I felt my entire body jerking, and then I hit the floor, hard.

I had no control. I was having a seizure. This had never happened to me, and I couldn't stop myself. My teeth banged against each other. My head was going to slam into a chair, but then someone cursed.

The floor shook as footsteps rushed toward me, and someone scooped me up.

"Get them out!" Kai held me, barking over my body. "I want the fucking medic in here. NOW!"

I flailed around. My hand hit his head. He cursed again, but wound his arms more tightly around me to still my movements.

That wasn't what he was supposed to do, but I couldn't tell him my EMT training. He carried me back into his bedroom, and we sank down on the bed, his entire body wrapped around me to keep me from hurting him or myself. When he heard my teeth clacking together, he grabbed for a pillow and shoved it into my mouth, then sank back and held me immobile.

I shouldn't have felt safe, but I did.

After a moment, I could feel the seizure slowing, and an intense exhaustion settled in. I heard knocking on the door, then footsteps coming in just as I fell asleep. Again.

CHAPTER ELEVEN

"Pssst, Ray ray! Pssst!"

I opened an eye and saw Brooke kneeling beside my bed, her eyes lit up and an excited smile on her face. Her cheeks were red.

I groaned, burrowing my head under my pillow. "Go away. You're too awake for me."

She giggled, then shoved my shoulder. "Come on. Get up. I want to show you something."

"What?"

She was so annoying, so awake at a time I knew was ungodly and wrong. So wrong. It was irritating how much of a morning person she was. Five am wasn't the time to get up and dance, but that was one of her favorite pastimes.

Thank God I bargained hard. I'd gotten her to do her dancing routine in the community room down at the end of the hall. It was a nice bonus that two girls we hated had their room directly underneath, and they hadn't figured out who the dancer was. Not yet. The time was coming, though. We were only two weeks into school.

"Come on. I mean it. I really want to show you something." She was so persistent.

"What is it?" I grumbled, but I sat up, rubbing my eyes. This was not right. I glared at her, dropping my hands to my lap. "You're not human."

She laughed again, ducking her head behind her hands. "Come on. Come on. Quick."

"Fine, fine." I crawled out of bed and reached for my slippers.

I was pulling on my robe, following her out of the room, when it hit me that I wasn't cold. I should've been cold. It was always cold this early in the morning.

"Wait." I stopped, five feet from the door. "Where are we going?"

She poked her head around and waved me forward. "You're going to miss it. Come ON!"

She was too annoying for this to be a dream. "Fine, fine, fine." I rubbed a hand over my face. I just wanted to go back to sleep. "But where are we going?"

She disappeared back into the hallway as I reached for the door.

Then I heard her words, and an eerie laugh echoing from down the hallway. "My execution, silly."

My eyes snapped open.

I was awake, and not back in Hillcrest, not following Brooke. To her execution.

My heart pounded in my chest. I was in Kai's room, in his bed. Fear paralyzed me for a second, as I remembered the last time I'd woken here, remembered everything. Then I scrambled out of bed, hit the floor running, and dashed into the main room.

I skidded to a halt.

I was alone. Completely. There weren't even guards inside.

I slumped down in a chair at the table and took everything in. So much had happened, and my mind was swimming. I felt like I was drowning, and Hider operatives didn't do that.

I'd been playing defense this whole time, just trying to catch up. I had to stop. I had to formulate a plan.

They knew everything. Blade. The Network. The Hider operatives who came to help me—I felt sick again just thinking of them. If I hadn't made that call, that guy would still be alive. His death was on me.

I had to make it right somehow.

Brooke.

She was another piece of the puzzle.

Kai didn't believe me. He was desperate to find her.

The possibilities were endless, and none of it would get figured out unless I got out of here.

I *had* to get out. Somehow.

Getting out of this room would be a good first step. After showering, I grabbed some clothes and runners from the closet.

With clammy hands, and a pulse that didn't seem it would ever slow down, I started for the door.

It swung open before I could get there.

I opened my mouth, thinking that had happened fast, but then Tanner strolled in. Hands in his pockets, head down, he walked like he was out for a stroll he didn't want to be on.

Noticing my shoes first, he paused and lifted his head.

"Oh, hey. You're awake. Good." He turned around and called back over his shoulder, "Follow me."

I wasn't going anywhere.

Well, shit.

I had to. I had to see if I could escape or find the other Hiders.

Tanner hadn't waited for me, but there were two guards outside the door. Sighing, I headed out, but I kept my head up. I tried to memorize the way to wherever I was going, which was ridiculous because I was just guessing at where Tanner had gone. I must've been correct for the most part, but after I made a turn down a hallway, the guard behind me cleared his throat and said, "Other way."

"Thank you." I glanced at him and veered to the left hallway instead.

After that they had to direct me down three flights of stairs and through so many hallways I lost count. I'd felt like I was going back to the main door where they'd first brought me in, but I wasn't certain. I was getting a headache trying to track where I was and look for escape routes at the same time.

I should give up. Or wait for an opening.

This was the fewest guards I'd had, but there were still two of them. I had no doubt that whenever I got to where I was supposed to be, there'd be more.

Then I rounded a last corner and saw I was on the main floor. I could see the front door, but Tanner hollered from the other direction, "In here!"

He was in the kitchen, an entire grand room with a long dining table taking up one side, and an open kitchen on the other.

Tanner stood at the marble countertop, frowning at a coffee pot. "You drink coffee, Ray ra—Riley?"

He was dressed in jeans and a sweatshirt with the hood pulled over his head. With a big yawn stretching over his face, he glanced to me. "Hmmm?"

I normally didn't, but I shrugged. "Sure." Maybe it'd help me stay alert.

My stomach rumbled, hurting. My throat was painful too.

He finished getting the coffee ready to brew, smiling as he punched the last button. "There. Ready." He patted the top of the machine, a look of pride flashing over his face. "I just got this new sucker. About time to see if its espresso really does remind me of Paris." He winked. "I doubt it will."

"Tanner?" Someone called from behind me.

A guy was coming in. His head down, a bag like an EMT's over his shoulder, he frowned at his phone on the way toward us.

"You in there?"

He lifted his head when we were about five inches from impact.

"Oh!" He skidded to a halt, and his dark eyes widened.

I should've moved. I saw him coming, but this wasn't a normal situation. I was starting to feel like I had to do everything the opposite of normal just to see what would happen—if an opening to run would occur or anything. At least that's what I told myself. The truth might've been that my reactions were slow, really slow, and as I'd tried to move aside for him, my body had begun to shake. A wave of light-headedness had come over me, and I swear I felt my eyes roll to the back of my head.

"Whoa."

A thud sounded, and two hands grabbed my arms, keeping me upright as I started to waver.

"She needs to sit down."

A chair scraped against the floor, and I sat on it. The hands grew gentle, soothing. They felt nice after the shock of everything. He knelt in front of me, and I felt his breath on my face. He lifted one of my eyelids open.

"Tanner," he said over his shoulder. "I told you to give her something to eat and drink before making her walk through the house."

The guy was right in front of me, and getting even closer. A light appeared, and he began inspecting my eyes, one after another.

"Uh..."

I caught sight of Tanner's elbow in the air. He was raking a hand through his hair again. His hood slipped off.

"I did. I thought I did? What do you want her to have?"

"Any kind of juice you prefer?" the guy asked.

He paused.

I realized he was asking me. "What?"

"Juice." He put the light away and began feeling my neck. "What's your favorite?"

The fridge popped open. "We have orange juice, apple, prune? Why the fuck do we have prune? And grapefruit," Tanner said. "We have grapefruit juice too."

They waited for my answer.

"Oh! Uh, orange juice is fine."

The guy in front of me, his fingers now pressing over my carotid for my pulse, said, "Give her a piece of toast too. With some honey. She needs her blood sugar up. Are you diabetic, Riley?"

He said my name like he knew me.

He did look familiar...

His skin was a slightly darker tone, but he had the same black hair, dark eyes, and full lips that all of the Bennetts had. His hair had a little curl to it, and he seemed younger. Or maybe it was the gentleness I felt from him. He had a baby face too, with a softness to his skin.

"Jonah?" I asked.

He was the baby.

He nodded, grinning slightly, but with a flash of sadness in the depths of his eyes.

"Hi, Riley. I'm sorry we're meeting under these circumstances. And especially after last night. The shock of what Kai did, mixed with how much you were vomiting and the fact that you hadn't eaten or drank much the whole time they were driving you, gave you a seizure—induced by the drop in your blood pressure and blood sugar levels. Are you diabetic?" he asked again, picking up a small machine and lifting one of my fingers. He squeezed just beneath the tip and poked the machine into my skin.

"Hey."

He put the machine away, setting it aside. "Your color is coming back, but you're dehydrated." When the coffee machine started whirring, Jonah scowled at Tanner. "That's not for her, is it?"

Tanner had two mugs in front of him. "Uh...maybe?"

Unzipping his bag, he pulled out a stethoscope. "It better not be. She needs liquids. Juice and water are all she can drink, at least for a while. If everything turns out to be induced by shock and not something else medical, she can have the coffee *later*."

He moved aside my shirt, just an inch, and pressed the stethoscope to my chest.

"Are you the medic?" I asked, as he put the other end in his ears.

Kai had called for one last night.

Jonah held firm for a second before moving the stethoscope to the other side, and then behind me. He folded it back up and put it away in his bag a moment later.

"No. I'm not."

Tanner smirked, watching us from the kitchen.

I took in Jonah's rigid shoulders as he moved in front of me again. "Did I upset you by asking that?"

"Not at all." But his tone had cooled. He motioned to my shirt. "I'd like to press on your stomach. Would that be okay?" His gaze found mine. "Are you pregnant?"

I blanched. "No!"

Shit. Was I? But no. That was a ridiculous question. There'd been a Tinder date six months ago, but that was the last time I'd needed to fulfill those types of needs. I wasn't a prude, but I enjoyed sex in a relationship. And because of my job, meaningful relationships were few and far between. Over the last five years, I'd dated two guys, and both relationships had ended after eight months.

I was a good liar. I didn't feel proud of that, but with the way I lived, I had to be in order to survive. But somehow the lying always put a wall between myself and anyone I might be involved with. I began to feel more and more empty the longer I was with someone, and that meant the only other option was Blade. But the romantic feelings weren't there with him.

"Okay." Jonah pressed on my stomach. "Do you feel pain in any of these spots?" He moved and pressed on four areas on my stomach. I shook my head every time.

With a sigh, he sat back and reached for the pricking machine. "Your levels are fine. You're not diabetic, so I'd surmise your seizure was stress induced, mixed with the havoc your body experienced yesterday. It can happen. It's rare, very rare, but I've heard of it before." He frowned, hesitating, but reached into his bag again. He pulled out some papers, sliding them to me with a pen on top. "I'd like to request your file. Would you give me permission to do that?" He indicated the papers. "This more protects me, just so you know."

I got what he was saying. The file was probably already with him. Kai would've demanded it, with or without permission, and that was just a way to cover Jonah's back in case it was needed. With what this family could do, I was relieved to see one member followed the law.

I nodded and reached for the pen.

His mouth pressed in a firm line as I signed. "It wasn't supposed to be like that."

He stood, staring at Tanner. I couldn't see his face, but Tanner didn't seem fazed.

He shrugged and yawned. "Don't look at me, little brother. You and I both know we don't make the decisions."

"Yeah. Well." Jonah bent down to pick up his bag, putting the strap over his shoulder. He looked back to me, one of his hands sliding into his pocket. "Drink the juice and have some toast. Tanner will get it for you. Wait with the coffee. You should be fine now, but you're dehydrated. You need to be replenished before drinking that stuff."

He gave Tanner one more lingering look. Then he went back out the door and turned down the hallway, not going to the front entrance, leaving me alone with Tanner. Well, Tanner and the guards—two by the door and more I knew were just outside.

Tanner picked up the glass of juice he'd poured for me and stepped away from the counter. He paused, seeing where I was looking.

Motioning to the guards, he said, "Hey, Marco?"

One of the guards inclined his head.

"Take off. She won't leave, and Jonah will be back. We're good."

The guard didn't move. He didn't say anything either.

Tanner's eyes flicked upward. A soft curse slipped out under his breath. "Fuck's sake, guys. She can't take me. You all are outside every exit, and there's no way she can leave the grounds. The girl is helpless, and she won't attack me either." His eyes shifted to me. "Or I don't think she will."

The guards' response was to cross their arms in front of their chests and roll their shoulders back, raising themselves to their full heights.

Tanner growled, "Kai is the boss, but you're forgetting this is my place too. I can make your lives hell if I want to. Get gone. I mean it."

The two now shared a look, and Marco relented. "We'll be right outside the front door."

"Yeah." Tanner waved at their backs as they turned to leave. "You go stand there." He moved toward me as they left, closing the door behind them. He placed the juice in front of me. "Drink."

He stepped back to the counter as two pieces of toast popped up.

"Kai is scary, but so is Jonah if his orders aren't met."

I picked up my glass, taking a sip. The juice felt refreshing, and my stomach growled, as if remembering it was beyond the empty mark.

Tanner began to butter the toast.

"Jonah's a doctor?" I asked.

"Mmm-hmmm."

How did one brother become a doctor when another killed people for a living? I eyed Tanner. He was pulling fruit from the fridge. What did he do? How did he fit into this family?

"Did he kill the others last night?" I asked instead.

Tanner paused, straightening a little, his eyes growing more alert. "They're alive."

He picked up the plate of toast and bowl of fruit he'd put together. He walked them over to me.

"And they aren't here, if you're hoping to go look for them," he added. "They were moved to a different facility."

My mouth watered at the smell of the toast and the sight of the strawberries in front of me now. I hated that. I wanted to go through all levels of resistance, even a hunger strike if it came to it, but I couldn't. My stomach growled like a volcano ready to blow.

Tanner softened his tone. "Look." He sat across from me. "We took you because you're our best shot at finding our sister. That's all. If you help us, you get to go back to your life. It's as easy as that."

I glared. "You kidnapped me. It's not that simple."

He snorted. "Please. You can tell the prime minister we took you and nothing would happen. You're on the up and up with your job. You know our family can't be touched."

I scoffed.

He lifted an eyebrow, his smirk knowing. "Don't underestimate my brother. That's a fatal mistake if you do."

I straightened, holding the glass of juice in front of me. Its coolness calmed me for some reason. "I don't know where Brooke is. But even if I did, why would I help you find her? If Brooke went missing on her own, I'm sure she did it for a good reason."

Like she was scared of her brothers, or one of them?

Like she didn't want to be murdered the way her oldest brother had been, or their father?

"Brooke wasn't in the right frame of mind when she took off," Tanner countered. "Trust me on that." He leaned forward, his eyes boring into mine. "You know how close I was to her. I know you do. She told me how much she talked about me to you, so remember how much I loved her back then? It's more now."

He leaned back just as Jonah returned. "We all love her. A lot. We're looking out for her, for her safety."

Jonah slowed, hearing the last of his brother's words.

Tanner was right. I did remember how close she was to him, and how she adored Jonah, who was all grown up now.

"You were ten when Brooke left Hillcrest," I said to Jonah. "That'd make you twenty-three now?"

"My birthday was last week. I'm twenty-four." His answer was stiff, and he went into the kitchen.

He was a doctor at that age? That wasn't possible.

As if reading my thoughts, Tanner grinned. "Little Jonah's a genius. So take heed, Ray ray." A smile spread over his face. He was taunting me. "Whatever escape plan you're thinking of, it's already been thought out for you and taken care of. Between Kai and Jonah, every detail has been handled. Your best bet for getting out of here is to help us find Brooke."

I took in how assured he looked, how resigned Jonah seemed, and I remembered how they'd captured me, how they'd handled the gas station, and how everything had been calculated and planned out last night. My heart sank.

They were right.

I had to help them find Brooke.

Her image flashed in my mind—her social media pictures from the news—and I remembered holding her after Kai and his father drove away. I remembered how she'd sobbed in my arms, and I hardened inside.

Fuck. Them.

CHAPTER
TWELVE

I had three ways to leave.

Find Brooke. Escape. Or put them in a situation where they needed to let me go.

As I drank my orange juice, ate my toast, had a second glass of juice and then finally a cup of coffee, I savored every taste, because if worst came to worst, a hunger strike was a last resort. But even then... I ran through the scenarios. They could put a feeding tube in me.

I winced at the thought.

I hoped it didn't come to that. I really didn't. Another seizure, maybe? Jonah said it was rare and didn't think I'd suffer one again, but I could fake it? Could I do something else where they'd be forced to take me to a hospital? Maybe. That was another last resort, so escape first.

I'd have to try. They kept telling me it was pointless, but I needed to find out for myself.

And that meant I had to be in my best health, so I asked for a third piece of toast as I ate all of the fruit Tanner had given me.

I wasn't thinking about the Hider male they'd killed. I couldn't. I couldn't even focus on Brooke. Escape was it for me. If I could just get out of their estate, I knew Blade would be waiting for me. He would've traced all the phones to this location. His tech skills were nearly unmatched. He was the best, and he was an asset the 411 Network utilized often. We'd been placed near

Calgary for a reason. It was smack in the middle of the distribution line between Canada and the States.

I sat in the kitchen with Tanner and Jonah, who seemed content to sit in silence, for another hour before I started getting tired. Jonah noticed first.

"You need more rest to heal. You should sleep."

They called the guards, who took me back to the other part of the compound. I thought they'd take me to "my" room, even though I'd only been in it for a short time, but they didn't. They took me to Kai's apartment.

They left me alone, taking up their spots outside the door, and this time I did a more thorough search of the place.

The vents were too small to fit in.

The main window in the living room looked out over the same cliff the deck did. If I wanted to escape from this room, I would have to fall to my death. So that meant I needed to be able to move around the house more freely. There had to be another option elsewhere.

I really was tired. Jonah was right. I needed rest, so I crawled into Kai's bed and tried to not notice how good the sheets felt until I faded off.

. . .

I woke to darkness.

The curtains were pulled back from the glass doors, so moonlight filtered in, but it wasn't much. Then I sensed what must've woken me. A figure moved in the closet, and I heard rustling sounds. Clothes. Clothes being removed. A hanger clanging against another.

I didn't say anything, and after a moment he moved out to the main room.

Light flooded in from the bathroom before it faded, and I heard water come on. The light shone again when the door opened before it was flicked off.

The clock beside me said it was three in the morning. I had slept all afternoon and through the evening into nighttime.

My bladder was uncomfortable—that could also have been what woke me.

I didn't hear Kai come back, but I sensed him again. He paused at the end of the bed. "Should I turn the light on for you? Do you need the bathroom?"

I croaked, sitting up, "Yes. Thank you."

He flicked the light on, and it was blinding. I closed my eyes, keeping my head down as I got out of bed and hurried around him. I felt his gaze the entire time. The air electrified as I moved past him. I felt like I could breathe easier the farther away I got from him, and once I shut the door, I felt better.

Maybe just his presence had woken me?

I was pretty sure he intended to sleep with me. Was that why I was in his room? He hadn't pushed it before, and I hadn't considered it. Tanner had made no moves. Jonah either. The guards were all respectful. There'd been no lewd comments, no suggestion of anything sexual. But was that all done after tonight?

My body was calm. I wasn't reacting the way I should be in a kidnapping situation. It seemed as if old friends were keeping me away from home, but I could choose to leave if I wanted. That's how it felt to me, but that wasn't the truth.

I needed to wake up to this situation.

Had there been something in that juice earlier? I'd watched as Tanner poured the first glass. He hadn't put anything in it, and he'd poured himself a glass later. He drank from the same pitcher. I saw him pour the coffee. Had he put something in my mug before putting the coffee in? But Jonah hadn't wanted me to drink it. That didn't add up with them drugging me.

I knew I was dehydrated from the night before. I'd vomited everything out of me and cried away the rest.

My body really was exhausted from the shock.

Now I was in Kai's bed, sleeping, and he'd offered to turn the light on for me? He was being kind, when I knew he was cold and ruthless.

My head began to ache, and after relieving myself and washing up, I was nervous to go back into the room. I was nervous about dealing with Kai Bennett.

Where had he been today?

I knew the storm from last night was coming again. Kai was back. Kai was the one who would demand my assistance.

I sensed him on the other side of the door. Again there'd been no sound. I didn't see his shadow, but I knew he was there before he spoke.

"We're going to sleep. That's all, Riley."

A lump formed in my throat.

Again with him being kind. Patient. Calm.

My body leaned toward him, as if he were the shelter for me in this storm.

I gritted my teeth.

I needed to remember he'd killed that man. I needed to remember Cord and their father. Brooke had been scared of him.

But.

Even as I tried to remember all of those things, my body was still drawn forward. I sagged toward the door, wanting to open it and step out. He was seductive without trying to be seductive.

My hand shook as I opened the door, and there he was. My stomach jumped to my sternum. My heart picked up its pace.

He wore only sweatpants, the waistband hanging low. I couldn't help myself. I took in every single muscle of his chest and stomach. Even his hips were defined. He straightened from where he'd been leaning against the doorframe and his eyes darkened, turning completely black as he looked me over too.

I became self-conscious in only a T-shirt and a pair of boxer briefs I'd found in his closet. I'd changed before crawling in bed after breakfast.

I was wearing his clothes, with no bra.

His gaze settled on my chest. I felt my breasts hardening.

"Tanner told me you didn't kill the others," I blurted, needing to think of something else, to change the mood. "Is that true?"

It worked.

Kai's eyes whipped to mine, and though he didn't move, I felt him pulling away. A wall slid between us.

His face hardened. "Yes. Your friends are alive. Your Network was notified of their capture, along with yours."

They already knew. I had notified them, but I held my tongue.

His eyes began to smolder, and a taunting glint showed as he said, "But then again, you already knew that since you're the one who called them."

Now I snapped to attention.

How had he known? Had the Hiders told him?

He chided softly, "You think one of my men left that phone by accident?"

Everything in me fell to the floor. Hope. Rebellion. Strength. It was gone now, and I knew what he said was correct. Everything had been thought out, even the bait for me to take.

It was then I realized the real reason they'd taken me. It all clicked in place.

I'd been a fool.

Despair washed over me. "You didn't take me because you thought Brooke notified me, did you?" It was true. I felt it now, and I saw an arrogant look flare over his face. "You took me because of the 411 Network."

He'd kidnapped me, knowing I would call them if I had a chance. And I did—exactly what he wanted.

His tone was soft, but it sent chills down my back. "Your friend Blade isn't the only tech specialist at the top of his game. We have one of our own." He leaned toward me, his breath an irritating caress on my face as I closed my eyes. I couldn't move away, but I wouldn't lean toward him.

He moved closer until I could feel the heat from his body. He was an inch away. I could hear him breathing.

"Your friend does not know where you are, and your cooperation is no longer needed. Your network is looking for Brooke for us, to get you back."

His hand touched my arm, zapping me with the contact. His arm curled around me, tugging me against him. Sensations seared through my insides. He bent down, his breath now on my neck.

"With or without your help, I will get my sister back, and then you will be released. Until then..." He ducked, swinging me up into his arms.

I gasped, my arms grabbing his neck in panic. But I didn't need to. He cradled me against his chest as he returned to his bedroom. He moved to the side of the bed I'd been lying on, closest to the balcony, and laid me down.

He stared at me before pulling back, and I couldn't move.

"I didn't intend this, if it matters to you. You were supposed to be taken and put in a nice, comfortable room. You were supposed to be given anything you wanted, except your freedom, and your Network would hand-deliver my sister to me for your safety. I wasn't even planning on talking to you, except to ask about Brooke, but here you are."

His hand went to my face, his thumb on my bottom lip. He traced it, and I couldn't suppress a shiver.

It wasn't a bad shiver. That was the problem. I would never understand my reaction to him.

He stepped back, his hand falling away, and triumph flared in his eyes. "Sleep tonight, Riley. That is all I ask of you." He moved to the other side of the bed.

I slipped under the covers and felt the bed move as he joined me. The light went off a second after that.

"What happens if I kill you in your sleep?" I asked. "You trust me to sleep here, with you?"

He laughed softly. "No, but for some reason I can't make myself have the men take you away. So for now, you stay. If you kill me, then you'll die as well."

"Are you going to hurt your sister when you get her back?"

He didn't laugh this time. "She thinks I will, but no. She ran with the wrong assumption in her mind. That is all I can say."

"Why?"

He sighed, barely a foot away from me. I could feel it.

"Tomorrow we can talk. Perhaps you'll find some answers. Until then, I am tired. I have been traveling all day and had many meetings. I want to sleep. Sleep, Riley."

But I didn't, even long after he did.

I heard his breathing even out, and I tried rallying inside.

I made myself remember that male Hider. I remembered seeing the guard pull the trigger, the spray of blood, and the way his body slumped to the floor.

He died because of me, and I vowed I would find his family.

I tried to summon the energy and courage to slip from the bed, get to the kitchen, and find a knife. I envisioned stabbing it deep inside Kai.

I had to make that guy's death stand for something. I had to.

That promise was the only way to make it right in my head. Because instead of getting up, I fell asleep.

CHAPTER THIRTEEN

I slept three hours.

I could tell my body had caught up on sleep when I woke, because I felt good. I felt sane. And I watched Kai sleep for the next hour.

Now that I wasn't sleep-deprived or in shock, I could think more clearly. I reviewed everything that had happened—with Kai, Tanner, Jonah, everyone, everything.

I was weak. That's the only explanation I had for why I wasn't running right now, or fighting right now.

I hadn't had sex in six months. There was that too.

I was attracted to Kai Bennett. No matter who he was, that was just a fact. After last night—feeling my body wanting to go to him while my mind screamed at me to keep away—that was the only explanation I could justify. I was weak, and I hadn't lusted after a man since that Tinder date. And even that guy's effect on me had been minimal compared to Kai Bennett's.

No. Brooke's brother.

I had to pull back. I had to erect walls between him and me, because I knew what I needed to do. First names weren't a part of it. *Names* weren't a part of it. He was Brooke's brother. He was the reason she'd run. He was Cord's murderer, their father's killer.

Murderer. Killer. He was those things too.

Hider training told us to strip away our humanity. It would be there in the times we needed it, but to get to the abused, we had to walk into hell. We had to be prepared for whatever was on the other side. When they'd taught us this, I'd thought of my mother. I'd thought about how she'd been beaten within an inch of her life, how he had left her to die and called someone else to take care of the body. That Hider—though my father had no idea he was with the Network—hadn't known what he was walking into. If my father had caught him, backtracked for some reason, or followed up, that Hider would've had to kill him. Because if he hadn't, I had no doubt Bruce Bello would've killed the Hider and my mother.

That's what I needed to do this morning. I lie here, beside this man, and began to strip away my humanity.

When we Hiders opened the door, saw the survivor, realized the scene was safe, our humanity came back to us.

Except sometimes it didn't.

I hated that, and I was ashamed because of it.

It was why we did what we did, but when we opened those doors, sometimes I didn't feel a thing for the survivor. I wouldn't feel a thing until we had already taken them where they needed to go. It was usually on the drive home that my humanity came back to me.

The car would be silent. I would be riding in the back or next to either Carol or Blade in the front, and I would gasp when it returned.

No one ever looked over at me. No one asked. I didn't know if they knew or understood, but it wasn't until then that I shed a tear for what we'd done. We'd helped someone, and I was grateful.

But I was also thankful because I'd gotten through it, and so had my team. Blade and Carol were like my family by now. I'd spent almost more time with them than anyone else. Almost.

Sitting up, I slipped from the bed, stood, and looked down at this man sleeping.

It wasn't right, because at a time when I needed not to feel, that's all I was doing. I still felt so much confusion over how I could lust so much for this murderer. I felt the same disgust with myself that I'd felt all those times when I'd needed to feel my heart and hadn't.

I usually pushed it down. Now I didn't.

I allowed the disgust to grow to loathing. I loathed myself. It filled every inch of my body, every pore, every cell, every hair until finally, finally it moved past me and onto him.

It was my own self-hatred, but I allowed it to spread beyond me.

I couldn't think. If I did, it wouldn't work. Padding around the bed, I did what I'd vowed to do two days ago.

There was a knife block in the kitchen, and I took one of the smaller ones. I knew it was just as sharp as the others, and I could wield it with better precision.

I went back to the bedroom.

The sun had begun to rise outside.

A small glimmer of light was beginning to warm the room. It was just enough. I could make out his sleeping form.

I paused in the doorway, gripping the knife.

I knew what would happen. If I killed him, he'd said I would die too. That meant I would have to do this, then bolt.

I probably wouldn't make it, but I had to try. I would never get this chance again. I knew that with certainty. It was now or never.

I raised the knife—

—and his eyes opened.

I launched forward at the same time he shot upright. He caught me in the air. The knife flew out of my hand, and he rolled us so I was beneath him. I tried to fight, kicking at him, but he only shifted so his entire body was on top of me.

I tried to punch him; he grabbed my arms and slammed them down on the bed.

Every inch of him was plastered against me.

The whole thing happened in less than three seconds, and not a word was spoken between us.

His eyes were heated and angry, his jaw clenched. A vein stuck out in his neck. His eyebrows pulled together, and a buzz sounded at the door.

He cursed under his breath, jumping off the bed in one lithe movement. He pointed at me as he left the bedroom. "Stay."

A moment later, he opened the apartment door. He had a brief conversation before the door shut again, and the lights in the apartment came on. He strode back into the bedroom. I hadn't moved, and he glared at me a second.

"Get up. Get dressed. We're leaving."

There should've been a knot in my throat. But there wasn't anything, just acceptance. My body was heated, my breathing shallow and fast.

I sat up. "Are you going to kill me?"

He snorted, pulling clothes out of his dresser. "Don't tempt me." His eyes raked over me. "Your Network called. They found Brooke."

Brooke? No.

There was no way they could work that fast, even if there were two Blades. It was a trap. It had to be, but I didn't say anything. This could be my opening. If I didn't kill Kai, I could escape. I just had to be ready.

"Riley."

Why did he have to sound so tired?

"Get dressed."

He left. I heard the apartment door open, close, and lock a moment later.

The knife seemed to mock me where it lay on the floor. Ignoring it, I stood and dressed.

CHAPTER FOURTEEN

"Did you get in trouble last night?"

Tanner sidled up next to me as we waited on the front steps of the compound mansion. He looked toward Kai and the guards, who were chatting down on the driveway. It was early, around six-thirty, and a cool breeze shifted around us, along with a bit of fog. It gave an eerie feel to the atmosphere.

Which I wasn't feeling. Because I was pissed.

I was mad I hadn't made my move in the first place, instead of sleeping next to Kai. And I was mad that when I had made it, I'd failed. Somehow I was even mad that I'd made the move at all. Nothing made me happy this morning.

And I was still kidnapped. That put a damper on things too.

I scowled at Tanner. "Do not start."

He bit back a laugh, jostling his shoulder with mine as I heard a groan behind us. Jonah came to stand on the other side of his brother, rubbing his hands together. He dropped the same EMT-like bag he'd had yesterday at his feet before reaching inside his jacket to adjust something. Then he hooked his bag back over his shoulder.

Both Tanner and I watched him.

Jonah looked over, raising an eyebrow. "What?"

"You're going with us?" Tanner asked.

Jonah shrugged, holding back a yawn. "I figured I could get a ride. Kai just wanted me to come check on her." He nodded to me.

"And she looks good, so I have another rotation I want to finish before the weekend."

Tanner looked at the sky before smiling wide and thumping his brother on the back. "Jonah's in his second year of residency. He's got what? How many years left before you're a real surgeon?"

Jonah grimaced. "Five, you asshole. And I'm a surgeon now."

"You know what I mean." Tanner laughed, drawing the attention of a few of the guards and Kai, who were still talking on the driveway.

I hadn't been ostracized or told to stand here by myself, but it must have looked like I was being punished, which Tanner had picked up on. It was probably me—I did feel like a child being disciplined. It was stupid. And irrational.

But mixed with the weirdness I was feeling about my failed attempt to kill Kai—regretting it and not at the same time—I was certifiably messed up. That was me.

I scowled because I hated feeling this way.

All my life, I'd known what I wanted. I was clear on my path.

Before Hillcrest, my sole purpose had been to avoid my father and tend to my mother. When I went to Hillcrest, my mission had been to learn, to have fun with Brooke, and to stay at Hillcrest as much as possible (even over the extended holidays). Then after Hillcrest, my goal had been to survive. That was it.

Everything changed when the 411 Network approached me.

After that, my purpose became being the best Hider operative I could be. That meant finishing my education, training, and accepting the post they assigned me to. My mother was in love with another man. They'd had another child and a second not long after that, and she was fulfilling her goal of just living. That was a big middle finger to Bruce Bello, though he didn't know.

One day, I hoped to share the news with him that he'd failed in killing us. I included myself in that because I knew it would've happened one day if I'd stayed around. It'd been inevitable. A man like that never changed.

See? My whole life had been clear and concrete, until now. Now my head was all muddled up.

Despite my circumstances, I enjoyed spending time with Tanner and Jonah. Yet I was worried about Brooke. And I was kidnapped. I hated Kai Bennett. Or I thought so. Yes, I did. I did. But my body didn't.

Fuck me.

I was a mess.

"Let's move." Kai stepped aside as an entire caravan of SUVs rolled in, stopping before us.

Tanner and Jonah started toward one of the middle ones. I followed until Kai called out, "You're with me, slicer."

I whipped my head around, narrowing my eyes.

Had there been a glimmer of a grin on his face? No. His expression was stoic, as it had been the whole time we stood there.

Tanner frowned. "Why? She can roll with us."

Kai didn't spare him a look, only ducked into an SUV two down from us. "She goes with me. That's final."

I didn't miss the sympathetic look his brothers sent me before I went over. Kai had taken the seat farthest from the house, so I didn't have to go around. A guard stood at my door, waiting for me, and I ducked inside, trying not to appreciate the warmth and aroma of sandalwood. It reminded me of back home, with Blade and Carol.

Kai had his briefcase open on his lap, and he was going through some papers. He gestured to the console in front of us, "There's coffee or tea if you want it." He shuffled one piece of paper behind the other. "It's not scalding hot, in case you were tempted to throw it on me." He shuffled a second paper behind the pile.

I stared at him.

There wasn't anything else I could do. I didn't know what to say, and a gurgling sound emerged from my throat. I gulped it down, embarrassed.

The guards closed the doors, and it was quiet. Almost peaceful.

I'd expected two rows of seats like in the SUV I'd ridden in to get here. But this one had just enough room for Kai and myself. Two doors opened in the front, but there was a separator between us and the guards. I couldn't see them, or hear them, but I felt the SUV dip under their weight as they got inside.

What did one say in this situation? I'd tried to kill him. I'd failed. And now he was offering me coffee or tea.

"I had to try." So I guess that's what I was going to say.

He paused in moving the papers. I could see him look my way in the window's reflection, and with a jolt, his eyes met mine there too.

He showed no emotion though. "I know." And he went back to reading his papers. "I would've too."

What? I looked, but he was ignoring me again.

Then the cars started, and I had a feeling this was how it was going to be for the entire trip. Total and complete silence.

CHAPTER
FIFTEEN

I was right.

We were now on hour four, and my bladder was screaming. I hadn't wanted to, but I'd succumbed to both the tea and the coffee. I drank the tea first, because that's what I would've done at home. Tea and berries: my morning routine, along with a good workout or yoga. Blade sometimes joined me. Carol never did. She'd watch us do yoga and crack jokes while she crunched down on her chip of the week.

The tea hadn't fulfilled me, and I'd itched for the coffee. After my two cups yesterday, I was starting to understand why everyone was obsessed with it. There was an addictive quality. I was now wanting to go to the bathroom and also wanting a second cup of coffee.

I was returning to my American roots, it seemed—not with the bathroom part, the coffee part. My mom used to love the stuff. So did my dad...

My stomach took a sudden dip down.

I hadn't talked about Bruce Bello in years, and I was now sitting next to someone who knew him. Who knew the situation, fully.

"What is he like now?"

I asked the question before I realized I was going to. My voice sounded hoarse, as if I were half scared to ask, and I suppose I was. I was terrified of the answer.

Kai had settled down in his seat, reading on his computer, but he looked up.

I didn't look over, but I could feel his gaze. I kept my head turned away.

I heard him close the computer. "Your father is one of the stupidest human beings I've ever met."

I looked over.

His nostrils flared. His eyes were fierce.

He folded his hands over his computer, holding my gaze. "I met him when I was fourteen. He was having a meeting with my father. He was a fool. My father used yours. He transported our drugs alongside his products, and your father had no idea until it was too late. There are many factors on which to base your father's stupidity, but that was the first I remember." He broke away, turning to his window. "There's not been a good meeting with him since."

That lump in my throat was back. Growing.

I pressed my hands together, sliding them between my legs to still the shaking. "You still do business with him?"

"He's a means to an end. That is all." Kai looked back, his gaze piercing through me. "Would you like me to stop working with him? If I do, he will go out of business. He will lose all his companies. Your cousin will leave him, if he hasn't killed her by then. He will suffer."

The way he said that, I could tell it wasn't a new idea to him.

My lips parted. "That's what you were going to do to him? I thought you said you'd kill him."

He didn't even blink. "I could do that easily. He would get angry, curse us, proclaim he doesn't need us. He would be lying, though, and he would soon learn he needs us. He would come back to us, at some point. He would beg even. You could be there. You could walk out and shoot him, if you'd like."

God.

He offered murder like he was offering me coffee.

I shook my head, my stomach twisting. "I don't yearn to kill him."

There was silence.

A full minute.

And then he said, "You're a liar like your father."

"I am not!" I hissed. "I am nothing like him."

He quirked an eyebrow, undisturbed. "You want to kill your father. Admit that, at least to yourself. Just like you want to kill me, half the time."

I closed my eyes. I wasn't going to take that bait. He knew I was conflicted. He was too. So maybe because of that, I confessed.

"I daydream about revealing myself to him. I want to see the look on his face when he recognizes me, when I tell him my mother and I are both alive and he failed."

"And then you want to shoot him?" I could hear his smile. "Or use a knife as you tried with me?"

Could I slice my father? Push a knife deep in his throat, or chest?

I envisioned the tearing of his skin, his tendons, and how I would embed that knife in his muscle. How he would spasm, his mouth gaping at me. He would grab for the knife, but he'd only hold it. If he pulled it out, blood would explode from him. There'd be a certain look in his eyes when he realized he was going to die, and at my hand. Blood would trickle from the wound, coating his hands, his chest, then run down his pants to pool at his feet.

It would be warm blood. I would probably be sprayed with it.

A sick feeling took root in me, and I knew Kai was wrong.

I shook my head again. "No, I don't want to kill him. I just want him to know he failed and never to be able to hurt us again."

"You'd like him ruined then?"

The hairs on the back of my neck stood up, and I shifted my head to him.

"Why do I get the feeling you'll do just that if I say yes right now?" I murmured.

His eyes narrowed, but the lines around his mouth softened. "Maybe I'm looking for an excuse to get rid of Bruce Bello? Maybe helping out my sister's friend is good enough."

I scoffed, trying not to feel affected by his words. "Then who'll transport your drugs for you?"

"We aren't in the drug business anymore."

Oh. My shoulders relaxed.

"We transport guns now."

Oh! My shoulders slumped.

"But to answer your original question, your father is worse than he was when you were a child. He's more vain. He's weak. He's greedy. He's more violent. He barely remembers to show empathy or consideration even to keep up appearances, and he needs to die. Whether at my hand or yours, that's up for debate." Kai spoke succinctly, as if he were at a business meeting.

He turned and pressed a button on his door. "Let's take C route and pull off at the next gas station. Miss Bello needs the bathroom."

He released the button, opening his laptop once more.

"How did you know?"

He didn't spare me a look. "You've been shifting in your seat for the last thirty minutes, and glancing at the coffee with both yearning and regret for the last ten." He lifted his gaze to me. "You're not as hard to read as you hoped you would be. It's a quality you might want to work on if you continue as a 411 Network operative after this."

Well then.

He went back to working, and I was effectively dismissed.

I tried to rally up indignation, disgust, or even anger. All of them failed me. For some reason, I was more mystified than anything.

That was another emotion I'd never felt before.

CHAPTER SIXTEEN

The ride after our stop was more comfortable.
Tanner must've gone to bat for me, because Kai allowed me
to ride with him and Jonah when we left the gas station. They told
me stories about Brooke, starting from when she left Hillcrest and
continuing through just before she'd disappeared. I knew they
skipped over the bad parts, like their father's death or whatever
happened that led to Brooke going missing, but it was nice to hear
about her.

It felt like my old friend was back with me, and she was just as
vivacious and adventurous as she'd been with me at school. Tanner
told most of the stories, with Jonah jumping in. He spoke quickly,
seeming excited to be able to add something to the conversation.
But Tanner was clearly the one with the closest relationship with
her.

Just as it had been in the Hillcrest days.

They were cautious when speaking about Kai, but sped up as
soon as he wasn't involved. Both were smiling, laughing.

The last few hours sped away like that, until I realized we'd
been traveling for eight hours.

"Why don't you guys fly?"

They quieted, seeming startled by my question.

I looked between them. "I mean, it'd save you time. Right?"

Jonah coughed and turned toward his window.

The car went from feeling light to being suffocating. I frowned.

Tanner responded, his voice low, "Cord died in a plane accident."

That was how he'd died?

Tanner frowned. "Shit. What'd Brooke say about how he died?"

I must've reacted.

I shrugged, suddenly interested in my hands. They were dry. Very dry. Too dry. I needed lotion.

"Nothing, just...that he died."

I was still looking at my hands when Tanner snorted. "Right."

The conversation ended, and we rode in silence for another twenty minutes until Jonah said out of the blue, "She talked about you all the time."

A shiver went down my spine.

They were talking about her as if she were dead, not somewhere else.

I tried to shake that feeling. It was wrong. She was fine. She *would* be fine, wherever she was.

"Really?"

"Yeah." His head rested against his headrest, and he swallowed before adding, "She never shut up, actually. It was sweet in a way, but annoying too." He opened his eyes enough to squint at me. "No offense. It was just that she acted like she was back at school, even up till last year."

Tanner coughed, and whether it was intentional or not, Jonah quieted.

The brothers shared a look before Tanner glanced down, then murmured in an almost distraught tone, "It was six months ago. She changed six months ago."

Why?

What happened?

Those questions burned in my throat, and I wanted to know all the answers. I wanted to know the adult Brooke, what she'd been like before she changed and how did she change.

"Yeah." Jonah's eyes closed again. "Six months ago."

I looked between the two. What the hell had happened?

Ask them!

It was as if Brooke was yelling at me. I imagined her voice, crying out in my head.

"What happened six months ago? How did she change?"

Please don't shut up now. Please don't remember I'm the enemy and shut me out.

I held my breath, worried they'd do just that.

"I don't know." Tanner expelled a sudden rush of air. His eyes were bleak, flicking up to mine before sliding to the window. "She just changed. She seemed happy, bubbly, and then nothing. Something happened. Whatever it was, that's why she's gone."

"Because she's scared of Ka—"

"Stop!" Tanner said sharply. He glared at Jonah, controlling his voice. "Family first, Jo."

Jonah's eyes clasped shut a second. He raised a hand, rubbing his forehead before letting it fall to his side again. He sighed. "Yeah. Right. Yeah. My bad." His eyes were bleak when he glanced at me. "Sorry, Riley."

Damn.

It'd been building, and then nothing. A gate slammed down, stopping the flow.

Disappointment filled me, but I had a feeling I'd be in this car for another few hours. Another opportunity might present itself.

CHAPTER
SEVENTEEN

The stop was sudden.

We were whizzing along, and then suddenly our vehicle veered to the left, then right, and we skidded to a halt. I grabbed my armrest to keep from falling over, and after the second veer, Jonah slammed an arm over my chest, cementing me in place. The two guards were holding on themselves, but trying to watch out for Tanner and Jonah at the same time.

"What the hell?" Tanner said once we were at a complete stop, but he should've held his breath.

The doors flew open. The guards jumped out, guns already drawn, and they stood point for a second. Then, they put their guns back in their holsters and leaned down.

Almost speaking in unison, they said, "Mr. Bennett, please exit the vehicle."

Jonah and Tanner shared a look, both frowning, but they got out.

I'd started to follow Jonah when the door behind me slammed shut, then locked, and the guard facing me bent down. He nodded behind me. "Not you, ma'am."

Ma'am? Really.

"But—"

The door behind me opened again. I turned to see Kai Bennett getting inside, taking the seat Tanner had vacated.

A guard stood outside his door, but Kai motioned to him. "I'll be fine. Go in the front."

The door shut.

"What's going on?"

Kai didn't answer, but he didn't need to. The front doors opened. The vehicle dipped down as two men got inside, and a second later, we were moving forward again.

I twisted to look behind.

Tanner and Jonah were standing on the side of the road. One vehicle remained with them, along with four guards, but the rest were following us.

Kai sighed, taking out his phone. "Change of plans." His dark eyes came to rest on me, and I tried not to feel the weight of them. His eyebrows dipped down momentarily before they cleared and the same impassive expression came over him.

He turned his attention to his phone. "Sit back, Riley. No matter your worries, you are fine, and you will be fine."

This guy—I wanted to yell at him, scream at him. I wanted to rail that what he was doing wasn't "fine" and I had plenty to "worry" about.

But I didn't.

Because I wasn't a complete idiot.

Then—fuck it. I guess I was. "Say that to the Hider you killed," I spat.

I looked out the window, biting down on my tongue. I'd already messed up. I shouldn't have said that. It was like poking a bear, or a panther. A very dangerous and deadly panther.

He was Brooke's brother.

I tried to tell myself that, calm myself down a little bit.

Brooke's brother. He did care for her. Or I hoped he did. He had taken her out of school because he wanted her with him, and I remembered that slight pause before he got into the SUV when I'd first seen him. He had been worried about Brooke.

He was capable of that emotion, at least.

Who was I kidding?

Why was I kidding myself? That was a better question.

His response was quiet. "I didn't kill your Hider."

"What?" I felt the blood draining from my face.

His eyes were still hooded, but tired. I saw the bags under them.

"We rigged it, fastened a blood bag under his hat. The gun was blank, but the force of the air was enough to puncture the bag. Your man knew ahead of time what would happen. He was to play dead or the next bullet would be real. He played dead. Your reaction sold it the best." His lip tugged up for just a second before falling back. "Thank you for that."

"Wha—" That made no sense. "Why would you do that?"

"As of three hours ago, we let the other Hiders go. We felt your Network needed further motivation. Your man was kept isolated like you. He's still with us, but I've no doubt the others relayed that we already killed one man, and we'd have no problem killing you next."

"Why, though? They were already looking for Brooke." I swallowed over a knot. "Weren't they?"

"They gave us a time and place to meet, but it was too soon. They found my sister too quickly."

I nodded. "Because it's not true, you mean? That's what you're saying."

"Letting the other Hiders out wasn't for your Network. It was for one person in your Network."

For...

My mind jumped ahead.

"For Blade." Because...

"My information tells me he's in love with you. If the Brooke they found is fake, he'll find the real one." He held up his phone. "And he says he did. He sent me new coordinates for a meeting."

Blade was in love with me?

Sadness hit me first. Not shock.

That told me everything.

Maybe I knew, in a back part of my mind. Maybe I'd known for a while and had shoved it back there so I didn't have to deal with it.

I looked away. I couldn't bring myself to face this man, this monster that might look like a goddamn angel, but was most definitely a murderer. He'd lied about killing that man, this time. But there'd been others. It didn't matter.

And he knew about Blade. He'd used Blade. He'd used someone I cared about against me, and according to his brothers, it was the same thing he was doing to his sister. Brooke still cared for me. Tanner and Jonah had said as much, and Kai was using me to find her. Against her wishes.

"Fuck you," I gutted out. I couldn't stop myself.

A rage built in me. It bloomed, filling my chest.

"Fuck you," I said it again, blinking to clear my vision.

"You didn't know about his feelings?"

My throat burned.

It wasn't his place to make me face it, to force the time I'd have to deal with it. That wasn't his place.

Fuck. Him.

I didn't reply. I didn't trust myself right now.

"You don't love him back."

Even that statement, because it *was* a statement, not a question, infuriated me.

I rounded on him, my eyes blazing. "It's not your place."

He studied me, not reacting. I felt his gaze over every inch of my body, and he almost lazily looked back up to meet my eyes. His head tilted to the side.

"No, it's not. But you're forgetting *your* place."

I felt slapped.

He was right.

He murdered people. I saved them.

I almost scoffed until he added softly, "I will do anything to find my sister, and love is the best motivation there is."

I had looked away, but damn him. I lifted my eyes, against my wishes. As always, something about him drew me in, his words lured me.

Our eyes locked. I could almost hear the jail cell click in place, with me on one side and him on the other. He dangled the key in front of me, laughing, and I was helpless to stop listening to him, hopeless to find a way out.

That's how I felt until his next words washed over me.

"I thought at first to use you to find my sister, but seeing you, I knew you would never turn against Brooke. Because of love. You love her. I don't know if it's as a friend, as a sister, or because she brought a moment of good into your life, but for whatever reason, I know you are loyal. I respect that, but if I can't use you in one way, I will use you in another. There are always angles."

He tipped his head forward, his eyes almost admonishing me. "I'm very good at my job, and there are always ways to get what I want. Finding my sister is what I want." *Right now.*

He didn't say the words, but I heard them.

There was no judgment in what he had said. He talked to me as if he were educating a student, filling me in, letting me know what to expect from him.

Maybe that's what he was doing?

He'd told me I was a surprise to him last night.

Maybe I needed to turn off the emotions and listen to him as a Hider. My training said no emotions. I was embarrassed because in that regard, I knew he was outdoing me. He was winning. I didn't know quite what the battle was, but I knew I was losing.

"Blade sent you new coordinates for Brooke then?"

He loved his sister. Perhaps I could turn the tables? Get *him* to talk.

He smiled at me, and I knew he was laughing. I saw it in his eyes.

"I've been doing this all my life. You're playing catch-up, but it is fun to see."

He sat back, turning away and pulling his phone out.

The conversation was done. He had dismissed me.

And damn him, because now all I wanted to do was to get him to talk.

Instead, I sat back and plotted.

CHAPTER EIGHTEEN

When we stopped again, it was in the basement parking lot of a hotel.

Vehicles surrounded us, and I was stunned that Kai had let us get so close to others. The guards stood around us. Kai stepped to the side and talked to one of them before the man nodded and left us, hurrying across the lot.

A door closed in the distance.

We could hear conversation, a laugh, a baby crying.

"We're in Kelowna."

I didn't know what surprised me more, that we were in a small city a few hours from Vancouver, that Kai had told me, or that Blade had sent us here.

I only said, "Oh."

Kai eyed me again, his eyebrows up. "You're not surprised? You expected this?"

I shot him a look. "I thought you were better at this than I could ever be?"

He grinned. "I am, and you seem confused. I'm wondering why."

I shrugged. "Maybe I'm just surprised you told me where we are."

He laughed. "Maybe I'm lying, checking to see if you'd be surprised at our location."

The guard was returning, hurrying with a hotel worker alongside him.

Kai glanced over and saw them, but turned back to me. He ducked his head down, stepping close, and everyone else was pushed aside. It was just the two of us.

"I thought you'd be happy to be returned to your friend."

I flushed, but it was an angry flush. I was heated all over. "I would be happy, if that were the case. If it is, you get your sister, the sister who ran from you. And maybe I don't trust you, and I don't believe you'll hand me over when and if everything works out." My eyes narrowed. "Maybe I don't believe a word you say."

He was silent, observing me.

I had a feeling he was considering my words, sifting through them.

And then I knew he had been, because he said, "I don't believe you."

"What a surprise." I sneered.

He stepped even closer, softening his tone. I could feel the heat from his body. "You have claimed over and over that you don't know where my sister is. That's what I don't believe. You *do* know where she is." He stepped back, and when he spoke again, tone matched his gaze, both suddenly cold and calculating. "My sister isn't here, but it'll be fun to find out how your friend thinks he can fool me."

With that, he turned and started forward.

I was stunned enough that I didn't move, and a guard had to grab my arm and guide me forward.

I almost stumbled over my feet, but I couldn't go there. I couldn't think about Brooke, or Blade, or what was going to happen next. If I did, I was going to do something to get myself killed. And I couldn't do that. Not yet.

I had people to live for. I had a mission to live for.

Pay attention! I heard Blade reprimand me in my head.

He was right, or my training was right.

I had to take note of what we were doing, always. I had to remember everything.

We went to a back elevator, in a back hallway. It was the cargo elevator, the one the workers used for food and laundry and who knew what else. It took us to the top floor, and the hotel worker seemed nervous. She dropped the key card twice before the guard used it instead.

The doors opened.

We stepped out to a small hallway, turned immediately to the left, and another door opened for us.

It was the penthouse. Or so I assumed because it was grand enough to overlook the bay behind the hotel.

It had a kitchen, a dining room, a living room, and there were three rooms just off the main one. Three bedrooms.

I knew, without looking, without asking, that Kai Bennett had rented the entire floor. He wouldn't let his privacy or security be challenged by having outsiders so close.

The worker spoke to him as I walked to the window, looking out over the pool and water beyond. She was still nervous, but there was also a hitch in her voice. She wanted to impress him. She would've slept with him. I heard that too in her voice. She was offering her body, and when he didn't reply, but his guard did, it was a rejection.

Why I cared was beyond me.

It just made me burn even more with hatred. I hated Kai Bennett.

He could fuck whoever he wanted.

The worker said her goodbyes, adding that if we needed anything, her number was on her card. She was the manager, I realized, but it didn't matter. She still wanted Kai, not even noticing there was a female in his presence being kept there against her will.

Maybe that was on me? Maybe I should've made it more apparent, but chancing a look at Kai where he stood a few feet away, I knew it wouldn't have mattered.

Power oozed out of him. I could've told her I'd been kidnapped, and he would've just laughed, saying I was making a joke, and she would've believed him. He could've said I was sick. I was bipolar. I was off my meds. Anything, and she would've believed him.

The door shut behind her.

Kai nodded to his guards, and they all dispersed as well.

I didn't look. I knew a handful would stand guard outside our door. They would all take their turns, and the rest would either sleep in the other rooms or relax.

For all the badness in him, Kai treated his guards well.

He spoke from behind me. He was close, but I didn't know how close. I didn't look to see. "You can have the room on the right."

I could've baited him, said something about not trusting me, not making me sleep with him, but I didn't. I bit my tongue, and I felt him leave the room. The other bedroom door closed.

I still remained. A full minute, maybe more. My eyes were blinded, with emotion or tears, I didn't know.

I felt trapped.

And helpless.

And... I wasn't sure the exact reason for either of those emotions, because under both of them was another one, one I didn't want to feel at all.

Instead of naming it, I turned for my room.

I stopped short in the doorway. He'd given me the bigger of the two rooms. This was the master suite, with a king-sized bed in the middle of the room and an ensuite bathroom—glass-walled shower, clawfoot bathtub, two sinks.

I turned and found that yes, there was a balcony, but as I moved toward it, my heart sank. Like the one at the house, it was at least thirty floors up.

There was no pool underneath, just the edge of a golf course. Two golf carts drove by down below, and I noticed Kai sitting on his balcony. He watched me, seeming almost curious as to what I would do.

"You're not worried I'll climb down?"

He frowned, just slightly. "Why would you, if I'm going to return you to your friend soon?"

He had me there.

The side of his mouth tugged up. "Unless you think, like I do, that your friend is lying to us?"

I straightened, my head rising. I grabbed the railing and my hands curled around it, tightening enough so my knuckles stretched.

"Blade wouldn't lie."

Not even a blink. "I would, for the woman I loved. There's nothing I won't do to get my sister back." A glimmer of a smile showed. "So yes, your friend would lie. For you."

I felt a punch from his words. Good or bad, I didn't know, but I felt it. I loosened my hold on the railing.

He stood, nodding toward the view. "Climb down, if you want. I'll just find you again." Goddamn him. He smirked now. "There's nowhere you can hide from me. And you know it." He turned to go inside, but said over his shoulder, "Sleep, Riley. You need some rest. We meet your friend in two hours."

Two hours.

My arms were suddenly shaking. I smoothed a hand over my stomach, trying to calm myself, but it was pointless.

I had two hours, until what?

Blade wasn't a liar. I knew him, but Kai was right. Blade might not lie, but he would set a trap. He would choose his words carefully, and I didn't have a good feeling about whatever was going to happen in two hours.

I just didn't know what I could do about it.

• • •

Two hours later, I hadn't slept.

How could I?

Something was going to happen, and it was going to be very bad. I felt it in my gut. When I heard Kai open his door across the suite, I sat up in my bed. I felt him coming toward me, literally felt him. There were no sounds. No warning, just a trickle of energy that spread over my body. I stood, crossing to the door just as I knew he was on the other side.

Holding my breath, I could hear my pulse pounding in my eardrums. After a moment I heard his voice. Quiet, a tender whisper. "Riley."

It wasn't a question, as if he were wondering if I was asleep and didn't want to wake me. It was a statement, resigned.

He knew I was standing a few inches from the door as well.

Reaching out, not saying a word, I turned the handle, and there he was. He was suddenly so close. His presence was overwhelming. I felt him sliding inside of me, taking over, and I gulped because my body responded to him, to his closeness.

He had a hold of me, whether I wanted him to or not. I couldn't deny it any longer.

Biting my lip, and feeling fucking parched, I asked, "It's time to go?"

I already knew it was. I raked my gaze over him, trying to clear the cloud of possession I felt from him.

He was dressed in black—form-fitting sweatpants and a long-sleeve shirt. His dark hair had been combed back, and those eyes... I tugged my eyes up, away from the way his lips had flattened. If his eyes were normally dark, they were black now, and they were darkening every second I held his gaze.

An emotion flickered there, then disappeared.

"It's time." He held out a bag. "Put these clothes on."

I hadn't even noticed the bag.

Embarrassment washed over me, and shame.

I needed to get a fucking grip on myself.

"Okay." I reached for the bag. We were both careful our hands didn't touch when I took it.

My heart tried to stampede itself out of my chest as I drew back, shutting the door with more oomph than I needed. I almost sagged against it. Almost. I caught myself. He would've heard. He would've known his effect on me, if he didn't already.

Who was I kidding?

He knew. He knew full well what power he had.

Biting back my humiliation, I emptied the bag onto the bed. A pair of pants and a shirt similar to what I had on fell out. Black runners. Socks. He had everything in here, even a sports bra and underwear.

I held up the lacy thong and arched an eyebrow.

Really?

As if sensing my thoughts, I heard him chuckle from the other side of the door. "Tanner picked the clothes."

Tanner.

Asshole.

But I grinned. That made it better, less embarrassing for some reason. With a sigh, I changed out of what I was wearing. Everything fit like a glove. The shirt and pants were incredibly soft, but firm against my body. I didn't want to think how much they'd cost, and the socks and runners fit. I felt better support with these shoes than I got from my normal workout shoes. The bra fit too. As did the underwear.

It was eerie how well Tanner could shop.

A hair tie fell out of the bag, and I swiped it up, putting my hair in a braid. I had showered before trying to rest and my hair was dry now. My fingers made quick work through the strands.

Shit.

Standing back, I recognized myself, but I didn't at the same time.

The outfit was similar to what I would've worn on a work errand, but the woman looking back was glowing. Her eyes were alive, blazing. Her skin was flushed with color. Her lips parted, seeming swollen.

I looked like a wanton assassin.

Double shit.

This was him. I knew it. It was his effect on me.

Biting down on my lip again, I looked away, turning my back to my reflection. If I looked this alive now, how had I looked before? A slicing pain split through my chest, and I struggled to get oxygen for a second.

Then, as I blinked, it passed.

I couldn't think about it. I just couldn't.

Blade. Brooke.

This was a mission, just like all my others. I didn't know the parameters. I didn't know the time, the place, the how, but I was a participant just as much as Blade and Kai were. Only I had limitations.

The door opened, and Kai stepped in, his eyes finding me instantly.

"Ready?"

I clipped a nod.

I was ready, for anything.

CHAPTER NINETEEN

Kai and I went down in the same elevator as before, only it was just us this time. When the doors opened, four guards were waiting. Two turned to walk ahead of us, and as we stepped out, the other two fell in line behind us.

We went to a white van with a plumbing company sticker on the side, and as the back door opened, Kai took my arm. He climbed in, pulling me with him, and walked us to the front where we knelt behind the driver and the passenger's seat. Six guards already lined both sides of the van, sitting on the floor like we were.

Two of the guards who had walked with us hopped inside, and the other two shut the back doors. A guard hit the locks from the inside, and the other two walked around to get in the front.

The van started forward, and we drove out of the hotel's underground parking lot in total silence.

The men weren't looking at me. No one made eye contact.

I gauged the distance, and after we'd gone three blocks, all the guards took out their guns, checked them, and put them back in their holsters. Two added silencers and held them on their laps, pointed down.

I glanced over at Kai, but he stared ahead. He didn't seem tense. His breathing was even. He wasn't sleepy, but he seemed calm. Then again, why wouldn't he be? This was probably something he did once a month.

Or more.

We traveled one more block, then turned in to another underground parking garage.

As we stopped, the doors opened, and all the guards jumped out. I started to follow, but Kai took my arm again. He held me back, shaking his head.

I stayed. So did the two guards in the front.

The doors were shut again, and we drove back out onto the street.

We went into another parking lot and got out this time.

The entire lot was empty, except for our van. I thought both guards would come with us, but only the one in the passenger seat got out. As we started forward, the van peeled out, hurrying to the street and turning left, back toward where we'd just come from.

Kai let go of my arm and stepped behind me.

The guard went forward to push a button on the elevator. It was already there. We stepped in, and the guard pushed the button for the sixteenth floor. This was another building that had thirty floors, but it wasn't a hotel. I could tell that much. There were no sounds as we went up, and we went straight to our floor. As the elevator doors opened, I realized it was an office building. We walked through a glass-walled lobby into the larger main room. Floor-to-ceiling windows made up the walls here too, and we walked all the way to the one at the north end.

The guard took out a pair of binoculars.

Kai took my arm and maneuvered us so he was standing in front of me, his back to where his guard stood. My back was to the elevators now.

I stared up at him, feeling his hand tighten on my arm before letting me go.

"What?"

"I know you've had training for your job. I know you can fight and handle yourself." He stepped closer, his gaze boring down into mine. His eyes were heated, smoldering with promise. "I am better than you."

I almost laughed. "Are you serious? You want to do a whole game of I'm better than you…"

My voice trailed off as he closed the distance. His hand held my elbow, and he pressed me against him. He was rock solid, every inch of him tense.

He was serious, deadly serious.

I swallowed over a lump. "Okay."

"I travel with fewer guards than my brothers because I am as good as my men, better than most of them." His hand tightened on my elbow, sliding up to the back of my arm. His fingers pressed in. "I am allowing you leeway by only bringing one of my men. The rest need to be on the ground. My man is here because of you, not me. I'm telling you this as a warning. Do not run, or you will get hurt. It's not just one guard you have to calculate taking down. It'll be me as well."

He pulled me all the way against him. I could feel his breath on me, warming me. A few inches separated our lips.

His eyes moved there, lingering before looking back up.

"Do not get foolish and make a mistake, thinking you can escape me here," he said flatly. "You can't."

His hand slid up, over my shoulder and around my neck to cup the back of my head. He closed the distance, his mouth almost touching mine.

"I do not want to hurt you," he whispered, his lips brushing against mine. "But I will if it means losing my sister. Remember that."

I couldn't breathe.

I couldn't move.

I didn't dare.

I didn't know if I wanted to, so I kept still, my eyes holding his, and when he didn't move away or kiss me, I knew he was waiting.

I nodded, my lips brushing back against his. I whispered, "Okay."

That was it.

He released me, stepping back, and I felt deprived of... something.

Something wrenched out of me as his body moved away. I wanted to pull him back. I wanted to feel him against me, but I gritted my teeth. I pushed that desire down.

I was fucked up—that was the only reason I could find for my attraction to him.

My father was a monster, so I was attracted to a monster.

That's why I felt this lust.

Disgust flared up in me, so much I could taste it, and I forced myself to step around him.

"I won't run," I told him. Then I went to see what his guard was watching.

I'd been expecting to be at the meet with Blade.

I'd been expecting he would step out of his vehicle with Brooke. Kai would have me. We'd meet in the middle, and whatever happened after that happened. Whether I'd stay and fight for Brooke, or if Brooke would actually go with her brother, I didn't know. I hadn't fully thought it out, mostly because I couldn't. I wasn't in the driver's seat for this one, Kai was.

But what I didn't expect was to not be involved at all.

At the glass wall, I looked down and saw two vehicles in the lot. Neither was the van we'd ridden in. They were SUVs. Kai gave me a pair of binoculars, and as I put them up to my eyes, I saw the doors open.

Tanner got out. So did I.

Not me, obviously, but someone who looked like my twin.

I was stunned.

She was wearing the scrubs I'd been taken in. Her hair was down, swept to one side. She was hunched over, purposefully hiding her face, and goddamn, she even walked like me. The bitch had studied me somehow.

Her/my hand came up and brushed some of my hair back, like I do.

Like I did just now—I caught myself, and cursing, I tightened my hold on the binoculars again.

She tugged at the bottom of her scrub top, just like I would.

She stopped, hesitating, and her shoulders rolled back, *just like I do*.

There, across the lot, was Blade. He was too far away to see it wasn't really me as he got out of the Chevy truck. I was impressed that sucker had even made it the whole way, and it told me he was doing this off the books. 411 didn't know about it. If they had, he would've been in an SUV.

"What are you doing, Blade?"

He paused, holding his arm up to his forehead to shade his eyes. He saw Tanner and her/me, then went to his passenger door. Opening it, a girl got out—a girl... She looked like Brooke, but it couldn't have been. He wouldn't have done that. I knew Blade. No matter how much he might want me back, he wouldn't trade in someone who was hiding for her life.

It went against his code as a 411 operative.

Kai leaned forward. I could feel the intensity rolling off of him.

It looked like Brooke.

Same dark hair, same build, same height as the girl I'd seen in Brooke's Instagram pictures. But...no way. It couldn't be.

"That's not her," Kai growled. He snapped a radio to his mouth, pressing the side button. "Abort. It's not her."

Tanner's hand went to his ear, then shot out to the girl beside him. We heard a shout over the radio before both turned and ran back for their vehicle.

I jerked forward, but there was nothing I could do.

Sixteen floors separated us.

I glanced around, but Kai was already in my ear. "Don't fucking think about it."

He motioned, and the guard grabbed my arm and began dragging me away from the window—but not before I saw all the guards who had come with us swarm into the parking lot below.

"Grab both of them!" Kai ordered. "Take them to the warehouse."

"No!" I kicked, trying to get free.

The guard wrapped his arms around me. He held me up and dragged me at the same time.

"NO!" I squirmed. Fighting.

I needed to get free. Blade was in trouble. Whoever was with him, she was in trouble too. I had to help, despite what I'd said to Kai.

I had to.

There was no other option.

"Enough! You promised!" Kai was in my face.

I shook my head. "No, no. Not my friend. You broke it. You broke your word. You never said you'd take my friend. You—"

God. I was so stupid, but I knew what I was going to do.

I was insane.

As he moved closer to me, I closed my eyes, reared my head back—and head-butted him.

"Shit!"

"Argh!"

Except I hit air.

Opening my eyes, I found Kai standing to the side, his eyes wide open and shocked.

"Jesus Christ, get her in check!"

The motion had upended the guard's hold on me, and I broke free of his hands.

I dropped, my body going limp, but as soon as I hit the floor, I rolled to the side.

This was so bad, so bad. I couldn't get away like this, so almost in one motion, I tried pushing up to my feet and running for it.

Except Kai was there.

He wrapped an arm around my waist and tossed his radio to the guard. Yelling over my head, he lifted me like I was a child. "Go ahead of us. Bring the SUV around to the side door. I got her."

The guard wavered. "You sure?"

I glanced at him, then looked again. The guard had blood all over his face. *Did I do that?* But then I was back to fighting to get free.

Kai held me in the air and wrapped one of his arms around both of mine, securing them to my sides, and he put his other arm around my legs. I could only try to get free the way I had with the guard, but Kai was ready for it. He braced himself, and as the guard held the door open for us, he ran for it, carrying me. He went sideways so I didn't get hit, but I was still a battling mess.

"Woman. Stop."

"Never!"

I couldn't even turn around and bite him, though my desperation levels were nearing that point. I wanted to rip a piece out of him, in a whole new way than I had ten minutes ago.

The elevator door slid open, and Kai carried me in while the guard remained on the floor. He dropped me to my feet, wrapping his arms around me and hooking one leg around mine so I felt like I was stuck between resting against him or falling on my face.

"Get it done!" he commanded as the doors shut.

The guard nodded, lifting the radio to his mouth.

"Goddamn you! Goddamn you, asshole!" I screamed.

He hit the button and a litany of curses left him. He moved before I could comprehend it and swung me up so my back hit the wall. He stepped in close, using his body to hold me up.

I felt even more helpless in this position.

His groin was right there, pressing into mine, and a whole different heat spread through me.

I clasped my eyes shut. No. NO!

I would not let my body go there.

He had Blade. He had the woman who'd helped him.

But, fuck—I felt him hardening against me, pushing against me.

"You fucking asshole," I whispered, broken.

He sucked in some air, resting his forehead near the base of my neck, his mouth lingering over my artery. I felt his lips there, brushing over my skin, before he spoke.

"You and me both," he whispered. "You and me both, Riley."

Shit. I didn't want this, but the fight still left me. I became dead weight in his arms.

He took my friend, *my friend.*

I couldn't let him hurt Blade. I just couldn't.

"Please don't hurt Blade."

He lifted his head, and his eyes softened as he took in my face.

"He's my family. My only family left."

His eyes darted from my tears, to my eyes, to my lips, and stayed.

He nodded. "I won't hurt him."

I strained against him, my arms still pinned. "You promise? You have to promise."

His eyes jumped to mine, and he raised an eyebrow.

I cursed. "You never said a word about kidnapping my friends. Never. You just said not to run."

"Which you did."

"Because you ordered them to take my friends!"

"Friends? I thought it was only him you cared about."

I didn't know who the woman was. She didn't look like Carol. She was taller, had a bigger bone structure than Carol's.

"I don't know who she is," I admitted. "But if she helped Blade, she's someone I'm indebted to. So yes, friends. Both of them."

Kai's eyebrows pulled together. When I licked my lips, his eyes moved there, his eyebrows lifting.

My neck felt warm. The heat was spreading, moving up my face until I knew my cheeks were red.

"I didn't mean to do that."

He grunted again. "Right. If you stop fighting me, I will not hurt your friends today."

"Today?!" I nearly levitated my entire body off of the elevator wall, my groin grinding up on him as I did. His hand dropped down to catch underneath one of my legs.

I had a hand free, and I used it.

I balled it up and swung.

He dodged me, then let go of my leg as he caught my hand and slammed me back all at the same time.

He was rock solid. If our clothes were gone, he would've been inside of me, but as it was, he just held me—face to face, every inch of our bodies pressed against each other. He moved his legs out, positioning my legs wider so I couldn't kick.

"Stop. Fucking. Fighting!" he yelled in my face.

"Stop. Hurting. My. Friends!" I spat back.

His eyes bulged.

Sexual desire pulsated through us. It was heavy in the elevator, and it was alarming, dangerous, but there was more.

There was real anger, because if I'd had a choice between fucking him or slicing that knife in his throat, I would've taken the knife in a heartbeat.

But I also wanted to fuck him.

My God, I was twisted.

Tasting my own disgust once again, I turned my head away and closed my eyes. I willed that animal lust out of me, but it wasn't going away. It was hot and heavy and pulsing, and I bit back a moan.

Just then, the elevator stopped and the doors opened. I opened my eyes.

Standing in the entryway, with four guards around him and guns pointed at him, Blade stared back at us.

CHAPTER TWENTY

"Are you fucking him?" Blade hissed.

We were sitting in the middle of the van. Guards surrounded us. The woman was in front of us, sitting with her head down and shoulders hunched forward. Her hands were in her lap as if they were tied, but I knew they weren't. Blade's weren't either. That was a liberty given to them.

I refused to glance over at Kai, who sat near me, his back against the side of the van beside his men. He almost looked like one of the guards—dressed the same, the same stony expression on his face.

"No. And we can talk later."

Blade glared at Kai. "Really? You sure about that?" He raised his voice. The words were for me. The attitude for Kai.

I couldn't stop myself. I looked over. Kai was ignoring Blade, his gaze focused solely on me.

I swallowed over a lump.

This wasn't going to end well, but having said that, no one had died. Yet.

I motioned to the woman in front of Blade. "Who is she?"

He shot me a look. "No one."

I frowned. She wasn't no one, but he gave me a second meaningful look and *ooh* now *he* wanted to wait till later to talk. I rolled my eyes. Fine. I'd grown accustomed to riding long hours in silence.

But this time we only rode an hour and a half before the van pulled onto a gravel road, then paused. The door to a large warehouse opened, and we drove inside. The warehouse door closed at the same time the van door opened. Three guards were there to greet us.

Kai got out first, going off with one of his men, their heads bent together.

The guards got out, and one by one, we were led out after.

Blade was taken to a corner, with four men guarding him.

They took me to a different corner, on the completely opposite side of the warehouse. Four guards also stood by me. The woman was left in the middle of the floor, with four guards taking point around her in a square. Someone pulled the van around to face toward the door, probably for a quick getaway if necessary.

Then we waited.

Minutes ticked by.

My body ached. The adrenaline from the hotel, then the nerves and the fighting in the elevator—it was all hitting me. I was thirsty. My stomach cramped from hunger, and I struggled to keep my head up.

One of the men must've noticed, because a guard brought over a blanket and bottle of water. He left them at my side, along with a second blanket folded up to use as a pillow. I felt guilty because they didn't offer the same luxury to Blade or the woman, but it was a battle to keep my head from resting there.

The minutes kept trickling by, and I gave up the fight.

I fell asleep.

· · ·

"Are you sure?"

A male voice was near my head.

A second male voice, "Yes. It's the same woman."

"She was with Riley's friend."

Not a question, a statement of fact. It was Kai talking, and he sounded confused.

I tried opening my eyes. I wanted to ask who he was talking about and then—

Darkness.

• • •

"I don't know anything!"

That was Blade.

I bolted upright, my heart pounding in my chest.

He was surrounded by Kai and more guards. I only had one with me now.

Seeing me awake, he cleared his throat. "She's up."

Kai immediately turned for me, coming back. He strode around the woman, whose head hung almost to the ground. Her hands were behind her back, but still not tied up. Her legs were crisscrossed in front.

Her position looked painful.

Kai ignored her. He knelt before me, looking me over. "You're okay?"

My chest clenched. I was his prisoner. He shouldn't talk to me with that amount of concern.

"I'm fine. Just tired."

He studied my face before nodding, and he stood up. "Come on." He took my arm, helping me stand. He picked up my water bottle and the two blankets and took me over to the van. He opened the back door.

A bed had been made there, and there was another water bottle and some crackers waiting.

"You can rest here while we get some answers."

Blade glared at me from across the room, but it wasn't as heated as earlier.

Kai waited for me to climb in.

"My friend?" I asked softly.

"Will be fine. It's the woman we're figuring out. You sure you don't know her?"

There was an edge in his voice. I gave him a more sharpened look. "What are you saying?"

117

"It would be beneficial if your friend told you how this woman came to help him. It would be beneficial for him...and you."

A wall moved back in place over Kai's face. He wasn't letting anything show, but I'd been around him long enough to know that wall was something. When he had to make a hard decision, when he was about to do something he knew others wouldn't like, that wall showed up.

I pressed my lips together and looked back to Blade. "I can ask him, but he won't tell me if he thinks you're listening."

"I can bring him over here. You can both eat."

"No." I shook my head. "Let us go out there—take a walk or just step a few feet away. I can ask."

Kai was back to studying me. "You would actually help?"

I didn't respond. I knew if I didn't help something I didn't like would happen. But I didn't want him to know that. I shrugged.

He tipped his head forward. "Fine." He signaled with his hand and went to speak to a guard. Immediately, the others hauled Blade to his feet.

"Hey! Hey! What are you doing?"

Hearing the panic in Blade's voice kicked me in the sternum. They didn't answer. They only dragged him to the door.

He twisted and struggled. "No! NO!"

Finally, he went limp like I had before. They kept dragging him until he saw I was coming too. Then he put his feet under him at least. Kai remained back, but a guard walked beside me.

Blade's eyes found mine. They were diluted with horror.

I swallowed over another lump, feeling my heart sink. Again.

"Riley, what's going on?"

I lied. "They want to talk to the woman."

He shut up, and a transformation came over him. He was angry. I saw the steam rising, and wasn't surprised when he jerked his hands free from the guards. They reached for him, but he shrugged his body away. "I'm coming," he growled. "Okay? Can I walk out of here on my own?"

With jerking motions, he began to move.

I didn't know why he was jerking. Poor circulation? But Blade wasn't like that. He did yoga twice a day. Maybe I'd slept longer than I thought?

Either way, he was walking almost regularly by the time we stepped outside.

I must've slept longer than I thought. It was dark outside. We were surrounded by trees and a bright moon, which gave enough light to show we were on a hill. I caught sight of two farms farther down in a valley. The woods seemed to stretch on for miles. They must've brought us farther out than I'd realized.

Small rocks had been laid down instead of pavement, and the guards spread out around us, letting us walk down the driveway.

Blade drew near me. "What's happening?"

"Are you okay?"

He nodded. "Yeah. Some of it's an act."

I got it. Make them underestimate you. It was a good act, but a little too good.

"Blade. I'm serious. Are you okay?"

He didn't reply at first, then ducked his head. "I fought back before. They roughed me up, just enough to subdue me. Once I stopped, they did too." He sneered at the nearest guard. "I have to say, for working for the Bennett family, they're scarily professional."

Yes. They were, but I'd witnessed how Kai took care of his men. He either didn't want to worry about turnover or he actually cared about them. Or who knows. He might've just trusted these guys and didn't want to burn them out.

I needed to stop giving Kai more credit than he deserved. Fucking attraction had started to blind me to what he did for a living: he was in the mafia. He was a bad guy. He did bad things.

"Yeah," I said faintly, my stomach growling. "I'm surprised too." I eyed him again. "You'll be okay?"

"I'll be fine as long as we get away or maybe get some food." He gave me a lopsided grin. "It's good to see you. I haven't said so before now."

He was right. I stopped and we hugged.

"It's good to see you too."

His arms still around me, he said into my ear, "The woman found me. I don't know who she is."

I whispered back, "What do you mean she found you?"

A shudder went through his body. He burrowed his face in my shoulder. "The broadcast went through the Network's service. I saw he'd released the other Hiders, but killed one. A day later, she was knocking on my door saying if I wanted to go after Kai Bennett, she would help me."

I stilled.

That didn't— "She sought you out?"

He nodded.

She'd recruited him.

"You don't know her?"

"No—" he began.

A bloodcurdling scream ripped through the air.

Everyone outside ran for the warehouse.

The guards got there ahead of us, and as the door opened, I could see the woman reach for one of the guard's guns. There was more shouting, and then a gunshot.

The woman's back arched, and she crumbled to the floor.

No matter what Kai said, I knew there wasn't a blood bag for this one. The woman was dead. Blood poured out of her forehead.

I stopped in my tracks, staring at her lifeless body before lifting my head.

Kai stood over her, the gun in his hand. He was the one who'd shot her.

Then the door slammed shut in front of me.

I didn't comprehend anything after that, not right away.

Blade did. He grabbed my arm and whisper-shouted in my ear, "LET'S GO!"

They'd left us alone.

I couldn't think about it.

I turned. Blade had started to run, and I took off after him.

They would find us. Kai had promised that. I had no doubt he would, but Blade needed to escape. I didn't trust Kai with Blade's life. I didn't know if I trusted him with mine, but it didn't matter right now.

We ran.

I was breaking my promise, but I didn't care. Kai had broken his too.

My heart was in my chest, but as I took flight behind my 411 operative partner, I shed the woman I'd become just being near Kai Bennett.

Each step I took away made things clearer. I was returning to that 411 operative Kai knew I was. My steps grew quicker, more assured, steadier, and the emotion drained from me.

I became calmer the farther away I got, and then everything clicked back into place.

My mission was to get free.

CHAPTER TWENTY-ONE

We could hear them yelling.

We were already over a ridge and down another small hill, out of their sight, by the time they realized their mistake.

But it wasn't soon enough.

That thought plagued me. *Not soon enough.* Not for Kai. Not for the way he had everything planned and calculated ahead of time. It didn't make sense, but I pushed forward. I had to.

Blade and I sprinted past trees, their branches whipping against us. He stumbled once, but rolled right back to his feet. Our Hider training came back to us. Regulate your breathing. Don't overexert yourself. Keep your head up to see the best. Shoulders in a comfortable position. I pumped my arms when I grew weaker. Push off your heels. Roll through your toes in a circular motion. Envision your feet as if they're wheels. Keep going.

Just.

Keep.

Going.

We ran. It started drizzling, and we ran through that too.

We kept going downhill. There were two farms. We should've been close by now.

But that thought still bothered me. Kai had messed up, big time. But he didn't make mistakes.

If that were true, then he'd wanted us to run.

Right?

The other option was to stay, unless it'd been a test. I'd failed if that was it.

But no. That was a mind fuck. If you're given a chance at freedom, you take it. That was a golden rule for humanity.

"There!" Blade shouted, pointing ahead at a light.

It was one of the farms. Veering toward it, we paused just before breaking from the tree line. A large red barn loomed in front of us, the paint fading and stripped off. A large fence circled out for livestock, but there were no animals. The fence was broken in more than one place, and the grass grew tall. It hadn't been mowed for a long time. There was a small cabin structure behind the barn, but the door was half gone. A side of the house had fallen in on itself. No one lived here, hadn't for a long time.

"There might be shelter."

Blade started forward.

I caught his arm. "No."

"Come on." He motioned to it. "I know it's not ideal, but we need a break from the rain. At least for a little while."

I shook my head. "No, Blade. It's not right. Something doesn't feel right."

"What are you talking about?" He raked a hand over his face, wiping some of the rain away. It didn't matter. More fell down from the tree above us. "I need a break. Five minutes, then we push off again."

He started forward, and that's when I saw the camera. It was positioned at the top of the barn, angled at us.

Right at us.

Oh shit.

A bad feeling sank in my stomach.

I saw the second camera just as Blade stepped from the tree line.

And the first camera moved with him.

They were watching us. That's why they were late in chasing us.

Oh my God.

He kept going, and that camera kept tracking him. The second was moving around, scanning up and down the trees. It was looking for me.

"Blade," I called out. "Do not stop. Do not look back at me."

His shoulders tensed, but he did as I said.

"They're watching us. There's a camera on you."

"Go," he yelled back.

I shook my head, though he couldn't see. "I can't."

"Go, Riley!" He kept walking forward. "Go! I mean it. Find Carol. She'll help."

But I couldn't. My stomach clenched in a tight knot, but I knew I wasn't leaving him. Blade had a better chance with me as a captive than me free. The Bennetts had no loyalty to him. At least Tanner and Jonah cared about me. I had to trust that, trust that Brooke loved her brothers for a reason.

"I can't go."

I gritted my teeth...

"NO, Riley!"

I stepped forward.

The second camera snapped to my position. I stopped, my arms out, and because I hated just giving in, I raised my middle finger.

The back barn doors burst open, and all those guards from the warehouse came streaming out. Kai was in the middle, walking at a more sedate pace. His gaze landed right on me. He wore the same mystified expression as before.

Two of the guards grabbed Blade, another two headed for me.

I held my hands out. "If you grab me and shove me to the ground, I will kill one of you."

They paused. One glanced back to Kai, who nodded, still walking forward.

"I'll handle her," he said. He nodded to Blade. "Take him."

They put Blade in one of the SUVs.

Kai took my arm. He walked me to another SUV as the other one pulled away at high speed.

"Was that all a setup?"

TIJAN

Kai glanced at me as the door opened. I got in the back, not fighting, and slid over. He got in beside me. The door closed, and we took off. We only had one guard with us.

Kai was becoming more and more lenient with me. That was good, very good. I glanced over at him.

He was on his phone, typing, but said, "Marcus, can you put the heat on full blast for Miss Bello? She's chilled to the bone."

I refused to feel anything for his thoughtfulness. He was the reason I'd been out running. It was nighttime. It'd been raining. I was soaked.

He finished whatever he had to do on his phone, put it away, then reached behind him for a blanket.

He put it over my lap. "Get warm with this."

I eyed him, pulling it up to cover myself.

There was no anger. There was almost nothing on his face, but there wasn't the wall I'd grown used to seeing.

Without looking at me, he rested his head against his seat. "We let your friend keep his phone. He tucked it next to his junk. He doesn't think we knew it was there, but we did. He walked through a full-body scan. We thought he might use it when you ran for your escape." He stopped and looked at me now. His eyes were piercing. "Did he?"

My mouth dropped.

This was why it hadn't felt right. It wasn't just the cameras.

Goddamn him. Goddamn him!

My nostrils flared. "Were you watching the whole time?"

No hesitation. "Yes."

"The woman? Was that a show?"

Still no hesitation. He answered freely. "No. She's the head of a victim's advocate group. She's been after us for years. Her son died in a shooting. She thinks we're to blame for her son's murderer having his gun in the first place."

"Was she right?" I bit out.

"Maybe." His eyes dipped before coming right back up. Still no emotion. "There was no serial number. We don't typically

125

transport those guns, but we have in the past. Her son was murdered by his lover. I have no idea if we're to blame or not."

Why was he telling me this? This was more than I needed to know.

Then I knew. "Did you put a tap on me? You heard Blade tell me about her, didn't you?"

His eyes enlarged, just a fraction of an inch. "No. We were given confirmation that she approached your friend, not the other way around. He didn't even know her, did he?"

I shrugged, my jaw hardening. "Does it matter? She's dead. You killed her."

"She got one of our guns—"

"Bullshit! I know you don't make mistakes. She was allowed to grab that gun." I shouldn't have been yelling, but I was. Too much had happened over the last few days. "You wanted a reason to kill her, and she gave you one. Self-defense. Your only mess-up is that I saw it."

I quieted.

He didn't reply.

And then—*fuck.* "You meant me to see that, didn't you?"

Of course he did. I closed my eyes, my head hanging forward. I felt a headache coming.

"You wanted me to see because if I hadn't, I would assume it was a blatant murder. Blade would've said the same, but we both saw, and if need be, we'll testify it was self-defense."

Of course.

My God, of course.

Not a goddamn thing happened without Kai's calculation behind it.

He was cold, ruthless, and not human. No one with humanity could plan all of this out to the umpteenth detail.

"Did you have cameras in the woods?" My voice was dull, bleak. It made me cringe, just hearing myself.

"Yes."

Honesty. That was one good trait he had. Maybe the only one.

"Of course, you fucking bastard."

There was no fight in me anymore. Those words left me on a surrendering sigh, and I turned toward the window. We were moving fast. The trees rocketed past us. Here I was, locked in this vehicle. I was warm, but moments ago, I'd thought I was running for my life.

What a fool I'd been.

"You thought if you let us go, Blade would call for help." I already knew that was the plan. I was starting to catch on to his methods. Slowly. "You were going to trace the call and see if they led you to Brooke. Weren't you?"

A pause.

I felt him watching me, but I refused to look at him. I refused even to search him out in the window's reflection.

"Your friend said he knew where Brooke was," he said. "He failed to bring her. He wouldn't cooperate and answer our questions. We had two options: put him in a situation where he'd show his cards willingly or make him do so with force. I promised not to hurt your friend, so I chose this route. I would do it again."

His phone buzzed. He took it out of his pocket and read the screen before replying and putting it back. "And you were wrong. While you were running, he did stop and make a call. We have a new target."

"Who?" I turned to him.

He looked away this time. "We'll find out."

CHAPTER TWENTY-TWO

I'd been shut out.

We didn't go back to the hotel, and I had no clue where they'd taken Blade. We drove up to another huge house, and they took me to my own wing. Yes. Wing. Again. It wasn't the same house, but once I stepped out on another balcony, high above another death-defying fall, I recognized where we were: their Vancouver estate.

This was home for Brooke, the home she always used to talk about. I knew from those stories that there was an Olympic-sized pool, a tennis court, and a lazy river where she would go tubing with Tanner and their friends. There were more houses on this estate, and a garden that had its own maze.

Brooke loved this home.

She spoke about it with such fondness. She had also talked about her father's study, though when she did there was no warmth in her voice. There was fear. He'd conducted his business in that room, which had its own entrance.

Sighing, I had to stop myself.

I was thinking back as if this were a common occurrence, as if Brooke had opened up to me about these memories. She hadn't. These were small snippets I'd gathered from a comment here and there, spread out over an entire year.

She'd talked about the tennis court, about swimming, about the river. She'd mentioned her father's study. One time she mentioned seeing a man enter through the side door.

But I'd listened and absorbed everything, because that was the kind of girl I was. It was the same now.

It was day three of me being in this house.

My wing had its own kitchenette, and a coffee machine too. I could pick up the phone and ask for any food I wanted. I was in the lap of luxury, but it wasn't mine.

This had been Brooke's life.

There was a small-theater-sized screen in the living room, and a sectional couch that had a bed in the middle so it was one giant square.

I couldn't imagine this life.

Mine had not been like this. There'd been wealth, yes, but everything was overshadowed by my parents, by my father. I'd slept in the hallway most nights, a blanket with me and nothing else. I'd had to sneak back to my room each morning.

I'd had a chef who cooked for me, but it wasn't normally what I wanted. It was whatever my father ate and left behind. I was never allowed to eat with him. My mother usually took her meals in her room. If she didn't, she still couldn't eat with me, only with *him*. So while I'd also had a gilded cage growing up, a line of terror had run through my background.

I didn't remember a time when I wasn't scared my father would snap, find me, send for me.

I didn't feel that with Kai.

Maybe I should've.

I should've feared for Blade's life. The logical part of my brain told me to think about that, but my instincts told me he was safe, just as I was.

I let out a breath and reached for the remote control. I was changing the channel when I heard a soft knock on my door.

I looked over from the couch. "Yeah?"

I expected a guard to walk in with dinner. It was that time, and they always knocked. If I didn't answer, they told me my food was outside the door. Of course they were there when I opened—if I opened—the door, but they never came in unless I granted them permission.

This time the door opened and Kai walked in.

I sat up straight, my heart slamming against my chest.

It'd been three days since I ran from him. I'd had no word from him since.

He looked good.

I tried not to notice, but I did.

My eyes ran over him, taking in the way his shirt fit his chest, showing the leanness of his stomach and falling in just the right place over his pants. He looked all business, his hair combed back. I had to pry my eyes away from the rest of him.

I didn't want to see the knowing smugness in those dark eyes, or the smirk that curved his mouth.

"Where's Blade?" I scowled.

He stopped. I heard a soft sigh before he took a seat on the couch parallel to me. He leaned forward, resting his arms on his legs, his hands folded together over his knees. He angled his head toward me, a shadow falling over half his face.

"I brought a chef in. The guys said you haven't eaten dinner yet. Would you have dinner with me?"

I frowned. "You're not telling me? You're asking?"

"I'm asking." He inclined his head. "Tanner and Jonah are coming later tonight as well, if you'd like to have drinks with them."

I studied him, really studied him.

That wall was there, but there was more. A lightness? But that didn't make sense, not for someone like Kai Bennett.

Still, I was curious.

I sat up, stiffly, and shrugged. "Sure. What time?"

"Dinner will be in thirty minutes. Will you have enough time to dress?"

I scanned over his clothes. He could've been on the cover of a fashion magazine.

I sighed. "I'm guessing you don't do dinner in sweats?"

A grin tugged at the corner of his mouth. "For the right occasion, always." He stood, nodding toward the closet in the bedroom. "There are dresses in there, or you can dress however you like. I know Tanner and Jonah will be coming from a night at the club. It's your choice."

And with that said, he strolled out.

I hated to admit it, but it was good to see him. It was good to see anyone, talk to anyone. The guards didn't count. Though I'd considered trying to have a conversation with them.

Okay.

I had tried. They ignored me.

Hearing Tanner and Jonah were coming gave me a little kick of excitement too.

I missed Blade. I missed Carol.

I missed my routine of going to work, working out, and being a Hider operative.

I missed my normalcy, which wasn't that normal, but it was to me.

As I dressed, I knew I needed to question Kai about Blade. I wanted to make sure he was safe, was okay, and if I could, talk Kai into letting him go.

I was nervous and grew even more so when I'd picked the outfit I was going to wear.

I didn't want to go too dressy, but I heard what he was telling me without saying the words. Tanner and Jonah would be dressed up. Everything they wore screamed money. So maybe it was them in the back of my mind, maybe it was Kai, or maybe it was the hope that maybe I could talk Kai into letting Blade go, or maybe there was a part of me that didn't want to feel like the outcast. Whatever the reason, I chose an elegant black pantsuit. The middle plunged down all the way to my stomach, but sheer lace covered the midsection.

I stepped back, looking in the mirror, and again, I didn't recognize myself.

I was a far cry from the Hider operative who dressed in scrubs, workout clothes, or whatever set of clothes my "cover" had me wearing.

Blade, Carol, and I had dinner out once or twice a month, but nothing fancy.

When I left my father, I'd left that world behind.

This would've been me if I had stayed, if I had lived.

If.

That was a big word there.

I'd been happy with Blade and Carol, but being here, coming back to this world, a small *what-if* had started to take root in me. It wasn't the *what-if* of Brooke staying at school, or of somehow growing up with the Bennett family. It was what-if my father had been a different man, if my mother hadn't been abused by him, if I hadn't been scared of living in my own home—that what-if. What would life have been like if I'd had a normal family?

Not even wealthy.

If we'd had a meal at a restaurant? If there'd been no factories or business conglomerates, no privileged schooling, just a father, a mother, and a child? A home with three bedrooms instead of three wings? Or one bathroom instead of one entire servant quarters?

What would that life have been like?

I sighed, fixing my hair back into a high bun, and I even put on makeup. All those thoughts were useless. That wasn't the card I was dealt growing up, and in the end, I was alive. I had a mission, an important mission to focus my life, and that was good.

I was good.

I slipped my feet into a pair of sandals, but I felt naked walking out of that room without a sweater, runners to run, or any type of covering I might need if I had to make a break for my life.

No matter the thoughts swirling in my head, that part of me would never be gone. But for the first time ever, I began to wonder if that's what I wanted for the rest of my life.

The guards trailed behind me as I left my wing.

I wasn't sure where I was going, but I walked in the general direction of the main part of the house. The hallway wound around, coming to a second-floor landing, and I crossed to the stairs. I could hear the sounds of cooking in the kitchen, which was behind the stairs. The layout was similar to their other house, and I walked in feeling a little more at ease.

Until I saw Kai.

He stood in the shadows at the window, a glass of bourbon in his hands, and his profile took my breath away.

Moonlight lit the entire bay, and lights from boats and homes beneath him put a soft glow over his face. I faltered mid-step.

The attraction burst inside me, heating me, making me ache, and I clamped my mouth shut in reaction.

I hadn't asked for these feelings. They disgusted me on the regular, but he'd been gone for three days, and it was all hitting me full force now.

But Blade. I couldn't forget Blade.

I couldn't forget myself. My situation.

I was here against my wishes, but as Kai turned to look at me, a dangerous new *what-if* edged its way in alongside the others.

My hand shook, and I tucked it behind me, meeting his gaze across the room.

His eyes warmed, a softness shining there, and he nodded. "You look beautiful, Riley."

So did he.

I smiled and ducked my head. "Thank you." A wave of nerves hit me again, and I had to stop and breathe to calm myself. It didn't work. I was even more nervous.

"Would you like a drink?"

"Please." I raised my head.

He turned his back to me as he poured a glass of wine.

I was glad for the small favor and smoothed a hand down my front. Sometimes that helped. It didn't tonight. I began to think nothing would take the edge off until Kai turned back, a full glass of red wine in his hand.

He held it up. "Brooke always liked this wine. I thought..."

I nodded. "Thank you. That's perfect."

"Perfect?" He raised an eyebrow, handing it over.

I grabbed the stem of the glass, avoiding his hand, and I knew he took note.

He stepped back. "Perfect is a big word, especially for someone who's still here against her will."

I paused in raising it to my mouth. "What?"

He motioned to the table.

There was a bowl, two plates, three glasses, and two sets of silverware for every seat. Every glass and plate had a gold rim at the edge. It was another reminder of this world I was visiting—a world where I used to live, or I should've.

Why was I thinking like this?

I loved being a Hider operative. And that wasn't this world.

It never would be.

I sat and pulled my chair up to the table. "When are you going to let me go?"

There.

I had to leave, because staying here was messing with my mind. It was muddling everything.

"I thought you were going to bargain for your friend first."

There was the Kai I knew. We were back on solid footing. I was the 411 Hider, and he was my kidnapper.

I looked up, feeling more settled inside. "And if I asked that? What then? Would you actually grant that?"

He took a sip from his glass before putting it on the table as he sat to my left at the head of the table.

"I have a proposition for you." He motioned to the table and the room. "That's the reason for all of this."

"A proposition?"

"Yes." He nodded, his mouth pressing tight before relaxing. He raised his chin. "I let your friend go home."

"You did?"

Surprise spread through me. My hand tightened on my chair.

"Your Network has been unable to find Brooke. Your friend has no idea where she is. He was bluffing to try to get you back. We followed up on his call, and the person we found had nothing to do with my sister. Now, I'm in a place where I've exhausted most of my options." His eyes pierced mine. "I fully believe you know where my sister is, but the normal ways I would force you to tell me are...unavailable, so I have a different proposition for you."

"You let Blade go?"

I was still stuck on that one.

"I let him go as a gesture of goodwill to you. He will not make claims of being kidnapped by my family—to the law or to your employers. As far as they're concerned, he attempted to get you back by himself, and it went bad. He failed. He is back home, and I've been told he was put to work immediately."

Oh God.

I heard what he was saying. "You have people in the Network. They're giving you information."

It made sense—that's how he found me, how he knew Blade was acting on his own.

"Yes, I do."

"That's how you knew about me this whole time."

"Yes." He gentled his tone. "Brooke asked me to keep tabs on you. She worried about you."

It didn't help. I already knew this, and it *so* didn't help. I felt a sting of betrayal. The Network was sacred. No one was supposed to be bought. We were all pure. That's what I'd thought. That's what I had believed this whole time.

We were good.

Looking at Kai now—he was bad. But since I'd been held by him, the lines had become more and more blurred. And now, hearing there was someone in the Network working for him, fury flared inside of me.

"I believe you know where my sister is," Kai continued. "I will not be convinced otherwise, but you won't tell me. I'm loath to force the issue. I've tried, and I'm not willing to resort to the lengths that are my last options. So..." He reached for his glass and took a healthy sip from it, gritting his teeth before putting it back on the table. "...here's another play."

He paused. His eyes were steady on mine.

"I'll tell you the truth. All of it."

CHAPTER TWENTY-THREE

My answer was swift. "Okay." I raised my head, rolled my shoulders back, and waited.

I didn't have to wait long.

Kai leaned back in his seat, picking up his glass. "Brooke ran, but she wasn't alone. She ran away with her boyfriend, a member of a Milwaukee-based mafia family, Levi Barnes. He's not in line to take over the family business, but he's connected to them. His father is the youngest of Mildreth Barnes' sons. Brooke ran with him because she overheard a meeting where I was told Levi was informing on his family to the FBI."

Ice ran down my spine.

She wasn't afraid for her life. She was scared for her boyfriend's. It all made sense now.

"Brooke knows I've recently been more ambitious in reaching out to the Midwestern part of the States, to the families who run those territories. She assumed I would either kill Levi as a gift to his family or I would turn him over to them."

Rats got killed. That's just what happened.

I nodded, swallowing faintly. "I see."

"You don't." He leaned forward, moving without making a sound. The chair didn't squeak. There was no shift in the floorboards. If I hadn't seen it, I would never have heard him. There was an almost ghostly quality to the way he moved sometimes. Silent. Stalking. Hunting.

His eyes grew fierce now, pinning me down. "If you reveal what I'm about to tell you, I will have you murdered." He paused.

He meant what he said, and I forced my head to nod. The shiver wrapped around my entire body, but I had to listen. It was important.

"I want in on the Midwest. That's my goal, and I have done extensive research into all the controlling families. Brooke's boyfriend's family is weak. They're my way in, so my sister was wrong about my intentions. I have no wish to kill her boyfriend. I want to use him. He's going to be my way in to destroy his family."

Of course.

I hung my head, whispering, "You don't really want to find your sister. You want to find her boyfriend."

"No." I heard his chair move now as he leaned back again. "You're wrong. I want to find my sister because I love her, and because the longer she's out there..."

I looked up, his voice beckoning me, and I saw him nod toward the window.

"...the more unsafe she is. She's a Bennett. You think I'm the only one looking for her? I have enemies who would relish hacking her to pieces—while she's alive, while she's screaming my name, and videotaping it all for their sick pleasure."

He stopped, his eyes closed tightly. His jaw clenched, and then he shoved back his chair. His glass in hand, he dumped the rest of his bourbon down his throat before stalking to the liquor cabinet. "I have been protecting my family since I was a child. Against who is the only component that's changed." He poured his glass half full. Capping the bottle again, he remained there, his back to me. "I have to find my sister. I need your help to do that."

He looked back, his eyes stricken. "Please."

A lump formed in my throat.

God. I knew the danger of the Bennett name, but I couldn't shake the feeling that most of the danger was from the family itself.

"I can't," I whispered.

His nostrils flared. "But you know where she is."

I couldn't touch that either. I hung my head again, closing my eyes.

I suddenly wanted all of this to go away.

I didn't want to be in these clothes that reminded me of my past. I didn't want to be here in this room, with him, knowing he would do anything to find his sister. I wanted to be back at my home with Blade, with Carol, with my cover job as a nurse aide who spoke in inspiring quotes.

I missed being Raven, not Riley.

"Where is she?!" Kai roared, throwing his glass across the room.

It shattered against the wall, falling to the floor, and I didn't flinch. Not. One. Bit.

I shook my head. "I can't help you, and you know it."

He returned to his seat, and this time I refused to look at him.

The room was tense, the air thick and oppressing, and for a moment, I felt as if my father were with us.

I shoved that down. I would not cower. I would not be intimidated.

"Our father killed my brother," he said softly.

What? I looked up.

He wasn't looking at me. His gaze was trained on the table, but I knew he wasn't seeing what was physically in front of him.

His fingers tightened around the bottle he now held in front of him.

"Anthony Bennett was a sadistic father." He shuddered. His hand twitched, and his head shook slightly. "He was obsessed with power, and Cord was getting to the age where he was supposed to start taking over some of the responsibilities of the family. Our father didn't want that to happen. He knew Cord was kind—weak, in his eyes—but he saw how others reacted to him. They liked him. They approved of him, and the truth is they wanted a change from our father's rule. Anthony Bennett wouldn't have it. He saw years into the future where Cord would've taken over the business. He would've had our father killed." His eyes were so bleak. "That's the way of our life. So he got rid of Cord first."

He murdered my brother.

Brooke hadn't been talking about her other brother. She'd meant her father.

I never thought of it, but... A father who could kill his own child? Or a mother? A flicker of rage began heating me inside.

I should've considered the father first. I had firsthand experience in that cruelty.

"I'm sorry. I thought—"

"I know what you thought," he said, sounding tired. "A lot of people thought it. My father made the mistake of waiting before killing me. He didn't see me as a threat because I was only sixteen years old."

I knew what was coming.

A knot formed around that ball of fury inside me. It was all mixing together.

"I killed my father instead, and I paid off a family friend to be our guardian. I paid off the courts. I paid off everyone."

He stared at me. I expected a wall to fall in place, but it didn't. Though he wasn't hiding himself, he wasn't showing anything either. He was dead. That's what I saw when I looked into his eyes. Death.

"I did it the most humane way, at least in my opinion," he said. "I smothered him with a pillow one night, and he just stopped breathing. No one asked why we weren't seeking vengeance. Everyone knew."

"You had Brooke come home after that."

He nodded, his gaze moving away from me.

I felt unpinned, as if he'd been holding me up against the wall. I sat in a chair, but my legs jerked.

The sensation of falling was strong.

"I did. I didn't agree with sending her away. I wanted my family all together. It was time to bring some good into this house."

Those words resonated.

He killed to bring something good into Brooke's life, for their whole family.

He wasn't the ruthless killer I'd thought he'd been. He did care. He did love. He did feel pain.

"I'm sorry—"

"I don't care. Honestly." His shoulders lifted, and his eyes found me again. "I want to know where my sister is. I *know* she came to you the day after the news broke that she was missing. I know you drove her somewhere that next morning and you returned the same day. I know it was the third day you went to a tanning spa to hide the fact that you hadn't gone to Florida for a vacation. And the next day I had you taken." He stood there, his hands in his pockets, and his head fell forward, but he still stared me down. "I have proof of everything. I know you acted alone. I know you didn't tell your roommates. We have security footage of you along the way. For the rest, we were able to hack your friend's computer. The only thing I don't have is where you stashed my sister."

My hands started shaking.

My stomach turned over.

I felt like I was going to throw up.

My vision blurred, and spots floated around me.

He knew.

He knew almost everything.

He'd known this whole time.

"Tell me where my sister is."

I couldn't look at him. I couldn't betray her.

I couldn't—

"Riley!"

I jumped in my chair, shoving it back at the same time. It almost tipped over, but I clung to it.

Or maybe that was me almost falling out of it?

It was all rolling over and over in my stomach. It was forcing its way up my throat. I felt the pressure of it coming up, and I swallowed it back down.

Agent lockdown.

I heard my trainer's voice in my head, and as if she'd commanded me in present time, I felt the protocol happening.

My toes relaxed.

My legs stopped shaking. My knees calmed.

My thighs grew strong.

My hands rested on top of them, flat, fingers spread out. Ready.

I sat up straight.

My back was no longer against my chair.

My arms stopped trembling.

My stomach grew still.

My breathing evened out.

My shoulders squared back.

My chin rose.

My mind grew clear.

I was no longer Riley Bello.

I was 411 Operative Raven, and my mission was being threatened.

"Riley?"

My voice came out in a monotone as I recited the phrase they'd burned into our memories: "I will uphold my vow as an agent of honor. I will never break the promise a survivor has entrusted to me. I will never take away a person's freedom, even if it means giving up mine in their place. I am an operative of the 411 Network, and I will not break my silence."

I was gone.

"Shit," Kai murmured.

The door opened and another voice demanded, "What the fuck is going on in here?"

A third voice, "What did you do to her?"

"I think I broke her," Kai answered.

CHAPTER TWENTY-FOUR

Three weeks earlier

3:00 am

My roommates had gone to their bedrooms. I needed to go as well, but I couldn't. For some reason, I couldn't bring myself to move from the kitchen table. After they left, I got up to heat some decaf tea. It usually soothed me, but not that night. Or that morning. However you thought of it.

Knock, knock!

I jerked, instantly on alert.

Blade's computer had a warning built in. When someone crossed the driveway, it sounded. It was harsh and loud, so it would've woken everyone up long ago, but looking, I saw why it hadn't gone off.

Brooke Bennett stared back at me, and she hadn't come down the driveway. She'd come through the woods.

Her eyes were wide and panicked. She shivered, branches in her hair, and she waved her hand frantically in a circle to me. It was covered in a shirt. She looked drenched.

Opening the door, I stepped back. "My God. Brooke?"

"Hi," she breathed out, hurrying inside. A chunky sweater hung off of her frame. She was dressed in the same jeans from her Instagram image I'd seen on the news. She pressed her lips together, faint blue lines circling them. "Hiya, roomie."

I didn't think.

I grabbed her for a hug.

3:30 am

"Are you sure about this?"

She nodded. She had showered, changed clothes, and was watching through the window. "Yes. I have to disappear. There's no other way. He'll kill me if he finds me." She swallowed, looking back. "He can't find me."

Something fell to the floor down the hall, either in Blade's or Carol's room.

Brooke gasped, whirling and freezing.

She'd just started to look normal, color moving to her cheeks, but it drained from her again, leaving her pale.

I moved closer to her, dropping my voice to a whisper. "It would be easier if they helped us."

"No!" she hissed. "The less people who know, the better. I know I'm putting you in a bad place, but this is what you do. I'm so sorry." Her hand found mine, still a little cold and clammy. "Please help me."

6:00 am

My phone started buzzing.

Brooke glanced over from the passenger side of the truck. "Is that your roommates?"

I silenced it, then moved and pressed a pre-programmed message back before turning it off. "Yeah. They'll just think I went to the gym. I have a few hours before telling them I decided to stay for a slow swim or an hour massage. It'll be fine."

"Are you sure?" She was so twitchy. The panic never left her.

I nodded. "I'm sure."

She breathed easier and nodded, her head drooping. "Good. Thank God."

She had told me she was running from her brother.

She had told me *we* needed to go somewhere with a train station.

She had told me even I couldn't know where she'd end up.

143

She had told me the private detective she'd hired to find me only told her.

She had told me that same PI was killed the day before in a car accident.

She had told me that car accident, which might not have been an accident, had nothing to do with me.

She had told me all that to reassure me I was still safe.

At six-thirty that morning, I'd helped her disappear, while she'd lied to me.

CHAPTER TWENTY-FIVE

Present day

Cool hands touched the inside of my wrist.

I opened my eyes, lifting my head.

Jonah sat on the side of my bed, two fingers curved around my wrist while he gazed at his watch.

The rest of the night flooded back to me.

Kai had spoken the truth. He *had* broken me. The thought of giving up Brooke, telling him what I knew, was too much. So I went back to my training, and what happened next would give me nightmares for a long time.

It wasn't anything physical. It was emotional. I could see Kai, see Tanner and Jonah when they came into the room, but I was lost in the back of my mind. A different force was in charge of my body, and the only thing I could think about was not giving up my assignment.

Kai stopped pushing, but it hadn't mattered.

For an entire night I'd sat in my room in an almost catatonic state. I was awake, but could only repeat the vow I'd taken when I became a 411 Hider.

Tanner was outraged.

Jonah was concerned, taking my vitals and watching me as if I were his patient, and Kai was quiet. At first.

Then there'd been yelling, fighting, and Jonah had shouted at both of them to get out of my room.

"What time is it?" My throat burned, as if I'd been in the desert for thirty-six hours. I could only croak, that was it.

Jonah's head whipped up from his watch. "Holy shit." He let go of my pulse, immediately feeling my forehead with the back of his palm. "Riley? You're back?"

I nodded, and the movement made me want to vomit. I had a lot of that going on lately. "Yeah. It's me. I'm back."

"You scared us, and it's almost seven in the morning. I've been monitoring you all night."

I was grateful he didn't interrogate me then and there. He did a full assessment, checking my breathing, pulse, blood pressure. He checked my reflexes. He even pinched my skin for hydration. At the end of it, he stepped back, his stethoscope around his neck. His hands found his hips, and he frowned. "You're fine."

My head felt like it was splitting open. I rubbed at it, grimacing. "Could do with a painkiller for this up here, but yeah, I'm fine otherwise." I couldn't say the same for my mental status.

Even I was scared about what had happened to me.

I'd heard about operatives breaking down in the field, but it'd never happened to me. And I wasn't even sure if that was the same thing. Either way, it didn't sit right with me. I needed to be mentally strong at all times, not breaking and letting a stranger emerge in my place. Fucking weird, that's what it was.

"I need to go to the bathroom."

"Of course."

He waited to make sure I was steady on my feet. I wavered a bit as I stood, but my balance kicked in as I walked for the bathroom. I heard him gathering his bag and supplies, then the door clicking shut softly behind him a moment later.

I sagged against the door.

I did have to go to the bathroom, but I needed a moment to collect myself.

Holy. Shit.

I'd scared *myself*.

What happened? Was that normal? Was that going to happen again?

I didn't want to think about it, but it was pressing on me.

My hands began to shake again, and I ran them down my legs, taking deep, calming breaths to ease out the trembling. It didn't work, but fuck it—I never wanted to be like that again. Ever.

I was finishing up in the bathroom, washing my hands, when the main door opened again.

My bathroom door shoved open and Kai stood there, glowering at me.

"Are you okay?"

He didn't wait. He took two steps in, his hands slid into my hair, and he cupped my head. He stood close, intimately close, his eyes peering down at me. Searching. Questioning. As if my mental whatever-it-was had betrayed him.

"Are you okay?" he asked again, still gruff, but quieter. His chest rose up, jerking, and it held a second before lowering.

He wasn't mad *at* me. I felt it then. He was scared *for* me.

That realization opened a floodgate inside of me. I crumbled before I knew it, and I closed my eyes, tears slipping down my face as I leaned into his chest.

"No." I sobbed.

He cursed and lifted me in the air. He cradled me against his chest, walking back out to the bedroom. Sitting on the edge of my bed, he held me as if I were a child, pressed my head to his chest, and tightened his hold on me.

I tried not to completely collapse. But I did.

Kai was the enemy, or I'd thought he was. Now I didn't know.

I didn't know what was going on with me.

I didn't know if I should've helped Brooke as much as I had.

I didn't know anything, and I really didn't know why I just wanted to curl up in his arms and never leave again.

"No." I pulled back.

I could never go there, do that. Ever.

He didn't respond, but he did let me go and stand up. His hand ran through his hair, and he tipped his head up and turned slightly to face away from me.

"What happened to you?" he asked.

I answered him truthfully. "I broke. You broke me."

He glanced at me. "How?" His eyes were sharp.

I shrugged, sighing. "I don't know."

But I did. I felt it swirling inside me, and for some reason, I heard myself saying, "Protecting whoever I hide is a part of me. It's ingrained in me. I cannot break that vow. I was that vow. My mother is a vow. Do you get that?"

His nostrils flared, but that was his only response. His head hung low.

"I didn't hide her, but I did help her."

He lifted his gaze, and I swear, he stopped breathing. He went so still.

I couldn't look at him, not with what I was about to say, because this would destroy a part of me.

"It's exactly how you said. My roommates went to bed, but I couldn't sleep, and Brooke found me. She showed up at my door, drenched. It'd been raining that night. I gave her a ride to a train station three hours away. I hugged her, gave her papers for a new identity, and that's it. When I said I don't know where she is, I don't. She mentioned meeting someone, but I watched her get on a train."

"Where was that train going?"

"It was going to Winnipeg."

"You drove her to Edmonton?"

I nodded. "I took back roads. The kind that wouldn't have gas stations with security cameras."

"She's not in Edmonton. I had people check that place. They combed everywhere."

He began to pace, his head down, rubbing his forehead. His shoulders bunched tight, his shirt stretching over them.

"If she got off the train, there would've been video footage of her somewhere," he said, mostly to himself.

There wouldn't have been. Not if she moved the way I told her to move, head down, new hairstyle. New clothes. A hood or scarf or a hat to cover her face as much as possible. She needed to stick to far corners, move as little as possible. Use cash. And the other piece of information, the fake passport I gave her.

"You have to tell me where you think she is."

"That's all I know."

"You're lying. I can see it on your face. I know how to read you by now, very well. Please, Riley. No agenda here. No calculation. I'm not manipulating, threatening, nothing. I'm asking as an older brother. The longer she stays away from me, the more likely an enemy will find her. If she's with Levi, they will be found. His family probably knows by now he was turning evidence on them. They'll be out in full force too."

There was a nagging.

If she was with him, and he was working with the government... But no.

Or could they have?

"What?" He saw. He knew.

I shook my head. "Nothing." I frowned. "I mean, it can't..."

"What?"

"Just..." I still couldn't quite grasp it. "I know you have men in the FBI. Can you see if there's actually an active investigation into the Barnes family? Not where they're just taking what information they can get from him before deciding to open a case against them?"

His eyebrows lowered. He was deep in thought. "You think if there is, the government is hiding him."

"Which means they're hiding her."

"If they're together," he added.

No, the pieces were falling into place.

"Why would she go to you to hide if the US government was hiding her as well?" he asked.

This was not good. So not good.

"To either further hide her tracks or because they don't know they're hiding her."

Kai sank down on the bed next to me. Bending over, his elbows rested on his knees and he caught his head in his hands.

"Shit," he breathed.

My heart tugged. I didn't want it to, but it did.

"Call whoever you have in the FBI," I said softly. "Don't ask for her. Ask about him."

He didn't move at first. Silence filled the room for a few seconds, and then he reached over. His hand grabbed mine and squeezed, just for a moment, before he stood.

When he walked out, his shoulders seemed to sag in disappointment, and he looked as if he'd aged ten years.

He left through the bedroom. I heard the main door closing as he stepped out into the hallway.

A second later, I heard the soft tread of footsteps over the carpet.

I hadn't moved.

The door hadn't been open before Kai shut it. Whoever was coming toward me had been in the wing the whole time. They'd overheard everything.

Tanner stood in the doorway. "I can't believe you did that."

Yeah. Neither could I.

CHAPTER TWENTY-SIX

Tanner and Jonah kept me company for the day.

No Kai.

They didn't talk about him, and I didn't ask. We acted like we were friends having a movie marathon. They ordered pizza—or had someone make it. It just showed up, carried in on trays with anything I wanted to drink.

Tanner had a beer, and Jonah was drinking a green probiotic drink. I'd had one earlier as well. I kept to my tea for the rest of the evening. All day long, no matter what we did, I felt unbalanced. My hands weren't steady, and I knew it was because I'd given Brooke up.

I had broken my oath as a 411 operative. Would I be able to continue working with the Network? They would've understood. Hell, Brooke wasn't even an official client, but she was *my* client. She had been my person to help, and I'd given her up. It didn't matter that I hadn't told Kai where to find her. I'd assisted him in getting closer to her.

After the fourth movie, Tanner grabbed the remote and turned it off. "No more." He dropped it on the coffee table and sat back, his arms hugging a pillow over his chest. He burrowed into the couch, his ass toward me and his head in the corner.

"I'm fucking tired, and no more superheroes," he said, his voice muffled. "I'm superheroed out."

Jonah yawned, stretching his arms on the other side of me. The couch was ridiculously big, with thick, plump cushions, so I barely registered he was there.

Jonah groaned, standing up. "What time is it? I feel like I could sleep for a week."

Tanner snorted, still in that corner. "So says the real-life superhero. Give it up, little bro. You're going to be bouncing off the walls by tomorrow, wanting to go off and rescue people." He rolled over to sneer at his brother. "Save lives and shit."

Jonah frowned, another idle yawn coming over his face. "You sound pissed about that. Why you pissed?" His eyebrow went up. "I've saved your ass a few times."

He had?

I looked over Tanner, trying to see any scars.

Tanner rolled his eyes, sitting upright and rubbing a hand through his hair. "I'm giving you shit because Brooke ain't here to do it for me. That's what she does. She looks out for you, checks in with you, and gives you enough shit so your head don't get all swollen up from being the saint in this family."

Tanner sounded irritated.

Jonah grunted, grinning. "Yeah, right. She doesn't give me shit. I'm the brother she adores. She gives *you* shit so your head doesn't pop off and float away." Laughing to himself, he grabbed the beer bottles on the coffee table and the paper plates with leftover crusts.

He took them into my kitchenette area. I had a small sink, a mini fridge, a small microwave, and a coffee machine. All I really needed was a kettle for some tea, but I was growing a taste for coffee since being with the Bennett family.

As Jonah put the trash into the garbage can, a pillow whipped past my head and hit him square in the back.

Tanner growled, "Stop being perfect. We have staff to do that shit."

Jonah's mouth opened, his frown deepening. He finished putting the trash away. "You drunk, Tanner? You can be a dick at times, sober or not."

Tanner laughed, rolling over to stretch out on the sectional. His face smashed into the cushions once again. "Damn straight I'm a dick. And you know what? I would be more of a dick if Kai weren't so, so, whatever he is."

Jonah came over to pick up more of the trash.

I stood to help him.

"No, no. Sit." He waved me back down. "We came in here and made a mess."

"See!" Tanner barked. He flung a hand up. "He's being perfect. It's annoying."

"You're annoying." Jonah put down the paper plates and went over to his brother.

Tanner didn't know he was there until Jonah grabbed one of his legs and yanked.

Tanner's entire body came off the couch. Jonah kept pulling, sweeping him clear over the coffee table. All the garbage went with him, and Jonah finished with a yank so Tanner went sailing, almost to the wall.

"What the fuck?!" Tanner was up, charging his brother.

Jonah braced himself.

Tanner hit him in the chest. His arms wrapped around Jonah's waist, and planting his feet, he body-slammed him to the floor.

Jonah twisted out from under him, tucking a leg around Tanner's and flipping them over.

Tanner wasn't to be outdone. The two of them wrestled all the way to the main door, and after a bit, I started to hear their laughter.

"Check!" Tanner slammed Jonah back into the wall.

Both were panting and sweaty now, their faces red, but their smiles relaxed me.

"Ah!" Jonah laughed. "Get off me. You win."

Tanner relaxed, and Jonah shoved his arms off, kicking him the rest of way.

Tanner laughed too, falling back to collapse on the floor, his arms spread out. "Fuck." He was breathing hard. "That was fun. We haven't done that forever."

Jonah scooted up, his back resting against the door and a lopsided grin on his face.

"Yeah." He was still panting. "I work out, but forgot how damn heavy you are."

Tanner rolled over and whacked him on the leg with the back of his hand. "Shut it, little brother, or I'll kick your ass all over again."

"Yeah, right." Jonah shoved at Tanner's leg. "You used up all your juice in that match. I'd take round two."

"Fuck that."

"Fuck you."

"Fuck you!" Tanner bolted to a sitting position, pointing at Jonah.

Both paused, staring at each other, then began laughing again.

"We're fucked up," Jonah said, shaking his head.

Tanner grunted, falling back down. "Speak for yourself. I'm a stud. I'm not fucked up. I do the fucking up."

I coughed where I'd been sitting on the couch, watching. I'd loved it. I knew I had a stupid grin on my face. This was something I hadn't had growing up. Blade, Carol, and I weren't like this.

I'd once thought of them as family, but seeing Jonah and Tanner—no, Carol and Blade were friends. Co-workers. Not family. I didn't have this with them. If Brooke had been here, she would've been in the middle of it or laughing and shouting from the sides. Hell, she might've been coaching Jonah.

Another cough ripped up through my chest, and both of them snapped to attention. They got to their feet, coming over.

I waved them off, covering my mouth, and turned away from them. "No, no. I'm fine." Cough. "Really." Another cough. "I'm done." Two more coughs. "Now, I am. Really."

Nope. Lying.

I couldn't stop until Tanner had left the room, and Jonah went for his bag. He brought it over along with a glass of water. I took a sip, and it helped ease the coughs. He pulled out a cough drop and gave it to me. I eased back against the couch, my chest feeling weak.

"That sucks. I'm sorry." I waved toward where they'd been. "I didn't want to interrupt that."

Jonah shook his head, pulling out his stethoscope and kneeling beside me.

I leaned forward, knowing what he wanted.

He lifted my shirt enough to put it against my back. "It's fine. I think we both forgot you were here, actually. We haven't wrestled like that forever."

A pause.

"Deep breath."

I breathed deep.

"Exhale. Slowly."

I exhaled. Slowly.

"And another."

We repeated the process another three times before he moved to my front, his face looking away as he listened.

He was moving back, his stethoscope hanging around his neck when the door opened again.

Kai came in first, with Tanner behind him.

I felt zapped by his presence, and I sat up straight.

"You okay?" Kai's concerned eyes looked me over, lingering where my shirt was pulled down an inch before frowning and sliding his gaze to his brother. "Is she okay?"

"You said she was outside in the rain the other night?"

Kai nodded, standing against the couch, right behind me.

I tried to ignore him.

My heartbeat skyrocketed.

Being around Kai was *stressful*.

"She was. You think she got sick from that?"

Jonah gazed at me, frowning. "Yeah, maybe. She's got some wheezing in her lungs. Plus, she's been under a lot of stress."

See?

"It might've worn down her immune system." A hard look entered his eyes, and in that moment, he looked almost exactly like Kai. He scowled at his brother. "Lay off her. Whatever you have planned, just stop. She needs rest and relaxation, and being here, being around you isn't doing it. You're wearing her down. Literally."

"Hey..." Tanner moved to stand between the two.

But Kai nodded, pulling away from the couch. "Okay."

"Okay?" Tanner and Jonah parroted him together, their eyebrows raising.

"You shitting me?" Tanner added.

Jonah only said, "Good."

"I have to fly stateside anyway."

That got all our attention.

"Why?" asked Tanner.

"Did something happen?" Jonah said.

"Did you find her?" I chimed in.

Tanner and Jonah turned to look at me.

"What?" came a gargled sound from Tanner.

Jonah got quiet, stepping back.

Kai ignored them. "Maybe," he said to me.

My heart sank and leaped all at the same time. Maybe Jonah was right. Maybe I needed to stay away from Kai...and then I remembered it wasn't my decision!

I was being held there, against my wishes, because of someone I used to love. And if he'd found her, it was because of me.

And I still didn't know who to trust: Brooke or Kai.

Suddenly, I felt lower than low.

"Can I have a minute with Riley?" Kai asked.

"Yeah." Jonah nodded.

"Sure."

The last was Tanner, a gruff edge in his voice, but he followed Jonah. Jonah left his bag on the kitchenette counter, and I heard them moving for the door.

It shut quietly, and I could feel the emptiness left behind. The air felt more open, but also stifling.

Kai came around to sit on the edge of the couch, diagonal from where I was.

I didn't look at him. I didn't need to. I could feel every movement he made, every look he sent my way, every time he started to say something and didn't. Which he did, three times, while I sat waiting.

I swallowed over a knot. "You found her, didn't you?"

I'd done that.

"We found *him*. I told them not to move, in case she's there. I need to be the one she sees first. She has to see I'm not going to do anything to harm her or her boyfriend."

My heart squeezed.

He sounded so genuine.

"Are you lying to me?" I still didn't trust myself to look at him.

"No."

Another squeeze.

"I did that." Those words wrung out of me. *Fuck it.* "I gave her up. If you hurt her, I swear..." I glared at him, flinching when I saw concern in his eyes, the bags under them. "I will kill you," I finished.

There was no heat to my words, just promise.

He waited a beat, then nodded. "I believe you will." A trace of amusement lingered in his tone. "I told you I'd murder you if you told anyone what I said before. I mean that too."

I still glared at him, but I remembered.

He would murder me. I would kill him.

Fuck, we were almost perfect for each other—NO! No. No. NO. I would not think like that.

I forced myself to look away, feeling like I had to break cement to do it. "What will you do if it's her and she's fine?" *What will happen to me?*

He seemed to know what I was really asking because he replied, "You can go back to your life. Like normal."

Except nothing would be normal now.

"Are you going to be okay?" he asked.

I pulled a blanket over my lap. "I'll be fine. I'll sleep and get better." I gestured to Jonah's bag. "There's a doctor here. That helps."

"Yeah."

I knew without looking that he was rubbing a hand over his mouth. He was deep in thought; he was going to change something, I was about to be put through the wringer again.

"I was going to bring Jonah with me," he said.

"What?"

I looked at him, and I was caught. His eyes captured mine.

"In case Brooke needs medical attention."

"Oh." Guilt flared in my chest, warming me. "That's a good idea, actually."

He shook his head. "No. He can stay here. I'll bring someone else."

Of course. Again. What was one doctor to the head of a mafia family? He probably had a whole slew of them to call—EMTs, nurses, nurse assistants even.

And what was I doing here?

I was envisioning a gorgeous *Grey's Anatomy*-like *female* doctor—street and academically smart, gorgeous, who could save lives with nothing more than a straw. That's who he'd call to travel with him.

Nope. No jealousy here.

"Just be careful," I heard myself say when Kai stood up.

He stopped in surprise, but I pushed up from the couch and went to the bedroom, shutting the door with way more oomph than it required.

CHAPTER TWENTY-SEVEN

I t was three in the morning.

I heard a soft knock at my wing door, followed by bad déjà vu. I pulled on a wrap, went to the door, and opened it.

Kai stood on the other side.

No guards. Just him.

The hallway light had been dimmed to a soft glow, and he leaned back against the wall, his hands in his pockets, his head down as he waited. He didn't move, just raised those piercing eyes and asked, "Can I come in?"

My hand tightened on the doorknob. "I thought you'd left already."

"I'm going in an hour." He nodded behind me, his voice almost gentle. "Can I come in?"

Want swept through me, filling me, heating me.

Desire had been present between us for a long time, longer than I'd guess either of us wanted. And it was so strong at this moment, maybe it was because I knew he was leaving again, maybe it was the time of night, maybe it was because my walls were down for whatever reason. I tried to erect them, but I couldn't.

I just wanted him. It filled me so completely that it stopped me from talking for a second.

"Are you sure that's a good idea?"

There it was. I said it out loud.

He expelled a ragged breath. "Maybe not, but I'd like to come in anyway."

God.

An ache throbbed in me, and I fought against actually panting. This was ridiculous, but I eased back and moved into the living room.

I didn't sit. Something told me I should remain standing.

He shut the door behind him with a soft click, but didn't advance. He remained next to the door, his head down, his hands in his pockets, his shoulders hunched forward.

"I'm about to get on a plane—"

A plane?

"—and when I land, I'm going to have to do bad things."

The alarm that had crept up me when he mentioned the plane shifted to a different alarm, a foreboding one. He was warning me.

"I'd imagine. Levi gave up someone the FBI was protecting, right?"

He didn't answer.

My guess was right.

"And if your sister is with him, you'll take them both."

His eyes rose, holding mine.

I felt almost brazen now. "And if your sister isn't with him, you'll still take him. Just him." My mouth parted. My throat constricted.

I was playing a dangerous game, baiting him, but my God, he'd come to me. He brought me here. He'd pulled me into this in the first place.

"And you'll use him to force your sister to come to you. Right?" I didn't wait for his answer. "How?" I bit that word out as a demand, jerking toward him. My hands balled into fists at my legs. "How will you let her know you have him?"

He waited for me to finish. His eyes were heated, smoldering. I ignored it. A tingling spread through me, starting at the base of my neck. It intertwined with my dangerous addiction to pushing the envelope, walking the line, seeing how far I could go without toppling over a cliff.

Kai was the cliff.

I just wanted to fall free. Away from him. To him. In his arms. I wanted all of it, and my chest heaved.

I closed in so I was only a foot from him. "It won't matter. None of it. You might find your sister. You might force her into coming back to your fold, but if you threaten the man she loves, you'll have broken her. You'll have broken whatever childlike and pure bond there was between you and her as siblings." I took a step. "She'll never look at you the same way." A second step. My voice lowered, but it held venom. "But maybe you've already done that. Maybe you've already killed whatever allows a little sister to adore her older brother? This is just par for the cour—"

His hand slid around my neck, cupping the back of my head, and I stopped talking.

Every tendon in me stretched tight.

My pulse raced.

My mouth parted again.

The ache inside of me was agonizing.

I wanted him.

I couldn't deny it. I'd stopped lying to myself, but I still felt utter disdain for what he did, for who he had to be.

He pulled me to him, sliding my wrap down to fall on the floor. His eyes bored down into mine, just a few inches separating us, and I could feel how he held me suspended.

I felt his pulse too. It was as fast as mine.

"You may hate me. You may loathe me." His hand slid back from my neck and moved down agonizingly slowly, between my breasts to my stomach.

I gasped, and he slid his hand under my pajama shorts until they rested over my clit. I surged upward at his touch, my head falling back, everything in me starting to tremble.

One of his fingers dipped inside of me. "But you goddamn want me." And with that, a second finger joined his first and he took hold of my tank, his mouth slamming down on mine.

It shouldn't have been like this.

I was writhing.

I shouldn't feel the fire he'd just doused with gasoline ignite inside of me.

When his lips touched mine, flames surged, and I gasped into his mouth. His tongue slid inside. Everything exploded, and I felt his tongue searching for mine as his fingers began to thrust. I was coming undone, and all I wanted was to get closer, my fingers sinking into his chest and arms, then sliding around to his back.

I climbed up on him, and he growled, grabbing my leg and turning to shove me against the wall.

Holy hell.

His mouth took, but it savored and gave at the same time. He commanded me, taking ownership of me, but then he pulled back and softly grazed my lips.

I moaned, following him with my mouth.

I wanted more. I needed more.

"Fuck," he moaned. His hand slid down my neck, pushing my top farther down, and his fingers moved over my breast, cupping me.

This was wrong.

My body didn't care.

I was overheating, and I rested my head against the wall, falling back. I could only gasp for air as he moved down. He kissed under my bottom lip, his mouth tasting my jaw and scorching a path to my throat and down between my breasts until he circled over my nipple. He teased me, brushing his lips over me, then following with a sweep of his tongue.

I took a fistful of his hair and held him to me.

His eyes widened in surprise as he saw the need in me.

Lifting his head, he let me slip down in his arms until we were face to face. He watched me. I watched him. Holding me, he rocked into me over and over, his fingers flexing inside.

I wanted more.

His eyes softened and he slowed down, his lips nipping mine.

I bit back a whimper.

He nipped again, his gaze almost black with desire. But he held back, making me almost blind for him.

"You're killing me." I couldn't hold it in. I bit my lip, closed my eyes, and pushed against his hand.

A third finger joined the others, and I leaned back, my throat exposed to him. I grasped his hand to make him move faster, and he chuckled softly. He thrust into me, stretching me, filling me as his lips found my throat.

I felt fused to him, and I wanted him to keep moving.

He held back a moment before his fingers twitched.

"Ah!" I gasped. "You just want...?" I felt the scrape of his teeth and froze, a bubble of air caught in my throat.

He thrust hard, growling, "You don't know what I want."

"Kai!"

His palm grazed over my clit. He rubbed against it, his fingers finally, finally moving. Sliding out, then pushing in.

His mouth moved back up to take mine again.

I felt enslaved to him.

He continued thrusting, slowly, going deeper and deeper.

A frustrated gasp left me, and I snapped my legs around his waist. I arched my back, grinding on his hand. He held me tight as I began to ride him.

"Please. God!"

His mouth closed over mine before he whispered, "Not. Even. Close."

Then he began to fuck me, his lips drowning out my sounds. I grew frenzied, but still he took his time, coaxing me with kisses, his fingers. His hand tweaked my nipple before he pulled his mouth away. His lips covered me there as he grabbed my waist. His hand slid around as he pressed his groin close. He anchored me against the door and played my goddamn body like an instrument.

He strummed as his fingers pushed in.

He tapped out a beat as he pulled back out.

He kept the perfect pressure on me, and I jerked in his arms, my mouth ripping from his as an onslaught of waves crashed through me. I hurtled over that edge, but he didn't let me slow down. He started right back up, and it wasn't long before a choking scream ripped from my throat as I came a second time.

My body went limp. I was a puddle in his arms. Every bone in me had melted.

He held me up as I collapsed against his shoulder. Moving away from the door, he cradled my ass and the back of my neck. He walked me to my bedroom.

He laid me on the bed and stood over me, gazing down.

I must've looked wanton. My top was still shoved aside, my breast exposed, and my pajama pants had fallen low on my hips. My thong had been pulled over for his entrance.

I didn't cover myself. He took me in, looking from my legs, to my pussy, to my stomach, then up to my breasts and lips before finally meeting my eyes, his jaw clenched. His eyes were stormy, inflamed.

It awoke a calm in me, and I slid sensually over the bed. I had him captive now.

He tracked every move I made.

My gaze went to his pants, to the bulge there, the one I'd felt under me, straining.

I sat up, my strap falling off my shoulder, and moved to the edge of the bed, feeling a new throb in me.

He remained silent, watching me as I grabbed his jeans.

I pulled him forward, my hand resting over him. I looked up, meeting his gaze as I undid the button at the top, then slid down his zipper. I reached in, finding his cock, and I wrapped my fingers around it.

He hissed, his eyelids falling low but still watching me.

I brought him out and moved to take him in my mouth.

"No." He grabbed me, holding me still, his chest rising and falling rapidly.

"I didn't come for that." A bleakness shone in his eyes, before vanishing. "I want you to come with me."

I sat back.

He leaned down, slid a finger up my arm and pulled up my strap until I was covered. He adjusted my pants next, but first he slid his palm down my stomach, under my thong to bring it back in place. He arranged everything until I was covered.

Expelling a sharp hiss, he fastened his jeans back up and sat next to me. The side of his leg and arm brushed mine.

Facing forward, his head dipped down. "I came here tonight to ask you to come with me. I don't usually fly with loved ones, and you're included there."

I—what?

"Brooke loves you, and I know Tanner and Jonah are fond of you. No matter the circumstances of you coming here, you are considered a friend of the family."

I felt him watching me, but I focused on my lap.

"That means something to me. If I find Brooke, she won't travel back with me on a plane. I'll have her driven back. It's longer, but..."

He didn't have to say anything.

They'd lost Cord on a plane. He didn't want to risk Brooke.

"I get it."

"But," he said sharply, "it's too long a trip for me. I have to fly, so I'm making an exception. I'd like you to come with me."

"Where are you going?"

"New York."

I frowned. "Levi is being kept in New York?"

"Outside of New York, yes."

"Oh." My frown deepened. I picked at my pants, smoothing out wrinkles that weren't there. My mind raced.

What did this mean? My thoughts swirled.

"I'm sick!" I blurted. "You're going to get sick."

He fought back a smile. "I don't get sick. Ever."

Of course. I snorted. "You're not human."

He waited a beat. "Will you come?"

I wanted to go. That was the truth. But everything within me argued.

My mind: hell no.

My everything else: fuck yes.

I was still tingling from exploding in his arms a moment ago.

I looked up. "And if I wanted to go home?"

"I'll have Tanner ride with you." He didn't hesitate. "You know the truth about Brooke leaving. I'm trusting you with that information. No one knows."

"Not even your brothers?"

He nodded. "No one."

"What agenda do you have? What's your endgame here?"

"No endgame. I'm being selfish; that's all." He tipped my head up, raising my gaze to his. His finger caressed under my chin. "I want you to come with me. That's it."

Oh. Well. When he put it like that, I knew my answer.

"No."

CHAPTER TWENTY-EIGHT

I held still after giving Kai my response.

My heart pushed against my chest, beating hard, and he dipped his head in an abrupt nod.

"Fine." He stood. His hand fell away from my face. His heat left my side. There was no comforting weight on the bed with me.

I shivered, feeling coldness in the room and knowing it was him pulling away from me.

"I'll tell Tanner and Jonah to accompany you home."

My mouth fell open. He left the room with quick and decisive strides.

He was actually doing it. He was letting me go, after what we'd just done.

The shock lodged firmly in my throat and remained there long after he'd left, long after I heard the door click shut behind him, and even when a staff person came in and began packing a bag for me.

I stood, shaking. "Those aren't mine."

"Mr. Bennett said to pack you clothes since your scrubs are gone."

Right. Because they put them on a look-alike to trick Blade.

Everything hit me with a thud.

Fuck's sake. I'd been kidnapped and now I was aching because I got to leave?

My head began pounding.

"You can go with him, you know."

Tanner stood in the doorway, his arms crossed, one foot over the other.

"What?" I croaked.

He flicked his eyes to the ceiling. "I know what you smell like, darling."

The back of my neck heated. I snuck a look at the staff woman, but she didn't pause. She folded a shirt I'd worn every other day here. She knew it was one of my favored ones, then reached for another I liked.

"That's none of your business, Tanner." I stiffened.

"I know that. I just don't care. Listen." He gripped the sides of the doorframe and let himself fall forward, his elbows pointed out. He began pushing back and forth, his biceps bulging from the motion. "Yeah, how we brought you here was shitty. But you know our name. You wouldn't have come if we'd asked, and you wouldn't have helped find Brooke either. You know it. We know it. Kai's the one who has to make those shitty decisions—but make no mistake, if it wasn't him, it'd be me. We have a whole family full of sharks who want to come in and take what we have. We will not let that happen, any of us. We're Bennetts. That means something, even with Brooke."

He tipped his head forward, his eyes knowing. "And you know it too. What Kai should've done, and I'm assuming he didn't, was emotionally blackmail you. He should've said there's a damn good chance Brooke's going to do something stupid when she sees him on that doorstep. She'll get someone killed because she doesn't act rational sometimes. She jumps before looking where she's going. Kai could've said that, but he didn't, did he? Chew on that a second, huh?"

I swallowed over a hard knot. "What are you talking about? Who'd get killed?"

He shrugged. "Take your pick. Brooke. Kai. Brooke's man—and Brooke will then blame herself or Kai." He pushed off the doorframe, turned, and slid his hands into his pockets. "You should go, my two cents, but what do I know?" He strolled away, whistling once he got to the hallway.

The woman was done. My bag was packed and in her hand. She waited beside the bed.

I was going to regret this. I knew I would. "Put that in the vehicle Kai is leaving in. I'm going with him."

She nodded. "Of course. I'll notify him now since they're leaving the driveway already."

"What?"

But she was gone, hurrying out.

I blanked a second, then went into overdrive. I couldn't travel in my pajamas...or maybe I should? No. That was ludicrous.

I grabbed a pair of black leggings, an oversized black hoodie, a black tank top, a pair of underwear, and a bra. I went to the bathroom, changed, and washed.

What am I doing?

I slipped on a pair of black flats.

I have no idea.

Oh God.

My throat constricted. Panic clawed at my chest.

Grabbing a hair tie, I piled my hair into a messy bun and left my wing.

It took a second to figure out what was wrong.

I blinked, and it hit me. There were no guards.

I was completely alone.

Shit.

I didn't have a phone. I wanted a phone. I needed music when I flew. I hated not having music. Or a book? Maybe I should've grabbed a few from their library, but I was already off and weaving toward the front entryway.

Was I making a mistake?

After what we did—my body instantly warmed, and I bit back a groan.

It was going to happen again. More. More would happen.

But Brooke. Kai. I didn't want anyone to get hurt. Brooke would listen to me. She would. Tanner was right about that. She'd talk first, before doing something rash. Right?

Was this all a calculated move? Had Tanner been supposed to come in, lay on a guilt trip, and send me running after Kai? Because, fuck. That's what happened.

I stopped at the bottom step, the entryway beckoning me. A pair of headlights shone outside. They were waiting for me.

"He won't come in for you."

This time Jonah stood behind me, a drink in hand. He was dressed much like me, in a sweatshirt, but with sweats on the bottom.

"You'll have to go to him. He's been notified that you changed your mind, but the decision has to be yours. Totally. He'll wait, but not for long. He'll go without you, so decide quick. Otherwise, the next vehicles will be leaving in six hours. We'll take you back to your other life."

My other life.

He was right. If I went with Kai, somehow, in some way, I would be returning to my old life. But if I stayed, even if I went back to Blade and Carol, could I really return to that world?

I'd broken my vow.

I was still breaking my vow, now actually going with the person the hider wanted away from.

But...my eyes were glued to those headlights.

I knew my decision. I felt it deep down.

I went outside.

I hadn't ever really considered not going. I'd been fooling myself.

The door to the SUV opened. Kai sat to one side, and I got in.

The inside was warm, a slight trace of bourbon in the air.

I sat back, not meeting Kai's gaze, and smoothed my sweaty palms down my legs.

Had I just made a mistake?

Then he placed a phone in my hand. "For you to use."

I choked up.

I turned on the screen, saw the WiFi connected already, and knew what this really meant.

He'd just offered me real freedom.

Next he placed a pair of headphones on my lap.

Without another word, I plugged them in, put them on, and found some music. I slid down beside him, and it wasn't long before I fell asleep.

I felt... I didn't want to think about how I felt.

It was a way I shouldn't have. I knew that much.

CHAPTER TWENTY-NINE

Kai traveled via private jet.
I shouldn't have been surprised. Privacy and security were so important to them. It made sense.

We rolled up to the plane in a private hangar and got out. There was a slight drizzle in the air, a faint smell of manure underneath. I shivered, ducking my head as we went up the ramp.

"Welcome, miss."

The flight attendant gave me a professional smile, indicating for me to take a seat. I was surprised how big the plane was—ten people could fly with us.

I took one of the seats in the back, and one by one, the others filled with Kai's security guards. I wondered if more guards were coming, flying separately, or if he had a whole fleet to meet us when we landed. They kept the seat across from me open.

One guess who was going to sit there.

My phone buzzed, and I opened it up.

Hey.

Me: Who is this?

Blade.

I shot a look at Kai, but his back was still turned to me as he spoke to the pilot.

Me: How did you get this number?

Blade: Your man sent me a text with the number, said you'd be using it. You're with him for real?

Me: No. I'm with him for Brooke.

Blade: He's brainwashed you.

I waited a second before replying, my stomach rolling over on that one.

Me: Maybe. If he hurts Brooke, I'm going to kill him.

The phone rang, and I answered, "Hey."

"What the fuck are you doing sending that text? It's his phone. He's going to be monitoring your texts."

Kai turned now and made his way back. His eyes found me, took in the phone pressed to my ear, but he had no reaction. I shifted lower in the seat, getting more comfortable.

I lowered my voice, "He knows."

"He knows?!"

"I told him."

Blade sighed. "I don't know what game you're playing with him, or if that's what you're doing or not. Just...be safe, okay?"

My nerves were stretched so tight, I could've bounced a penny off them. "Oh, I will," I remarked as Kai took the seat across from me.

We hung up, and I busied myself picking a new song.

"You didn't tell him we were going to New York?" Kai asked.

I paused. "It's none of his business."

Kai frowned, but as I had in the car, I plugged in my headphones, buckled my seatbelt, and got cozy in my chair.

"You knew I would talk to him."

Kai shrugged. "What part of being here of your own free will means you can't make phone calls?"

"Touché."

He frowned, then grinned. "Touché." Sitting back, he pulled out some papers as we taxied to take off.

Once in the air, the flight attendant began serving us drinks and food. I asked for a blanket.

"There's a full seat in the back." Kai gestured behind us, and through a privacy curtain, I saw he was right.

It was almost big enough for two people to sleep on.

"I know you didn't sleep last night," he added.

"Do you?" Why did I bait him? I grimaced. "Don't answer that."

He didn't, just smiled.

I didn't know how to handle this Kai. He was smiling. He was kind. He was...not being calculating or ruthless, or holding the seat in a death grip.

"I thought you didn't fly," I said.

"I don't, if I don't have to." He shuffled his papers. "And fear isn't the reason we prefer not to fly. It's because why risk another loved one the way we already lost one?"

His eyes were steady on me. He put his papers down, turning to face me as he leaned over the aisle. His voice lowered. "I will do almost anything for my family, and if traveling by vehicle a few extra hours is it, it's an easy choice."

"But flying to New York..."

"A necessary evil. I don't have the time in my schedule to drive, and like I said before, you're an exception." His eyes heated before sliding to the back curtain. "You don't want to lie down?"

I was tired. I was wired. I was all of the above.

I was confused mostly.

I shrugged, holding my phone with the music. "I'm good for now."

He nodded, sitting back. He picked up the papers. "If you change your mind, I did pick this jet specifically because of that back area for you."

Specifically?

Wait.

"You have more than one plane?!"

CHAPTER THIRTY

Hour one, I was content.

Hour two, I was restless.

Hour three, I took the flight attendant's offer of a drink. I needed something to settle me.

Hour four, I went to sleep on the back seat. I left my phone and headphones in the other seat, so I could hear the background buzz from the engines. Every now and then, I caught a snippet of conversation from the guards. Their murmuring settled me somehow, lulling me into sleep.

Hour five, I woke to screaming.

I jerked upright, finding the flight attendant crouched on the floor next to me. Her hands covered her head, and she'd curled almost in a ball. She raised her head, and I could see she was terrified.

"What's going on?"

Another scream.

I scooted to the side, my heart jackhammering.

The curtain had been pulled shut, and I reached forward.

"Don't!" she hissed, grabbing my hand. "He'll kill us."

"Kai?"

"No. The man."

The man?

"You will die!"

That voice didn't sound human. It was high-pitched and animalistic, like a cat screeching.

I slipped to the floor to see under the curtain. A wall of men stood in front of me.

What do I do here?

Fear for Kai coursed through me, but my training also kicked in. Whatever was happening, letting the man stay in control was the wrong thing to do.

I moved to the opposite side, where the attendant was crouched. She watched me, her arms shaking. Tears slid down her face as she shook her head at me.

She knew I was going to do something.

I was stupid.

Kai had security guards.

They had a better chance of handling this, but where was Kai? Had he already been hurt? How had this happened?

The curtain moved an inch, and I almost gasped when I saw one of the guards watching me. He shook his head too. His face was deadly serious.

I mouthed to him, "What's going on?"

He shook his head, closing the curtain.

"—you want."

That was Kai. Some of my fear eased, just a bit.

"I want you to die!" Another strangled scream.

He must have a gun or a weapon if they weren't rushing him. *God*. What weapon? Was it pointed at Kai?

"I know, but there are people on this plane who don't deserve to die this way."

"That's where you're wrong! YOU'RE WRONG! They all deserve to die. They work for you. They should all perish. It's been deemed. YOU."

A thud.

"MUST."

Another thud. I could feel his footsteps through the plane. "DIE!"

TIJAN

There was a rush of thuds, as if he ran forward or someone ran at him.

I looked under the curtain, my heart in my throat, and the wall of men was gone.

Jumping up, I peered through to make sure, and I was right. They'd all rushed him.

"No, no." A clammy hand grabbed my arm. The attendant tried to pull me back. "Don't go out there. Please."

"AGH!"

I'd never forget that sound. It was like the bleating of an animal dying slowly, asking for help in its last moments of life.

I didn't think.

I tore my hand away from hers and rushed out, going to my seat and huddling down for cover. I could peer around it, just one eyeball.

The men were on top of a guy I didn't recognize. His skin had a green tinge to it, soaked from sweat, and his eyes were wild. One guard held a gun, just by the end, and two others patted the man down.

Kai stood over him, staring.

I recognized that set in Kai's shoulders. I knew what it meant. He was furious. But he was keeping it reined in.

One of the guards looked up at Kai. He gave him a firm nod as both of them stepped back. The others who had been pinning the man down stepped back too. All of them gave him a wide berth until only the man and Kai were left in the center of the plane.

Slowly, so slowly, Kai reached over and took the gun from his guard.

The man's eyes darted from it to Kai. They were almost vibrating in his head.

His lips parted. "What—what are you doing?"

That's when I saw that Kai had gloves on. And he was wearing a jacket, not one I recognized from before.

The man didn't have a jacket. He wore just a shirt.

A sick feeling rose in me.

Kai was wearing that man's jacket.

He had gloves on.

He was holding that man's gun.

"This is the third time you've tried to kill me and my men," Kai said calmly.

What? Shivers went up my spine. The hair on the back of my neck stood up.

"The first time, you went to prison. I let the police handle you."

Kai's hand fit around that gun like his own glove, like he'd been holding guns since he was three, like it was second nature to him.

"The second time, you went to a psychiatric hospital," he continued.

The guy began crying, shaking his head, moaning. He crouched down, covering his head with his hands the way the flight attendant had been moments earlier. He rocked back and forth on his heels.

"No. No. Please, no," he repeated. "Don't do this."

Kai crouched down close to him. "You lost your family to a drug deal. You blame me for those drugs. I took pity on you. I understand how grief can make you do bad things. I gave you mercy the first time, and the second time my sister pleaded on your behalf. She knew your wife, said you were a good man. You were a janitor at a hospital where she volunteered. My brother remembered you too, said you were a good worker there. That was the last time."

I sat back, no longer cowering behind the seat.

"No, no, please no. Don't do this. No, no, please no." He spoke faster, the words running into each other until he looked up and saw me. He stopped speaking.

Kai looked.

His eyes darkened.

He was mad at me. I didn't care.

I couldn't look away from this man. He was skinny, his face gaunt as if he hadn't eaten in days. Seeing me changed something in him. The crying stopped. He sat up. He no longer cowered.

Kai stepped back to give him space, stepping back again as the man stood.

The man never looked away from me.

Kai stepped to block me, but the man yelled, "No! No. I am about to die. I want to stare into the eyes of a woman."

A savage growl ripped from Kai. "Get her out of here!" he barked at his men.

"No! She's your woman, yes?"

There was no response. Two of the guards moved toward me, but I held them off. Shaking my head, I stood too. My legs were weak, but I wanted to see this. I didn't know why. Maybe I didn't want to be the one cowering in the back? Maybe I didn't want to put my head in the sand, knowing what was going to happen but letting Kai shield me from it?

I stepped out, putting a hand up as another of the guards tried to block me. "No. I want to give the man what he wants. We all know what's going to happen anyway."

He wouldn't hurt me. He couldn't. Kai wouldn't let that happen.

Something whispered to me in the back of my mind. I should stop this. I should try to help him. He was sick—that was obvious—but I remembered waking up to his screams. I remembered the flight attendant. I remembered the other two times Kai had spoken about.

Even Jonah, even Brooke. They wouldn't have fought for this man again.

They were Bennetts, like Tanner said. It blazed inside of me now.

Kai was a Bennett. Kai was the leader of the Bennetts. He would not let this happen again, and because of that, I said, "Let him see me. Please, Kai."

The last guard moved aside, so I stood a few feet behind Kai. The man shifted to the side to see me around him.

I was a ball of writhing nerves.

There's a feeling in the air when you're about to see someone die. Your gut clenches, and what's about to happen, you know is wrong. But thinking about it in that brief moment, I couldn't think of a time when someone's death had felt right. Maybe if life has been lived to its fullest or the person is crippled in pain with no hope...but I'd never seen that happen.

However, in this moment, I knew the wrong feeling wasn't about him dying. The wrong was about how he had lived, the pain and anger that must've been with him.

I was guessing because as I stared into that man's eyes, I only saw death. Whether it was his, his wife's, his child's, I didn't know. But I saw blackness, and I felt a cold emptiness creep into me. This man's look of death was different than Kai's, and maybe I'd think on that later.

He gave one last strangled scream, launching himself at me, and Kai shot him.

CHAPTER
THIRTY-ONE

I sat in the back of an SUV, a blanket around me, and I was... calm.

I shouldn't have been calm, but I was.

When we landed, the authorities were en route. Kai's men bundled me off the plane and had me in the SUV by the time anyone from the government showed up. The pilot had called in a distress signal. I still wasn't sure what happened. We should've gone through customs. I'd been stressing about a passport at one point on the plane. But Kai had it covered. He seemed to have everything covered.

I figured they'd tell the police it had been self-defense. But Kai had on the guy's jacket. He'd shot him in such close quarters that it could've also been argued as a self-inflicted shot to the head. A suicide.

Kai spoke to a police detective as the body was carried off the plane on a stretcher. No one took photographs or collected forensic evidence. It was wrong, but this was how the underbelly lived. And in some cases, thrived. Kai was thriving.

That man would be shuffled into a pile of paperwork. Maybe he would be mislabeled at the morgue. Maybe he'd be cremated sooner than normal.

Kai would make this go away.

He nodded to the detective, who put her notepad away. She spoke into her phone like a radio and moved past the stretcher into another vehicle. Kai talked to a few other men, some who had met us on the tarmac. They nodded and shook hands, and Kai turned toward the SUV.

A guard opened the door. Kai got inside, and as usual, it wasn't long before the guards got in and our caravan of three vehicles departed.

Kai only glanced once at me before settling back in his seat, taking his phone out.

We didn't talk until thirty minutes in, as our vehicles sped down the highway.

"You didn't eat on the plane," he said. "Are you hungry?"

My stomach dipped, but not because of that.

"You murdered him," I said quietly.

He put his phone away and turned to face me. "If I let him live—"

"I know." I just felt sad. "I heard. He didn't deny."

Neither of us mentioned that according to mafia law, the man should've been killed the first time. No exceptions. Kai had given him two. That was more than enough.

That's how they thought in that world.

My stomach shifted. That world. I was becoming part of that world.

Kai might've dragged me over the line, but he had let go, and I'd stayed.

"Hey."

I closed my eyes. I didn't need to hear concern in his voice. I didn't want to see it in his eyes either. If I did, I'd succumb. That was my pattern with Kai.

"We didn't go through customs," I said.

I caught his frown when I looked over. I kept my head down, the blanket bundled around me.

"We would've." A second of silence. He was gauging me. "Because of the shooter, we landed in a different location."

Still. *Customs.* I'd never snuck into a country where I didn't have to produce a passport, even if it was a fake one. That was a constant we handled with the Network. We had customs agents on our side who let the fake passports go through. They were sympathetic to the cause. That wasn't the case here.

"You had a passport for me?"

He dipped his head. "Yes."

"As who?"

"As your cover."

I spoke without thinking. "The Network would've known. I would've been flagged in an alert."

Silence sat between us, so heavy.

My employers would've known I was with him willingly, that I was staying. I hadn't thought about what they might be thinking, but now it was so clear it was like someone had grabbed my spine and ripped it out.

I would've never been a 411 operative again. I'd had my doubts already—but it was still my choice, my decision for when I had time to process it. But this would've taken it out of my hands. The Network would've expelled me the second my cover's passport was used.

I would've lost everything: Blade. Carol. Even my stupid cover as Raven.

My mission in life. Where would that have gone?

Where is it going now? A voice laughed at me, mocking me.

I blinked, shoving down the turmoil. "How was that man even on the plane?"

"There's a storage unit he hid in. It's accessible to us if we had needed to get in there."

"Why'd he wait so long? Why not right away?"

Kai shook his head. "He was working up his courage? Maybe he lost consciousness and came to again later? Maybe he was waiting for all of us to be sleeping?"

I picked at the edge of the blanket. My vision started to swim. "You seem fine," I said. It was an accusation. "You don't seem disturbed. Was this just another Tuesday to you?" A slightly unhinged laugh came from me. "It probably was. I mean, you're in the mafia. You control half of Canada. Have you moved into Toronto yet?" I hiccupped, which turned into a snarl. "You can't, right? You're not into drugs. There has to be a drug business in Canada. If you're not running it, who is?"

There was a look in his eyes.

I trailed off because I knew. "If you're not doing it, you're allowing someone else to do it."

His jaw firmed. "Dissecting my business is not the reason you're here."

"Right." I snorted. "I'm here to help Brooke, or to fuck you."

This was pathetic. *I* was pathetic, because it was true. He'd brought me for those reasons, and sadly, I'd probably do both. Even now.

"Goddamn you," I told him. "Goddamn you to hell."

CHAPTER THIRTY-TWO

I needed to get drunk. Fast.

As soon as we pulled up to the log house nestled among a bunch of trees and overlooking a river, I grabbed my bag and hightailed it inside. Security had already walked through. They were coming out as I walked in, ignoring everything.

I took the first set of stairs and climbed. Up. Up. All the way until there were no more stairs. I think I was on the third floor. I was a pro at figuring out which room Kai would want me in. I followed the hallway all the way to the back and went into the last bedroom. It was large, with its own sitting room and a library nook. A person could sit there and literally reach forward for their next book. The attached bathroom—shared with another bedroom—had a glass-walled shower big enough for four people to have a dance party. This would be my room.

I searched for the liquor cabinet. Not finding one, I went to the room across the hall, the one I shared a bathroom with. In the back corner, I found it. I reached for a bottle, not caring what it was. Pushing off the cap, I tipped my head almost at the same time.

I was guzzling it before I even left the room and entered mine.

The men were coming inside. I could hear their voices below. The aroma of pizza wafted up to me, and that meant one thing: I needed more alcohol in my system.

I did not want to feel this self-hatred.

I was weak. I was an embarrassment to the ideals I'd dedicated my life to: helping others, saving others, protecting others. I was with a man who violated all of those principles, and I should run. I *could* run now, but I didn't. I knew I wouldn't.

I would give in when he came to me. I almost had to. There was a yearning deep down. I craved Kai. I needed my first fix. I needed to feel him inside of me, claiming me, fucking me.

I sank to the floor, still clutching that bottle.

A part of my mind was still thinking clearly, a small part, but it was fast disappearing. I knew I was having a breakdown. Maybe it was from everything or just from that man on the plane, or the fact that *there was a man on a plane and everyone acted like it happened every day!*

I was losing it.

Clambering to the toilet, I cleaned out whatever I'd had in my stomach. Maybe breakfast from a day ago? Would that still be there?

The bottle in hand, I struggled back to my feet. Good. The more blitzed I was, the better. Though, I was more unsteady because I'd lost everything in my stomach, not from the drinking. Shedding my clothes, I stepped into the shower. I knew I couldn't wash it off of me, but damn if I wasn't going to try. I found everything I could've asked for. Shampoo. Facial cleanser. Even a toothbrush in a package.

But I only needed booze, and I chugged down another shot.

It didn't help.

I was dirty, inside and out. I'd never get myself clean, but I would try. Lord help me, I was trying. I scrubbed at my arm when someone stepped into the doorway. They could see me through the see-through glass, but I didn't care.

I knew who it was.

I raised my head and squared my shoulders.

He could see every inch of my body, and his eyes roamed. My breasts. My stomach. My pussy. My legs. Back up to linger on my pussy. A new level of self-loathing exploded inside me, because an ache for him was forming. Again.

I felt heated, my breathing hitched.

When he looked at my breasts, they hardened. My nipples craved him touching them, covering them. His eyes were black now, his lust showing. He parted his lips before he tugged his eyes up to meet mine.

I ached.

And I bit my lip because I tried not to let him see.

But he did.

He stepped forward, shedding his clothes as he came. He prowled. He stalked me.

His muscles rippled. God, those muscles. I was in a shower, and my mouth dried at the sight. That said everything. Every inch of him was defined, all the way to his stomach and past when he pushed his pants down. He dropped them on the ground, lifting his feet clear.

He toed off his shoes and socks. I knew he had a gun. But I didn't know where it was.

He paused right before coming into the shower, his boxer briefs still on, and he waited. He waited for me.

He was giving me this decision.

I stopped thinking. Stepping out of the shower spray, I walked to him. His eyes never left mine, and they grew hungrier with every inch of space that disappeared between us. I stopped right before him.

My body was slick.

His chest lifted in a slow breath. He still didn't move. He waited.

And then I lifted the bottle, took a last swig, and handed it over. He took it, set it behind him in the sink. And he waited again.

My chest rose, a small motion as I filled my lungs once, then closed the distance.

His heat. He was power. I'd felt it before, but not like this, not when I knew he was going to be inside of me. My breasts touched his chest. My hand skimmed down his side, following the dips and rises of his muscles until it came to his waistband, that one last bit of a barrier between us. My lips grazed over his shoulder as I began to push his boxer briefs down.

His mouth found mine, and that was it. He took command. Demanding.

He picked me up, walking back into the shower, and my hand found him. My fingers wrapped around his cock, and I held him as his tongue swept into my mouth.

He wasn't inside me yet, but I still felt him. He pushed all the darkness away. It didn't matter in that moment that he was the reason it was there in the first place. He claimed me, and if I were being honest, I would've admitted he'd claimed me long ago.

He pressed me against the shower wall, and I wound my legs around his waist.

Our mouths opened over each other, and I groaned, my fingers tightening over him.

A rush of air left him. He pulled back just enough to growl, "If you don't put me inside you in the next second—"

I lined him up with my entrance and pushed my hips down. He waited, letting the tip sink in before he dropped a hand to my waist and thrust the rest of the way.

There.

That's how we were supposed to be, as one.

Another savage growl left him as he dropped his mouth to my throat. He paused. He was waiting for me again.

I began moving my hips, rocking into him.

His hand slid back up my side, grabbing my breast and covering my nipple. He bent, his mouth taking one breast as he kneaded the other. Then he started thrusting. Hard.

I gasped, a shout working its way out of my throat.

There was no foreplay here. The entire time I'd been with him was our foreplay. This was now. Enough waiting.

I rode him as hard as he was fucking me.

I needed more.

I laid my head back against the wall, my mouth gaping at the pleasure coating every fucking inch of my body.

He moved in and out, forceful, and I met every roll of his hips.

Fucking hell.

In. Out.

Harder.

Deeper.

Faster.

I raked my nails down his arms, curving in and holding on for balance.

I slammed down on him until a guttural groan left him and his hand grabbed my waist. He held me still, then began thrusting harder. I didn't think he could've, but he did.

I screamed as I went over the edge and my body spasmed in his arms. My back arched and stayed arched as the waves rammed over me. I dissolved into a puddle as Kai stopped moving.

"Wha—"

He carried me out of the shower, still inside me, and took me to my room. Before laying me down, he pulled out, but immediately climbed between my legs once again. I wrapped my hand over his dick.

He hadn't come yet.

As in the shower, I lined him up, and he didn't wait this time. His hand flexed over my hips, and he moved in. He took his place, and then he screwed me. My entire body moved with the force of his thrusts, and before he'd finished, I felt another climax rising in me. Reaching blindly, I grabbed above me, taking hold of the headboard. Lifting up off the bed, I crossed my ankles behind his back and pushed back at him. He caught my ass, his fingers sinking into my skin. His mouth fell to my breast again. He tasted me as he came, exploding inside, and then I was meeting him.

I came apart in his arms once again, the fourth time in a span of twenty-four hours.

Easing out of me, Kai moved to lie next to me.

I could feel his heart rate slowing, and I knew he could feel mine. He draped an arm over me, his leg twined still with mine.

"I'm clean. I'm on the pill," I told him.

He nodded, his lips grazing my shoulder. "I know."

"You know?" I tensed, turning my head to him.

His fingers circled my breast. "Jonah forwarded your file to me."

Jesus. Even with sex, he didn't mess up.

I shouldn't have been shocked. I should've learned by now.

He ran his hand down my stomach, dipping between my legs, and one of his fingers moved inside of me.

I grunted, lying back down and spreading my legs.

I'd already come. I didn't know if I could handle another, but he began moving in and out of me, a slow fucking, almost lazy. As he kept going, I began to move with him. This time, the climax was a slow journey, like the best blanket I'd ever felt warming my insides until the pleasure built, built, and I snapped, the edge coming at me with breakneck speed.

I gasped, sweat covering my chest. Kai dropped his mouth down, teasing me, trailing between my breasts before running back up, lingering at my throat, then finally moving to my lips. It was a soft kiss, like dessert after a five-course meal.

My entire body was boneless. I was a puddle of contentment. The self-loathing was gone. I knew it would come back. It was inevitable. As long as I couldn't say no to this man, I would be on this ride of exhilarating highs and pleasure to dangerous lows.

The sound of someone outside my door had Kai stiffening next to me.

There was a knock. "Sir?"

Kai gave me an apologetic look before sliding off the bed. He snagged a blanket from the closet, draping it over me and bent to kiss me.

"Sleep, if you can," he whispered before standing up. "I'll be back."

He went through the bathroom and shut the door behind him.

A moment later I heard the door across the hall open and the faint sound of a conversation. They must've moved into his room.

I could've gotten up, gone to the bathroom, tried to eavesdrop.

I did nothing.

I fell asleep, just as he said.

CHAPTER THIRTY-THREE

Blade: I found Brooke.

The text came in at 6:43 am.

I woke up, hearing the buzz, and grabbed the phone from the nightstand. It took a second for the brevity of those words to sink in. Blade wouldn't lie. Not this time. The timing wasn't right for that. No. This was the truth.

I glanced over, but Kai wasn't next to me. The bathroom door was closed, so I couldn't see to his side. I decided not to think about where he might've gone.

I sat up and texted back.

Me: Where?

Blade: 44, 93

They were coordinates. I plugged them in and stared a moment.

I felt a burn starting in my gut.

The train went to Winnipeg. It made sense for her to go south on 29, then take 94 all the way to Minneapolis in Minnesota. It was a seven-hour drive. Seven. Hours. The train might've been longer from Edmonton to Winnipeg. How had no one considered this?

Me: How was she missed?

Blade: She stayed to the corners, like you instructed. Switched trains walking with an elderly man. She had a full disguise.

The disguise wasn't from me. The elderly man hadn't been either, but it was perfect. The elderly were overlooked so easily.

Me: I have my Raven passport. Can you book me on a flight...

I stopped typing. What was I doing? I didn't know where I was in New York. Turning on GPS could get me an Uber, but I had to be serious. Kai would know about these texts—maybe even knew already—and the chances of me sneaking away, getting a ride to the airport, getting on a flight to Minneapolis before Kai did were slim to none.

I'd gone into Hider mode.

It was a relief to know I still had it in me. It hadn't left me, like so much of my resistance had.

Instead, I texted:

Me: Can you narrow it down? House, apartment?
Blade: I did better. She's in a basement.

And he gave me the actual address. We only needed to drive up and knock on the door.

Me: Is she using a phone?
Blade: Working on that. If I get all this, and she's safe when the big bad brother finds her, does that mean you come back?
Me: If 411 will have me.

That was the truth. I wanted to go back. I wanted that normalcy again. Everything made sense as a Hider. I knew right from wrong, top from bottom, and I knew which side I stood on: the right side. If I stayed...

Me: Thank you, Blade.
Blade: Just be safe and come home.

I didn't respond, instead sliding out of bed and going to wash and change. My old clothes went back into the bag. I had it over my shoulder, sneakers on, a hat pulled low on my forehead when I left the room.

I didn't know what to expect. Maybe a small part of me just wanted to run from what was happening to me.

I turned down the hallway, moving briskly, and headed down the stairs. As I approached the front door, I didn't look behind me to see who was in the kitchen. Some of Kai's guards were likely awake; that was to be expected.

I wasn't expecting to see the entire group already in the driveway, throwing bags into the SUVs.

Kai stood next to the one we'd ridden in, his arms folded over his chest as he listened to one of the guards. They were looking at a map and a phone. Kai nodded before looking up. His eyes found me immediately.

I should've been used to feeling singed every time that gaze found me. I wasn't. The burn spread inside of me.

He didn't seem surprised at the sight of me, and I firmed my mouth. He already knew. They already knew.

They'd been expecting me.

I let out a sigh, coming down the steps and meeting him at the door of the SUV.

He reached for the door handle before I could, but didn't open it. He moved to stand close, his body heat warming me. "You and your pal had a nice chat."

I looked away. Most of the men were in their SUVs already. Only a few were waiting for us. One came behind me from the house. I could only assume he had locked up.

"What do you expect? I hide people, not find them. It's not a good feeling."

He still didn't open the door, and I looked up, meeting his eyes.

There were a myriad of emotions there.

After a moment he opened the door. I got in, and he shut it behind me, walking around to the other side. As the guard opened Kai's door, he sat beside me.

After we'd driven for a half hour in silence, I remembered something. "What about Brooke's boyfriend?"

Kai had been reading on his phone, and he lifted his head. "He's not a problem."

I frowned. "Kai—"

"Don't, okay?" His tone stopped me. "You hate me. I get that. And I get why, but your body doesn't." His eyes trailed down, warming said body even further as he went to my feet and back up. "As long as you remain in my company, can you shove the indignation? I am a Bennett. This is what my family does. You know this, and you stayed. Deal with your decision."

Well. Consider me slapped back.

He has a point, a voice whispered in my head, but instead of addressing that, I put my headphones on and turned up my music.

There was a slight sting in my mouth, though.

· · ·

Here it was. Here was the time, as I looked out my window on a private plane over West Virginia, that I needed to do some soul-searching. Kai had been right with what he said before.

I did know who he was. I knew the family he led. I knew the lengths he would go to, had gone to already, and I'd stayed.

I knew who I had let inside my body.

But I was still twisted up inside. I needed to decide: stay or go. Help Brooke or just leave.

Sleep with him again, or not.

It had to end.

It had felt right to get those coordinates from Blade. It felt right to get a text message about finding someone, so I had to go help that someone. That synced perfectly inside of me. It was what I was meant to do.

Then I walked out into the main cabin of the airplane and there was an entire envoy of mafia guards, as well as their leader. He was actually sleeping for once, his head resting back on his seat. And yes, I felt the tug inside.

Full lips. A jawline that melted me. Cheekbones that said, "Oh hello there." And those eyes that could undress me with a look. They almost had. But Kai's looks weren't the problem, though they contributed. It was more. There was something in him that beckoned to me.

I hated what he did. But I didn't hate him.

I lusted after him. But I loathed his job.

Still, my physical weakness—or whatever was going on—wasn't right. Remembering how I'd felt when I got Blade's text, I knew my decision. Kai wasn't the issue, not really. I wanted to remain with the Network. I wanted to keep helping people. I had to. It had once been me who needed help. It'd been my mother. There were others out there like us.

Kai and me, we had to end. No more.

I returned to my seat by the window and thumbed up my volume. Anything to distract me, because I didn't want to feel the boulder in my stomach.

CHAPTER THIRTY-FOUR

We landed in Minneapolis and were quickly swept into the back of a car this time, rather than an SUV. The guards had those. Kai and I had two guards with us, counting the driver, but it seemed more intimate, more quaint.

I looked over at Kai, who was watching out the window, and for a split second I felt like we were all friends road-tripping to see another friend.

"Aren't they supposed to have snow here?" I asked.

Kai turned to look at me, his eyebrows pinched together. "You live in Canada."

I kept my face neutral. "I know."

His eyes narrowed. "You're fucking with us."

It was summer. Of course I was fucking with them.

But I still hid my grin, feeling a bit punchy. "Can I choose the next house we stay at? I mean, you guys rent them, right? You haven't bought *all* of them..."

Kai's expression didn't waver.

Shit. He did.

"Really?" I choked out.

His nod was faint. "Except the hotel. And who said we're staying anywhere?"

That shut me up—for a moment. "We're going to Brooke right now? I thought there'd be a plan, a meeting time, blueprints plastered on the wall. You know..." I waved my hands in the air. "A whole marker board that we can flip over and start writing on the other side when a new idea comes to us."

He sat motionless. "Is that what you do on your 411 missions?"

"No." Look at that, my pants became so interesting. I dusted off some lint.

Kai must've taken pity on me. "We are staying somewhere," he relented. "But we're picking up my sister first."

Forget the lint. My head whipped back up. "We're going now?"

He nodded, returning to his phone. "Mmmm-hmmm."

"But—" My mouth was gaping.

They were moving too fast. Things had to be planned. I wasn't kidding now.

"What's the plan?" I snorted. "Going up and knocking?"

"Generally. Yeah."

Again with the gaping mouth. "Are you serious? You can't be serious. Brooke will…" Jonah had told me to go. Wait. No. Tanner said that. "Tanner said you needed my help or Brooke will do something stupid. She'll get someone killed."

Kai remained focused on his phone, scrolling up to read something. "Tanner lied to you."

"But, why would he lie to me?"

"Because he didn't want to babysit you?" Kai sighed, putting his phone away and resting his head against his headrest. He looked me over, a faint trace of amusement tugging at the corner of his mouth. "Tanner had a friend putting on a show at Fortune. He didn't want to drive all the way to Cowtown with you."

I… I had no words.

Not just because of Tanner, who was an ass, but because of Kai, who was smirking at me.

Smirking.

It was doing dangerous things to me. "Stop that."

And damn him, because he knew what I was talking about. His smirk only deepened.

"But Jonah said—"

"I don't know what Jonah said, but he wanted to get back to his job. He also didn't want to have to stay and babysit you."

"Both your brothers lied to me?"

He nodded. "They did, yes." There was a twinkle in those dark eyes now. He didn't look like the head of an international mafia family. He looked like a guy Carol would've fawned over if she saw his picture in a magazine.

I felt a flutter in my chest.

Kai was young for what he had to handle. He'd taken over the family at sixteen. And he'd murdered his father to do it.

Clearing my throat, I said, "What assholes."

"Can you blame them?"

No. "Jonah wanted to get back to his job?"

"His residency." Kai kept watching me as he spoke.

It should've been even more unsettling, but it wasn't. He was warm. He was being honest. I could see that, and somehow we felt like friends in this moment.

"He's wanted to be a doctor for as long as I can remember. It's difficult at times, though. Family comes first. A job like that, a family like ours, he gets caught in the middle a lot."

"He's young to be a doctor."

"He's a genius."

That's right. So was Kai.

My words were out before I realized I was going to ask. "How do you do it? Handle everything, think the way you do? How do you... I think I'd go mad just trying."

He rolled his head to face forward and lifted a shoulder. "I got it from my dad. I think the way he thought."

Which was why Kai had moved first.

"He sent me to college early, like Jonah. I had the scores for it, but he assumed I was going back after Cord passed." His mouth closed. His eyes grew hard.

He'd assumed wrong.

The unspoken said so much.

Knowing the monster their father had been, I found myself in a position I'd never experienced before. I was okay with what Kai had done. I was thankful for it.

"He would've killed you?"

Kai didn't respond. But he rolled his head to look at me again, and I saw it there. He would've, and that sent a pang through my heart.

I don't know what he saw in my eyes, but he reached over in response. I waited, suspended, as his finger tipped my head toward his and he leaned down. I reached up.

My decision faded, and our lips met.

Softly. Briefly.

A tingle.

It meant something.

He pulled back, and the flutters within me multiplied.

I turned back to the window. We didn't speak the rest of the ride.

I touched a hand to my lips after a minute, still feeling his there. And those flutters just kept flying around.

CHAPTER THIRTY-FIVE

I still wasn't clear on the plan.

I hadn't thought Kai was serious when we pulled into a driveway, but he motioned for his men to fall back. Two started to protest, but he just turned his back, grabbing my hand. Threading our fingers, he tugged me after him.

My eyebrows raised. *We're doing this?* On the flight, I'd decided we wouldn't be again. Then we'd kissed...

He leaned in, dropping his voice low. "If anyone is watching, a couple is less imposing."

Ah. Got it.

We were pretending. I could do pretending.

I bounced right into Raven's cover and smiled brightly at him.

His eyes widened, and he fell back a step.

Raven wasn't one to be deterred. I pushed up on my toes, placed my hands on his chest, and bounced up and down. "You know what they say." Another dazzling smile.

Kai had fear now. Real fear.

"Be the inspiration for someone every day, and be the reason that person smiles."

He cursed under his breath. "Your cover?"

"You bet!" I bounced back a step and gave him a thumbs-up. I pointed to the door. "Let's turn someone's frown upside down."

I started off, almost at a march.

I knew I didn't look like myself. With my smile in place, different clothes than when Brooke saw me last, and the sun going down, I was different. If Brooke was watching us come up, I hoped she wouldn't recognize me. Kai, on the other hand...that was his problem to solve. I knew the pretending to be a couple was more for curious onlookers outside, but if Brooke really was scared for her life, she'd have cameras set up and some way to be alerted.

The second we'd pulled into this driveway, she would've known. Or she *should* have, if she'd followed my instructions.

Kai caught up with me, tucking my hand under his arm, and I leaned into him.

"She's going to know it's you, if she's looking out," I told him.

"You're pretty convincing, though. I know you, and I'm having second thoughts on your identity." His gaze studied me a moment. "You're good at your job. You can change your perception by holding your head at a slightly odd angle, or having your hair parted on the wrong side. But it's more than that, isn't it? You change something on the inside and that emanates out, doesn't it?"

I grew quiet. Yes. That was a thing—change how you feel inside and people sense it. They sense it without even realizing they do. I've used that trick for many disguises, but I decided to keep it light.

"Har, har."

"I'm not joking." He flashed a grin at me, but tightened his hold on my arm and headed for the back door.

I was still waiting for his diversion. Anything.

But he went right up to the back and opened the screen door.

I shot him a look. "For real?"

He raised his hand.

"You're just going to—"

He knocked.

"—knock?"

Amusement flashed in his eyes as he stepped to the side, pulling me so I was front and center before the door.

"What if she has cameras?"

He let go of my arm and leaned against the wall. "This is my sister." He could've yawned from the alarm that *wasn't* in his tone. "If she's here, we're safe."

As if on cue, I heard from inside, "Coming! Hold on." Someone was running up some stairs.

"Kai!" I hissed under my breath.

He motioned to me. "You know what to do. Get her to open the door." He shook his head. "This is going to be anticlimactic. I feel like I should apologize to you for this."

"All of this—" I motioned between us. "—for a fucking knock on a door?"

He raised an eyebrow just as the person got to the other side of the door.

"The climactic part was finding her," he said.

"Coming! Hold on. This door jams sometimes."

It was Brooke. She was fumbling with the door.

She started to open it, but it got stuck. "Oomph! So sorry. Again. Crappers. I don't have the strength." One big tug and the door swung open, almost clipping her in the face.

I kept my face half turned, my eyes drilling into Kai's.

He'd been casual, but the closer Brooke came to facing us, all that dropped from his face.

His jaw firmed, and he straightened from where he'd leaned on the wall.

Brooke pulled the door all the way open and stopped, staring at me. "Uh... Where's the food?"

My chest lifted, and I pivoted swiftly to look at my old roommate.

Her eyes popped open and her mouth fell. "Wait! What? Riley?!" She started to step out at the same time Kai decided he'd had enough.

He spoke into his hand. "GO!"

And he moved forward at an alarming speed. He had grabbed her around the throat, pushing her inside, before either of us comprehended what was going on. Once inside, he held her against the wall.

"Wha—KAI!" She began twisting around, hitting at his arm.

"Kai!" I tried to pull him off.

His arm was cement solid, but I could see the hold he had on her throat was tightly controlled. He wasn't hurting her, just pinning her in place. She wasn't gasping for breath. I didn't think there'd even be redness when he let her go.

Her eyes were wild, taking me in too. She flailed and jerked like a wild animal.

"WHAT DID YOU DO TO HER, YOU ANIMAL? YOU PIECE OF SHIT. YOU MURDERER. YOU—"

"Enough!" he roared.

The front door of the house busted in, and his guards began a sweep.

Kai looked around, still holding her in place. "Who else is here, Brooke? Who else is here?"

She couldn't stop looking between us. "No one! And why is Riley here? What did you do to her? You brought her into this?!"

He snapped back to her, moving to invade her space. "No." His nostrils flared. "You did. You brought her into this the second you showed up at her house, and you know it." His jaw clenched, a vein pulsing at the side of his neck.

Brooke saw it too, and gave up the fight. Her head leaned back against the wall, and her hands fell to her sides.

She began crying instead. "What did you do to him? You're the reason he's not answering my calls today, aren't you? What'd you do to him, Kai?" Her hand balled into a fist. She raised it and pressed down on his arm. "Please, Kai. Don't hurt him. I love him. Please don't hurt him."

I backed away.

The guards were moving behind us. Three thundered downstairs.

Their yells of "clear" ricocheted around us.

"What is she talking about?"

Both Bennetts heard my quiet question. Both stilled.

Brooke frowned, her bottom lip pausing in its trembling. Understanding dawned, and her fist fell away from his arm again. "Oh, Kai." A whispered regret. "What did you do?"

"All clear," one of his guards yelled for the last time.

Kai dropped his arm from his sister and pointed downstairs. "Down. Now."

She pulled her gaze from me, meeting his. "What did you do to both of us?"

She didn't expect an answer. A defeated slump in her shoulders, she headed down.

I started to follow.

Kai's hand touched my hip, halting me.

He inclined his head, his voice so soft only I could hear. "Please don't think the worst of me right now." He caressed my waist a moment, then rested his forehead to mine and expelled a sudden rush of air. His entire body had been tense. Some of it now dissipated.

I watched as the tension returned, and he moved away, his head down.

"I haven't earned it with *this* one," he added.

He went downstairs to deal with his sister, and as was my pattern, I followed.

CHAPTER THIRTY-SIX

"Pack."

Kai pointed to the bedroom as soon as he got downstairs.

The basement was filthy. There wasn't a better word to describe it. The couch Brooke sat on looked like it had dried milk on one end, right over its mustard paisley pattern. The rest of the room wasn't any better. Empty water bottles filled one corner. Pizza boxes littered the floor. A television sat on a card table, a PlayStation on top and game controllers down below. A faint musty smell lingered, mixing with old cigarettes and dried puke.

The Network didn't use places like this. If the upstairs looked the same, I would've tagged this as an addict's house. The Network used empty apartments, houses that had been foreclosed. Not places like this.

Brooke remained on the couch, at the one end that seemed fine to sit on. Her hands were tucked between her legs, and her eyes narrowed on me again before she wrinkled her nose. Raising her chin, she rolled her shoulders back.

"I will not."

"You will too."

Kai went to the bedroom, grabbing a bag from the ground and throwing it onto the unmade bed.

"Kai, don't!" Brooke was off the couch, heading in.

He began rifling through the closet, tossing clothes onto the bed. He threw another handful over his shoulder. "Start packing, Brooke. I mean it. You are not staying here."

She grabbed the clothes from the bed and began putting them away in a drawer.

I watched for a second. There was something slightly comedic about this, and in that second, I knew Kai was telling the truth. This was a sibling fight. Brooke huffed, her eyes strained. She wasn't crying, pleading. She wasn't scared for her life. She was... annoyed.

She'd been wailing before, but the second he began to force her to leave, her chest puffed up in indignation.

"You lied to me."

I hadn't meant to say it, and both of them paused and looked over at me.

I stared at Brooke, the wind knocked out of me.

She bit her lip and her head folded down, but not before I saw the regret.

"You told me it was life or death. You told me if he found you, he would kill you."

I was floored.

My voice rose. "You have no idea what I've put myself through, what *you* put me through! Was your boyfriend worth it?"

She looked back up. A shimmer of tears rested there, ready to spill. "What do you know about him?"

I could feel Kai watching me, could feel the weight of his gaze.

I moved my head from side to side, resting a hand on the doorframe. My legs felt as if they could go out from under me. "Just that all this was for him. Were you ever scared your brother would hurt you?"

"Yes!" She clutched a shirt to her chest. "Levi is everything to me. Everything! He's my air, my food, my—my—my world! He's the sun and the moon and the stars..."

Then where is he?

If he was the reason for all of this, why wasn't he with her? Why had we gone to New York?

But I didn't ask those questions, because my loyalty had switched. I moved to stand behind Kai.

He cut her off, tossing the rest of the clothes on the bed. "Enough talk. Fill your bag or I'll have my men take you outside while I fill it. Those are your choices. Do it now." He brushed past, stopping to talk to a guard before heading up the stairs.

Brooke watched him go, and she broke out in a sob, collapsing on the bed.

"Everything is ruined. Everything I was trying to do. All gone." Tears slid down her face. "Did Kai tell you anything?"

I sat next to her, rubbing her back. "No."

Her whole body shuddered. "Levi and I met in Mexico. It was a spring trip with a few female friends, ones Kai approves of." She snorted, wiping a hand over her face. "Hell, I can't make just him the bad guy. Tanner and Jonah, they're as bad. But these girls are daughters of our colleagues, if you know what I mean. Other families."

Other mafia princesses. I bobbed my head. "Got it."

"Levi came along because he knew one of the girls, and we hit it off. It was a crazy week. If you've ever had a fling, think on that and multiply it by ten—instant love. And I mean it. I can feel it in every inch of my body."

She crumpled the shirt into a tight ball as she spoke.

"I know I can come off as frivolous and empty, a spoiled mafia princess, but I'm not. Levi saw that. He saw through what everyone else doesn't care to look past. I love him so much, Riley. I don't know what I'll do if Kai hurts him."

"Where is he?"

She shifted to face me. Her crying stopped. "You mean you don't know? I would've thought Kai would say something. He always had a soft spot for you."

What? "A soft spot?"

"Yeah. When I left school, he kept tabs on you. I asked him to in the beginning, but when you went into the 411, I told him to stop. He didn't. I lied about the P.I."

I snorted. "Really?"

But the soft spot...

"What has he said to you?" She drew her leg up and leaned forward. Her eyes grew determined.

A guard came down the stairs at that moment.

Brooke moved back, watching him.

"Boss said to finish up." He looked at me. "He wants you upstairs."

Brooke flicked her eyes upward. "Yeah, yeah. We're going." But she cast me a quizzical look as I stood and crossed the room for the stairs.

Kai was leaving the kitchen as I arrived, his lips pressed together.

I felt his fury blasting me. "Did she say anything to you?" he asked gruffly.

Really? A soft spot?

"Not really. Just that Levi is the galaxy to her."

His lips thinned, a shadow of a grin there, but it vanished right away. He stepped behind me, his hand coming to the small of my back. "Let's go."

I tried to look over his shoulder, to see whatever had made him so furious, but he moved to block my view.

"It's better if you don't see." His words were soft, but laced with authority.

I looked down and went outside, Kai still behind me. I started for the car, but he urged me toward one of the SUVs.

When I got in, he lingered in the opened door. "Do you want to ride with Brooke?"

I always kept myself walled in, protecting my feelings. But little by little, that wall to him was being chipped away. I felt anger and hurt at Brooke for what she'd done, but there was *more* for him. Just more of the other feelings.

"If you'd asked me that an hour ago, I would've said yes. But now, I want..." I took a deep breath, trying to see my way clearly. "You."

His eyes darkened. Desire, lust, and another ominous emotion wound its way down my spine.

"Give me a moment." Then he was gone.

A few minutes later, he slid back in next to me.

The guards led Brooke past our SUV into another one parked in front of us. Two guards got in on either side of her, and a minute later, our whole caravan was leaving.

We turned down the block, then went around the corner to the next block—the street behind the house Brooke had been in.

I felt the explosion through the SUV's floorboards. It was that powerful. Twisting around, I found myself speechless for the third time since coming to this state. I couldn't say or do anything.

I could only stare at the fire lighting up the sky, the dark black smoke swirling up around it.

Kai had blown up the house.

CHAPTER THIRTY-SEVEN

We drove north, away from the city.

We kept on for five hours before we turned off onto smaller roads, and finally we turned on to a gravel road again. This place felt similar to the New York home, with the driveway that wound back into a forest of pine trees for almost a mile. Finally we pulled up to the cabin, which perched on a cliffside overlooking a lake. It was still large for my standards, but not one of the oversized mansions we'd been using. Water stretched out for what seemed like another mile around us. We were so far up, it was a little scary.

Forest packed us in, with trees that seemed to stretch as far as the water did. Miles and miles. Stepping out and stretching my legs, I took it all in. A shiver went down my spine. I couldn't even see the roads out there, though I knew they were there. We'd just come from one.

Looking for even another house nearby, I saw nothing.

That shiver doubled, making the hair on the back of my neck stand up.

I wrapped my arms more tightly around myself, and Kai approached. He didn't touch me, but he studied me, his eyebrows pulling together.

"You okay?"

Brooke got out of her vehicle, her bag close to her chest. She marched past us, glowering. "Traitor," she hissed under her breath.

Something inside me snapped. "YOU LIED TO ME!"

I wasn't sure who was more shocked by my outburst. I think me.

"You have no idea what you have done, what lives you have uprooted, what futures you have changed," I told her in a fury. "No idea! Your lie had a domino effect. It brought your brother to me. It pulled me out of the life I was living, a life I loved. It brought me away from my roommates, my job, my mission in life—and it's not even just me. Hiders from my Network were affected by your decision. My roommate was affected. You, you—since leaving my father, everything has made sense in my world. Everything. I knew right and wrong. I was good at what I did. I loved what I did, and then your brother had me brought to him, and ever since then, everything has been turned upside down. All because of you. All because of your lie!"

I started forward, ready to slap her. But I caught myself.

No one said a word. Brooke gasped and jumped in reflex, but even she didn't speak.

They all would've let me hit her.

I stopped myself. *I* did. Not them. That clicked with me.

There was no moral compass here. They were mafia. They worked for the mafia. A slap was nothing to them, but that wasn't true for me. Not for the little girl who cowered before her father, or the teenager who ran from him, or the adult who was defying him.

I'd been waiting, hoping to lean on others for cues about what to do or where to go. Blade had helped with that before. Carol too. My job. Even the people we hid. But it wasn't the same here.

I was alone.

Breathing hard, my ribs feeling stretched, I lowered my hand.

But I did not apologize. I would *not*. It was wrong to use violence, but I wasn't wrong to have the emotion behind it. Just like it was wrong to act on jealousy. It was an emotion just like all others. You couldn't deny an emotion. If you did, that sucker burrowed down inside you and would work its way out whether you wanted it or not.

Am I jealous of Brooke? I asked myself.

I was.

I was jealous she had a family who loved her. I was jealous she had a family of brothers, because even though Kai was furious with her, he loved her. So did Tanner and Jonah.

My throat stung. "Words matter." My voice was hollow, but I had to still say it. "Actions matter. To be reckless with words is to be selfish, and combine that with power, and it is dangerous. Be better."

I walked past her. I walked past the guards around her, and I moved past the house.

There was a trail leading around the side, going into the woods.

I started down to it.

"He—"

"Leave her," Kai spoke over the guard.

I didn't hear whatever else he said. I had already slipped away into the trees.

· · ·

A twig snapped, and I looked up.

I had walked for a mile until I came upon a large boulder. It was on the side of the trail, stuck firmly into the ground overlooking a small clearing in the trees. The lake glistened before me.

I didn't move as Kai came to sit next to me. There was just enough room for two of us. Perhaps a third could've climbed on behind, but for now, two was perfect.

"I'll never be a Hider again."

He leaned forward, resting his elbows on his knees. "I wondered what that was about."

"You are a murderer. You hurt people. You traffic women across the nation." I caught his look and amended, "If you don't, you allow it. Drugs. Guns. There are so many horrible things you do."

He kept quiet, letting me talk.

"I loathed you." My gut rolled over. "I loathe what you do. I don't think that'll ever change."

He nodded, looking at the lake again.

I watched his profile, adding softly, "But I'm beginning to hate myself instead."

He tensed, his eyes closing.

"You are a big part of the 'bad' in life, and I was part of the 'good.' I was doing my part. That's what I told myself. I liked that feeling. In some small way, I was giving my father a middle finger because while he was in Milwaukee hurting someone, I was helping someone twenty hours from him. It meant something to me."

My chest hurt. I took a deep breath.

"Then your sister showed up, and everything was destroyed. It seemed like it took days, weeks, the last month, but in reality, it took only the moment when she decided to come find me. I helped her. I told her how to hide from security cameras. I told her to use a disguise, walk with someone else, literally *be* someone else. I didn't tell her to pretend to be an elderly woman, but she took my advice. She evaded you because of me. I thought I was doing the right thing."

It was a weird emotion, feeling at the precipice of two worlds. I'd been fighting against admitting this, but I couldn't any longer.

"I'm going back to my father," I said.

Kai turned to look at me, a strong emotion shining in his eyes.

I didn't name it. I looked away. I didn't care.

"He can't hurt my cousin. He can't hurt anyone else. He has to pay for what he did to my mother, what he wanted to do to my mother."

"I'll help you—"

"No." I was firm. "I want to do this myself. I have to."

He was quiet before nodding. "Okay. When?"

It was getting dark now. "In the morning I'll go."

He shifted to face me on the boulder.

I stared back.

One night. I'd give him one more night.

As if reading my mind, he nodded again. "Okay."

Then, because it'd been in the back of my mind this whole time, I asked, "Why'd you destroy that house?"

His mouth tightened for a second.

I didn't think he was going to answer, until, in a low voice, he did.

"You think I'm bad, but I'm not. I do bad things. Those people, whoever stayed there, whoever was a floor above my sister, they were bad people." A sadness came to him. He didn't move, or blink, or change his tone, but I saw it. I felt it. He gazed out over the lake again. "There was a room in the back that had pictures of children in sexual—"

I blanched. I didn't want to hear any more.

His jaw clenched. "Brooke was in *that* house. She was in the vicinity of people who could do *that*."

"Were they there?"

"No."

I had a feeling it didn't matter. I had a feeling he was going to find them anyway.

And I had to sit and think again.

I couldn't slap Brooke; that was wrong. But what I knew he would do? That was murder.

And I didn't feel any qualms about it, so who was the real hypocrite here?

CHAPTER THIRTY-EIGHT

Kai put me in a first-floor bedroom adjoining his through the bathroom, similar to the last place we'd stayed. Brooke was on the second floor. There was no third floor or I had no doubt she would've been put there. As it was, Kai had guards outside her door, outside the house, and in the hallways. Every door and large window had someone stationed there.

It was an odd feeling to step out into the hallway a few hours later, long after it had grown dark outside, and walk past the guards, not having them even blink at me.

I was free.

It was starting to sink in with me. I knew it, but feeling it was different.

"—don't understand why I'm not with Riley!"

I paused in the hallway to listen.

Brooke's strident voice was reaching maximum volume above me.

A low murmur responded to her.

"I don't care!" A slapping sound. "I want to talk to my old roommate. She was my friend first. Where is—"

I stepped forward and looked up. The hallway I'd been walking from my bedroom to the kitchen was beneath where she stood. A sitting room opened up next to me, the high ceiling going up to a loft on the second floor, so the hall outside her room looked almost like a balcony.

"I'm here," I called.

"Thank God," she said as she stepped to the railing. She started past the guard, wrinkling her nose at him. "I'm just going downstairs to be with my friend." She came down the stairs, and he followed.

"Good God, Eric." She rolled her eyes. "I'm not going to run. I know my brother has men everywhere."

"Anything you say, Miss Bennett. I just want to make sure you're safe."

She snorted, coming to the bottom floor and turning toward me. "Safe, my ass." Her eyes latched on mine. "I'm a prisoner of my own brother, can you believe that? That's insane."

"Imagine that." My tone was wry.

She laughed, and her whole face lightened. "Can I hug you now? Are we going to get in trouble if I do that?" She glared over her shoulder at Eric.

He didn't respond, just folded his hands in front of him.

She grunted. "Eric, I've seen you naked."

His Adam's apple bobbed up, paused, and he swallowed hard. "Yes, you sure have, Miss Bennett."

"Eric's family is close to ours. He grew up with us," she explained. "When'd you come to work for Kai? How long ago was that?"

He wouldn't meet her gaze, keeping his focus trained above her head. "I've been working for your family for five years, Miss Bennett."

She linked our elbows. "Eric used to run around naked with Tanner and me when we were little. We loved it when Samuel set up the sprinklers. We ran through them in our backyard."

I assumed Samuel was another guard. Or a groundskeeper.

"I see."

Brooke tugged me toward the kitchen. "Enough about Eric." She squeezed my arm. "Are you still upset with me?"

"Yes."

She burst out with a laugh. "Yes. Same Riley. You didn't mince words back then either."

216

I gave her a look. That wasn't true. I'd barely spoken when she knew me before. If she asked a direction question, I would answer, but I *did* mince words. I realized now how much I'd tiptoed around Brooke.

I'd wanted a friend. I'd wanted someone to talk to, someone to listen to me, to care about me. I didn't know how to demand that, so I cared first, I listened first. It was all coming back to me.

Eric was watching me. I glanced up, and he gave me a knowing look.

I looked away, clearing my throat. "Is Kai in the kitchen?"

"He's in the study."

"Where's that?"

Brooke tugged on my arm again. "Who cares? Let's get drunk. This place has wine."

We entered the kitchen, and she let go of my arm and went for the pantry. She opened the door to reveal a full wine rack just inside.

"See?" Her smile was smug as she grabbed two bottles and two wine glasses. "Eric, I assume you're not joining?"

He took position outside the doorway that linked the kitchen to the sitting room and moved so he could stare out one of the larger windows.

She snorted, shutting the pantry door and going to the table. Plopping down with a dramatic sound, she leaned back in her seat. "You have no idea how exhausted I am. This whole ordeal has been tiring."

She was telling *me* that?

But I sat. I was slipping into my old role without even trying. I only smiled at her.

She twisted the cap off the wine and poured two generous glasses. Pushing one toward me, she took hers and sipped. "Oh my gosh. That's so good. They always have the best stuff here." Her eyes narrowed, seeing I hadn't taken mine. "Do you not drink? I know we snuck wine in the dorms, but maybe you've changed." She perused me a moment. "You did look kinda hippyish when I saw your house."

"I'm not hippyish. That's my roommate." But she wasn't altogether wrong.

Being outdoors was my happy place. Raven had some hippy tendencies, and Raven and Riley had some similarities.

I straightened up.

I didn't want her telling me who I was. That was for her to learn from me. It wasn't her place.

"You're being judgmental, sister," Kai drawled, entering the kitchen.

My mouth dried at the sight of him.

He'd changed into a gray Henley and black pants. He was devastating in a business suit, lethal in athletic clothes, but with this shirt, he looked like power. Pure and simple—though there was nothing pure about his power nor simple about him.

Nevertheless, I felt a rush of relief, as if he were an ally coming to my defense. As if Brooke were my enemy.

I looked down at my lap, not wanting to see the way Brooke greeted her brother.

I didn't want to see her hostility, because I didn't think I could be hostile with a brother who loved me that much. Or maybe I'd see a fond resignation toward him, because while she didn't agree with his actions, he had moved heaven and earth to find her.

That meant something.

"I'm not being judgmental," she said.

Her reaction was neither. They'd just fallen back in place as if they were home, as if nothing had happened, as if they were arguing whether to play Monopoly or Bunko.

"You should take that back, *brother*." She mocked him. "I was just saying what I saw."

"You saw wrong." Kai took the seat beside me, reaching for the bottle and pouring a little into a glass he'd brought with him. "I saw the inside of her house. I agree with Riley. Her room was simple, straight to the point—a bed, a counter, a desk, a closet. That's it. Nothing extra. It's a room used for sleeping. That doesn't say hippy to me at all."

I looked at him. "When did you see my house?" *My room?!*

But Brooke wasn't having it. She propped her elbow on the table and pointed. "Okay. One, when did you see her house? Two, you were in her *room*?! Three, you're acting like there's something wrong with being a hippy. I have quite a few friends who are hippies. They're hilarious to party with."

Kai had kept a stone face before, but a grin cracked through now. He lifted his wine glass. "I never was. I was just guessing."

"Agh! You suck."

But he wasn't guessing. I saw it in his eyes.

He had been in my house, my room because he'd been right. I didn't have keepsakes or pictures or even a Chapstick out on my dresser. Nothing except my laptop. It sat center on my desk.

Brooke slapped a hand on the table, leaning forward, still gripping her wine glass. "Are you going to tell me what you did with Levi? I know you took him. Where is he? He's not with this caravan." She waved her glass around the room, indicating all the guards.

I could see three standing outside the window, two farther back in the woods, and another one right next to the house.

Kai just sipped his wine, eyeing his sister.

She made another frustrated sound, pretending to wring his neck in the air. "You drive me crazy sometimes."

"Sometimes?" he teased.

She succumbed, her face melting to a smile. "Yes. Annoying. You. You keep things from me, thinking it's in my best interest. But you can't make all my decisions for me. You're only four years older than I am, Kai."

"Four or forty. Same difference," he shot back.

"You're such a dick." But she was smiling, and she didn't mean it.

She loved him, as much as he loved her.

This was their relationship. Volatile, but well-meaning. Irksome, but loving. Reckless, but safe.

She was safe with him.

An ache burned deep in my chest.

I was jealous, again.

I wanted this relationship. Seeing it made me realize how much I hadn't had it growing up.

Blade. Carol. I tried to remember them, because they cared.

Not like family should care.

That voice was right. It stabbed me, but it was true.

I didn't want to feel ungrateful. Blade did care. I cared for him too, but since being taken by the Bennetts, old wounds were surfacing.

Suddenly, I didn't want to endure anymore. I didn't want to hear the fondness these siblings held for each other, so deep it was in the foundation of their entire beings.

I shoved back from the table. "Excuse me."

I should've said something better, more convincing, but I couldn't muster it. I fled to my room, shutting the door, leaving the light off. I stood in front of my window, my arms crossed tightly when the door opened.

"I'm sorry..."

I turned because I didn't recognize the voice. It wasn't Kai or Brooke who stood there.

It was a stranger, dressed head to toe in black.

He started toward me, a gloved hand in the air. "Your father se—"

No!

A white bolt of fear sliced through me, and then I screamed.

Best first line of defense: scream. Try to tear down the building using your vocal chords.

The guy cursed.

Behind a ski mask, I could only see his eyes. He sailed past me, and we locked gazes for a split second.

He launched himself through the window just as stampeding footsteps arrived and my door burst open. One, two, three guards ran through, guns drawn, and they went right to the window, the one with a gaping hole in it now.

Kai appeared, taking my arm, but when he started to pull me close, I resisted.

"You okay? What happened?" he asked, but two of the guards were listening too.

I told them, and one raised a radio to his mouth. He began broadcasting the details.

"What happened?" Brooke asked from the doorway, a guard's hand on her shoulder. She was pale, her eyes bulging. She held her hands in front of her chest. "Riley, you okay?"

I could feel Kai next to me, but I was shaken. I couldn't lie. Not because there was guy in this house, this bedroom, or even because someone tried to come at me.

It was my father.

Kai barked, "Everyone. Leave."

One by one, they did as he ordered, and the guard shut the door. Kai indicated for me to follow him. We went through the bathroom into the adjoining room, and he checked to be sure it was secure. He double-checked the patio door and the closet. The window. All for me.

I ran my palms down my jeans. They were sweaty. "My father knows."

I hadn't told the guards that part. Just that a guy came at me.

"He said, 'Your father se—' and then I screamed. Kai, he was wearing brown contact lenses."

He was still, so still. It would've sent chills down my back, but they were already there.

"Are you sure?"

I nodded. "Around six feet tall, medium build, and I noticed the ring of brown color on the white part of his eye. Colored contacts." A ball lodged at the back of my throat. There was no moving it, swallowing it, forcing it away. "He said *your father*. My father knows." And now the million-dollar question, "How does my father know about me?"

Kai turned to face the patio door. His shoulders were rigid. "Because someone betrayed me." He turned back, an apology in those dark eyes. "I made inquiries about your father's whereabouts when we returned earlier this evening."

Shit.

Shit.

SHIT!

Tears burned in my eyes.

I shook my head, wiping them away. I would not cry over that man. Ever.

I had made the decision to go after him, but this was happening too fast. I wanted more time.

"I'm sorry, Riley." A fierce promise burned in Kai's eyes. "I will find this man. He won't get off the estate. I can promise you that."

I shook my head. "How could he get someone here? How could he know this was where we were? I told you only three hours ago. No one could've... " Oh, God. Unless they were already here.

I was surprised, but Kai wasn't.

"It's one of your guards," I choked out.

"Yes," he hissed.

His dark eyes were nearly black now. The promise of death lingered in the air, filling the room.

"Kai..." My throat closed in on itself, around that boulder. "He knows. My father knows I'm alive."

That really started to sink in.

My vision blurred. Spots flashed around me.

I felt light-headed, and Kai began to swirl around me in a circle, the bed with him.

I was going to faint.

I realized what was happening, and then, it didn't.

Kai caught me in his arms, carried me to the bed, and stayed with me.

I lost track of time after the first hour.

CHAPTER THIRTY-NINE

I woke up in a bed, but not one I recognized.

"Where am I?"

Brooke shifted in her seat and leaned forward. "You're safe."

"What do you mean safe?" A pause. It all flooded back.

"Kai said you almost fainted. He wanted you to sleep as long as possible." Her hand covered mine. "You fainted before?"

"Yeah." My throat felt scratchy.

"Jonah's coming, but Kai talked to him on the phone. He said it was probably the shock of your father knowing about you and everything." She patted my hand before inching her chair closer. "I'm so sorry, Riley. I really am. When I thought to go to you, I didn't know any of this would happen, that Kai would pull you into this. But I should've. I was being selfish, and I feel horrible. I don't know how to make it up to you, but I'll try. I swear." She sniffled. "I've been selfish."

Yes. She had.

I looked away. "Where's Kai?"

"I don't know."

I turned back. She seemed solemn.

"What do you mean? Kai isn't here?"

She shrugged. "After you must've fallen asleep, Kai came out, and he was at another level. I've never seen him like that. Between you and me, he was terrifying. I thought he was going to kill some of his men right then and there."

The traitor. My father.

I remembered that part now.

Kai wouldn't return until he had dealt with the traitor. I was sure of it. Jonah was coming, so all the questions I wanted to ask, there was no point.

Instead, I asked, "Tell the truth. Why'd you run?"

Brooke straightened up, her hands falling to her lap.

She expelled a frustrated gargle, her eyes flicking to the ceiling. "I wasn't lying about it being about life and death. Kai found out something about Levi, and I'm terrified of what he'll do with the information. I love this guy, Riley. He's the one for me, and I couldn't bear it if my brother destroyed us." She snorted, leaning back in her seat. "I mean, if anyone's going to screw things up, it should be me. Give me a chance here to mess things up myself."

Raking a hand through her hair, she shook her head. "I'm a mess these days. How are you?" She gave a self-deprecating laugh, but her eyes focused on me. "You seem well, actually."

"I thought Kai kept track of me?"

"He did, but I stopped asking for the reports. You went into the Network, and I knew you'd be safe."

That was a year after she'd left school.

I snorted. "Thanks for your concern."

She winced. "I know, I know. Going back after my dad died, it was different. Kai was even scarier. Tanner was pissy all the time, and Jonah turned in on himself. He wouldn't leave his room some days. We were a *mess*. I'm a mess now, but we were worse then. I mean, Kai was sixteen. Our uncles kept trying to become our guardians, but Kai fought them on it. I don't even know how he did it, but finally, they stopped. That probably took seven months. Seven months of hell—not knowing if we'd have to leave each other or what. Even the actual law came in a few times, social services and such. Kai bought them off right away. It's such a joke sometimes. Our family gets away with murder."

That was the truth. Literally. "Yeah..."

Brooke kept going, even a slight cheerful note in her voice. "Kai said something about your father. He knows you're alive?"

I wasn't sure how to answer, or if I even wanted Brooke to know.

I used to trust this girl. She gave me what I desperately needed. Security. Safety. Acceptance.

"You hurt me when you lied to me." It stung to admit that.

She folded her hands together in her lap. "I know." Her voice softened. Apologetic. "Are you mad that I involved you or that I lied?"

"Lied," I said immediately. That was the truth. "I don't mind that you involved me. I would've helped you anyway, but you lied to me. You didn't need to lie to me. If you hadn't, I could've helped you better. I would've understood."

She tilted her head, questioning. "Has Kai said anything to you about Levi?"

Some of my anger faded, but not all of it. I was torn between so many things, and between more than a few people.

I shrugged. "We were in New York for a day; then we came here."

"New York?" She sat up straighter. "Where in New York?"

I shook my head. "I don't know. We didn't go anywhere. We were at a house, and then we came here."

But that first night... Kai went somewhere that first night.

"Oh. Levi had to leave for a trip. I thought he went to Boston, though." She sounded disappointed. "Okay."

We were silent for a moment.

"Are you going to run again?" I asked her.

She was the one to shrug now. "I don't know. It depends on Levi, on where he is."

"You can't get ahold of him?"

"I couldn't before you guys showed up, and now Kai took my phone. He gave me a computer that doesn't have wifi. When Tanner or Jonah call, the guard gives me the phone and stands there. I'm only allowed to speak into it, that's it."

That was a bit much, but Kai had said he wanted to use Levi. He was his way into the Barnes family. I wasn't even going to try to guess at what he was planning.

Unease crept down my back.

"Can I ask you something?"

I nodded, surprised. "Sure."

"Are you sleeping with Kai?"

My mouth went dry. I stared at her.

"I mean, you can tell me to piss off. I violated our trust, and he's the one who's been watching out for you since school, but are you?"

"Why are you asking?"

"Because I like you. We were friends once."

I flinched. That's what she thought of me? A week ago, I was ready to go down with guns blazing for her. I'd been too loyal. I had put too much stock in our old friendship, and I felt more than a little bit stupid.

"I thought we still were," I countered.

"Of course. I mean, you know, *if* I still have your friendship. I lied to you. I used you. I get it. Jonah would hold it against me for years if I did that to him."

I grinned. "Not Tanner?"

She snorted. "Fuck no. Tanner'd just critique my lies, maybe say what I did was shitty. I'd have to do more than run away to piss off Tanner."

"And Kai?"

"And Kai." She took a breath, sadness coming over her face. "Kai will love me no matter what, but he's never trusted me. Kai doesn't trust anyone. He grew up being molded the way our father wanted him to be. Cord got some freedom. Tanner, me, Jonah— we were all given our roles to play in the family, but it wasn't anything to do with the business. But Kai's role was to take over. When Cord turned eighteen, I think my dad realized everyone was looking at him to take over. Kai was sixteen when Cord died. He was supposed to be groomed for another two years."

She shook her head again. "Kai won't even ask me about Levi. He knows why I ran away, but I'm back with the family, and that's it. Once he thinks I won't run again, he'll drop all the extra safeguards, but until then, I'm in a luxurious prison." She gave me a wry smile. "He's even shipping in Tanner to entertain me."

"Really?"

"Jonah's coming too, but more to check on you. I've no doubt he'll want to go back to his hospital once you're cleared. I've not seen Kai since." She gestured out the door. "I know he calls in quite a bit. The guards keep poking their heads in, asking about you."

Speaking of which, Eric entered the room, a phone in his hand. "He'd like to speak to Riley," he said.

Brooke nodded, staying put.

"In private," he added.

"Oh!" She got up, shooting me a quick grin before turning to him. "If you wanted some alone time with me, you just needed to ask. You don't have to be all coy, making up a lie to get me out of the room."

A faint flush came to his cheeks, and he coughed. "Ma'am—"

"Ma'am! Ha." She slapped his bicep, moving past him. "You slay me, Eric. Come on." She gestured to me. "Give her the phone so they can have phone sex, and maybe you and I could do the real thing?" She winked, reaching behind her to shove open the door and step out.

He stayed put a second, not making eye contact. Then with a jerk, he handed me the phone. "Sorry, ma'am. Just set it aside when you're done. I'll be outside."

He practically shoved the phone at me and bolted for the door.

I raised the phone to my ear, but as soon as he was out the door, I heard Eric shouting, "CODE PURPLE. CODE PURPLE."

"What's happening?" Kai said in my ear.

"I think Brooke made a run for it. I'm hearing code purple."

He started laughing. "She won't get far. She hates the outdoors, but that's not important. How are you?"

How was I?

I sighed, not even wanting to ask myself that question.

"What?"

"Huh?" I asked.

"You sighed. What were you thinking?"

I did? And then I laughed. "We sound like a couple. The old 'what are you thinking' question."

Aaaand, silence.

Things just got awkward.

Why'd I say that? What was the point?

I glanced down, and started to pick at my blanket. "I'm sorry. I shouldn't have said that."

"Why did you?"

He didn't sound upset, just curious.

I shrugged, though he couldn't see me. Pressing the phone tighter to my ear, I leaned back on the bed, my head finding the pillow.

"I don't know, to be honest. I mean, I hate you."

"Of course." His tone was dry.

"I tried to stab you."

"It was a good try." Wry this time.

"I thought you killed that guy."

"As is typical when relationships are starting."

My mouth twitched at that. "You kidnapped a bunch of my friends."

"I kidnapped *you*."

"Oh yes. Good point."

"That's what I'm here for."

I settled into the bed, the warm baritone of his voice washing over me.

I yawned. "I saw you shoot a woman."

"Foreplay."

I laughed. "You baited me into running away from you to see if Blade would let any information slip."

"Which I hated doing, by the way. I didn't like thinking of you being cold."

"Aw, thank you for that."

"I care. Sometimes." A pause. "Don't get used to it."

I laughed again. "You burned a house down because you cared."

"I more had it explode than burned it down, but yes." He chuckled softly. "And thank God these phones are encrypted."

My mouth snapped shut. I'd forgotten. "Oh, shit. I'm sorry."

"You're fine. We use them for a reason."

Right. Because he's in the mafia.

I screwed my eyes tight, rubbing my forehead and feeling a pressure there. I'd been enjoying myself, but one reminder about our true reality, and everything came rushing back.

He was mafia, and not just any mafia. He was *the* mafia. Other mafia feared him. And he was gone, probably doing mafia stuff. Which was why I didn't ask where he was.

"What are you going to do about my dad?" I asked. Everything had changed from our conversation on that boulder.

"I'm going to kill him."

The pressure moved to my neck, spreading down my shoulder blades.

"Because of me?"

"Because he got a man inside my team. That doesn't work for me." He bit out, "Ever."

"Why do you tell me these things?"

"You asked," he said. And after a moment added, "I only share what's pertinent to you, and what I feel you will hold in trust. I don't tell you the secrets I know will violate your moral compass." He dropped his voice low. "I wouldn't do that to you."

But there it was. The issue with us. I was on one side, he on the other.

My throat stung.

"What are you going to do with your sister and her boyfriend?"

"What I told you before."

He was going to use him. "Brooke too?"

He was quiet a moment. "I love my sister. I'll take care of her, like I always have."

"And what if she wants something different?" The sting in my throat morphed into a different pain, which ran all the way to my fingers. "What if she wants to be free one day?"

"Then..." His voice was soft. He had to know what I was really asking. "I would let her go."

I exhaled sharply. All the molecules in my body relaxed, all at the same time.

I opened my eyes, a tear sliding to my cheek. It was a good tear.

"Okay," I rasped.

"Okay."

I could still hear an alarm going off outside my room. "Brooke will be okay?"

"She'll be fine. She's not stupid." A beat. "*That* stupid."

I laughed softly. "Okay."

"Okay." He mocked me softly, but I could hear his grin through the phone. "I have to go, but I'll be back soon."

That felt good. It shouldn't have, but it did.

I smiled into the phone, slinking back down into the bed. I tried not to say it, but who was I kidding?

"Hurry."

CHAPTER FORTY

"...Leave her alone until she wakes up."

"I know. I'm just saying, I should check on her."

"Kai said to leave her alone!"

The other voice sighed. "That's what I just said. I'm going to check on her—"

"Kai said—"

"I don't care what my brother said!"

The conversation was taking place outside my door, and though it'd been a soft lull at first, now Brooke was almost yelling at whoever she was talking with in the hallway.

"Eric—"

Eric. Ah. The security guard she enjoyed flirting with, even though Levi was her heaven on earth.

"They're idiots."

I looked over to the window, not alarmed but comforted instead. Kai stood there, his hands in his pockets. He'd been turned to look outside. Hearing them start to bicker again, he raked a hand over his face.

"I apologize for both of them," he said. "If I could fire Brooke, I would."

"You're here."

A brief nod. "They don't know I'm in here, though. They think you're sleeping, and they have strict instructions to leave you alone until I arrive."

"You snuck in?"

It was early in the morning, early enough that it was still dark. The slight coloring on his cheeks indicated he'd just gotten in himself.

"I snuck in. Brooke called Eric into her room down the hallway for a second."

"Would you fire Eric?" I pushed myself to a sitting position, scooting back to rest against the headboard.

He came over, keeping his voice quiet as he stood next to me. He reached idly for my hand, caressing my fingers. "Eric was purposefully assigned to Brooke. They dated when they were younger. If anyone will watch over her, Eric will."

It felt right to be in here with Kai, him holding my hand, having this intimate moment while they were out there.

And that felt wrong.

I coughed lightly, my fingers squeezing his for a second. "They dated?"

He nodded, almost absentmindedly. "Eric's from an old family. I owed his uncle a favor, more than one, and he called it in. They're no longer active in the mafia lifestyle, but Eric wanted to learn. He might be a security guard now, but he has promise. He'll step in and bring his family back into the fold one day. He's not ready yet, though."

Another thought came to mind. I felt a tug in my gut.

"And if Brooke were dating him again, that'd tie your families together?"

He'd been gazing at our joined hands, but he looked up. The corner of his mouth tugged up too. "No. I'm not like that. Brooke can date who she wants, but she'll have to make a decision to either bring that person fully into the family or keep them out. There'll be no in-between."

There was an ominous note in those words.

I echoed, dully, "You're either in, or you're out."

He nodded. "Something like that." His eyes held mine for a measurable minute before he let go of my hand and moved onto the bed beside me. I started to scoot over, but he clamped a hand on my waist, holding me in place. There wasn't enough room until he lifted my leg to lay it over him.

"Are you feeling better?" he asked.

Gah. I almost didn't hear him.

"Yes." My voice was raspy again. "You? Comfortable there?"

The barest hint of a smile graced his face, and his eyes began to trace down my body. "I am, actually." His hand slid to my stomach, lingered, and began to move down.

My heart picked up. So did my body heat.

I felt a throb beneath his palm, wherever it moved.

He rested it just under my belly button, pausing on the curve. The end of his palm pressed above my clit. He wasn't watching me, only staring at his hand. "On the phone you were asking about yourself, not Brooke."

My mouth watered, as if I saw a mirage in the distance during a twenty-mile trek over the Sahara.

"Yes."

His hand moved down another inch. The slightest hint of pleasure coursed through me—a shot, a zing, a tingle. He held his hand against my clit.

Not much separated us. A sheet, my underwear, and the softest material I'd ever worn for pants.

The conversation outside the door quieted as everything about Kai took my focus.

The way his finger began rubbing over my tummy in a slow circle.

How if he pushed down, just the slightest bit, I would need to bite down to suppress a groan.

My heartbeat picked up. My breathing grew deeper. And that throb only increased. It had become a yearning, a thirst, and my mouth kept watering.

"If I would let you go, if you wanted that."

Another inch and I felt him right there, right on the throbbing.

I tried not to squirm, but I wanted him in me.

I was damn near panting for it.

"Yes," I whispered, my eyelids growing heavy. I watched him, my chest rising and falling, faster and faster.

He began tugging the sheet away, but kept his hand in place. It bunched around him, as if he were a dam.

"And do you?" he said softly. "Want to be free?"

You're either in or you're out. His words flashed in my head again.

"Brooke left, and you went after her," I pointed out.

His eyes flashed, and his hand pressed against me, grinding over my clit. "She left without being safe. Her boyfriend is an added complication, but if Brooke wanted out, I would let her go, as long as she was safe."

I licked my lips, gasping as he lifted his palm and began to pull the sheet over me. It was a caress, the slow slide of that sheet. The texture teased me.

"So you wouldn't completely let her go?"

"If I knew she was safe, yes."

My mouth fell open. That sheet grazed over me, a whisper in the air, sending pleasure through me.

My mind felt muddied. *What were we talking about?*

"You're feeling better?"

"What?" The sheet finished its caress, and I arched my back.

His other hand went to my stomach, and he slid it up to the bottom of my breasts. He smoothed over my ribs, then circled one of my breasts. Applying the slightest pressure, he tugged me until I was sitting—my forehead close to his, my breast firmly in his hold, and his eyes holding mine captive.

His thumb ran over my nipple.

I groaned, lust flooding me.

His eyes dipped to my mouth. "You are feeling better, right?"

"Uh-huh."

I was feeling better. So much better. Every cell in me was awake and throbbing with need.

I lifted a hand, touching his face and drawing him back to look in my eyes. "The door?"

"Is locked." His eyes darkened, meeting mine.

That was all we needed.

I reached and his mouth met mine.

God. This kiss.

He applied pressure, demanding, commanding, until he pulled away. "Are you sure you feel okay?"

"*Yes*." I slid my hand down his arm and entwined our fingers before I moved them between us. I put them exactly where I wanted them and reached up to draw him back to me. My hand slid around his shoulders and my fingers sunk in. "I want you."

There were so many reasons I shouldn't, but I was done. At this moment, I only wanted one thing.

Him.

• • •

Kai stayed with me most of the day, but we didn't talk.

There was an ominous heaviness in the air, as if holding me wasn't enough for him. He took me again, and then again, each time a little harder, a little more desperate, but always making me explode in his arms before he finished himself.

As he came, he never looked away. His eyes held mine, memorizing me, burning into me. Something told me to hold my words, to feel, to be present, to be here with him because something was going to happen. Something bad. Something that would take him away. But none of that mattered today. This was him and me.

The loathing and disgust, the feeling of compromise, I set that all aside.

It was as if this day was special, as if it would hold a place in our memories forever.

Around six that night, I sank down on him, my breasts on display for him to feast from, and I let my head fall back. He pushed up into me, and anchoring a hand to his chest, I began to roll back and forth.

I rode him.

His hands grasped my ass, his fingers pushing into my skin enough to leave handprints, and he growled, sitting up underneath me. His mouth latched onto one of my nipples. He sucked, and licked, and tasted, and I kept riding, moving faster and faster.

Reaching around me, he slid a hand up the middle of my back. Goosebumps broke out over my skin just before he wrapped a tendril of my hair around his finger.

"Wha—"

He tugged on it, holding my head back.

I kept moving on him, taking him in deep, clenching around him, but I looked to see what he was doing.

His hand tightened even more.

"Kai!" A breathy groan from me.

Another savage growl erupted from him. I felt it all the way in my pussy. Letting go of my hair, his hands went to my hips. He lifted me, setting me on my knees, and moved behind me. Fitting between my legs, he arched me farther up for him and thrust in from behind.

"Kai..." Another groan as the sensations of him moving in me built, heating me. I'd never had this much pleasure, not all at once, not in one day, and I felt like I could scream until I had no more voice.

My body tightened. I felt it coming.

He kept stretching me, digging deeper, then pausing, rotating inside, and finally I erupted.

"AGH!" The first waves crashed inside of me, then another, and another round of waves. My body convulsed until I settled back and realized I was still kneeling.

Kai had a firm arm wrapped around my waist, holding me up as he continued to pump inside of me.

He hadn't come yet.

"Kai." I took his hand, lifting it from my waist and pressing a kiss to it. Then I leaned forward, giving him a better angle. "Fuck me."

He gripped my thigh as he began to do as I said.

He fucked me hard.

As he finished, he held still inside me. I felt his body trembling, but he didn't pull out. He kissed my shoulder, running a lazy hand down my back.

"I can't get enough of this." He said it as if he were talking to himself, a quiet murmur. But he held me firm and dropped a second kiss to my forehead before pulling out, and we fell to the bed together.

He wrapped himself around me, his entire body stretching as he yawned against the back of my shoulder. "God, Riley."

I felt his forehead press to the back of my neck. And as before, spoken as if I wasn't supposed to hear him, he murmured, "How am I supposed to let you go?"

I didn't answer him.

I couldn't.

I didn't know myself.

CHAPTER FORTY-ONE

"Well, hello there."

A dark greeting alerted everyone in the kitchen to my presence.

Tanner stood by the kitchen counter, a glass in hand. He smirked and tilted his head, giving me a knowing look. "What a coincidence. You were in bed all day. Kai just 'arrived' even though we saw his guards earlier." His mouth flattened.

There was an ugly glint in his eyes, but he took a sip from his drink and looked away as Brooke came toward me.

"How are you feeling?"

She was happy to see me.

Tanner wasn't.

I glanced over. Jonah appeared from a back hallway, his bag in hand. He saw me and motioned for me to go to the table. As I did, he came over, set down that bag, and began to check me over. Once he had his stethoscope inside my shirt and had leaned over me, Kai chose that moment to walk in.

He paused, looking at us, until Brooke's voice broke the silence.

"Kai!"

She and Tanner had gone back to the counter. She was making drinks for everyone.

No one had asked. She volunteered.

She grabbed something she declared was a pumpkin-tini and brought it over, full of smiles. "Big brother returns." She pushed the glass into his hand and kissed his cheek. "We've missed you." She patted his cheek and turned back to her drinks.

Tanner picked his up and raised it to his mouth with the same smug and taunting look in his eyes. "When'd you get in?" he asked. "I know your guards showed up at ten this morning." He waited a beat, his eyes sliding to me and back. "Or did you *come* much later?"

What Tanner said was disrespectful, a challenge. It wasn't meant in a teasing manner. Everyone in the room knew Tanner had sent a shot in Kai's direction.

To say I was mildly curious about how this would go down— yeah, that was an understatement.

Even Jonah stopped assessing me.

He pulled his stethoscope out and stepped back to watch.

Kai wore an Oxford blue Henley shirt, the sleeves pushed up to bunch around his elbows, and jeans that molded over his powerful legs. His hair was tousled, and the whole look made my mouth water.

Tanner had on ripped and trendy jeans with a white fleece hoodie, and his hair was combed back. His eyes were angry, a dangerous note in them, but as he gazed at his brother, that look lessened.

Kai didn't react. He didn't blink. He barely moved, and yet real danger began swimming around him. The air in the room grew tense, thick and oppressive, and it was all because of Kai. His dark eyes blackened, and his lips thinned, and he reached over to fiddle with one of his sleeves.

He spoke almost casually. "What's your problem, brother?" He didn't look at me, but directly at Tanner. "Is it that I might be sleeping with her? Or is it that you're only second in charge?" He took a step closer, his nostrils flaring. The casual air evaporated. His lip lifted in a sneer.

He was done messing around.

"Let's not forget the fact that I'm the one who murdered *him*." He paused. "For us."

Jonah stepped away from me. I heard a quiet, "Shit," under his breath.

Brooke's eyes were focused on the floor, her hands laced together in front of her.

No one said a word. This fight was between Tanner and Kai.

I couldn't speak about the other stuff, but I could talk about myself. I rose and cleared my throat.

Jonah frowned at me. Everyone frowned at me.

I ignored all of them and said to Tanner, "If I am sleeping with your brother, I don't understand how that's your business."

Tanner snorted. "You kidding? How is it *not* our business?" He flung a hand in Kai's direction. "You never should've been pulled in in the first place."

"Uh, hello?" Brooke shook her head, blinking. "I pulled her in, not Kai." She held a hand out. "If you're going to blame anyone for Riley, that should land on me."

Tanner turned to her. "You didn't know what you were doing. Kai—"

"Kai," Brooke raised her voice, speaking over her brother, "was following a lead. That was it. I pulled her in." She tapped her chest. "Me. I did that. Not Kai, and of course he's going to follow up. She works for the 411 Network. Their whole mission is helping people disappear. If he'd showed up and asked all nice, there's no way she would've helped." She snorted. "Kai had no other choice, and you know it."

Tanner glared at her. "You're supposed to be on my side."

"No." She held her hands up, palms toward him. "At this point, I'm on Riley's side. You all love me. For her, I have to make it right. Sorry. Don't ask for blind support, because you ain't getting it from me, not in this instance."

Tanner rotated his head, seeking out Jonah.

"Uh..." Jonah laughed beside me. "Not here, brother. Not with this one."

Tanner cursed. "You both suck." He looked at Kai, then me. "You *all* suck."

Kai sighed, his shoulders suddenly relaxing. "You're not angry at me for pulling in Riley. You're not angry that I'm sleeping with her. You're not even angry that Brooke ran away." He went to the kitchen counter, putting down the drink Brooke had given him and pouring himself a glass of bourbon. "You're mad because you don't want to be a Bennett, but you are." His tone went soft. "We all are."

I held my breath as I gazed around the room.

There were identical expressions of resignation on all of them. The only one who had a flicker of mutiny was Tanner, but after staring down Kai for another beat, that flame went out.

He lowered his head, tightening his hold on his drink, and tossed it back. "Fuck that."

He dropped the glass on the counter, letting it slide and bounce toward Brooke, who caught it before it could shatter on the floor. Grabbing the rum, he left the room.

"Fuck you all," he added as he disappeared.

After a moment, Kai came over to the table.

"She's okay?" he asked Jonah.

Jonah was looking the direction Tanner had gone, but he turned his attention to Kai. "Yes. Yes." He blinked a few times, shaking his head. "She seems fine, better than how she was at the house. She needs lots of liquids and rest." He pointed where Tanner had gone. "Is he going to be a problem? Because, I mean..." He glanced at Brooke. "We're all Bennetts. I hate this too, but it is what it is."

Kai was looking at me, his eyes warming. "No. He'll be fine."

"Kai—" Jonah started.

"I'll handle him. Remember, you and Brooke get a semblance of a normal life. He doesn't even get that."

There was a lot I didn't understand, and a part of me was dying to know more, but another part was just glad nothing else had happened.

Kai nodded toward me. "Just make sure she's all right." He left without a word to anyone else.

Brooke waited a moment before picking up two glasses and bringing them over to us. She perched at the table, wide and eager eyes darting between Jonah and me.

"Is now the wrong time to tell you Levi proposed to me before?"

Jonah had picked up his stethoscope, but it clattered to the table. He pinched the bridge of his nose, groaning. "Brooke. For fuck's sake."

"What?"

She looked between us, asking again. "Bad timing?" She lifted a shoulder, still smiling, and changed topics.

"So, you're fucking my brother?"

• • •

"Do I want to know what that was all about?" I asked Kai later in his study.

I'd stayed downstairs with Jonah and Brooke. Brooke kept inventing new drinks, making us try them, and he and I spent most of the time playing rock/paper/scissors to see who'd do the tasting.

Jonah took most because he kept insisting I needed water, not booze, but I still participated. I had a good buzz going by the time I went to find Kai.

The study was bathed in a deep pine aroma, which fit with the massive paintings of forests and mountains hanging on the wall. A tan-colored rock chimney climbed the far wall.

I'd come into the room on the first floor, but I looked up to see the second floor lofted above. The entire back side of the room was floor-to-ceiling bookshelves—a book lover's paradise.

Kai sat behind a grand desk facing the chimney, the rest of the room, and where I'd come in through the doorway.

I'd asked about earlier as I walked into the room, but I had a different question in mind now. "You don't have a ladder that I can use to swing from one side of those books to the other, do you?"

He stood. "No. Why?"

I shrugged, walking in a circle to take everything in. "No reason, just a fantasy from another world."

He came to stand next to me, but slid his hands into his pockets.

I wished he had moved closer. I wished he would touch me, but he didn't so I didn't, and things felt confusing for a moment.

He watched me, his eyebrows raised. "You're drunk?"

"Tipsy." A pause. "More than tipsy."

"Brooke's influence." He sighed.

"Yes." I nodded. "But also yours, Jonah's, even Tanner's. And mine. I decided to be Brooke's test bunny."

Now he smiled. "Test bunny? I've not heard that phrase."

I lifted a shoulder. "I like it better than guinea pig. But I like guinea pigs too. They're funny when they run and hop. Did you know they did that?"

"I didn't, no." His mouth wasn't smiling anymore, but his eyes were.

I began to feel self-conscious, but in a good way, because someone I liked was giving me attention and making me happy. Butterflies were out en masse.

"I haven't felt those in forever."

"Those what?" Kai tipped his head, a little tilt to his mouth. He was enjoying this conversation.

I flattened my hand over my stomach. "Nothing." I grinned, looking down. I could feel my face getting hot. "Nothing."

"You're teasing me." There was a lilt of a laugh in those words. "I don't remember the last time someone teased me."

I'd hit his arm before I realized it. Then I blanched. "Oh—oh! Hi." My face had to be beet red by now.

That's when the laughter started.

And once I started, I couldn't stop. I laughed enough that I needed to hold on to Kai's arm.

"I"—*ha!*—"don't"—*hee hee*—"know what's"—*snort*—"gotten into"—*hiccup*—"me!" I gasped, sucking in air to try to drown both things at once. Once I started hiccupping, it was the same result. I was done for.

Kai stared as if my skin had turned green. Patting my back, he asked, "Am I supposed to scare you? Something with peanut butter?"

That made me laugh harder.

I shook my head, holding a hand up, which he took in his.

God. That made me swoon and laugh at the same time.

This was not something Kai had dealt with before; that was obvious. Finally, with tears streaking down my cheeks, I was able to respond. And I was officially embarrassed. I'd never laughed like this, not even with Blade or Carol.

"Sorry. So sorry. I'm under control again."

I pulled my hand from his and rested it on his chest.

This felt good. This felt right, standing here, so close, just being normal.

I swallowed over a sudden lump.

"Sorry." I wiped the back of my hand over my cheek.

He used his thumbs to clear the rest of my tears away. His heart picked up under my hand, and I tipped my head up, our mouths so close together, but so far apart at the same time.

He just needed to lower his an inch, or I could've leaned up, and our lips would've met.

Heat rushed through me, spiking my pulse.

He lifted his hand, touching where a lone tear lingered at the corner of my mouth. "You're happy tonight."

Yes. In some ways. I tilted my head back, meeting his gaze. "It was like old times with Brooke. She's happy."

He nodded, his eyes falling to my lips. "And that makes you happy?"

"I was hurt by her lying to me, but yeah. It does." My throat swelled as I remembered my time with her. "She made me feel normal when I roomed with her."

But it was more than that.

"She didn't look at me with guilt or fear, or like she knew a secret about me that I didn't know myself," I continued. "That's what all the adults did, and I wasn't allowed friends. Not really. My mom didn't want anyone at the house, and my dad didn't want me at other people's houses. He couldn't control what I'd say." I nodded to myself. A smile tugged at my lips. "Brooke was my first friend. She was the first to give a damn."

"And I took her away."

My eyes lifted to his, but I didn't see regret or pity. Just understanding. I felt it inside of me, deep in my core.

I spread my fingers out over his chest, enjoying the feel of that *thump-thump-thump*. Strong and firm. Like Kai himself. Assured. Confident. He damn well knew what he wanted, and he would take it, or do it, or demand it—no matter what anyone said. He was going to do what he was going to do, and everyone else better get out of the fucking way.

I envied that about him.

If I'd been like him... Pain sliced through me.

I wasn't in this room anymore. I was back there, back on the day they'd told me she was gone.

Now. Now was the time to tell him. There was no more hesitating or second thoughts. I couldn't doubt myself, because it was time for him to pay.

"I want to help you hurt my father," I told Kai. Hardening, I said again, "I want to help you kill my father."

His eyes darkened. "I'm going to kill your father regardless."

"You said you would help me before."

"That was before he turned one of my guards against me, before he sent him to you. He changed the rules of the game. I'm taking him down."

He began to move away. I grabbed his wrist and stepped in to him, bringing our bodies in contact. "But I want to help."

He gazed at me for a long time before he gently extricated his wrist from my hand. He cupped the side of my face instead.

He said, "No."

And he walked out of the room.

CHAPTER FORTY-TWO

"No?" I walked right after him.

"I said no," he tossed over his shoulder, going down a hallway.

"I want to know why."

He took a back hallway to the kitchen. Brooke and Jonah were still in there. They'd moved to the table, two bottles of wine and a box of pizza open between them. Their conversation paused as we came in.

"You're not ready," Kai said as he turned the corner.

"What do you mean I'm not ready?"

Brooke's mouth fell open. Even Jonah seemed startled, though I wasn't sure the reason for their reactions.

Kai picked up one of the wine bottles, along with the two glasses.

"Hey!" Brooke sputtered, but she quieted after she looked at Kai's face. "Never mind." She swept a hand out. "Proceed."

He inclined his head and moved forward, back out into the hallway. I followed, and he spoke over his shoulder.

"You want to hurt your father, but that's all right now. You're not ready for the rest."

I thought we were going to my bedroom, but he turned left when he should've gone right. Where were we going?

There were stairs, back stairs, and we were going up.

"Where are you taking me?"

I heard a soft chuckle, and he held up the wine. "Keep following. You'll thank me." He glanced back with a cute grin.

Cute. I wanted to smack my forehead.

Kai wasn't cute.

He was hot. He was sizzling. He was alluring.

He wasn't cute.

But holy hell, there was a dimple, and my knees buckled. I'd never seen that dimple before.

I scowled. "Guys shouldn't be allowed to have dimples."

He barked out a laugh. "Come on." He transferred the wine and glasses to one hand, reaching behind and taking my hand with his free one.

I had a moment. One moment.

Time slowed down.

I looked down at our joined hands, at his smile, at the wine in his hands, at where he was leading me, and a thrill spread through my body. It tickled me from the inside out, and I had to contain myself because it was like we were normal.

Like we'd been to dinner and a movie and this was the end of our date.

Or hell, maybe we were on the second or third date. We were going somewhere to drink wine and neck—like normal couples.

We were a couple.

Wait. Were we?

What was going on here? Where were we going? And I didn't mean that literally, because I could see he was taking me to a room over the garage. The roof was slanted, with a skylight above. A large couch that was really a huge bed sat underneath, and as if all the romance movies had conspired against me in this moment, I saw it had begun raining.

It was officially the sappiest moment of my life.

Sigh.

I let go of Kai's hand and stood in the doorway.

He turned, backing toward the couch/bed, holding the wine out. "What's wrong?"

That dimple. He knew damn well the effect of that thing. It was a weapon.

He smirked. "Don't like skylights?"

I growled, "Dipshit."

He tipped his head back to laugh. "Come on." He put the wine and glasses on a stand next to the couch, opening a drawer to pick up a remote. He hit a button, and I watched a partition on the slanted roof slide away. A television screen moved out. It was large enough to fill the entire ceiling, so lying down, it was as if we had front-row seats to our own movie theater.

"Here we go." Kai looked at me, turning the screen on. "What do you normally watch?"

"Not politics." I said with a straight face.

Actually, that was all we watched. We had to, in case a new ruling made our job harder.

Kai chuckled and turned to the movie channels. "Fair warning." He paused on a romantic flick. "I've not watched a movie for...forever." He glanced at me. "I can't remember the last time I saw a movie."

I snorted, shaking my head. "Do the latest action one."

"Yeah?"

Another firm nod. "Yes. No chick flicks for me."

"Okay." He selected a movie that had just hit the theaters two days ago. How he got it here, I wasn't going to ask. I wasn't even going to be surprised.

I spread out on the couch and got comfortable.

Kai shut the door, casting the room in complete darkness except for the movie and the random flash of lightning above us. He crawled onto the couch with me.

"Did you want some wine?"

Instead of answering, I rolled over, grabbed the wine bottle, and moved back. I held it up in salute. "Let's be a little dangerous tonight."

Another soft laugh, and then he took hold of me. He lifted me up, scooted back, and deposited me on his lap. I could feel him hardening beneath me, and he stretched me to completely rest on him, my head nestled against his shoulder.

He skimmed a hand down my front, his fingers grazing the side of my breasts. He took the wine from me. "No glasses?"

"Nuh-uh."

I felt his chest vibrate with a laugh before he tipped the wine back to take a sip. He handed it back after he was done, and I grabbed it, almost desperately.

I needed it. I needed it to ward against what was going on here, because I was crumbling more quickly than I wanted to acknowledge.

I shouldn't have been this ridiculously happy for something as cheesy as a movie, a private room away from the rest, and a thunderstorm overhead, but I was. I felt so much that my throat was clogged, and I slurped that wine down, trying to push my feelings out of the way.

"Hey." Kai ran a hand up my back, sliding deliciously around the front before he took the bottle from me. "What's that about?"

"Nothing."

He didn't ask again, but he didn't need to. He was watching me. He knew. Taking a sip himself, he settled back, his hand running down the side of my body, sending sensations in its wake.

Throbbing.

Building.

But I ignored them. I settled back in his arms, resting my head against his shoulder, and I tried to ignore the way he ran a hand down my arm, and how his palm smoothed over my stomach, how his fingers traced over my skin.

I moved, hoping the throb would lessen, but it didn't.

I was beginning to pant.

Goddamn this man.

The movie was on. Someone was speaking. I couldn't care less. I was way past trying to follow, so I turned, my mouth half on his neck, and I asked, "What did you mean before about how Tanner didn't have a semblance of a life and the others do?"

He stiffened beneath me, pausing the movie.

"Really? You want to know now?" His eyebrow dipped.

I was half crazed and desperate from feelings I really couldn't afford to be feeling for him, so I nodded. "Yep."

"Okay." He leaned back, and I did what I'd been fighting against.

I moved to straddle him, but I sat back, leaving some space between us. I could feel him beneath me, and though he was hard, it was as if he didn't even know.

"There's a council in Canada," he said.

"A council?" I echoed. My mind raced.

God. I'm falling for him.

I can't fall for him.

He nodded as if I was listening, as if I totally understood every word he said, as if my world wasn't crumbling to pieces inside of me.

"There was a mafia war years ago, and it was so bad that our ancestors decided it'd never happen again. Too many innocents died." He ran a hand down my arm, grazing the inside of my wrist. He circled it, feeling my palm. "So they made a council instead."

"A council?"

I was repeating myself, and my heart jackhammered away.

"Yeah." He frowned, his eyes narrowing. "And because our father was a jackass and soulless and ruthless, he became the leader of the council."

Oh. Wait a minute.

I shifted up, my eyes flying to his. "So that means..."

He nodded again, his thumb running over my palm. "I'm the leader of the council. It was put together not just to end the war, but to help fight against the government." He paused, his hand tightening briefly over mine. "Or fight against the US because they always want to know what we do up there too."

Of course. That made sense.

I bit my lip. "And Tanner was mad because..." I had no idea why he was mad.

"Because he's second in line." Kai shifted. Grabbing my waist, he picked me up and pulled me to sit higher on him. Only a few inches separated us again, and I could feel his dick throbbing, hard and demanding entrance. I felt him twitch below me, and I had to bite back a groan because I wanted to give in. I wanted to let him sink inside me.

"So you..." I couldn't talk. I didn't even know why I was trying.

"Yes, me." He was teasing. I heard it in his tone. He knew exactly how he was affecting me. His hands fell to my hips, tipping me into him even more.

He leaned forward so his mouth grazed over my throat. "Yes. Me. I'm the head of the council because I'm the head of our family."

"And if you fall, then Tanner..." I was dazed. My pulse thundered in my ear. I felt him begin to kiss up my throat.

What were we talking about?

His arms tightened around me. "Tanner takes over, and if he falls, Brooke is next in line. She's a Bennett. One of us has to maintain control over the council. If we don't, that won't be good. At all."

Yes. The council. Of course.

Good God, he started to kiss my chest. He began to move south, licking all the way between my breasts.

This was never going to get old.

Ever.

I cradled the back of his head as he lavished his attention over me, and I knew this was never going to go away. I'd want him kissing me, licking me, tasting me, sliding inside of me until I was long past being old and about to hit my grave. Even then, I had a hard time imagining I wouldn't crave the feel of him still.

"Kai," I moaned, damn close to telling him all of it.

"Mmmm?" He lifted his head, those torturous lips pulling away from my skin, and I gazed down at him.

What was I going to say?

Need. Want. Desire. Those were the only things in my head. I didn't know anymore. I couldn't think right now

"Nothing," I rasped. "Nothing at all."

He lifted his mouth, and I brought mine down to it.

The movie began playing again. The rain continued.

And we were both soon groaning.

CHAPTER
FORTY-THREE

I had five days.

Five days of feeling Kai inside of me all night long. Five days where I'd wake and reach for him, where he'd roll inside of me or I would straddle him. Five days where we didn't leave the room until a late lunch. Meals were spent around a table, laughing, hearing stories from his siblings. Even Tanner began smiling halfway through the first day. Brooke loved cooking, so we enjoyed her gourmet meals—apparently she'd always wanted to be a chef.

Jonah left first, returning to his residency. He only had a few days' leeway, and his time was up.

Tanner was next, needing to return to the Vancouver home for the family business. I didn't ask what he did for them. No one offered that information.

Brooke, Kai, and I were left now.

Sitting up in bed, I glanced at the clock. It was a little after four in the morning, but I knew the other side of the bed was empty without looking. Rolling to the edge of the mattress, I tucked the sheet around my naked body.

Kai stood at the window, an arm braced against the wall beside the window frame. He wore sweatpants, which hung low on his hips. The full moon outside bounced off the lake, and I could see every muscle in his shirtless back. The shadows fell over them, gracefully showing me a path along his spine.

I moved to his side, the sheet trailing behind me, and he brought his arm to my waist, tucking me next to him.

"I woke you?"

I rested my head against his shoulder, feeling content and secure. "I don't know what woke me. What woke you?"

He was still gazing out the window. His hand tightened on my waist for a second. "I never fell asleep."

Something was wrong. "What's going on?"

Now he looked down, and I saw regret before he masked it. "I'm going to Milwaukee today."

We were still tucked in the northern end of Minnesota—only lakes and forest forever.

"You're driving?"

He shook his head. "There's a little airport thirty minutes away. We'll leave from there."

The moon cast half of him in shadow.

"You and Brooke are going to drive north, back to Vancouver."

"What? But—"

"It's safer that way."

Cord.

The plane accident.

He didn't want to risk us.

Fine. On *that* matter. But something else remained.

"I told you I would help with my father. Remember?"

He lifted his head back to the window. His jaw clenched. "We talked about this."

"Wha—"

"You." He rounded back to me. "Us. That changed everything." He pointed to the bed.

I fell quiet. How could my heart plunge in one second and soar in the next?

"He knows I'm alive. I want to see him."

"I'll bring him to you."

"Why are you going to Milwaukee?" I pulled out of his arms and faced him, folding my arms over my chest. The sheet rustled as I adjusted it.

"That's family business."

Which meant it wasn't my business. But I knew better.

"You're going to deal with my father, aren't you?"

He began to move away, but I grabbed his pants.

"You can't do that without me. It's my right."

"I said I would bring him to you."

He didn't get it. Or maybe he did. Suddenly, it felt so important to be there, to see him, to be the one to walk into a room when he wasn't expecting me. I wanted to make him feel unbalanced, to have him feel a small portion of the fear he'd put me through, put *us* through.

"Why are you doing this?" I choked out.

Kai's hand came to my arm, but I shrugged him off, stepping out of reach.

His tone was apologetic. "There are too many factors up in the air. I need Brooke away from Milwaukee. I need you away from Milwaukee. Your father knows about you. He's already tried once to get you. I can't run the risk—"

I shook my head. "This is total bullshit. You never said a word, but I know you caught the guy, whoever he'd embedded in your organization. You wouldn't have come back to me if you hadn't. It's safe for me again. You have a million guards. Your security team is unlike anything I've ever seen. You think twenty steps ahead. Don't tell me it's unsafe for me there, that you can't risk me—"

"Because it's the truth!" He got in my face, backing me up. "I cannot risk you. I *won't*. I've had my mother taken from me. My brother. I won't risk anyone else, and I won't apologize for that. I care about you. Whether it's rational or not, I won't chance losing you."

That stopped me cold.

I was angry, determined, I wanted to fight to go with him, to have my own vengeance, but hearing this, hearing him—I blinked back sudden tears.

He gentled his tone. "If there's even a chance he could get to you, do you know what I would do?" He moved closer, his hands finding my arms, circling to my back. He pulled me to his chest and tucked my head under his chin. I felt his voice vibrate through his chest. "I would rain hell over *everyone* connected to your father."

A shiver went down my back.

"I am not the good guy here. I am everything you've ever called me. I'm a murderer. I'm a bastard. I'm ruthless. I'm calculating. I will kill everyone your father holds dear, everyone who has helped your father, and I will *relish* it." He pulled back, tipping my head to meet his gaze.

What I saw there doubled my shiver.

Death.

He was promising it to me.

"I will not gamble with the lives of those I care about, and you're one of them now." He stepped back, his hands leaving me, and I was suddenly chilled to the bone.

His head lowered, and his eyes locked with mine. "You are *not* coming with me."

Got it? I felt the sentiment, but he didn't say the words.

He didn't say anything else as he went to the closet and pulled on a shirt, then a sweatshirt. He didn't say a word as he finished dressing and picked up the phone by the bed.

"I'm ready," he said into the phone.

He paused, looking at me.

I didn't know what to do. I couldn't fight him. He wasn't going to budge on this matter.

The door clicked shut behind him, soft but final.

• • •

The door opened again ten minutes later, but it was Brooke who slipped through.

I tightened my hold on the sheets. "Wha—"

"We have one hour, literally one hour."

"What are you talking about?"

She moved inside, and I was able to see her better—hair pulled into a low ponytail, dressed all in black, even her runners. Brooke always smelled of perfume, but today she smelled of nothing. Not even soap.

She pulled her backpack off and opened the front pocket. Dumping passports, phones, and money, she pointed at it. "Kai is leaving for Milwaukee, and whether Levi is going too or if he's being shipped in a different vehicle, I don't care. I just know my man is with him, and whatever move he's making with the man I love, I'm going to be there."

She looked at me. "You can make people disappear. It's your turn to disappear, and you're taking me with you."

"But..." I was already looking through everything she'd dumped on the bed.

We had different IDs. Plenty of cash. I stopped counting after I saw ten rolls of hundreds. I picked up one of the phones. "Burners?"

"You got it." She folded her arms over her chest, raising her chin.

My mind raced, but I wanted to go.

Something sparked inside of me.

This. This was right.

This was what I did.

"Your brother has people in the Network. We can't call them."

"Already on it." She pulled out her phone and showed me a screen of text messages.

I recognized an alias Blade had used one time. Just once. It'd been him, Carol, and me, and we'd snuck out to a nightclub and didn't want the Network to know. He was a goddamn genius.

I felt myself smiling.

"I'm in."

She looked up and made a praying motion. "Thank God." A quick squeal, and she was on her phone. "Okay, your friend is two miles from here to pick us up. We need to trek two miles through the woods in an hour."

"Why an hour?"

I was off, running to the closet to change. There was no time for modesty. Brooke was about to see me naked, and I tore through the clothes, throwing them into the room.

"You have a bag for me too?" I called.

"Of course."

"Put those in there."

"Okay."

I felt my heart in my throat. The clock had started ticking the second Brooke entered the room. I was wasting time, and we needed all the time we could get.

I pulled on a shirt. "You work out?"

"Yes..."

I held back a groan. She sounded hesitant. "What do you do for conditioning?"

"I swim. Sometimes." She snorted. "Hardly ever."

Fuck. If it was just me, I'd run there in under twenty minutes, give or take a few because of the foreign terrain.

Which reminded me, "Why an hour, Brooke?"

"Because that's all the time we have before the next shift of guards switches at the security cameras."

I wasn't going to ask.

Shit.

I had to know. "What happened to the other guards?"

"I might've drugged 'em."

I paused, one second, then yanked on my pants. Socks. Shoes. I had an extra set of clothes in the bag now.

"And I gave one an entire bottle of laxatives."

"What?!" I popped my head out.

She cringed, standing with both bags over her shoulder. "I'm pretty sure he'll have to go to the hospital." She brightened up. "But bonus! That might help us."

I glared. "No, it won't. Protocol will be to check on both of us before they dispatch a team to the hospital. We have *less* than an hour now."

"How long do you think?"

I led the way to the back patio. I paused before opening the door. "It depends on when someone finds him or he finally calls for help."

"Oh." She cringed.

"What?"

She dug inside her bag and pulled out a radio. "I figured we could use it to listen to them."

Oh. My—I grabbed her face and kissed her on the cheek. "Sweet Jesus, you're brilliant."

She shrugged. "Just tried to think what you'd do. You helped me the first time, so I thought we could help each other this time."

I took a breath. I didn't think the door was alarmed. I had stepped outside the other day and nothing happened. Then again, Kai had been with me, but it was now or never. Outside was our best shot. We'd run into guards inside.

"Wait." Brooke pulled out her phone and showed me a map. "This is where we're supposed to meet your friend."

"Okay." I showed her as much as I could. "There's a small window outside here where I never saw a guard walking. We'll have to go north, then swing to the right."

"I'm ready." She gave me a nod, letting out a breath. Her bottom lip trembled, but we weren't running for our lives here. We weren't running for freedom, not really. We were running to follow Kai to Milwaukee. There was irony in there somewhere, and I was sure I'd laugh about it someday. Just not right now.

I opened that door, and we headed out.

CHAPTER FORTY-FOUR

I t's a peaceful feeling.

I know that sounds ridiculous, but it is.

Running in the woods, with just the person beside you, knowing time is running out, knowing the day is coming, knowing you have one goal: to get where you need to be before they find you.

It calmed me in a way I hadn't felt in so long.

The part of my soul that needed to know my purpose, to understand the why or why not, the part of me that reared up if I wasn't following my morals, that part was quiet. That part was content, because it was right to run free. It was right to go to Milwaukee. It was right to confront the man who'd been the first monster in my life.

There was no longer any confusion in my head or heart.

But Brooke's breathing was already uneven behind me.

She'd let me take the lead, and I was using the age-old way to find our path: following the North Star. Once we'd cleared where I last saw guards standing before, we turned so it was on our left side.

Using the map Brooke had showed me, I'd memorized the myriad of roads near the house. There was one main paved one that went alongside the lake. It wound all around it, but Blade wouldn't be waiting for us on that road. He would pick a gravel one, and not the second- or third-best gravel road. He'd pick the fourth one, one that looked like little more than a long driveway, and he'd park just on the other side of a hill. So he'd see the oncoming lights from a car, but they wouldn't see him.

This was part of being a Hider that we rarely utilized, but we had training for it.

I enjoyed this part more than the others in my unit. I took to the outdoors better than they did, though even I didn't know why. It rarely mattered. We usually drove from motel to motel. At some points, we'd have to meet someone. They would lead us through a hotel, or a restaurant, or a school to the back, where we'd get in another vehicle. That was how we'd travel once we got the person who needed saving. Going through was rarely a straight shot. They liked to have us use two or three different routes, in case someone tried to track us.

There were a lot of rich and powerful abusers out there. They had access to main road security footage, to dirty cops, to almost anyone who would take a few extra bucks for a peek at their camera systems. Which made relying on trusted allies and assets already certified through the Network so important.

My mind continued to turn as we ran.

If Brooke had notified Blade, and he was already here, that meant she had known about Kai's travel plans days ago. It would've taken that long to get Blade here and for him to have a cover story in place to hide his whereabouts from the Network.

I was banking on the fact that he'd have a plan ready. We didn't have the Network's allies and assets, which meant we'd have to keep to back roads as much as possible—as off the grid as we could be, using the least visible roads, which meant it'd take us so much longer than Kai to get to Milwaukee.

I bent my head forward. One foot after one foot. Keep going. That's what I had to do.

"Agh!" A twig snapped, and Brooke cried out.

I whirled, grabbing her arm before she crashed into a tree.

"Oh, shit shit shit! Oh no." She moaned, grabbing for her ankle. "I think I broke my ankle."

Our hour was slipping away. I could see it shortening before my eyes.

She knelt down, wrapping her hands around her leg, as if to prevent the pain from spreading. "Riley! It hurts so much." Tears streamed down her face, and she gasped for breath.

By my calculations, we had a little over a mile, more likely a mile and a quarter yet to go. I looked around, but even if we'd had rope for me to build her a crutch, we wouldn't make it. They would find us.

"Can you make it?"

She looked up, her face pale and getting whiter by the second. She shook her head. Her eyes were dazed, half panicked. "I think I broke my ankle! For real." Her voice hitched on a sob, pain laced with a twinge of hysteria.

I'm sure this was scary for her. But broken ankles could be fixed. Being in the woods, I'm sure that didn't help, but those guards wouldn't hurt her.

I didn't want to think of it. It felt wrong, but...

"You should go." She said it for me.

I gazed at her, long and hard. You didn't leave your co-agent behind, and Brooke had become that for me, but I wouldn't get to Milwaukee if I stayed. That was just the truth.

"Go. Wait! Here." She was still sobbing, and now wheezing. She pulled her backpack off and thrust it at me. "Take it. I mean it. Go, Riley. Go. I know your dad is down there. It was seriously shitty of Kai not to take you with him, and he knows that. For what it's worth, I think my brother loves you. He might not know it yet, but he does, and I know he'll feel bad about not taking you with him, but he won't come back for you. He just won't."

"How'd you know he was going to Milwaukee today?"

She quieted, rocking back and forth from her ankle pain. She didn't answer. Her lips pressed tight together.

"Brooke. Tell me."

She clenched her eyes shut tight, shaking her head, then sighed. "Fine. Fuck it. I know because Eric told me. Do not tell! Kai will kill him, literally. He let it slip one night, said he only had three more days of this shit. He hates when I tease him, but he tends to slip up because I rattle him. He doesn't even know I heard him. I just guessed on the Milwaukee part because that's where Levi's family is." She was panting now. "Oh, God. This hurts so much." Sweat rolled down her face. "Not that I don't love you and love having gotten to know you again, but can you go? I'm about to die if I don't get a painkiller in me stat."

I still hesitated. It feels wrong to leave an injured person behind. It's rooted deep in your core.

"Go! For real!" She waved at me frantically before holding her ankle again. "This is really starting to throb. I'll hold off as long as I can before calling for help, but seriously. Get the fuck out of here, or I'm two seconds from calling and not giving a damn if they catch you. I'm in that much pain."

I still hesitated.

"Go," she croaked. "They'll send Tanner back to me, and I'll try to talk him into flying the coop, but I can't beg you again. I'm dying here, Ri. Just go. Seriously. Kick my brother's ass when you find him too."

When she reached for the radio, I was out of time.

I backed away, still feeling wrong, but I knew I needed to go.

When she raised the radio to her mouth, I turned. I was full-out sprinting within seconds.

I'm coming for you, Dad. I'm coming for you.

CHAPTER FORTY-FIVE

I heard the guards shouting and dogs barking just as I ran down the last hill. A rusted white minivan was pulled over on the road with only two tires on the gravel, and I knew that was my ride.

As I jogged toward it, the back door opened.

Blade greeted me, a dark green blanket full of camouflage ribbons thrown over his shoulders. He waved me in, and as soon as I was inside, he gave me my own blanket.

"Hi!"

Carol sat behind the wheel. Dark red sweatpants, a banana-yellow hoodie and her hair in curls wasn't even the icing on her disguise. It was the cigarette between two of her fingers.

Carol didn't smoke.

"Let me guess," I said, trying hard not to smile. "A tired, middle-aged mother." It was good to see them, both of them.

"Yep." She blinded me with a smile so I could see her yellowed teeth, and she pointed to the bags under her eyes. "And this isn't makeup. I stayed up two full nights for you."

"The alarm was raised?" Blade looked into the woods behind us.

I moved to the side. "She's not coming. She rolled her ankle and couldn't make it the rest of the way."

"That's too bad." Blade reached around me, shutting the door, and then he lay down in the back. "Get down here."

There was a whole setup of boxes and bags of Christmas ornaments. Nestled in between everything was enough room for two people to lie down. I knew as soon as I got down there, he would reach up and pull the rest of the stuff over us. They'd made the back look almost like a hoarder's minivan. It was perfect.

I began climbing back. "Drive north. They'll expect you to go south or even east. Go the opposite direction. We can hit the interstate and make up time that way."

Carol shot me a look in the mirror. "Pffft. You act like this is my first day on the job." She waved me down with her cigarette. "Get down, you mafia-kept woman, and let me rescue your madamhood."

I grinned at her. It *was* nice to see them again.

Blade tugged me the rest of the way, and a second later he'd pulled the boxes and everything over us. A wood frame held everything in place and kept the weight off of us. We had a cozy little cocoon down here.

A second later Carol was coughing. She muttered, just loud enough for us to hear, "I'd make the worst smoker ever." Another smattering of coughing. "Okay, guys. It's about to get cold. I have to open the window."

A draft hit us moments later.

Blade tucked the blankets more firmly around us.

He lay beside me. In the past he would've suggested we share a blanket to conserve heat. He didn't make that suggestion today, and I knew Kai was the reason.

There was a sadness in Blade's eyes, one I hadn't seen before and was hard to see now.

"Are you mad at me?"

He closed his eyes, rolled to his back. When he opened them again, he wasn't looking at me. "No."

"You're sad, though."

Did Blade love me? I didn't know. Kai said he did, but it wasn't my place to ask. The only thing I could control was whether I stayed with Kai at the end of all this. I should've regretted what I'd done, but I didn't have it in me. Not anymore. Not after being with him for the last week, waking up in his arms, being claimed by him. I felt all those dark and delicious sensations rolling around inside me all over again.

No. I couldn't regret Kai. At least not yet. Not until he did something so bad there was no turning back.

Was that wrong?

Even that question felt bleak to me.

Kai had a pull over me that I couldn't put into words.

"What does the Network think?"

"I don't know what—"

"Come on, Blade. Like you haven't hacked your way into those emails. This is me asking."

He was quiet a moment.

"They think you're compromised, but there are some who want to bring you back in, make you an asset."

They wanted to use me, turn me against Kai. While I stayed with Kai.

"He traffics in women, and drugs, and guns. I mean..." Blade turned to me. His words were fierce. "How can you be with him, knowing that? He is what we stand against."

I could've explained that Kai didn't traffic those in, except guns. I could've explained that he wasn't a bad man; he just did bad things. That he was the leader of his family, of the council, and he did both of those jobs to keep his family alive.

But I didn't. My loyalties were now with Kai, and he would want me to say nothing. An ache formed in my chest at that realization.

I loved him. I had fallen in love with him. Even now, even as I was sneaking to follow him, I would go back to him.

I couldn't explain any of that to Blade, one of my oldest friends, who had done so much for me and was currently risking his job for me.

Wait. Was he?

"What does the Network think you're doing this weekend?"

He hesitated before responding, his voice dull and low. "They think we're at a festival in Cowtown."

He was lying.

I knew Blade. I knew his tells. He'd hesitated. Blade. Did. Not. Hesitate.

I had one guess: they were already moving forward with bringing me back in. They wanted to turn me against Kai.

Well, then.

"He has people in the Network." I rolled my head to look at Blade directly.

There was no use pretending. I didn't want that for this friendship. He and Carol were too precious in my heart. I could not be fake, letting their mission wedge even more between us.

"If you're going to try to turn me against him, you have to know that. He has people inside. He knew things even I didn't."

"What are you—why are you saying this to me?"

"You know why."

He flinched before looking back at me. His eyes were haunted. "It's the only way I could keep my job. If he has people there, they're staying quiet. The Network was furious that I tried to get you back without them."

Now I was the one flinching.

The woman who helped him was dead, because of Kai.

You should get used to it. He's the mafia, for God's sake.

That voice. I hated that voice. My reason, my sanity, but also my reprimander. That voice got quiet whenever I was in Kai's arms.

"Heads-up. We're about to get tested," Carol said.

The car slowed to a stop, and her window rolled down.

"What?"

I bit down to keep from laughing. Carol had been chipper, her usual mood, moments ago. She groused at the person now. I could hear her take a drag from her smoke.

"Shit," she grumbled. "Here. Hold this."

"Ma'am?"

"What?" she snapped. "It's a cig. Jesus. You were smoking one too. I can smell it on you." She rifled through something. "Fuck. Damn." A thud on the bottom of the van. "Those little fuckers. They took my wallet. Why'd the fuck they take my wallet?" she growled. "I'm going to murder my own children. Do you hear me— wait." She gulped. A sweet voice now. "I mean, I'm not actually going to do that, Officer. But look…" Irritation. Impatience. "They wanted pizza last night. I bet that's when they took it, forgot to put it back. Or no… They wanted to go bowling today, and the mall! Those little shits went to the mall, when I told them specifically not to. I'm raising ingrates. Those little criminals—"

"Okay, ma'am." A rapping on the top of the car. "You're free to go."

"You sure? I wasn't speeding. The traction on these tires sucks too much for me to go fast. Another thing I need to fix. I tell you—"

The guy was brisk. He was done listening to her. "Here's your cigarette. Thank you for your time."

We heard him walk past us.

Carol took a drag, still grumbling under her breath.

His car started up, and he passed us by.

"See you later, pig."

I couldn't hold back my grin. She was a piss away from being a method actor.

Another moment, then, "He has feds on his payroll *and* local cops. Who are you sleeping with, Ri?"

I groaned. "It's complicated."

She laughed, rolling up her window and starting forward again. "Just hold on a bit. We have a plane waiting for us. Your boyfriend ain't the only one with some connections."

"The Network?" I asked Blade.

He shook his head, his first faint smile showing. "A friend of Carol's."

"Damn straight. I heard you. Tinder's good for a few things other than a hook-up."

"Carol, are you dating someone?"

She barked out a laugh. "You're not the only one who's got someone new and exciting in their life. My guy just happens to have his pilot's license and a buddy with a plane. Took a bit of coercing, but he said he could fly you to Milwaukee."

"Well." I grinned at Blade. "Hot damn."

"Hot damn, indeed!" Carol laughed again. "And hold on. I'm going to put the pedal to the metal, if you know what I mean."

We turned into a small airport. I didn't think it was the one Kai had flown out of since we'd driven for over an hour, but it was small. It was isolated. And there was only one plane getting ready for departure.

As soon as we parked, Carol went over to a guy coming out of the hangar.

Blade got out behind me, stretching a little. We'd stayed in the back until the last ten minutes, so our legs were a little knotted up. Rifling through a bag, he pulled out some papers and handed them over.

"Those are numbers to call for resources."

"Blade."

He kept going, pulling out a phone, a smaller envelope, another fatter envelope. "You can't use the phones Brooke gave you. He'll have figured out which ones were taken and have trackers on them. There's money."

I had both backpacks from Brooke. If there were a tracker on anything, we already would've had guards pulling in for me. I was safe, but I took the phone he gave me. Checking the back, I asked, "Not a Network phone?"

He shook his head. "No. I didn't want to risk it. Like you said, he has people in the Network too." He paused a beat. "The Network didn't want to risk it." He looked away. "You're right. They green-lighted Carol and me to come get you, but they want to know who his people are. They're not risking anything. Everything I'm giving you is off the book so no one can find you. Even me. The envelope is sealed, and the envelope inside that envelope is sealed. No one's seen it except the manufacturer."

And the manufacturer wouldn't give two shits. They were just doing a job. I was safe.

"Where is he flying me into?"

"Not Milwaukee. You'll fly to South Riddance. It's a small airport past Milwaukee. You'll have to drive back, but a rental car should be easy for you to get."

It was a good plan. If they were looking, they might not look at flights that didn't go to Milwaukee. It'd be an oversight on their part.

"Okay."

He glanced at Carol, who was still talking with her pilot friend, before he pulled out another smaller box. "Put this in your bag. You know what it's for."

My mouth dried. It was a gun box.

I doubted there was a permit for it, but I put it in one of the bags anyway.

"He could lose his license."

Blade glanced back at Carol's friend. "Don't get caught."

I hoisted my bags to my back. Blankets. Clothes. I knew what was in the backpacks: cash, credit cards, the phones to use, fake identification. I had everything I needed to start a new life. It was a bit of overkill, all this to sneak into Milwaukee under Kai's watch, but if I knew Kai, I would need it. He'd have his resources looking for me nonstop. I'd have to go all the way underground.

Carol and her friend walked toward us.

I asked under my breath, "We're certain this guy is legit? He's not on anyone's payroll?"

Blade looked at me from the corner of his eye. "You mean on Bennett's payroll?"

I didn't answer because that *wasn't* what I meant. I looked at Blade, and his eyebrows shot up.

"Carol swears she met him by chance, on Tinder. They've hooked up for six months."

But he could be a setup. He could be working for the Network. And maybe I was becoming paranoid? Too many times going around the block with Kai? He was making me see moves in a game that wasn't being played. Maybe.

Blade came to the same conclusion. "Ditch him as soon as you land."

"That was already my plan."

The guy nodded to me as he walked up and shook my hand. "You ready for this flight?"

Carol hugged me. She hugged the guy. He climbed into the plane, and she went back to the minivan, leaving only Blade and me.

He gave me a smile, another sad one. "Until we see each other again?"

There were words to say, sentiments to express, and tears I was trying not to shed. All I did was nod and promise, "I'll see you again."

As I climbed in and watched Blade go over to where Carol was waiting, I felt the same thing I'd seen on his face.

Sadness.

Everything was about to change. I felt it coming on like an impending doom. The pilot yelled at me to buckle up, and moments later, we were hurtling down the airstrip.

CHAPTER FORTY-SIX

I was being dumb.

This hit me as we flew over Milwaukee. I was being *so* beyond dumb. Yes, Kai had said I couldn't go with him to see my father. But I wasn't a captive, and I had snuck out of there like I was. Both Brooke and I had. I'd continued to hide, using this friend of Carol's to take me the rest of the way. Disappearing was a skill I had, but it wasn't one I needed in this instance.

Maybe?

I didn't know.

God. Why was this so hard?

"You ready to touch down?" the pilot yelled at me over the system.

"Yes!" I yelled back. I was cold, I had to pee, and I was ready to try to right my world again.

Once we landed, I grabbed my bags and nodded to him. "I need to head to the bathroom."

He pointed where to go, and because I didn't really know if he was just Carol's friend, I disappeared again. I did have to pee, but I needed every advantage I could get. Bypassing the bathroom, I swiped a set of car keys hanging in the hallway. I went out to the lot and walked around, pressing the unlock button. In the second to last row, I slipped behind the wheel of a Taurus and headed into town.

The GPS was set up on one of the burner phones, and I put in an auto repair place. Not the one with the best website, but one that didn't have a website, one that had Yelp reviews from local customers. I pulled in and used *their* bathroom.

We had landed during business hours, though it was getting late.

After I peed, I asked for a female employee, because there usually was one. When she approached, she was older—gray hair, makeup done. I couldn't tell her exact job title, but it didn't matter. I could see in her eyes she'd been around the block.

"I need a car," I told her. "My boyfriend is in the mafia, and I'm running from him." White lie. "I need anything you can give me. I have cash for something cheap and desperation enough to let you know I stole the car I drove here in."

She hesitated, scanning me up and down.

I wore the same black clothing I'd had on when I left the house. I was sure I smelled. My hair was pulled low into a no-nonsense ponytail. If I needed to sell being on the run, I'd hit that out of the ballpark.

She ran a hand over her face. "He hit you?"

I didn't want to lie any more than was necessary, so I chose my words carefully. "I just have to get as far as I can from him."

"You stole that cash from him too?"

My eyes flicked up. "No. Cash is good. A friend gave it to me."

She still hesitated. "I don't want to get in trouble."

"Look, the car won't be reported for a while. Maybe even a few days." I glanced up to the cameras. "Wipe the footage, then call in a random car. You have cars parked here all the time. I know how auto shops are. No one's going to look twice. You can say your footage clears every few days anyway."

She wanted to help. I could see it, but a girl showing up with cash, a stolen car, and a story about a connected mob boyfriend spelled trouble.

A hoarse "Please" finally sold it.

She let out a sigh, nodding. "Drop your keys for the car on the floor and give me a second." She disappeared behind the counter, returning a few minutes later. She slid an envelope over to me. I could see there were keys inside. "That's to the Chevy truck out back. Leave what you can for cash. I had a friend who got beat up by her boyfriend, so I get it."

"Thank you."

I reached inside one of the bags, took a few hundred-dollar bills, and held them out to her. The envelope pocketed, I did as she said. I dropped the keys to the Taurus on the floor and headed out. The store had been empty, and as I got to the only Chevy truck in the back, I knew she was either erasing the security footage or calling the cops.

Either way, I pushed down on the pedal, though as I headed out of town toward the interstate, I had to admit I wasn't sure who I was even hiding from at this point.

Kai?

My father?

The Network?

Or maybe myself.

CHAPTER FORTY-SEVEN

I didn't have a full plan.

The first day I got to Milwaukee, I set myself up at a B&B—one where I had my own exit and entrance—before I hit up a library and forged a new library card. Fake name, fake address, everything fake, but it worked. I got the card. That got me access to the library's internet, and from there, I searched for my father.

I wasn't going to search for Kai. I worried if I did then he'd find me instead. My dad was the next thing. I was going radio silent with everyone else, at least until I knew for sure what I wanted to do here.

The first article that popped up was an event my dad would be attending in two days.

The second was my obituary.

Prominent local tycoon's wife and daughter both dead. Authorities are investigating.

Jesus. I felt sucker-punched.

Clicking it, I read the story of my car accident, and how my mother's own car accident six months earlier was now looking suspect. The fucker had been investigated. *Good.* I felt some satisfaction. He deserved it. He deserved that and more, so much more.

There was a small write-up on my funeral. These were all articles I never could bring myself to search for and Blade never offered to get for me. But I saw the picture of my father grieving.

He had a hand to his face, his head bent like he was crying, and a woman I didn't recognize trying to console him.

He was faking it.

My father never cried. Ever. I wondered once if he even had tear ducts.

I got out of there, clicking on other articles.

There were more than I expected. He had gotten national coverage too; and his mafia connection was mentioned in both national stories. No doubt it was the reason for the articles in the first place.

My throat thickened, just thinking about him, about the reason for those articles in the first place.

My mother.

It still hurt. I thought I was over it, that everything had been pushed into the right categories and boxes and I was this professional, no-emotions operative. But that wasn't the case. It all swept up in me again.

I usually felt the hatred. That was never far away when I thought about my father, but today, looking at his face, his name, and remembering that time, I felt mostly just pain.

By the time I left and went back to the B&B, I had a plan formulated, and I picked up the phone in my room. I dialed the number at the house we'd most recently stayed at since I didn't have any other number on hand.

"Hello?" Tanner answered.

"You have my number?" I didn't introduce myself. He would know. I didn't wait for a response. "I'm going to hang up."

There was no hesitation. "Okay. Brooke's ankle is fine, by the way."

I paused, then put the phone back on the base.

I didn't know how long it would take, but I watched the clock and began counting.

It took twenty-three minutes.

Knock, knock! "Let me in. Now."

I let out a sigh, stood, and opened the door. I stepped back, seeing Kai's tight features glaring back at me.

I pressed my hands together. "The door wasn't locked."

He moved inside and shut it with a kick.

I'd expected him to come to me, to reach out, touch me. He did nothing. He remained just inside the door.

"It has to be your decision," he growled. "Everything has to be your decision."

His eyes were hard, his mouth pressed in a flat line.

He. Was. Pissed.

"How long have you been here?" he asked.

Oh boy.

His eyes were locked on me, unmoving.

I swallowed. "A day."

He shook his head. "A day. You've been here a full fucking day?"

Well, it was closer to a day and a half with the traveling included, but I didn't think he cared about that.

"*How* did you get here?"

I gave him a look. "Are you kidding?"

"No, I'm not! I'm not fucking kidding. How did you get here?"

"My job is to help people disappear. That is what I do, what I'm good at. You do mafia shit. That's what *you're* good at."

"I'm good at keeping my family safe. *That's* what I'm good at."

"Come on. I mean, did you really think I wouldn't get here? You really thought I would let you confront my father without me? He's my dad. Mine."

"And he deserves to die."

He was growling, nearly shouting, but he rubbed a hand over his jaw. He was trying to calm down. He looked down. "You flew, didn't you?"

Aw shit. "Yes."

"Goddammit, Riley!" Back to shouting.

I had to take a step back.

He wasn't moving, but it didn't matter. The air writhed around him, his words like punches. Everything was tense and riddled with fury.

Stark shadows fell over his face, making his cheekbones prominent and unyielding.

"Why are you mad?" I asked.

"I'm mad because I give a shit about you." His hand went to his hair, running briskly through it. "Maybe it's irrational, but my loved ones don't fly. It's my rule. It's the one thing I held on to when I took my father's position. Everything else I gave up. Everything. People I cared about, friends, girlfriends. School. A normal life. All of it was gone the second I took the head council position. It fucking matters, and it's one small way I'm reassured my family members are alive. You have a shot at living if your car is tampered with. There's no shot with a plane once it's in the air. No shot."

He cared about me.

His loved ones.

And his girlfriends.

It was petty of me, but...girlfriends? More than one?

His hands went to his hips, clearly frustrated. Bent, broken, but still here. Still standing. Still in the room with me.

"Brooke thinks our mother died from an illness. She didn't." His now-tired eyes flicked up to mine. Pain flared there. "Our father killed her, and he didn't act alone. I've never told anyone in the family this."

"How'd she die?"

"With her lover." His nostrils flared. "With Cord's father."

Oh—OH! My mouth fell open.

Kai sat on the edge of my bed, resting his elbows on his knees. He stared at the floor. "I was told by a source that her lover's family killed them both. They're a member of the council as well. And I've never been able to prove it, but my father helped. I know he did."

"No one knows?" I sat next to him, wanting to touch him, comfort him.

He gave me a look. "Not about Cord, but come on. Jonah doesn't look like us. It's obvious she was a cheater. And who could blame her? Her husband was a monster."

I winced, hearing my own thoughts flung back at me, words I had spoken before too.

He stood, pacing the room. "Fuck. I don't even know why I'm telling you this." He stopped suddenly and shot me a heated look, one filled with anger and loathing and worry.

The worry got to me, melting me. His tone, not so much.

"I don't care where you decide to go. I honestly don't, as long as you're safe. You're not a captive, even though you snuck out like one. If you and Brooke had demanded to come to Milwaukee, what'd you think I would've done?"

"Taken away our phones and kept us locked away in a log mansion?"

His mouth closed with a snap. "Yeah. I see your point, but you're not Brooke. You don't have a boyfriend that could fuck everything up for this family like she does. You have a logical head on your shoulders. Brooke would get pickpocketed by teenagers at the mall if she didn't have guards. That's actually happened. She has no life skills. You saw what house we found her in."

Yes. The house he had exploded.

He did care. He did love.

He was angry with me about flying. He was telling me about his mom. He connected them together, somehow. A way to lose me, another person he lost. I was going with caution, but I had a gut feeling here.

He needed to talk, if even for this one time.

"You said your mom died with her lover, but how exactly did she die?"

He closed his eyes, his head falling back. He let out a soft "shit."

I waited. Instinct told me to wait, to be quiet, to let him fill the space.

"They made it look like a mugging. A random fucking act of crime, but it wasn't. She was stabbed three times, once in the throat, and the knife lodged in the side of her skull."

Holy fuck.

He didn't move, his eyes fixed on a point in the wall. Unmoving. Unseeing. "The guy bled out. They nicked an artery to make it slow and painful. Their wallets were gone. That's how they

TIJAN

got it classified as a mugging gone wrong, but it was an execution. The only better way to have done it was a bullet to the forehead, have them on their fucking knees, but they didn't go that route. I don't know why. No one was fooled, except maybe my siblings."

I itched to move closer to him, to touch his arm, his side. "How do your siblings think she died?"

The smile he gave me was ugly. My soul cringed.

"Sudden-onset cancer."

I almost choked. "Are you serious?"

"My dad set up a doctor's appointment, sans my mother. The doctor showed him a file, told everyone about the diagnosis, and she was 'whisked off' to hospice. She was supposedly dead days later." He shook his head. "She'd been in the fucking morgue the whole time, her body on ice until the funeral."

My head swam. For him. For his mother. For Brooke, and the rest.

"I'm—"

He turned to look at me. "Do not pity me. Don't you fucking dare." His eyes flared with hatred, but it wasn't for me. I knew that. It still felt like another punch, though, almost as bad as seeing my dad's articles earlier.

"This is how we die in my family," he seethed. "Violently. Harshly. Cord's death was made to look like a plane accident. I made my dad's look like it was natural causes. My mom's was a mugging. The end is the same. We die. You want to be here? You want to be a part of this? You want to be locked in like I am? Because the end is the same. No matter what. Today. Tomorrow. Ten years from now. Twenty, if you're lucky. The end is the same. Someone will decide they want you dead, and it'll happen. In this life, we wish for natural causes. I would love to die in my sleep, or even from an accident, as long as it's a true accident. I don't want to die because of someone else's calculations, but I have a hard time imagining I'll get that lucky."

I narrowed my eyes at him. For once, I wasn't cringing, flinching, biting back sympathy.

279

I rose to my feet, slowly, and locked my chin in place. "Who do you think you're talking to?" Did he really not remember? "My father used to beat my mother on a weekly basis, sometimes daily. I was sent away to Hillcrest because she feared he'd get me too. He wanted her dead. Remember? He would've killed me. You said it before, he'll probably do the same to my cousin one day. I was born in darkness just as much as you. Maybe yours is darker, I don't know, but it's not like I ever decided to be normal. I didn't like the 'light' life. I helped others disappear too. What do you think we see when we find them? Those people are at their lowest. They're fighting for their lives. And we've been too late. Have I told you about those times?"

My voice sounded dull, echoing inside of me.

I kept on, though. He had to hear this. "Girls who got away from their pimps, who called for help. We get to a lot of them too late. We find their bodies. Or we show up to an empty hotel and get word a week later their body was identified in the morgue. Trafficked girls too. It's not just rich assholes we save people from. It's all walks of life. Girls who left home trying to get away from an abusive father or mother, get lured in by the promise of easy money, and get hooked on drugs. Prostitution. It's those too." I stepped toward him, my voice soft as silk. "Those girls you turn a blind eye to, who are trafficked in your territory, in your country. Those girls."

He watched me come toward him, his gaze matching my tone. Like a loving snake waiting to pounce.

"What would you like me to do in those situations?" he asked.

"Stop them." *Easy.* "Make that go away."

"Just like that?" He gave me a hollow laugh. "You don't know anything, do you, little girl?"

Oh, that fucker.

"I know the reason you reacted so violently to those people Brooke was staying with was because you recognized the signs." This was the ace up my sleeve.

I stood almost toe-to-toe with him. "I know she was being groomed, and she didn't even know it. She was living in that filth.

It would've taken one bored night where she went upstairs and had a drink with them. One drink. One drug. A second night of drugs. More and more until she forgot why she was with them in the first place, until she was desperate and would've done anything. Or she would've started while she was high, out of it enough where they could use a camera on her. Right?"

I reached out, my heart jumping all over the place, but my arm steady.

I shouldn't have, but I touched his chest.

His heart was racing just like mine, unsteady and erratic. Out of control.

I licked my lips and stared at his chest as it rose and fell under my palm. "You said no one was in the house, but that wasn't true, was it?" I didn't wait for the answer. I didn't need it this time. "You had those people killed, and you burned down the house to destroy the evidence." My eyes lifted to his now. "Didn't you?"

He stared right into me, slipping past my walls, my barriers to see me naked and stripped bare for him. But I saw him, just as much as he saw me.

Slowly, he reached up until his hand curled around my neck.

He pulled me close, crushing my hand between us, and as he bent for my lips, he said, so softly, "You're goddamn right I did. And I'd do it again."

Then his mouth fused with mine.

CHAPTER FORTY-EIGHT

No words. None at all.
Just right now.

Need. Want. Claim.

Mine.

Our mouths battled, both of us trying to dominate the other. I was almost bursting with need.

I needed to feel him.

I needed to touch him.

I needed to claim him.

I didn't care where we were. We could've been in the middle of the street, but I needed his touch on me, his body on me, his everything on me.

I needed him. My feelings were hot. They were demanding. They were dirty and complicated. They were everything in the gray part of life.

As we pushed against each other, our mouths laying claim, he ripped off my shirt. My pants. I dragged my nails over his, trying to tear it off.

"Fuck," he breathed, his hand sliding between our bodies, pushing inside my underwear, and then finally me.

I paused, gasping for air as I felt him inside of me. I'd been thirsting for this touch from him since he left. The time away, the day, had been too long, and everything was muddied around me.

When he was in me, the world righted. I wasn't confused anymore.

It was him. It was me. It was whatever this was between us, and as a second finger joined the first, I arched backward from the pleasure pulsating through me.

He moved his fingers, owning me, and his mouth trailed over my exposed throat, my chest, to my breast, then to the other. He suckled, tasted, licked, caressed.

God. I loved this man.

I hated him, but I loved him, and clamping a hand to the back of his head, I knew my need for him wouldn't be satiated with just one time. It'd be over and over again until I couldn't walk, until I couldn't crawl, until I couldn't even think about moving again.

That time might never come.

I knew, as his mouth switched to my other breast and his fingers pumped inside of me, that I was gone.

I growled, grabbing for his pants. I took out his cock and wrapped my hand around it.

If he owned me, I would own him too. It'd go both ways, or I would burn everything down around us.

I wound my legs around his waist, and he had a moment's notice to pull his fingers out. He caught me under my ass, and I lowered myself over him, sheathing him inside of me.

He held me, our eyes meeting, and we gasped at the sensation. I began moving up and down.

The surprise was gone. His eyes went black, and his hands tightened. He crashed me into the wall, pinning my hands above my head. His mouth went to my throat, and he began to suck, making me feel things I didn't know a person could.

I moaned, my legs tightening around his waist.

He moved my hands together, securing them with one of his, and his free hand went to my clit. He rubbed and teased as he took control, as he thrust in and out of me, pushing, shoving almost violently.

I could only hiss out, "Yesssss" through my teeth. I was blind with desire and drunk with pleasure.

Something crashed to the floor.

He kept thrusting in me, deeper and deeper.

He was making me his, but when had I not been? Really? Then his mouth found my breast again, and I was gone, lost in the darkness of our coupling.

He pushed in, out, in, out until I felt myself coming. An explosion crashed inside of me, and I screamed, gasping as it ripped through me, leaving me trembling in his arms. Once I was done, he carried me to the bed. Then he pulled out, moved me to my knees, and stood behind me.

He gripped my shoulder and molded himself over me.

His cock found my entrance, and as his teeth nipped at my skin, he pushed back in.

No. I'd been wrong. This. This was him claiming me.

One hand held my breast, the other held my waist, and as I turned back for him, his mouth found mine, and he fucked me until he came too.

It was rough, but it was us. He opened a channel inside of me where dark things happened, a place most people didn't want to acknowledge. Not Kai. Not me. He'd found it in me, made me look at it, and then he took me there and was making it my home.

I shouldn't have wanted it. I shouldn't have wanted him, but I could no longer deny that I was his.

Everything had been leading to this point—the time when I would seek him out, when I would follow him, when I would make him come and get me. We were there now, and I hadn't known until this moment.

I'd known everything was going to change when that plane left to bring me here. Now I knew how complete that change would be.

I rolled to my back, and he fell down next to me—both of us panting, sweating, tingling—and then his hand found mine and he squeezed. He curled toward me, his leg moving over me, holding me in place, and he pressed a soft kiss to my shoulder.

"Don't leave again," he murmured.

I squeezed back; that was all the energy I could muster. "Never."

And there, we both fell asleep, my world completely changed. I just didn't know if it was for the better.

CHAPTER
FORTY-NINE

I woke and rolled over. It was still dark outside.

Kai sat on the edge of the bed, his back to me, his elbows resting on his knees. I sat up, scooting over to slip my legs around both sides of him. He tensed at first, then relaxed as I rested my cheek to his back, breathing him in.

He caught one of my hands, tugging it to his chest. "Do you regret anything?" he asked, his back rumbling with the question.

I held still a moment. He was asking so much.

"No." I relaxed. I squeezed his hand. "Not one thing."

He raised our hands, pressing a kiss to them. "Good." Instead of turning to me, he reached behind him and dragged me around to straddle his lap. I raised my arms, resting them on his shoulders. I grinned at him, easing back to take in his entire face.

His hair was tousled. I could see soft lines of tiredness around his mouth, but his eyes were alert. Awake. He reached up, his fingers sliding to cup the back of my head.

He drew me close, my forehead touching his. "You're here now."

"I'm here now."

"I have things to do here."

"I know." My hand twitched. He felt it, raising his eyebrows.

"Will you be okay with that?"

"I came to see my father." But there was more. I'd come for him too. I just didn't know it until I got here.

He nodded, his fingers tracing my sides. "I want to remove your father from his company." He paused, observing me intently. "And I want you to replace him."

I leaned farther back to really take him in.

There was a guardedness, a resigned expression behind his eyes—as if he was warning me, but also waiting for...something. I didn't know what.

"Okay?" I asked.

"Are you willing to do that? I can have someone replace you, if you want. If you're willing to help me."

I grinned. "We're back to the original proposition then?"

His grin was rueful, but ominous at the same time. "You came here of your own volition. I won't send you away. I'll only *make* you do something if it's for your safety. That's it. I promise." He looked me over. "I don't promise often."

My mouth was suddenly parched. "Okay. I mean..." I licked my lips. "Yes. I'll do what I can."

"I need to remove your father from the Bello Company, and I'll put you in his place. If you stay, it's up to you. It can be real, or it can be for show. I can have Tanner come down to act as your spokesman. That's all up to you."

Why was he telling me this?

What else was going to happen?

But I nodded. "I'll do it."

And as soon as I said those words, the butterflies were back, and this time they had steel-edged wings. That meant so many things: I would reveal myself as not being dead to the public. I would have to face my father. It had been a nightmare for half my life, a revenge-filled dream, a goal, and now—I gulped—a reality. A whole tornado kicked up inside of me.

"What about my cousin?" I asked.

Kai shook his head, closing his eyes and tugging me against him. I looked into his eyes, seemingly closer to him than I'd ever been before. He wasn't guarded now. He seemed to be seeking comfort in me, in my embrace.

Some of the tornado lessened.

He moved to kiss my neck and breathed out, "She won't be a problem."

I tipped back, a finger under his chin as I raised his face. "Why not?"

A shudder went through his chest. He gripped my hand and held it between my breasts, his thumb sneaking out to graze one. "Because she's a non-factor. She's not his daughter. She's not related to him by blood at all. She is his mistress. That's it."

"Not girlfriend?"

"Mistress is more appropriate. Trust me." His gaze hardened. "She doesn't matter to him, not after he sees you again."

"Is she the only one who might have a claim to his position, though?"

"Only if they were married. They're not. I checked."

"I thought they were engaged."

"An engagement doesn't beat out a daughter. And when you're presented to him, he'll champion you. I promise."

The dark shivers I'd begun to equate with Kai went down my spine again. He was planning something, but this time, I wasn't on the other side. This time, I knew I needed to trust him.

"Okay."

"Okay?" His grin showed, becoming infectious.

Those damn dimples too.

I laughed, shaking my head. "You look like a little boy who got his favorite piece of candy."

His eyes darkened. "Because I did." He hardened beneath me and leaned forward, his eyes holding mine until I felt his lips on my throat. They were now commanding, and the throb within me burst into a full-fledged fire.

My breathing quickened, along with my pulse, and I tipped my head back as his mouth began to explore. Down. Down. Nuzzling between my breasts, then sweeping over to take one nipple into his mouth. His tongue wrapped around me, kissing me, tasting.

A full body sigh left me, and slowly, inch-by-inch, he lowered me back to lie on his legs. My head came to rest just over his knees. I was stretched out for his feasting, and as he released one breast, he moved to the other. He took his time, making my entire body clench, tremble, and tighten, only for him to do it all over again.

He moved farther down.

Farther.

All the way until I felt his lips on my clit.

He was bent almost in half, and his tongue pushed inside.

I gasped, sensations coursing through me, setting everything on end.

He kissed and sucked, thrusting his tongue in, then licking, while his fingers rubbed over me. It wasn't long before I was gasping, air caught in my throat, and I exploded for him.

A few moments later I still wanted him, but that had mixed with a languid contentment. Every bone in my body melted as he readjusted us, laying me on my back and moving between my legs. He crawled up, holding himself above me, his muscles rock hard, and then he pushed inside. He watched me the whole time.

Dark. Delicious. Desire.

All of it rolled together as he moved inside of me. This was different than before. This was a meeting of the souls. He was tugging me farther into his world.

A tremor wound up inside of me, like a snake, and once it worked itself all the way to the top of my head, I exploded once more.

He was right behind me, falling over me, his body quaking and trembling with his release.

I lie beside him as his heartbeat slowed to match mine.

He ran a hand down my side as he eased out of me. I couldn't form a thought or even a word. We had started to fall asleep when there was a shuffle of feet outside my door.

"I say, this is my house. My business," a sharp voice protested. "You let me in there. I need to check on my customer. It's my right!"

A low male voice spoke to her.

"I said what I said! I ain't moving."

Another shuffle of feet and a soft, reluctant knock on the door.

Kai tensed for a second before pushing up. "Hold on."

He jumped out of bed, moving with ease and athleticism. Flashing me an apologetic look, he dressed and moved to the door.

He opened it, and I sat up in bed, tugging the sheet to cover me.

His guards were there. And I was able to get a glimpse of the B&B's owner.

"Ma'am."

I almost snorted. That word coming from Kai was a new one. He said something more, shutting the door so I couldn't hear the rest.

"I want to see for myself," the owner said after a moment.

Swallowing my amusement, I climbed out of bed. It was time to go anyway. We'd stayed in this cocoon for as long as we could. Her presence just brought the inevitable. I hurried to dress and wash up, grabbing the little I had pulled out of my bags and stuffing it back in. I gazed around the room, still hearing the owner arguing with Kai.

I snagged what he'd left behind, but it wasn't much.

I went to the door.

"—assure you, I—" Kai stopped when I opened it.

The guard moved aside.

Kai took in my bags and nodded behind me. That guard slipped inside, and I knew he was clearing the room, making sure nothing was left behind.

"Mrs. Gambles." I had a wide smile on my face and held out my hand. "Thank you for letting me stay." I nodded toward Kai. "But you can see it's probably time to go."

She looked over the crowd of men in her hallway.

"You in trouble? Why are all these strange men here?"

"Everything's fine. I promise. I paid for the night, yes?"

"You did." Her tone was still untrusting. "I won't hesitate to call the police, you know." She stared hard at Kai.

"No! No." I took Kai's hand. "We're good. Thank you."

Kai glared at her, seeming a bit bewildered.

I tugged him behind me as I started down the hall, the guards jumping into action. They led the way, two falling in behind us, and I was even more mortified when I saw some of the other customers standing in the living room, their mouths gaping at the whole show. Three SUVs were parked on the curb, waiting for us as we left the house. As we approached, the door opened on the one in the back.

I went in first, Kai's hand on the small of my back to guide me.

We waited for the last of the guards. A minute later, he came out and got into the front seat of our SUV. He twisted around, holding out what I'd completely forgotten.

My gun box.

My stomach sank.

CHAPTER FIFTY

"You were going to shoot your father?" Kai finally asked. He'd been silent during the car ride here.

We were in house number thirteen million, but it wasn't really a house. It was more of a warehouse somewhere outside Milwaukee with the upper floors renovated into living space. That was our domain. All the guards were beneath us and around us.

I ignored Kai, dumping my bags on a couch and wandering around. There was a loft set above, but the main living floor was large. At one end, I was surprised to see a sliding door with a deck attached. It overlooked the lake, and we were quite a ways north of the city.

We were almost in our own world. Again.

"Riley!" Kai snapped from behind me, banging something down on the table.

I jumped, looking back.

His neck was tense, every muscle rigid. His jaw clenched.

I gave in, wandering back. "Yes."

"Elaborate."

I raked my hands through my hair, then hugged myself. "Blade offered me the gun, and I took it. I wasn't totally sure what I wanted to do when I saw my dad, but I took it to shoot him." I frowned. "Why are you mad about that? You've offered the exact thing, for me to kill my father."

He didn't answer, just stared at me as he breathed out through his nostrils. "I need a fucking drink."

I followed him into the kitchen area. "You're confusing the *fuck* out of me."

He ignored me, opening a cupboard, slamming it shut. He moved to the next and repeated the same vicious motions.

"What's going on with you—"

"You!" He whirled toward me, his face twisted. "You. You're what's wrong."

I fell back a step, feeling slapped in the back. "What? But—"

He picked up a glass and threw it against the wall. It shattered into pieces, falling to the floor.

My mouth fell right alongside it. "What is *wrong* with you?!"

"You—"

"Yeah," I cut him off this time, surging forward. "You said that already. Me. I'm wrong. But it's not me. It's you. This is what you've said since the beginning. You wanted me against my father. You offered to bring him to me to be killed. Then you said you would kill him anyway. Now you want to use me against him, and what?" I flung my arms out wide. "Why are you shocked that I brought a gun to actually do it?!"

"Because it's you!" he yelled. "It's you." He lowered his voice, his hand raking through his hair. When he looked back at me his eyes were stricken, haunted.

He paused, and when he spoke again it was almost a whisper. "Because—because I've fal—I *care* about you. I more than care, and I don't know what the fuck to do about that."

Those words almost shoved me on my ass. "What?"

He twisted around, both his hands in his hair again, his shirt stretching over his back. "Yes! Everything you're saying makes sense. Killing is something I don't think about anymore. I wish I did. I wish..." He snarled. "I wish I gave a damn about who I kill. It's him or us. That's how—"

"Him?" I said faintly.

"What?"

"You said him or us."

He frowned. "Us or them. It's us or them. That's how I grew up. That's how we Bennetts are."

"No." I shook my head. "You said him or us. Who's him?"

But I knew. My gut was twisting on it.

I gentled my question, "Who's him, Kai?"

He couldn't look away. He flinched. He tried to turn away, but I hurried over and caught him. I touched the side of his face, holding him in place.

"Who, Kai?" He had to say it. "Who? Say his name."

He jerked out of my grasp, walking away.

"Kai!"

"What?" He flung his hands out, stopping. But he didn't turn around.

"Turn around."

He didn't. He didn't respond either.

"Kai."

He took another step. Here we were again. I was chasing him. I was following him.

"Kai." I sighed. "Look at me."

"Why?"

He did, though. He looked, with sheer defeat on his face. Every inch of him looked like it'd been through the wringer, as if a truck had hit him.

"Why?" he said again. "This isn't goddamn therapy. You know who I meant. You know who the monster was who created me. You called me a monster before. Well, I learned how to be one from someone."

His eyes narrowed, a dangerous spark in them. He started for me, slowly.

"A monster created you too, but you didn't turn into one. I'm about to do that for him," he spat. "I'm taking you into my world, little by little. And you're coming."

He raised an eyebrow. "You're supposed to fight me on it. You're not supposed to come, but you are. One touch and you fold for me, and a part of me loves it. I thrive on it, but a part of me hates it. A part of me is disgusted when I touch you."

I flinched. He was disgusted when he touched me?

"I am everything that's bad in this world. You are everything that's good, and I am turning you into me." He choked out, "I hate myself when I look at you. You reflect everything wrong in me, every time I'm inside of you."

His words were like whips, cutting into me, but there was goodness too. I closed my eyes, forcing myself to breathe out through my nose, forcing myself to focus on the good. There was good.

There had to be.

Find it. Cling to it.

Keep it.

Maybe he was making me bad, but I was making him good.

There was this fight, this dance between us. Good versus evil—but I wasn't perfect, and Kai wasn't evil. He just did evil things. He was good that had been twisted into something darker.

I didn't know what to say to any of that, so I went with what I knew to be true.

"I care about you too."

"Don't, Riley."

I shook my head. "I care about you, and I know I'm changing, but I can't stop it because I care about you." He intoxicated me. "I more than care about you—enough to see this through."

And here was another truth. If I walked from him now, I would be shattered.

I turned to that glass, broken in pieces. That would be me if I walked, if he walked, and it was fast becoming too pronounced for me to not acknowledge it.

"You said I can't leave again. You can't either."

He rubbed a hand over the side of his face. "What are you talking about?"

"I can't leave. You can't either."

"Riley—"

"Say it!" I went to him. "Say it. Now."

"What are you doing?" He shook his head, hands on his hips, and he watched me come. His nostrils flared. "What are you playing at?"

"You think this is a one-way thing? You make demands, and I have to follow? I don't think so." I stopped just out of reach, forcing myself to hold firm. "Say it back."

He continued to watch me, something sparking alive in those dark eyes of his.

"Say it."

"Say what?"

"That you won't leave!" I shouted. "That you won't cut and run when something goes wrong, because something always goes wrong—"

"No shit!" he snarled. "I'm in the fucking mafia. Everything goes wrong with us, and we're the ones who do it. We do that. I do that. I give orders to kill. And sometimes I want to be the one who pulls the trigger."

"You're being a dick."

"I *am* a dick."

I met him face-to-face, toe-to-toe. "Tell me something I don't know."

He reached up, his hand curling around the back of my neck, and he pulled me close. I went up on my tiptoes, my lips square against his, but we weren't kissing. We were both breathing hard.

I couldn't look him in the eyes, not this time. "Tell me something new. I know who you are, and I know what you're doing right now." I reached up and grabbed ahold of his shirt. I yanked him against me. "You cannot scare me, so stop fucking insulting me by trying. *Again.* You don't want me to shoot my father, fine. I won't, but let's not pretend that's what this temper tantrum is about." I shoved him back, making him let go of me. "You're falling in love with me, and you're pissing your pants because for once in your life, you don't feel in control."

He stared at me, long and hard, and as I could've predicted, he turned and walked out.

The door slammed shut behind him, causing me to jump.

Fine.

I started to turn, but there was nowhere I could go. Instead, I picked up a glass and threw it against the wall.

Fuck him!

But as it shattered and fell beside the other, it did nothing to make me feel better. If anything, I had a sudden compulsion to glue both glasses back together.

CHAPTER FIFTY-ONE

Kai hadn't been back since he'd stalked out, but exactly eight hours later, Brooke arrived. Didn't take a genius to figure out he'd called in a replacement. Jonah had come too. He gave me a quick assessment and declared it'd be my last one. I was healthy once again.

Brooke and I spent the first hour catching up. She told me how she'd called the guards from the woods, and they'd found her and had her checked by a local doctor. Brooke said the doctor had been "gorgeous beyond words." Though it was only a strained ankle, it was still painful and "so worth it." Her words. Not mine.

Afterward, she said they'd grilled her about my whereabouts for a few minutes, and that was it.

She shook her head. "I swear, they broke speed limits getting me to you. What happened?"

There was a sour taste in my mouth, but I only shrugged. "I'd rather just get drunk than talk about it."

And she didn't push. Jonah either.

As we opened the first bottle of wine, Brooke said Tanner had been sent north again. As we finished the second bottle, she went on to say that since she was here, she wanted to sneak around Kai's properties. She was convinced he still had Levi somewhere and was "bound and determined" to save the love of her life.

I frowned. "Not to second-guess you, but you're awfully flirtatious with Eric and a certain doctor."

"Doctor?" She glanced at Jonah, who was working on his computer next to us.

He didn't look at her. "She's talking about Mr. Gorgeous Local Doc you were raving about earlier."

"Oh!" She laughed, slapping her hand on the table. "That's funny. No, no. Levi is the love of my life. I'm just flirty. That's all." She glanced over her shoulder, but there were no guards on our floor.

I had no doubt they were standing outside the door.

"I like flirting with Eric. He messes up if I really push him. How do you think I get half the information I do?"

Jonah sighed, closing his computer. He pushed his glasses up his nose. "Brooke likes to act as if she's being held hostage by our brother, but that's not the case. We're Bennetts. There's a responsibility that comes with our family surname. All of us hate it, but if we have to step up and bear it, we will. Brooke's constant flirting is her rebelling against those responsibilities."

Brooke glared at her glass of wine.

"I know." I nodded. "Kai told me about the council."

Both of their eyes widened.

"He did?" Brooke asked.

Jonah frowned. "Why would he tell you that?"

I shrugged. "I don't know, but he did. Is that bad?"

They shared a look.

Brooke lifted a shoulder. "I guess, I mean, I hope not. I'm sure it's fine."

But she seemed to be reassuring her brother more than me. Her dark eyes fixed on me, almost accusing. "Aren't you just sleeping with Kai? I mean..." She leaned forward, pushing her wine aside and dropping her elbows on the table. "Kai doesn't spill the beans about anything when it comes to our family. At all. Even to us. We only know half the shit because we're Bennetts. We have to know. You know?"

I nodded. "Mmm-hmmm." A closed smile. "We're just... having fun together."

Jonah snorted, sounding like his sister for the first time ever.

As if reading my mind, Brooke flashed him a smile. "Ha! What was that?!"

Jonah reddened before gathering his computer and making up some excuse to leave us for the night. After sharing another bottle of wine, Brooke took the bed, and I took the couch. Jonah went somewhere else. I didn't know where.

• • •

In the morning I woke to Kai frowning over me. "Why are you on the couch?"

I yawned and pointed. "Because yooooour sistah clai-ahed the bed."

I finished my yawn, remembered why this was even an issue, and glared at him. "Why do you care? You left."

And I might've been a bit hungover. There was a definite pounding just behind my forehead.

He ground his teeth together, glaring toward the bed while he answered me, "I had work to do. Don't take it personally."

I rolled to my feet, then whoosh. Head rush. I sat back down and waited for it to pass. "You took off at an opportune time, you know."

He was heading to the kitchen, but shot me an annoyed look over his shoulder. "If I'd stayed, we just would've been in bed all day and night. You know it. I couldn't risk that."

Maybe. But the words I'd said to him were still hanging there, uncomfortably.

Brooke sat up in bed. "Hey, big brother." She smiled wide, scratching her head, messing her hair further. "Man, wine sleep is the best sleep. I only need a few hours, but those hours are efficient, you know? It's like." She snapped her fingers. "Get to sleep. Sleep. Sleep. And bam, wake up. And here we are." She held her arms out toward Kai, whose back was to her. "Big badass brother is here to order us all around some more."

She gazed around, frowning. "Where's Jonah?"

Kai answered, his back still turned to her, "He's at a hotel."

"A hotel?! Can I go there too?"

"No." He finished getting the coffee ready and hit the button, before sending his sister that same annoyed look. "I wanted to give you a chance at saving the love of your life. He's in Milwaukee, you know."

She gasped, scrambling to her knees over the blankets. "Really? You'll let me see him?"

"I said save him, not see him." He raised an eyebrow, mocking her. "Isn't that your mission in life? Save the traitor to both our families?"

Her head moved back and her mouth closed. "Why are you being mean?"

"Being mean?" His eyes grew chilled. "How am I being mean? Maybe I'm annoyed that you keep professing your love to a guy who was turning evidence on his family."

Her cheeks grew red. "They're barely illegal," she mumbled.

"Doesn't matter," he countered. "That makes it worse. Have you asked yourself why he was doing that? He's not in line for any power in the Barnes family. He's not affected by anything they do. He's far removed, and yet he weaseled his way in just to get dirt on them. Why don't you ask yourself that question: why would he do that?"

"Stop it, Kai." She picked at her shirt.

"Brooke," he said firmly.

And as if feeling the same beckoning I did when he spoke, she raised her eyes. They were filled with pain now.

"I can only think of two reasons why he'd go out of his way to do what he did. Either he's hoping to open up some positions where he can step in and take over or he's being blackmailed. Which do you think is the realistic answer?"

She looked down. Her bottom lip trembled. "You're being mean."

"Well, I'm also pissed off that you convinced Riley she needed to run from me to come down here." His jaw clenched again. "You know that's not the truth."

She looked up at him, eyes blazing. "It's not so clear cut, and you know it. You're not letting me see Levi—"

"Because he's turning evidence against his family, and I don't want you to get pulled into that! What do you think they would do? It's really easy for his deal to go from just his family to being about ours too. Turn in the mafia princess—or better yet, give us dirt on her so we can blackmail her. You were doing something stupid, and you know it."

"I never would've. You have to know that."

He scoffed. "And I never thought you'd defy your family for a *rat* either. How can you not look at him and see what he's doing to his family?"

It was like the bad mood from yesterday had spread so he could torment his sister, but I had to admit he was asking good questions. Hard questions, but ones that needed answering. I also began to realize why he was pushing Brooke.

Because she didn't want to face it.

She had the wool over her eyes—she'd put it there herself—and she was fine with that.

Even I knew how dangerous that was.

"Because she's in love with him," I offered.

"Riley, don't—" He lowered his voice, though.

"Love is blind. It's a cliché for a reason. She doesn't want to see what he's doing." I turned toward the bed. "But Brooke, you have to answer him. You have to hear what he's saying."

Her eyes went to mine, hurt. "Don't team up with him."

I rose from the couch. "But if these things are true, don't you want to know who it is you're loving? If he's like this now, what could he do to you?" I met Kai's gaze for a moment. "You love him. What then? You get married? You bring him into the family? You run the risk of him turning on you too?"

I hated what I was saying. It was hurting Brooke, but this wasn't about Levi himself. She had to see that. It was his betrayal. Once a cheater, always a cheater. It could just as easily be once a betrayer, always a betrayer.

"Kai's trying to protect you from yourself, just so you know. You should appreciate having that in a brother." I turned and locked eyes with him. "I would."

An emotion flickered in his depths before he pressed his lips together.

Brooke made a gurgling sound. "God, Riley. You're sleeping with him; that doesn't mean you should take his side. I'm your friend."

A friend who lied to me, but then again, Kai wanted to murder my father. And so did I.

"I'm on *your* side. Kai is too. But you're right." I turned back to look at her. "Maybe I'll go hang out with Jonah today."

I'd headed for the bathroom when Kai called after me. "If you leave, let the guards go with you."

I paused, turning to walk backward.

It was a different feeling, this freedom with a leash, but I understood. I'd just been advocating a form of this to Brooke, so I nodded. Kai and I needed to talk, but right now, I felt like heading out.

With an entourage.

So that's how Jonah and I came to be sitting in the back of an SUV, heading toward the Lakeshore Wharf.

"Where are we going?" he asked.

"The Wharf. It's been so long since I've been there. I want to see what's all still around."

He tugged at his shirt collar, watching the businesses go by as we whipped down the back streets. "We don't really do touristy stuff. This is weird."

"Come on." I patted his leg, looking out my window. This had been my home once upon a time. It felt good seeing it again. I'd missed it. "Think of it this way, Kai was laying into Brooke about why she loves Levi. I'm getting you out of an uncomfortable family drama."

"Well..." He sat back. "When you put it that way, you're completely wasting your time."

"What do you mean?"

He raised his eyebrows. "Brooke and Kai don't talk, really at all. Kai barely talks to anyone. If he does, it's just to bark orders. And we realize he's the head of our family. There's a shared respect we all feel for him and what he's done for us, but you need to understand, there's no confrontation with Kai. He tells you how it is, and you can either accept it or not."

"And if you don't?"

"Then he'll bring it up later." He rolled his head from side to side, moving back to watch out his window. "Mostly until his point is proven right."

Well, there was that.

After a few more turns, we pulled up to the front of the wharf.

Jonah made a sound. Everything was bustling with activity. "I can't even remember a time we did something so normal like this."

"Normal like being a tourist?" I couldn't hold back my grin.

Forget Kai for the day. Forget Brooke. Forget everything. A part of me wished it'd been a different brother beside me, but I was still happy to experience a little piece of my old home again.

Jonah's eyes clouded over. "You know we're not going to blend in."

I lifted a shoulder, tapping on the door, and the guard opened it from outside. When I'd learned to do that was beyond me. But it felt natural.

I got out and began noticing everyone noticing us, and that part didn't feel so natural, but falling in step as two guards started ahead of us *was* second nature now.

They did attempt to blend in with the crowd, but it was an awkward fit. If someone broke through their circle around us, one of them stepped forward and steered the person—or a child, one time—away.

Still, I wasn't going to let it stop us, or stop me.

We picked up some breakfast first, but we didn't sit down. Eat. Grab. Go. Let's keep it moving. The guards nabbed some food too. They tried to sneak their eating, but when one saw me watching him, he just smiled and finished up his breakfast sandwich. These guys moved almost as one being. They had their ways, and an hour later, after hitting some shops and the Ferris wheel, I saw more guards coming and switching out. So that was how they did it.

One ride on the Ferris wheel wasn't enough, not for me. For Jonah, yes. But he was trying to be a polite companion after I caught him wincing as I steered him toward the wave swinger. I heard a mumbled "Oh, God," but he climbed on next to me and rode like a trooper.

I took pity on him after that.

We did the carousel next, though I selected one of the benches in the middle.

"Thank God." He sighed.

I laughed, tipping my head back.

He smiled. "Sorry. This is just not what we do."

"That's what you said." I shifted slightly to face him. "It's not what I do either, to tell you the truth."

"Yeah. I can see that." He eyed me. "Is it weird for you? To go from a life where you were a professional Hider to this?" He waved to the guards around us, one going up and down on a pink tiger.

I bit back a laugh. "Yes. But right now, I'm only focused on the next step."

He nodded, not asking what that was, and I was grateful because I didn't want to lie to him.

"Can I ask you a question?"

His eyebrows rose. "Sure."

"Do you have a girlfriend?"

His eyebrows went higher.

"I'm not asking for me." My grin was easy. "I'm just wondering how that part of your life fits with everything else."

"Oh." He settled back against our bench, mulling it over. "It doesn't. I mean, there are questions, but we learn to lie. Every Bennett is born an amazing liar. We've had to become that just to function sometimes. As far as a girlfriend..." He paused, his cheeks becoming pink.

I sat up. I'd thought I was fishing in an empty barrel here.

"There is a girl."

"A girl?"

"She's another resident."

"Resident?"

"Ah." He laughed shortly. "A doctor. She's in my year. We work at the same hospital."

"How do you do that, by the way? What with the constantly leaving for family things."

He rubbed at his eyebrow. "To be honest, Kai rarely calls on me. This whole thing with Brooke threw all of us for a loop. We were scrambling. Then he brought you in, and I knew what Brooke had done wasn't the normal little tirade she sometimes throws. It was more serious."

"You didn't answer the first question, though."

"Oh. Yes. Uh, I'm in trouble, to be honest." He bobbed his head forward in an easy, smooth motion. "But having my last name as Bennett helps. Kai will just step in, grease some wheels, and I should be fine."

Why wasn't I surprised? "That's how it's done? He bribes your way through medical school?"

He frowned. "Yeah. It's part of our world. If I want to have some semblance of a normal life, I have to accept that." His frown deepened. "I'm just grateful to have this time to become a doctor. This never would've happened if my father were still alive."

"What do you mean?"

"He sent Brooke away. He killed Cord. He would've killed Kai too. Who knows what he would've let Tanner and me do, or get away with. He didn't even let me live with the family."

"What?" My heart twisted.

"I was sent to live with an aunt. He didn't want me around the rest of them. I got to see them on holidays or if Cord or Kai insisted they visit me."

The pain in my chest doubled.

He shrugged and swallowed tightly. "It is what it is. I look different. He treated me differently."

"I'm sorry."

He coughed, shifting in his seat. "Kai changed everything. He brought Brooke and me back...but yeah, to answer your initial question, we compartmentalize." He coughed again, blinking rapidly. He flicked a hand to the corner of his eye. "Brooke falls in love every two months. Tanner doesn't. I don't know what he does. He rarely talks about women. And I..." He quieted, flashing me an uneasy smile.

I grinned back. "You have a girlfriend."

"That I lie to every day." His laugh was uneven, forced. "But that's how it is. We lose our footing with the council, and we'll all be wiped out."

"What?!"

"You didn't know? I thought Kai would've explained..." He trailed off again, frowning. "Sorry. I thought you knew."

"No," I gasped. "What do you mean you'll be wiped out?"

"Um..." He hesitated.

"Tell me, Jonah."

"We're only at the top because they fear us. They fear Kai. If someone moves against us, they'll have to kill us. All of us. It's literally all for one, one for all with us."

My head swam. I had no idea.

No wonder Kai was so concerned about who Brooke fell in love with.

"Thank you for telling me. I didn't know."

"About that..." He bit his bottom lip. "Can you not tell Kai you found out from me?"

I barked out a laugh, a little louder than I meant. "Yes. Of course. Yes."

And then, because we hadn't covered it, I asked, "What about Kai and his love life?"

The ride was coming to an end. Jonah reached for the top of the bench in front of us. "Kai has women in every city for his needs." Then he stood and glanced at me. "I mean, that was before you. I think?" His grin turned lopsided, and he hopped off like his life depended on it.

I sat rooted to that bench.

Kai had a woman in every city? But of course. I cursed myself. How stupid was I? To think I was special? I'd been brought in because of his sister's actions, not his.

It hadn't been his choice. Though maybe that didn't matter.

I stood on wooden legs and moved to where Jonah was waiting for me. The guards moved in behind me, and we were tourists for the rest of the day. But my spirit wasn't in it anymore. The thought of Kai's other women plagued me, sitting heavy on my shoulders. I only did one silly face in the photo booth.

I really threw myself into the movie at the theatre. And by throwing myself, I mean I sat in the darkness and pretended I was into it. Silently. Soullessly. Just imagining all those women at Kai's beck and call.

Of course he had them.

He was powerful and gorgeous.

I was foolish not to have thought about that earlier.

It was dark when we emerged, and if someone had asked me what movie we saw, I would've had no idea. A guy was in it. That's all I remembered.

"Where to now?" Jonah asked.

We had switched places at some point after the carousel. Jonah had begun to enjoy himself, and I was the one not really here. I could hear his reluctance to go home. Hell, I didn't want to go there either.

I moved behind him. "I think there's a beer garden here."

He brightened. "That's a great idea. We should call Brooke and Kai."

CHAPTER FIFTY-TWO

Brooke burst on the scene like a four-year-old colt getting her first run through the field. She zipped in, ignoring the guards in front of her, her arms swinging and her braids flying. Almost in sync. Spotting us in the back, she stopped and did a hop-skip-jump before twirling around and landing on the seat across from me.

"Hi, guys," she said in a rush, smiling from ear to ear.

Dressed in leather pants, a silky, shiny skin-tight tank top and a faux fur vest, she had glammed up for the night. Her hoop earrings swinging with her braids, she was embracing her freedom.

"Finally, finally, some booze and boys." She clapped to herself, doing a little shuffle in her seat. "I'm free!"

Jonah and I had picked the back table for a reason. It afforded a modicum of privacy, and there was a walkway beneath us, so if we had to do an emergency getaway, we could go out that way. Plus, just as we figured, the guards were already spreading out to surround us on both fronts.

The place was full, and all eyes were on us.

They'd been watching us since we entered. Two of the guards had taken position at the bar. One was trying to lean against a post, pretending to be on his phone the whole time, but people noticed. Another guard had claimed an entire table behind us. When the staff tried to fill it, he walked off with them, and I saw the manager coming out seconds later.

That table remained empty the whole night. I could only imagine they'd paid them well for it.

The attention from the other customers followed Brooke, because who acted like that? Apparently Brooke did, and I now remembered a time we went to a mall and she decided to start dancing in the food court. I'd forgotten she had that side. She didn't care who was around. If she felt something, she did it. Tonight, she'd wanted to come in swinging, literally.

As she grabbed a menu, I knew who else was coming.

I felt him. A little tingle on the back of my neck.

He walked in at a more sedate pace, with no dance moves, but it wouldn't have mattered how slow or fast he came. Power and authority rolled off of him in waves. His aura filled the entire beer garden, and even the staff paused to watch him walk past.

I heard someone whisper to their friend, "Is he famous?"

"Sssshhhh," was the response.

The closer he got, the more evident it became that guards were following him. More whispers started. Someone pulled out a phone, but the guard closest to her moved to block her. He said something, and the phone disappeared. I had no clue how he managed that, but I tried to fixate on it, focus on that woman whose eyes were suddenly much bigger than they'd been mere seconds ago, because while I was watching her, I wasn't watching him.

Closer. Closer.

The tingles rose in power, zapping me. But I was calm.

When I looked up, he was staring right at me, a mocking glint in his eyes. He smoothed a hand down the front of his shirt, as if stroking a tie that wasn't there, before he folded into the chair beside me. He moved the chair over as he sat, and his thigh pressed against mine for a moment before he settled in his seat.

"What?" I asked.

He didn't answer, shaking his head before turning to face the manager as she approached.

"Mr. Bennett." She folded her hands in front of her, her head dipping as if she were going to bow, but decided at the last second just to lower her head in a brief nod. She cleared her throat, her neck becoming red. "It's a pleasure to have you here tonight."

Oh, yes. That guard had really schmoozed her.

She reached up, tucking a strand of her hair behind her ear.

She was a plain-looking woman, and she wore the same uniform as her staff: a white button-up shirt over black dress slacks. The only thing setting her apart was the manager tag on her blouse and the fact that she was the one greeting us.

Kai spoke to her as Brooke leaned over the table, talking over them.

"All I have to say is if there's a chance we can get this one—" She pointed at Kai. "—to a nightclub, I will have died and gone to heaven."

Kai shot her a look, but continued speaking to the manager. She had stepped closer, bending her head, and oh—what a coincidence—the top three buttons of her blouse were open. I was fairly certain only one had been opened when the first guard bought the table behind us.

Shifting in his seat, Kai reached over to touch my side, but he continued as if he wasn't aware of the touch. He knew. His fingers pressed into my side before drifting to the top of my leg. He so knew. I caught the faint grin teasing his mouth. He was enjoying this too.

He must have seen me eyeing the manager like a starved hawk seeing a rival falcon on the next perch. And why I was using animal metaphors was beyond me. I needed to get out. Well, I needed to get out more than I had today.

Maybe a nightclub visit was in order...

But no. I had plans.

There was a reason I'd asked to come here, had asked to stay here. I just hadn't entirely figured out my plan. But glancing at a nearby clock, I saw I still had time.

"Thank you," the manager finished, nodding before she left.

Kai leaned back, putting an arm over the back of my chair.

I stiffened.

Brooke and Jonah noted the movement, but Brooke didn't stop talking.

I tried to tune in. She was asking for Jonah's recommendation on the first shot for the night when Kai touched my shoulder, pulling me back into his side. He moved his head as if he were looking past me, his lips right next to my ear.

"You abandoned me earlier," he said, his breath tickling me. "I could've used your backup."

I turned my head just slightly so our eyes could meet. "You were handling it just fine. Besides, you left me in the lurch earlier than that."

"I had work to do."

He eyed me, daring me to bring up my parting words from our argument.

A flush worked its way up my back, my neck, and he felt it, his hand moving to the back of my neck. His thumb began rubbing in circles, which caused another tickling sensation to vibrate over my skin.

"Is your work done?"

Now he smirked. "You tell me." He looked meaningfully over his shoulder.

I followed his gaze and gulped.

He saw the clock too.

He knew. Of course he knew.

His thumb kept rubbing. The manager returned with three servers in tow. Each held a tray overhead. The manager set up a long table just off to the side. She spread a cloth over it, and one by one, the servers put the food and drinks on that table. They were setting up a buffet, complete with a bartender who had moved to a portable bar in the corner of our space.

Brooke squealed, heading to the bar right away. "Shot, please! Give me a sex on the beach." The bartender reached for an already opened bottle, and a guard stepped up. He'd merely looked at the bartender before the manager went over to have a word with her employee. Within a few moments, all the already opened bottles were pulled and sealed bottles took their places.

As this was happening, a guard came over and tasted some of every food on the buffet.

He was testing, and it hit me what was happening. They were making sure nothing had been tampered with.

I had fallen in love with a mob boss.

I'd forgotten for a moment.

A wave of doubt hit me, but just as quickly, it was gone. I'd gone down this path. I had tortured myself over what I was doing. I had decided.

I had chosen Kai.

Jonah said before it was all of them together—one for all. Sitting here, seeing how the people around us seemed mesmerized by Kai, I began to think about power shifts. Everything was balanced out. What would happen if Kai forced one of the illegal trades to grind to a halt in their country? What would replace it? I wasn't naive enough to think something wouldn't, or someone wouldn't. Everyone wanted to make a dollar, and bad fucking people could be ingenious.

That's why Kai kept Jonah close.

Jonah was good. Jonah was a genius, but so was Kai. The intelligence must've been passed on through their mother? No, Kai had said he thought the way his father had. Both his parents must've been highly intelligent.

"What's wrong?"

Kai pulled me from my thoughts, leaning forward in his chair.

Jonah had joined Brooke at the bar. He shook his head as she pushed a drink toward him. The guards had moved back. The servers were gone, the manager too. In our little bubble, we had a small bit of privacy.

"I know you don't have a hand in the drug business, but if you pushed to eradicate it, what would happen?"

He didn't blink or pause. He didn't even question why I was asking. "A new drug would happen. There's always something new coming down the pipeline. New guns. New drugs. New form of sex slaves. That's just the tip. There's gambling. Black market for organs, for bodies, for anything you want. Credit cards. ID theft."

"Do you control all of that?"

A beat. Two. Then, "I know enough about it."

I gave him a rueful grin. "That's all you're going to tell me?"

"Why are you asking?"

I pressed a hand to my chest, as if to keep it from exploding. "I thought I could help do something. Anything. But learning about it all, I'm left with this helpless feeling of how can anything be made better when the bad is always there?"

He held my gaze. The way he paused was significant before he reached over to cup the side of my face. His thumb ran over my lips, his eyes darting to them before rising to look tenderly into my eyes, taking my breath away.

"In the world I live in, it's hard to be good. But I will try. For you." He tipped his head down, his forehead resting on mine. "I'll do what I can. I promise."

I closed my eyes, his words filling me up inside.

He wiped away a tear on my cheek.

That meant more than I could put in words.

It meant the world to me.

It meant that I could stay.

CHAPTER FIFTY-THREE

B rooke was drunk, dancing alone beside the table.

Jonah was also drunk. He kept giggling, resting his head on his arm braced on the table, his shoulders shaking. He would stop, stare off, and repeat.

It was past midnight now. The beer garden had closed. I was sure Kai bought out the rest of it. Most of the staff had gone by now, but the manager remained. She approached to let us know she'd kept a lone chef on in case we wanted anything from the kitchen.

Brooke's hand shot up. "Ooh! Quesadillas! Please."

People still walked along the wharf, but most everything closed at midnight. I looked over at bright lights moving around at the end of the pier—some kind of event. We had watched couples walk past us in formal dresses and tuxedos. Glittering gowns. Pink. Black silk. Sequins. The rich and powerful. A few looked our direction with quizzical expressions, but none came over to investigate. Heads bent together. Hands came up to cover their gossiping mouths.

Maybe they'd been wondering, while attending their extravagant event, about who had been in the beer garden. There would be rumors that it was someone famous, a celebrity, or perhaps even a government official, because that's what they did. I remembered that from my time with my family.

There'd been whispers and rumors about my mother too.

The two girls approved to go shopping with me in the mall had proved that. They'd asked if it was true that my father caught her having a torrid love affair and she'd really died trying to run away with her lover.

It twisted me up, remembering, and it didn't help that I could've sworn one of those same girls had walked past us twenty minutes ago. Her hand had been tucked in the arm of a middle-aged man. Slender. Beautiful. And hungry eyes, because she'd been one of the ones to watch us for a bit.

"Did you see him?" Kai asked.

I whipped around, wandering farther down to the very edge of the beer garden. I wasn't even sure if I was still within its borders. I'd taken some stairs down to a sidewalk. I could still hear Brooke's laughter in the background, mixing with music and mingling with the beat coming from the event.

I sighed. "How long have you known?"

"That your father is supposed to be attending that event or that that's the real reason you asked Jonah to play tourist for the day?"

"Both?"

He moved to my side, but he didn't touch me.

For some reason, I appreciated that. He let me stand on my own, not overwhelming me.

"The second the guards told me where you were going." He slid his hand into his pocket, tipping his head back, still eying me. "It's public knowledge that he's supposed to be attending tonight." Kai smirked. "If he didn't show up, people would notice."

People would notice regardless—I realized what he was saying. I gaped at him. "You're going to take him tonight?"

But of course. That was why he'd come here. Not to spend time with us, his brother, his sister, but because of my father, because it was already in the plans.

It burned.

I looked away. "Jonah and Brooke have both told me how much you usually *aren't* around. Tonight meant the world to them."

"Hey." He cupped the back of my head and turned me toward him. "Look at me."

I turned, but I closed my eyes. I didn't want him to see how it hurt.

This was the same Kai. An agenda. Three, four, five steps ahead, and I'd thought... It didn't matter. I'd been stupid.

"Hey." A more insistent urge from him. "Look at me."

Fine. I did.

And my chest was held suspended.

His eyes damn near smoldered, a fierce expression in them I couldn't place.

"You bringing my family here, me coming and spending time with them, with you, has meant the world to *me*." He drew me toward him, and goddamn, I was going. I couldn't resist. He dropped his tone, his eyes dipping to my mouth. "This is not something that would've happened before you. I doubt it'll be something that happens after—after we leave here again. But never, ever think my family is not first. They're the reason I am who I am."

"Where would you have been if we weren't here tonight?"

"In a hotel. Fucking you."

I coughed. "Ah." Some of the burn eased. Or, well, it was washed away by a scalding pot of fire instead. A whole different type of burn took its place.

He rested his forehead to mine, his hand leaving my neck to trace my bottom lip. "I'm going to send my siblings back with some men. Stay with me. See this out."

He was inviting me into the darkness with him, but I was already there. With this one, I'd gotten there first.

I nodded, and he stepped back. He went to speak to one of his men, and after a moment, with a short nod, the guard went to do his bidding. Kai turned back toward me. He didn't stop. He moved past me, snagging my hand. He pulled me with him, his fingers twining with mine, and we were off.

His men were ahead, some on the opposite side of the wharf, and more trailed behind us, but for the first time, they completely blended in.

A thrill went through me.

Kai pulled me ahead, but still remained in the shadows. We weren't dressed for the event, though that didn't seem to matter. Just as we got to the event's main entrance, a roar went through the crowd and almost as one, they turned around to look where we'd come from.

Kai tugged me back, continuing to twist, maneuver through the crowd. I realized he was doing it on purpose. His head was down, his shoulders hunched forward. He had put on a somewhat meek air, so no one paid attention. That amazed me, given who he was, but it was working. For now.

Once we got to a better spot, almost at the very edge of the pier and tucked behind a small booth that was closed up for the night, Kai let me look back.

I did, and the world stopped.

Time stood still. Everything in me paused because walking down the middle of the pier, as if he were king of the fucking universe, was my father. On his arm, my cousin. It was an odd thing, seeing her. A smugness on her lips, her eyes gleaming and greedy as she sauntered beside him. She wore a gold, sequined gown, strapless, and her breasts were almost popping out.

It should've sickened me, seeing them together. She was my mother's niece. There was no blood relation between the two, but he was my father, and she was my look-alike. Except she wasn't. There was something in her that looked nothing like me.

And they looked like they belonged together.

She was bad, just as much as him. I didn't know why, what she'd done, but I could tell she belonged there. On his arm seemed the perfect place for her.

I must've made a sound because a couple in front of us turned around, and Kai pulled me farther back.

"Can you handle this?"

I whispered through gritted teeth, "I want to murder both of them."

A low chuckle was my reward. He smoothed a hand down my back, resting over my ass before moving around to the front of my hip. He moved my back to his chest, and I could feel his lips grazing the side of my throat. He pushed my shirt aside, nibbling on my shoulder as his hand began exploring. He ran it across to my stomach, his fingers slipping inside my pants, and I almost fell back, leaning nearly my whole weight on him. My head rested against his as he kissed me.

He moved us farther and farther back until no one could see us. We were separated from the crowd, and with a few movements, he untied the tent opening for the booth.

He pulled me in, tying one string back in place, and then he was on me.

"What are we doing?" I asked between kisses.

"Damned if I know." His hand moved inside my pants, and I had a second's warning before his finger was inside of me.

This was insane.

My father was outside, talking. He looked like he was about to put a show on for this crowd, and we were in here. Kai kissed down my throat, his other hand holding my ass as he pumped his hand in and out of me.

My knees buckled.

He pulled out, but only to turn me around. Moving his leg up between mine, he held me in place. His fingers moved back into me, but more gently this time, sensual. He pushed in, in, so far in, and his mouth began tasting my throat. He kissed and caressed me as he moved his fingers back out, going deliciously slowly.

I panted, my need mounting. My entire fucking body burned now. My head fell back to his shoulder and I moaned.

"Ssshhhhh." He turned his head, his mouth catching mine.

"Is someone in there?"

I almost groaned again. Goddamn. We were going to be caught.

But then, "No, ma'am. Please move along." A guard stood outside. Of course.

"But—"

"Move along, ma'am. Please."

Kai's hand swept up under my shirt, moving my bra aside and wrapping around my tit. His thumb rubbed over it. "We're protected," he breathed. His hand slid to the other tit, cupping me, scorching me. "You make me lose control. My God. I can't—I should be out there, watching your father, and instead, one touch from you and I can't—I have to have you." His fingers picked up their pace. In. Out. In. Out. I felt him almost all the way to my stomach, and I rode him, moving my hips over his hand.

I grasped his arm, holding him still, and I moved faster. Harder.

Until a rush exploded in me.

I came quietly, but it left me boneless, and I couldn't move. My entire body twitched from the after effects. I could barely raise my head.

A low moan slipped out, and Kai's arms tightened around me. He pressed a kiss to my mouth, then my jaw, my chin, my neck before he just held me.

I could feel his cock under my thighs.

I reached for him, but he tensed. "No." But he sounded reluctant. He moved me off of him, slowly. His hands lingered, running down my arms, and when I could stand, he stepped in behind to hug me. His lips found the curve between my neck and shoulder, and he wrapped his arms around me.

I knew neither of us wanted to go back out there.

I wanted to stay in this tent. It felt good in here. I wanted this Kai with me at all times—loving, caring, tender. The man who could make me lose my bearings and bring me so much pleasure I almost saw fucking stars, but out there was a different Kai. He would have to be cold, detached, ruthless.

A shiver went down my spine.

That was my Kai too, but he scared me.

He sighed, nuzzling my cheek before lifting his head. "We have to go. I have to go. We have some time. You can stay in here, if you want. For a few more minutes."

"When are you taking him?"

"Soon."

I didn't know how it was going to go down, and as Kai slipped out after squeezing my hand, everything in me yearned to pull him back in.

I yearned to keep him with me in this pocket of time, because when I left, there was no going back.

I'd come with the intention of hurting my father. I'd made my decision earlier. I was going to stick with it, but almost a lifetime could separate me from deciding that and now doing it. I was on the precipice. And if I failed, Kai would be there. Hell. Kai would do it anyway. He was half doing it for me; I knew that. And I wouldn't really have to participate, but I was here.

In my old life, you had a moral decision in times like this.

If you see what's going to happen and stand aside, you're just as guilty. To be innocent, you must step in, you must try to help stop it. I was not going to do that this time. So I was a part of it all.

I was guilty. It didn't matter if I pulled the trigger or not. His blood would be on me. But there was more going on. Here I was with Kai. If I went with this, I was choosing him.

But that decision had already been made too.

Hadn't it?

We still hadn't finished our argument. I'd said those words to him, calling him on loving me and not knowing how to handle it. His answer had been to leave.

He left. Then I left. Then he made me climax so fucking hard I couldn't stand afterward. So I still had some things to sort out.

Grabbing a chair, I sank down onto it.

That's when I heard him. My father's voice from outside.

He was laughing, boasting. It was funny how it hadn't changed, even since I was twelve. That sound still made the hairs on the back of my neck stand up. He made my stomach roll over in disgust just as he always had.

When I'd heard him bark orders in the house. When something made him furious at a meal—if there wasn't enough salt or he suddenly decided we needed ketchup even though he'd banned it, saying it was "beneath his palate." The way he'd sounded when he had colleagues over, how he spoke to my mother in a way that forced her to be nice, be polite, and not say a damn word. She'd better fucking smile or she wouldn't be able to walk the next day.

From his beating.

His laugh rolled over me, and I felt nausea moving up my throat. It was the same laugh he'd used when I'd heard him bring a woman to the house. He'd taken her to the basement, and I knew there were others. My mom knew too.

I'd been nine, but I knew what he was doing with her.

My mom.

I hadn't seen her in so long. It was three years ago that I saw her for the States' Thanksgiving Day. It was one holiday we both enjoyed, and that day was special to me. She had met someone a year after leaving my father. It'd seemed quick to me, because that's when I'd left too, but I had no place for any emotions other than happiness that we were both alive. Safe.

She had someone who loved her, protected her, and while he didn't know about her past, I also knew what else she was trying to tell me.

She was going to start over. I never told anyone, but that's why I became a Hider.

I agreed to the separation from her because I wanted her to start over. I didn't want my face to be a reminder of her past, of the torture he had put her through, and I found a new purpose in life.

I was better. I was alive. She was alive.

She'd had two more children, a boy and girl. I'd seen their pictures. Blade kept track of them for me. Both were in sports, getting top scores in their years. I was happy for them.

I was proud.

They were close to the age I'd been when I went to Hillcrest. Somehow, knowing I was about to face my father, that hit me hard. It sat with me, giving me a sense of life's brevity.

I'd been thirteen when I thought my mother died, fourteen when I found out she was alive, and still fourteen when I lost her again. All because of him.

And suddenly, here I was now, burning with renewed loathing.

CHAPTER FIFTY-FOUR

I stepped out of the tent, and a guard nodded for me to move a few steps behind a podium.

"You okay?" Kai was next to me in a heartbeat, his hand finding my elbow.

I looked over his face. He was tired. He was tense, but he was alert. I recognized the other look in his eyes. He was hunting. He was my father's predator, and I swear, a part of my heart swelled, though it shouldn't have.

I nodded, feeling everything from my chest down go numb. I no longer wanted to feel. "I'm good." I nodded again, firming my shoulders, raising my chin. "I'm ready."

He stared at me, a full five beats before his hand fell to mine. "Good." He moved to stand beside me, facing where my father stood.

He was talking to another couple, an older man and woman. My cousin was beside him, her arm around his waist, and his hand spread over her back. It slid down, cupping her ass, and remained there. She pressed closer to his side, touching his chest and tilting her head back for a laugh.

This was another world.

This would've been mine, if he'd let me live.

I would've been one of those girls in a sequined dress, arm candy for another man. Perhaps that wasn't always the case, but my father would've wished it. He would've wanted me to be with someone who could bring him more power, more money, just more, more, more. And if I hadn't, he would have gotten rid of me.

I fought back a full-body tremble.

Kai felt it. He glanced at me.

I ignored him, raising my head again.

He let it pass. He was biding his time. He would hunt his first prey, then target his second one: me. But that would be after.

As he turned back to my father, my thoughts wandered again.

I searched for a good memory of my father, but I had none.

That said something, didn't it?

Most dads, even if they're assholes, still leave some cherished memory with a child. But I had none. I only remembered when he would hurt my mother, when he would bark at her or me at dinner.

I remembered the effects of him.

I remembered how she would shake at the dining table, how she would spill soup from her spoon if she did something he didn't like.

I remembered how everyone was so tense when he was in the room, in the house. I remembered the maid crying, running from the room.

I remembered how he'd yelled at our butler. I remember how the chef had cooked six dishes one night, just in case he hated one of them, which he did.

I remembered all the bad.

I tried. I really did, but I couldn't remember the good.

There was no love in me for my father, and because of that, I ached. There should've been one thing I loved about him. There was nothing.

I was cold as I stood on Kai's arm, watching the man who'd helped bring me into this world.

I felt no warmth for him. Not even a flicker.

• • •

We waited for two hours.

Most everyone was drunk, laughing, giggling, tripping over their dresses. The men tried to help hold up their dates, but they were just as drunk. They would topple forward, grabbing onto each other and laughing. There was so much laughing.

I didn't feel like laughing.

I didn't feel anything.

I moved when Kai did, and I remained silent, biding my time.

"I thought you said soon before."

Kai's arm tightened around my waist. He turned his head, his mouth nuzzling just beneath my ear. "I did. I was told he was going to leave after his speech."

His speech.

I suppressed a shudder. I'd been in the booth, remembering my mother when he was speaking, and I was glad. I didn't think I could take both, not at the same time.

"That was two hours ago."

"I know." His hand found mine, and he squeezed. "Patience. That's all I can say."

For the first hour, my father had moved through the crowd, talking, laughing with people. I worried he would find us, but Kai was always moving us out of his line of sight. He never saw us. Our guards raised some interest, but not much, and I'd been surprised at that.

One was on the dance floor now. Another two were laughing loudly, encouraging the patrons to drink by the bar. A few were lounging at tables, talking with people as if they were long-lost friends. And there were still more. Two were behind us, standing near the water as if wishing they could be fishing. The nearest ones were the most at attention, keeping an alert eye on their boss. Or their leader.

Kai was more their leader than their boss.

I'd realized that too, watching them and him for the past two hours.

He had been a leader since the beginning.

He waded into the fray. He didn't stand back, letting them guard him. He was right with them, on the forefront of whatever was happening.

I remembered how he'd been the one to shoot the man on the plane. How he'd been the one to shoot the woman at the warehouse. Him. Not his men. In his way, he protected them as much as they protected him.

That was another reason anyone who went against him would lose.

He didn't command his men's loyalty. He'd earned it. I saw it in Eric. He wasn't a guard. He was more. He was from another family in the council, and it'd been Kai he wanted to learn from. I knew he would use Eric's allegiance someday. Kai did nothing without reason, without carefully analyzed thought.

Kai smoothed his hand up my side, his finger brushing against my breast. He smiled. "You okay?"

Was I? I thought about my father, why we were there, and the memories that had surfaced about my mother.

I moved my head up and down. "More than okay."

Kai's eyes grew hooded, and he held his thumb to the side of my mouth. He pressed there, feeling my lips, his thumb slipping past them for a moment, just an instant before he smiled.

"Good. Because it's showtime."

• • •

I'd like to say the plan was elaborate and *Ocean's Eleven* style, but it wasn't. It was very simple.

The event finally wound down to the point that only a few people remained. My father was one of them. My cousin was either drunk or beyond exhausted, and she stumbled alongside my father as Kai drew me along the wharf, out to the edge. We trailed them, but neither seemed to notice, and for once, I didn't see any of our guards around. Though that didn't mean they weren't there.

Once we got to the end of the wharf, my father stopped, my cousin next to him. He was focused on his phone and looking down the street.

He was waiting for a car.

Kai drew us up behind them, thirty feet separating us, and he watched.

An SUV turned in, idling in front of them. My father and cousin got in.

The SUV pulled out, and another SUV replaced it, but this time, Kai and I were running. I got in the back. Kai got in the front. "Go when ready," he said into his phone.

Two more SUVs sped past us, moving to intercept my father's SUV until it veered and the driver hit the brake. As it stopped, the guards ran from the other SUVs, surrounding the one my father and cousin were in. They pulled the doors open, pointed guns in their faces, and yanked them out. My cousin was thrown to the sidewalk. The man in the passenger seat of my father's SUV raised a gun and hit the driver in the head with it. The horn sounded until his body was tugged to the side, and that was all they stuck around for.

They forced my father into one of our SUVs, the guards slammed their doors, and off they went.

All over in thirty seconds. Kai's men worked as a well-oiled machine. My father never stood a chance.

I turned just as we shot forward and caught a glimpse of my cousin, her eyes wide in shock.

She was pale, her mouth hanging open before moving into a cry.

But those eyes. I wouldn't ever un-see them.

I recognized the look. It was the same I'd had when I learned my mother was dead. Cousin Tawnia had been traumatized. This moment, this memory would be forever burned on her consciousness. She would never be the same.

I didn't want to think that or feel it, but as I turned back in my seat and faced forward, I knew it was true.

And I had been part of doing that. Whether it was for good or for ill, it just was.

CHAPTER
FIFTY-FIVE

There's this sense in the air when something important is about to happen.

It's a feeling around you, but inside you too. Like something doesn't make sense, like something is off, like impending doom is an invisible freight train and you can't get out of its way. You're on the tracks. You can hear it. You can feel it. You can even smell it, but you can't see it.

You just know it's coming for you.

Riding in that SUV, hurtling down the streets of Milwaukee in a caravan of two other SUVs, I felt that feeling.

I looked away from the window and watched Kai in the front passenger seat. His jaw was strong, his shoulders relaxed. He didn't seem rigid, or tense, or anything other than calm.

Serene.

That's the word I was looking for, but that way of describing what was about to happen seemed wrong too. I didn't know what Kai had planned, but I knew he did have a plan. He always did, and I knew the end result would be my father's death. Somehow.

My stomach should've clenched at that.

I should've felt ready to have a nervous breakdown. But I didn't. I only had a feeling of something dead in the air, and how fucking helpful was that?

We drove north to the same warehouse I'd slept at earlier.

All three SUVs sped into the parking lot, into the warehouse, and hit their brakes. The guards emerged all at the same time.

There was a lot of yelling.

A van pulled in behind us, then a second van.

Guards dispersed, four going to each van. They opened the back doors. More shouting. Commands in the air.

They brought a man out with his hands tied behind his back and a bag over his head. He wore black clothing, same as the guards—a black suit, but athletic shoes to run in. His clothing was wrinkled and torn, and he smelled as if he hadn't changed clothes or showered in days.

Out of the second van came a guy wearing dirtied and ripped jeans, and a T-shirt whose ends stuck out underneath a ripped sweatshirt. Two halves of the sleeve dangled off one arm, which was a mess of bruises and redness. Dried blood. A rash. Other scars.

As the guards hurried him past me, I saw that the scars were rope burns.

His arms were tied in front of him, and he had a bag over his head too.

My dead feeling only intensified.

Prisoner one was taken to an office on our right. The second was taken to a side office.

Then they pulled my father out, his hands tied with rope and a bag over his head too. A guard replaced the rope around his wrists with a zip tie before gripping his arm and leading him into the office on the right.

Kai stood outside my door, waiting for me. Watching me.

"Where are Brooke and Jonah?" I asked.

"On their way back to Vancouver."

I had a fleeting thought that maybe it was for the best. They'd both been drunk. They could sleep most of the way. Then that thought left and the emptiness returned.

Finally I asked, "Why am I here?"

Kai didn't need me for this. Maybe for my father, because I'd asked, but not the other two. And who were the other two? How long had he been planning this? How long had he had them?

He frowned before stepping closer. "Do you not want to be here?"

Did I?

He waited.

I looked down. I'd told him I did. Gone to huge lengths to make that statement, actually. I'd told him I wanted to be a part of this because of my father, that I wanted to destroy him, but I wavered now.

Kai stepped closer, his hand sliding around my neck and his fingers threading into my hair. He lowered his forehead to mine. "You don't have to be here. You really don't."

He cupped the side of my face, and I leaned down, savoring his touch and closing my eyes a moment.

When I opened them again, he was watching me. Like always.

Waiting. Like always.

Being there. Like always.

I was so goddamn torn inside.

"I'm scared to see what you're going to do," I whispered.

That was the truth, in the most real way I could put it.

"Why?" He cocked his head to the side.

My hand rested over his. Why? I'd asked myself that question, over and over again.

The truth. Stick to the truth.

My hand shook over his. "Because I'm scared of what it'll do to me."

I gripped his hand, pressing it to my chest. "I'm not an idiot. I know you're more than likely going to kill all three of those men, and while I have chosen to stand at your side, to stay at your side, I am twisted about the right thing for me to do." I took a breath. The words came faster than I could process them now. "The Hider in me should try to stop you. But as the child of one of those men, I want to stay to see vengeance play out. The woman in me is scared. I'm just scared."

Kai wrapped his arms around me, and just like that, I felt certainty and strength swirl up inside of me. But it wasn't mine. It was his. He was giving it to me, or I was absorbing it from him. Either way, I knew I was one of Kai's now, just as he'd said.

I was one of Kai's—his hostage, his lover, his friend, his confidant, his enemy.

I was his, but he was mine too.

Or was he? Could Kai actually belong to someone?

As fast as that possessive need rose up in me, it vanished.

"What do you need from me?" he asked.

His honesty was brutal. And melting me.

"I need to know what I am to you. I am changing the framework of who I am because of you, so I need to know it's worth it." I paused a beat. "I love you, even though I shouldn't. I do."

His eyes darkened. His lips parted. And he was kissing me.

It was a possessive claim. Hot. Commanding. His tongue swept to meet mine, and I moaned into his mouth, pushing up on my toes and wrapping my arms around his neck.

I don't know when I'd fallen for him, but I had, and I couldn't change it.

I could never go back to the life I led before—to either of the two lives I'd led before.

He pulled back, his lips resting over mine. "Wait for me. I will say what you need to hear, but not now. Not here. Wait. Can you do that?"

"I don't have much choice." My grin was rueful.

The corner of his mouth tugged up, and he kissed me again, then pressed a kiss to my forehead. He breathed against there for a moment. "Just wait. Please."

Just wait.

Those were my instructions.

He gave me a third kiss, then led me to the first office. Once inside, he put me in a dark corner, up against the wall. A man sat in a lone chair in the middle of the room, a single light trained on him. The rest of the room was dark.

I knew I wasn't the only one standing in the shadows.

Kai walked forward. He made no sound. He was like a ghost again.

He sighed. The sound was so loud in that room, and it was everyone's cue.

We were about to begin.

He turned to a wall and spoke, "Bring them up."

It took a second, but a videoconference image came up and filled the entire wall. In it was a table, in a room similar to ours, and around the table sat eight individuals—three women and five men, all middle-aged or older.

A woman sat at the end, her gray hair swept up into a bun at the top of her head. She wore a black turtleneck sweater, black-framed glasses, and minimal makeup. She was the image of classy, elegant, and wealthy.

She was in charge of the gathering.

She folded her hands on the table and leaned toward a microphone in front of her. "Okay, Kai. We're all assembled. What is it that you want us to know?"

Kai glanced once in my direction before walking forward and folding his hands in front of him. The next two words had me swallowing because it wasn't what I was expecting; they weren't who I was expecting.

"Welcome, Council," he said.

CHAPTER FIFTY-SIX

The elegant woman leaned forward, folding her hands over each other, and regarded us. "You sent word two days ago to assemble. We're here at this ungodly hour, and when we get done, I still have to travel home. I'll be missing my granddaughter's birthday party, so let's hurry this along. Who do you have behind you?"

Kai pulled the bag off the guy.

His face was badly bruised, and swollen on one entire side. His lip had been busted and dried blood still caked on top. One eye barely opened.

I shifted farther back against the wall, because I recognized that eye.

"This is the security guard who approached a guest of mine on behalf of Bruce Bello." Kai's eyes narrowed as he waited for their reaction.

A few of the council members bent together, starting to talk.

"Okay. Okay!" The woman slapped her hand on the table, shooting the members a glare. "We're here to listen to the Bennett family. Stop talking." She regarded Kai again. "We're all aware of Bruce Bello and that you have his daughter in your care. She's the guest this man approached?"

"Yes." Kai turned to the man. "You've been my guard for four years. Have you always been working for Bruce Bello?"

The man coughed, jerking forward.

We waited until he was done.

He lifted his hand to wipe his mouth. There was blood on it. He took a second to compose himself. "No. I was a faithful and loyal employee until I received a coded email from Bello just a few weeks ago."

"And this email said?"

God. Kai was emotionless. His demeanor said each and every question he asked would be answered. This man had been tortured into submission.

"He had a picture of my daughter in a man's arms. He was holding a knife to her throat. The email said I was to do what he wanted or he would kill my little girl."

"And what were his instructions?"

"I was to kill his daughter to save mine."

Kai lifted his eyes to mine at that very moment. No reaction. No shock. No remorse. No sympathy. He knew all this already.

He knew, and he hadn't told me, but then again, why was I surprised? This was something my father would do.

"Any other instructions?" Still so cold, Kai turned away.

"Yeah." The side of his mouth he could still use tipped upward in an ugly grin. "I was supposed to kill you, or as much of your family as possible. Bello said he would pay me good if I did."

Kai folded his head down. "Thank you."

The spokeswoman cleared her throat, drawing everyone's attention. "And his daughter, Kai? I assume you've helped resolve that."

"I have. She is safe." He turned to the ex-guard/my father's would-be hitman. "Your wife and daughter will be cared for. I give you my word."

It took a second.

Why would he speak that way? Why wouldn't he just say they were safe and being cared for, not that they would be cared for? Why did the man's head jerk back, his eyes glistening with tears as he nodded.

"Thank you," he said hoarsely.

Kai turned back to the council.

"Sir?"

Two men entered our room. Kai had been given a signal without anyone knowing, but it wasn't them who spoke. It was the ex-guard.

He saw the men coming and leaned forward. "Sir, if I can say something?"

Kai faltered.

I held my breath.

I expected Kai to listen to him without emotion, being his ruthless, cutthroat self. He was the head of the Bennett mafia and no one else in this moment, but he didn't turn to his past employee right away.

He looked to me first, and pain flashed in his eyes. It was there, then gone.

He grew resolved again, his face tightening up. Only then did he look back at the man.

A tear slipped down the man's face. "I know what will happen to me. I betrayed you, and there's a code. I broke that. For that, I apologize. I truly am sorry I didn't come to you when I received that email. I just—" He looked away. "I wanted you to know that, and I know you'll care for my family. Thank you."

Death.

That was the penalty.

I shrank back against the wall. Kai was going to have this man executed because he'd tried to kill me.

As if sensing my turmoil, Kai regarded me again. His eyes were piercing, blazing with an unnamed message, and I gasped silently.

He held a hand up for the men, then brought it down.

The two men each took an arm, and they walked the disgraced guard out of here. Kai watched me as I watched him. There was no fight in the man anymore. He went willingly. He was already dead, and he knew it.

Kai wanted me to see this, all of this. There were two more to come. Why would he want me to see this? To scare me? To warn me? To ready me—

Bang!

I jumped, clamping a hand over my mouth at the gunshot.

Kai had come over and cupped the back of my head. I would've hit the wall, but he cushioned my jerk. My eyes were wide, staring into his, and I couldn't stop myself. A tear slipped down my cheek.

He bent forward. "Ssshhh. They can't see you. I don't want them to know you're here." His eyes closed. His forehead rested against my cheek, and his thumb rubbed the side of my jaw. "Trust me. Please." He lifted his head again. "There's a point to all of this. I promise."

My heart pounded, but I reached up and grasped the back of his head, pressing his mouth to mine in a hard kiss. "Go. Do what you need to."

His hand slid down my arm, and he pressed a softer kiss to my mouth before pulling away.

He returned to the front of the room, center stage for his council, before motioning to the door again.

It opened, and they dragged in my father.

My ribs were beginning to ache, but Kai said to trust him. I would do that, though it took all of my strength to remain in that room.

Kai whisked the bag off my father's head. He was struggling, trying to run, and grunting around the duct tape over his mouth. The guards forced him down into the chair. He kept bucking back, the chair scraping against the floor, and Kai waited. The council watched.

No one spoke a word.

Kai waited for his prisoner to be subdued. The council was merely waiting for the next point on the agenda. This was their business meeting. What PowerPoint presentations were to others, interrogating/torturing/executing a prisoner was to them. Only one had even protested the time of this meeting. There were looks of resignation on the others, as if a late-night/early-morning get-together was common for them.

This was so far from what I had once been, but I lifted my head toward Kai and knew I wasn't going anywhere.

We waited five more minutes as my father fought. Finally, two more guards came in and produced leather straps to wrap around him so he couldn't move an inch in that chair. They even secured his head. He could only move his feet, and all he did was loosen his shoes enough to kick them off.

Finally, after another ten minutes, he stopped. A sudden deep sigh left him, and if he could've hung his head in defeat, I had no doubt he would've.

The four guards stepped back, and Kai moved forward.

"This is Bruce Bello."

The spokeswoman snapped, "Yes. We know. Why are we being subjected to this? You are the head of this council. You do not need our approval for any of this. Just execute the men as you see fit. It's my granddaughter's birthday, Kai. A birthday. She wanted me to have tea with her and her ponies. As a grandmother, I will only get a few of these years before she grows up and replaces her love for me with her phone. Get to the point!"

Kai was unfazed. "There is a point, and I'll get to it when I get to it." He pointed at my father. "As you all know, this is Bruce Bello. He's been running a distribution line for one of our families."

"Yes. Yours."

"I cut ties with him. He's remained working with another of our members."

Now there was more of a reaction.

The spokeswoman's eyes sharpened, and she leaned forward. Her hands flattened on the table. Around the table, more of the council began talking to each other. Their voices were no longer just murmurs.

She lowered her head, her eyes locked on Kai. "What exactly are you saying here? Stop pussyfooting around. Come out with it if you're going to accuse one of our members of something."

Again, Kai was unfazed.

He turned to my father. "We've not had the time I needed to question you, or to insure your cooperation, so I'm going to tell you this now."

My father's eyes had been scanning the room frantically, but he stopped and stared at Kai. Some of the wildness lessened.

Kai stepped closer. "It is in your best interest to be forthcoming."

He leaned down, placing a hand on either side of the chair's back so he had my father trapped. He spoke softly so I could hear, but I didn't think the council behind him could.

"You will die at the end of this, but how is up to you. It can either be quick and as painless as possible, or it can be slow. I can make your death take weeks if I want to. It's your choice."

My father began scanning the room again, then closed his eyes. He moved his head up and down, the barest minimum of a motion because of his straps. It was enough.

Kai pulled off the tape over his mouth, all at once.

"Agh!" My father spat out blood. "Fucking hell, Bennett."

"You will cooperate?"

My dad glared at him, still spitting out pieces of tape and blood. "Yes. I'll fucking cooperate, but only if you tell me where my daughter is."

Kai went still. His eyes narrowed to slits. "Why? So you can hurt her further?"

"So you can finish this job for me."

I stiffened.

Kai tensed.

"That bitch of a wife of mine slept with my business associate, but I could never prove it. She was worthless, hateful. She was a waste of my years. That girl too. Both of them been fucking up my life."

He was still going, but I closed myself off.

I had known, and hearing it, hearing that he'd had no regard for us, this was nothing new. I'd always known.

"—and she was a fucking spoiled brat. We sent her away so I never split her head open on the floor. Couldn't have that stain on my tile, you know. That stuff was fucking expensive. Sturdy. I humped my maid there a few times, so I knew it could clean up, but damned if I wanted blood there. Fucking bitch. She and her mother. I wanted both of them gone. Couldn't stand either of them."

He was still talking, poison spilling from his lips, and he didn't even notice Kai was no longer paying attention. He was watching me.

A look of pity crept into his eyes, and I bared my teeth. "Don't!" I mouthed. He hadn't wanted my pity either.

A hardened expression firmed over Kai's face, and he straightened up. "That's enough, Bello."

"I know you got her. If she ain't in this room, she's around. She's got to be. I know she's your new fucking pet. I had pictures sent to me. You think you're the only one with spies? Well, I got mine too. I have images of you fucking her so hard that I jacked off to 'em. Tawnia got it hard that night, but she loved it. She was lapping it up. Bitch was moaning, crying all over me, but damned if she didn't come. She came hard. Screaming the whole time too."

"Shut him up, Kai." The spokeswoman's nose lifted in disgust. "Who has he been working with since you cut ties?"

Kai didn't turn to her, only raised an eyebrow. "Bruce?"

My father shut up before his eyes darted downward. "I ain't been working with anybody. I'm doing my own thing."

"I told you. Hard and long, or quick and painless. Your choice."

Hatred radiated from my father's face as he snarled back at him. "I'll tell you. I'll tell you everything, but you gotta promise me something. You kill my girl. Finish the job. I don't want her to have anything of mine. Bitch doesn't deserve it." He tried to spit from the side of his mouth, but he couldn't move his head enough. The spit landed on his arm, just missing Kai's face.

Realizing that, his eyes bulged out. "Oh shit. I'm sorry. I didn't mean..." He stopped again, glaring once more. "No, fuck you. Fuck you, Bennett! I know you ain't going to do shit. You ain't going to promise anything. I'm not saying a wor—"

Kai's hand moved in a flash toward my father's side, and a gargle choked out of my father's throat.

More blood came out of his mouth, and he spasmed.

Kai's hand moved back, a knife in it. The tip was covered in dark blood.

He pressed the tip to my father's leg to clean it off. "Now, I can start your slow death if that's what you really want. Or, you can answer the *fucking* questions. Your choice."

My dad gurgled again. "Goddamn you—"

"Do you want me to slit your throat here and now?" Kai slammed his hands down on my father's shoulders, and a hoarse scream ripped from my father before he began sobbing.

I winced. Those sobs came from deep inside of him.

"Goddamn you. Goddamn," my father choked out. Tears streamed down his face.

Kai stepped back, turning to me briefly before rotating back to the council. "Did you order the death of your wife?" he asked flatly.

My father frowned. "Yes."

"Did you blackmail one of my security guards to kill your daughter while she was in my care?"

"Yes."

Kai paused. Then, "Are you in business with the Guaranno family?"

"What?!"

"Hey—"

"What is going on?"

All of those protests were from the council. Two of the members shoved back their chairs, turning red-faced to the spokeswoman.

Not Kai. The spokeswoman.

One of the other women spoke clearly, "What's the meaning of this? Jillian?"

The spokeswoman paled, her mouth gaping. "We—sit down. Everyone. Sit down." She hit the table again with the base of her palm. "I said sit down!"

She seared Kai, half growling. "You better get to your goddamn point or I will—"

Kai spoke over her, calmly. "Bruce Bello, are you still in business with Jillian Guaranno?"

He waited.

"Yes."

He stepped closer to the screen. His question was directed to my dad, but he wasn't facing him. "Have you been in business with the Guaranno family for the last five years?"

"What?"

"Jill!"

"This can't—"

But the spokeswoman was silent, a resigned shudder passing through her. Her head bent down.

"Jillian!" The same woman on the council pounded on the table with her knuckles. "What is going on here?"

But the rest of the council had fallen silent. They were listening for the rest.

"What was your business with the Guaranno family?"

My father hesitated, his side still bleeding. "Gun distribution."

No reaction from the spokeswoman, but the others seemed to suck in a collective breath. The other woman murmured as she sat down, "Oh, Jill."

"What were your instructions?" Kai asked.

"To undersell your product. I'd offer yours first at a higher price—higher than you wanted them sold—and if they did sell, I'd pocket the extra money. If they didn't, I'd offer them the same gun at a cheaper price. Those always sold."

"What else?" Kai grated out, staring down the spokeswoman.

As he did, a door in the back of the room on the screen opened, and I recognized some of the men going inside. One approached the table, moving silently. Only the members facing his direction saw him, and none gave it away. They looked at him, then looked away.

It was Tanner who came to stand directly behind the spokeswoman. He didn't say or do anything. He was waiting, as we all were.

My father's strained voice filled both rooms. "She had me shipping black market products too."

"What?" This came from the elderly man in the council. But unlike the others, he didn't ask questions. "You dirty fucking whore!" He shoved back his chair, his voice rising. "None of this was approved. We're a council. You have to approve this shit. Underselling the Bennetts' gun distribution, then what? Underselling my trade too? You're going to die tonight, Guaranno. You're going to die a horrible and slow death!"

"Mr. Bello," Kai called for attention again. Still. So. Fucking. Calm. "Do you have anything else to share?"

"No."

But that was enough.

These were matters that directly impacted the council, and even though I didn't know them, I knew what Kai had exposed was a lot. One family had gone against two others. Everyone knew what would happen next.

Kai motioned for the guards in our room, and they untied my father. They half-dragged him, half-walked him out the door, and I almost went with them. Was that the end? The big fucking finale?

It couldn't be, but the door shut before I could go with them, and I felt Kai's hand at my wrist. He tugged me back. He gave a reassuring pat to my arm and left me back in my spot.

I waited for the gunshot. Half wanting it, half knowing I would hate it.

It never came.

CHAPTER FIFTY-SEVEN

"Jillian." Kai was speaking to the council again.

She lifted haunted and stricken eyes to him.

"Do you have anything to say?"

"Don't kill my children. My grandchildren. Please."

Kai asked the others, "Any objection to the execution of the Guaranno family?"

"What? No!" She was rising, her hand in the air. "I said no! No. Don't do that. They're innocents. They aren't a part of this world. My granddaughter—"

While she'd been talking, one by one the council members held up their right hands. As soon as the last one was done, Kai nodded to Tanner.

Taking out a gun, he pressed the muzzle to the back of her head and—I turned away.

Bang!

Jillian stopped protesting, and I heard a thump.

I held firm, my eyes tightly shut as I heard a soft sniffle. I couldn't tell if it was in this room, if it was me, or if it was someone on the other side. The chair scraped against the floor, and I heard another hard thud followed by the sounds of a body being dragged across the floor.

A door opening.

A door closing.

And silence.

Another sniffle.

A man coughed.

A second cleared his throat.

Kai still waited.

I couldn't look. Maybe I should've, but why? Why see what I knew had happened?

The door opened and closed again. I didn't hear footsteps, but I heard the chair moving again, the sounds of something wiping over the table, the floor. This went on for a minute before the door opened and closed one more time.

"None of the Guaranno children will be harmed," Kai said. "The grandchildren either. Only Jillian, her two brothers, and the two eldest sons will be greenlit. They are the ones involved in their family's business. I am within my rights as leader of the council to make this order, but are there any objections?"

A beat.

One more.

No one objected.

Finally, the oldest man said, "You do what you need to. We will follow the Bennett family."

"As of this moment, the Guaranno family is no longer a member of the council, but we need a ninth person to vote on this next matter so there can be a majority. I'd like to request my brother Tanner vote in her place."

"We have a personal matter?" the third woman spoke, the one who had remained quiet throughout all of this.

Her face came into the light. She was in her mid-forties, with dark hair that hung down to her shoulders and pearl earrings. She wore a light sweater over a shimmering top, and her face had the slightest blush, matching her soft pink lips.

She didn't seem angry or shocked, just aggravated. "I thought that was enough for the day."

"One more, Rose."

She nodded, leaning back in her seat. "Very well." She looked to one of the other men, one with a full head of black hair and a rough glint in his eyes. "Richard, you okay with this?"

"Yeah. Yeah." He nodded. "Get on with it."

Kai turned to one of the guards in our room, and he opened the door.

The third prisoner was dragged inside and put in the chair, but he wasn't strapped in like my father. There was little to no fight left in him.

The bag was removed, and unlike the other prisoners, this one seemed content to merely sit there. There were no bruises on his face. No bloodied lip or swollen features. He didn't even seem tired. What I had mistaken for no fight was just an acceptance. It was as if he'd been asked to come in for an interview he didn't want to give.

He was young, maybe twenty-four? He had light brown hair that looked as if he'd just run his hand through it, honey brown eyes, a tilted mouth that made it seem as if he were permanently amused, and dark eyebrows that somehow gave him a rounder-looking face with chubbier cheeks than he actually had.

He would've been a cute-looking frat boy if this had been another life.

"State your name," Kai said.

The guy grinned up at him, that top lip curving in a lopsided grin. "Levi Barnes."

"Why have I brought you into this questioning today?"

Levi shrugged, lounging in his chair. "Probably has to do with the fact you don't want me with your sister, but more likely it has to do with the fact that I was turning evidence on my family."

A hush fell over the council. They had begun to talk amongst themselves, but they all perked up at that last bit.

"Why were you turning evidence on your family?"

"Is this from the Barnes family in Milwaukee?" one of the council members asked.

Only Levi seemed to take offense at that statement. His grin slipped, and his eyebrows drew closer together.

Kai nodded.

"I'm not a *this*," Levi protested. "I'm a fucking person."

Kai ignored him, addressing the others. "I'd like the room for the council members to be locked down."

"What?" one of the men barked.

Rose moved forward again. "What's the meaning of this?"

"Lock it down, Tanner."

Tanner was already moving. Two doors opened, and more guards streamed in. His guards, not anyone else's. I recognized so many of them. They lined the inside of the room before the doors were shut again and deadbolted firmly in place.

Every person in that room was now a prisoner. Kai had taken complete control.

I tried not to react to this, but I couldn't ignore the tingle that ran down my spine, the way it curled toward my stomach and began to warm me.

Kai looked at me once before turning back to Levi. He stood right next to him, speaking down to him. "You have a secret about my family, don't you?"

"What is going on here, Kai?" Rose demanded. "I don't like being a captive to your men. We all have men. We all have families, and I'm not saying that in the way Jillian was. My family will hunt yours down if you don't get—"

"I'm getting to the goddamn point!" Kai yelled, his calm exterior slipping. "Sit your ass down. NOW!"

She quieted, her mouth clamped shut, and a second later, she sat down. I watched how she swallowed, her jaw trembling before she raised her chin.

"Kai Bennett, you cannot speak to another—"

"I can, and I will, and you might want to keep quiet so you can understand where the hell I'm going with this!"

"Kai—" another member began.

"Shut up!" He burned them with a look. "All of you." Without waiting, he rounded to Levi. "Tell them what your family was hired to do. Now!"

But he didn't. Levi held back, his eyes skirting around the room, passing over me without a second glance and lingering on the door before facing Kai again.

"Shit." He raked his hands through his hair. "That's what this whole thing was about, wasn't it? Not about me turning on my family or having a fling with your sister. It was about the other matter. Look, man." He started to get up.

A guard pushed him back down, hard. Levi barely noticed. He held a hand up, imploring Kai. "I had nothing to do with that. That was my uncles, and to be honest, they're all right bastards. We're basically nonexistent on the market in Milwaukee. Another family's pushed us out. We just have a few businesses, a couple gambling circuits. That's all."

Kai waited for him to stop blabbering, and once he was done, he repeated, "Tell them what your family was hired to do against mine."

Levi cursed. He began shaking his head, groaning as if he were in pain. "I can't do that. I mean—shit. I can't. I *can't*. The stuff I was turning on my family was petty. Nothing big. Nothing like this. I can't—no. Don't make me. Please. I love your sister—"

"You don't love my sister. You just called her a fling."

"I know. I know, but there's feelings there. Right? Man, I had plans. I was gonna—" He searched for words.

He was stalling.

"I was gonna ask her to marry me. I was gonna—yeah. Yeah! I had it all planned too, until you picked me up. I was heading to Minnesota to get her. We were going to go back to Mexico, get married there. I wasn't even turning evidence, not really. It'd been a setup by the local cops. They set me up with child pornography."

Oh God.

My eyes opened again. I was starting to see the dots.

Oh my God.

"They confiscated my computer, put that disgusting crap on there, threatened to take me in if I didn't give them something on someone," Levi whined. "So whatever. What I did tell them was minor, so minor. Just a slap on the wrist."

Kai was letting him hang himself. The more Levi said, the worse it was for him.

I'd helped Brooke get to Minnesota, but he'd been the one to find her a place to hide. Those people had been his connections. That meant...

A string had tightened inside of me, twisting all my organs around and around each other, all into a nice, tight bowtie.

"Tell them. Now."

So quiet, but so lethal.

I saw Rose close her eyes in surrender. She knew what was coming, whatever it was.

"Fuck!" Levi yelled before slumping in his chair. "Fuck! Fuck! Fuck!" His hand went through his hair once more before he shot forward in his seat, sitting on the edge, his feet bouncing up and down. "Fine. You want to know what they did? We killed your mom."

I deflated. And I looked at Tanner in the other room.

He had been expressionless until now. Now his eyes were wide, his eyebrows high and his mouth open. He reached forward, grabbing the back of a chair in front of him.

A few of the council members cast him sympathetic looks, but not Rose. Not Richard, and not the elderly man. I didn't know what families they represented, their last names, but I didn't think it mattered. Somehow, in some way, they were involved, because all three were eyeing the guards around them.

I suspected there was a policy that council members couldn't sit at the table with weapons. So they were sitting ducks for whatever was coming their way, set forth by Kai.

"Explain."

Levi eyed Kai, shaking his head. He just kept shaking, and his leg started bouncing up and down. "You're a dick, you know that?"

Kai hadn't been watching him, but his dead eyes slid his way now. He stepped closer. "Start talking, or I'll start torturing. Happily."

Levi stalled for one more moment before giving in. "Fine." He looked up, already flinching over what he was about to say. "About twenty years ago, my family got paid to make a hit look like a robbery. My two uncles did it. It was supposed to be just the woman, but then a second order came through for the guy too."

"And that woman was?"

"Already said," Levi huffed out. "Your mom."

"And the man?"

He was quiet a moment. "Her lover. Randall Ritzo."

Tanner's eyes cut to the elderly man, and in a second, he had his gun out. Two steps and he brought the butt of the gun down on the back of the man's head.

No one said a word. No one.

The elderly man fell forward, his head hitting the table hard, but he lifted a hand to the back of his head. "What the—" He pulled his shaking hand back, blood on his fingers. "Why the hell did you do that? Randall was my son!"

Tanner growled, taking the man's head and grinding it into the table again. "My mother, you old fuck! You killed them, didn't you?" He scowled at Kai. "You knew about this? THE WHOLE FUCKING TIME?!"

Kai didn't respond, only turned to Levi. "Finish. Tell them the rest."

Levi let out a long-suffering sigh. "You're going to kill me after this, aren't you? Don't matter if Brooke loves me or not."

In response, Kai pulled out his gun. He pointed it at him. "Tell them." He cocked the gun. "Now."

"Yeah." He raised his voice. "Yeah, the order came down from the Ritzo family. It was his son. We didn't get the purpose of killing your own kid, but whatever. Families have done worse, especially in our world. So yeah. My uncles killed 'em. Both." He scowled right back at Kai. "That order came down from your dad too. Both your fucking families were behind it."

"And one was already dealt with."

Kai didn't take his gun away. Instead, he stepped even closer, putting the muzzle right against Levi's forehead. "Finish. Once and for all."

Levi's eyes closed then opened again. He looked tired, gaunt.

He stared past Kai, past the gun. "A deal was struck afterward. Your dad, Ritzo, and the other broad's family all went in together with a side business. When you killed Senior Bennett, his end was scooped up by Dick Delaney there."

The Richard guy scoffed, but he tugged at his shirt. "You're lying now, Barnes."

"You're a rat." The Rose woman seethed, but she was nervous too, shifting in her seat, still eyeing the guards closest to her.

The only one not raising an argument was the elderly man, who Tanner had let lift his head back up. Blood trickled down his forehead. He tried to wipe it away but left a smear across his entire face.

"What was the trade?" Kai narrowed his eyes. "I'm getting fucking tired of prompting you for this shit. You want to live, you spill everything. I won't ask again."

Levi's eyes jumped to his. "You're going to let me live? After all this?"

"I care about my sister."

Renewed hope lit Levi's gaze, and he straightened up in his chair. "Yeah. Uh. For all those up there who don't know what our trade was, it was..." He chewed the inside of his cheek. "Sex trade. Illegal porn. All that shit. I was the pointman down here. My family didn't want to deal with that, so yeah, I was creating openings in the family. All them up there on the council knew about it too. They were helping me turn evidence on my family so I could step into the leadership role and bring the sex trade down here. I also had to scope out the competition. There's a big ring in Ohio, but we had plans to eliminate them. Just hadn't gotten to that part yet, if you know what I mean."

He stared at Kai for a second before continuing. "Those three were never going to bring the rest of you in on the trade. Too much money and too messy with the fact that none of them were cleared to be doing sex trafficking. Only one cleared for that was the Guaranno family, who..." He looked, then frowned. "I don't see up there anyway."

Kai pushed the gun against him again, just a slight pressure before stepping back. "Is that all of it?"

"Yeah." He eyed Kai warily. "That's all of it. Except, my family didn't know what I was doing. Just me. They got their asses handed to them from another fight down here against a rival family, so after they did the hit, they got paid, and that was it. I'm the one who reached out, said I could help bring it all to Milwaukee. I targeted your sister, told that group I had power over your family.

I was supposed to get some bad shit on her, then blackmail her to get to you. They wanted to take you down. Those three are ambitious fuckers, if you ask me." He waved to them. "The only reason they let me in was to get at you, because I'd already started boning your sister."

"Right," Kai clipped out, turning to the council again.

Two guards now stood behind those three council members. Rose. Richard. Ritzo Senior. Tanner had moved back, his eyes closed. He was counting to himself, his chest heaving.

"You've heard enough," Kai said. "I motion to execute Rose Montieth, Joseph Ritzo, and Richard Delaney immediately. Cora, you start."

The last woman raised her right hand.

The man beside her did as well.

And again.

Again.

Tanner was the last, but in his right hand was a gun, and before Kai could say a word, he pressed it to the back of the old guy's head and pulled the trigger.

I watched this time. I couldn't look away.

In a sick way, this was riveting.

After all this work, all this planning, bringing everyone together, waiting all those years, and having it all come to fruition now—Kai could never leave this life. This was who he was, how he thought, how he lived, how he breathed. Or was it? Pulling my gaze away, I felt him watching me, and I winced at the pain in his eyes.

Maybe...

I began to pull away from the wall.

Maybe this wasn't how he wanted to be, but I heard Jonah's voice in my head again. If he fell, they all fell. Then I thought about what they'd wanted to do, what they'd wanted Levi to do to get at Kai. I didn't know what to think, how to determine what Kai might possibly think.

Without a word, Kai raised the gun to Levi, his eyes holding mine.

He pulled the trigger.

CHAPTER FIFTY-EIGHT

After the executions concluded and both rooms had been cleaned, Kai faced the council.

"There will be an opening at Bruce Bello's company. I would like to insert his daughter as CEO. She can be acting or the real deal. We will use Bello's trucks and his distribution line for the rest of our businesses, and we can expand farther south at a later time."

Four members were gone from that council.

Tanner hadn't sat down. He remained in the back, but his eyes were blazing.

"If he has a board?" Cora asked. "If there's pushback for some reason?"

"Then we *push back*." Kai scanned the rest of the members. "All in favor?"

One man chuckled. "As if we're going to refuse you anything right now, Kai."

Kai didn't smile back. "All in favor?"

Four right hands raised.

"I have another proposition, and it's one you will not like." He glanced in my direction, though his eyes didn't quite meet mine. "There is tighter legislation forming against sex trafficking. I would like the council to pull out completely from that trade."

Cora's forehead tightened. "It's good money, Kai. We're in the business of making money."

"It's stupid money. It won't be worth the risk in the future."

"But—" She started to argue again.

"We'll open more casinos. We'll have added revenue coming in from the Bello line, and that company will give us a foothold in Milwaukee. We can use that, spread out, gain more traction. The ring in Ohio is too strong. I've looked into it. I don't want to go against them, not right away."

"Kai—"

"We'll lose," he spoke over another protesting member. "We lost four members tonight. That's four families gone and out of business. We will cover the Bello base, move farther south into the States, but each of you can pick up the revenue left behind by those families."

"Except the Guaranno family. Besides the gun business, their approved trade was sex trafficking. Who's going to miss out on that money?"

"Whoever that is can be brought in as a new partner with my next business venture. It's in the future, but I think it will be competitive. I can only extend that offer as a way to make it up to that other family."

They seemed to mull it over, and then prepared to vote. This time to get out of the world I had asked Kai to help with, and to make the changes he'd proposed.

The vote would go through.

I stopped listening and could only stare at him.

He'd done that for me. There was no new legislation. Sex trafficking was one of the easiest crimes to commit with good money, and he knew that. He'd lied through his teeth. For me.

It wasn't long before the council members left, looking relieved to be able to do that, but the feed didn't end. Tanner remained in the room, and so did Kai. He sat at the head of the table, glaring at his brother.

"How long did you know?"

Kai didn't waste time. "After I killed our father. He had encrypted notes that I deciphered. I figured it out then."

"You are a fucking piece of shit."

Kai didn't respond.

Tanner rubbed the bridge of his nose. "Randall *Cordell* Ritzo. That's his full name. Cord. Did she—was Cord—" He exhaled sharply. "You know what I'm fucking asking."

"Yes, he was Cord's father. Mom had a diary. She talked about her affairs in there."

"Jesus Christ." He pushed back in his chair, his arms folding over his chest. "How'd you get *that*?"

"That's a story for another day, but Tanner..." Kai's voice dropped, almost comforting. "She was unhappy with our dad."

"But her first kid? I'm surprised he didn't kill her immediately." His tone grew hoarse. "Are you his kid? Me? Brooke?" A bitter laugh. "We know Jonah isn't, but how many others?"

Kai didn't respond.

"Kai." Short and curt.

"Brooke and I look like him, but you have a rounder face, so I don't know. Is that something you care about?"

Tanner stood slowly. "You ever keep me in the dark again, and I will kill you. I don't give a shit what that means for the rest of us. You got that? I don't get left in the dark. Ever."

Kai inclined his head. His eyes cast my way. "If you want in, you have to be in." He looked back to Tanner, heat forming in his eyes. Finally. After all of that, he let the real Kai shine forth. "You don't want to be treated with kid gloves, you start acting like a fucking adult. You want in? You take over the Bello Company for Riley."

Tanner looked for me, and so did Kai.

I stepped forward, crossing the room till I could be seen on the screen.

Tanner's nostrils flared. "Is that okay with you?"

"Yes," I breathed out. I didn't want to be involved, or as minimally involved as possible. "I will announce that I'm alive, and with whatever happens, I'll take over, then you can step in. You can do what you want with it."

I didn't want anything of my father's.

"Okay." He rolled his shoulders back. "Then I'll do it."

"Good." Kai touched the back of my elbow lightly. "I'll see you when you get down here."

He glanced to the side of the room, and just like that, the image was gone. The call was done, and in a few seconds, the remaining guards had exited the room. It was only Kai and me.

"Are you sure that signal couldn't get hacked or watched by the government?"

"Yes." He stepped in cautiously. "We're safe. I make sure of it."

He was making sure I was okay with his touch too.

I grabbed his hands and stepped into him. My arms slid around him, and I rested my head to his chest.

He'd fulfilled his promise. In one afternoon, he'd done more than I ever could in an entire lifetime as a Hider.

He'd helped. Even though he was in the mafia, he'd still done well today.

"Thank you," I murmured, feeling his hands sweep through my hair.

His arms tightened around me, and I felt his lips on my shoulder. A deep, shuddering breath left him. "You don't hate me?"

I pulled back to see him. "Is that why you brought me in here? To loathe you?"

"No." He bent back down, nuzzling me. "To tell you the truth, I don't know why I brought you in here. I wanted you here. I wanted you to understand this world better. I wanted you to see that you don't have to regret hating your father, in case you did."

I felt his tension and reached up, my hand cradling the back of his head. My fingers began running in small circles, comforting him.

"Is that what you do? Regret hating your father?"

His body tightened, then relaxed. "No, but you're better than me. I can see you feeling that. I wanted to line everything up for you and let you deal with your father, but I can't bring myself to let you go or haul him in here."

I laughed softly, "So let's not. Let's handle him another time.'" I tipped my head back to grin up into his eyes.

He lifted his head, his eyes darkening, dipping to my lips. "That sounds perfect."

I framed his face with my hands and nodded my head, feeling his arms tighten around me, knowing he wouldn't let me fall.

His body was riddled with tension and knots. What he'd done just now, pulling all of that off, I could only imagine how much energy it had taken.

"Let's go upstairs."

His lips were on mine almost before I finished speaking, and he swept me up in his heat, the tingles already spreading through me, his arms holding me fast. He carried me out of the room, to an elevator, and we rode it to the next floor.

CHAPTER FIFTY-NINE

Kai was standing shirtless at the window, looking out at the lake when I woke up in the morning. He had a coffee cup in one hand, and his other rested against the wall.

Fuck. A magazine cover right there.

I pushed back the covers, reached for a robe, and padded over to him.

He grinned, bringing his arm around me as I fit in next to him.

I slid my arms around him. "Did you sleep?"

A half laugh/half snort came from him.

We hadn't slept, hardly at all.

There'd been a frenzied need in Kai, a desperation to release whatever demons had been in him through the long night before. The first time had been rough. The second slow and loving. The third had been in the shower. For the fourth, he took me from behind. And still, a few hours later, he reached for me again, pushing inside and watching me the entire time.

I was sore as I leaned against him.

He smoothed his hand down my back, resting it on my hip. "I told you to trust me last night." He stepped back, his hand finding mine. He set his coffee down on the nightstand and pulled me toward the closet, where he handed me an oversized sweatshirt. I pulled it on, along with a pair of pants. He tugged a Henley over his head and led me to the elevator.

His guards were waiting for him, and they fell in step around us.

We all walked outside, then down to the lake's edge. There was a small dock with a boat tied to it and two people waiting on it.

As we stepped onto the dock, one of them stood up.

His hood was pulled over his head, but after a moment I recognized him and faltered. It was the first prisoner from yesterday, the guard that had been blackmailed by my father.

He extended his hand, tears glimmering in his eyes. "Thank you, Mr. Bennett. Thank you." His voice cracked. "This means a lot. You have no idea."

Kai shook his head before stepping back to stand beside me. He nodded to the other man. "You gave him his paperwork and everything?"

The man nodded. "Yes, sir. He's set to go. New ID for him and his family. I'll drive him up, make the drop so he can reunite with his family, and continue to my normal fishing expedition. I'll take good care of him."

It was then that I noticed the penguin—small, but pinned just inside his coat collar. He'd been watching me, waiting, and I stepped closer to Kai's side.

Kai was using a Hider operative for this man.

A look passed between the Hider and me, a shared understanding. He knew who I was too.

I... I had no words.

The fact that Kai had done this, that he was using my previous employers for the very mission I'd held so dear to my heart—it meant more than I could've imagined.

Kai shook hands with the boat driver, the ex-guard again, and they prepared to go. His arm came down around my shoulders, and he pulled me in close, leaning his head down to rest against mine.

We watched them pull away, then head north on the lake. As they disappeared, the guards moved back to give us privacy until it was only Kai and me on the dock.

I tipped my head back to see him. "You kept him alive?"

He nodded. "He was one of mine. He should've come to me straight away, but he was one of mine. The council thinks he's dead, and that's all that's needed. If I hadn't killed him, they would've tracked him down and done it themselves. Knowing that, he'll stay hidden and silent for the rest of his life. If he shows again, he knows what will have to happen. But he was one of mine first. I take care of mine."

Kai had an odd look on his face, his eyes distant, a slight frown. Then, shaking his head, he cleared the look away and draped his arm over my shoulders. We walked together back inside.

For once, things felt right. Things felt like they'd be okay. Finally.

. . .

So much seemed to have happened right after the council meeting. Kai told Brooke about Levi—the truth of what he'd been planning and doing, and the truth about how he'd met his end. She'd broken down.

Kai had asked Eric to be here when we broke the news to her, and he was at her side. I'd glanced around as she wept, my heart tearing for her pain. I wasn't sure who was going to go to her. So when both Eric and Jonah hesitated, I started.

Then Kai surprised everyone. He'd scooped her up first, cradling her like she was a child. He'd rested his forehead to hers, whispering something over and over again.

Jonah and Eric seemed as surprised as I was.

But Kai knew what Brooke needed. He'd held her for a good hour, carrying her to the couch and holding her almost on his lap. Jonah had sat on the other side of her, his hand on her arm. Both brothers had tried to be there for her.

I'd sat on the floor, within reach if Brooke needed me. Eric did the same.

I could hear Kai whispering to her.

"We're here for you. I'm here for you. I'm so sorry, Brooke. I'm so sorry." He was almost rocking her back and forth. "We love you. Tanner loves you. Jonah loves you. I love you. We're here for you. We will carry you. I'm so sorry."

Jonah's hand had clenched her shirtsleeve. "We love you, Brooke," he'd croaked out. "We're fucking Bennetts. You're a fucking Bennett."

She passed out after another hour of crying, and that night, Kai was the one who'd carried her to the vehicle. Jonah had walked behind, holding her bags, and Eric went with them. Kai placed Brooke inside the SUV, draped a blanket over her, and kissed her forehead.

She'd looked shattered. Pale. Her face was tear-drenched, but when Kai stepped back, she'd reached for me. "Riley."

I went to her, hugging her, and I kissed her forehead as well. "I'm so sorry, Brooke."

She nodded, sniffling. More tears slid down her cheeks. "I loved him. I did, but he betrayed me." Her voice broke, and a hard look flashed in her eyes. "He had to die."

I wasn't sure what to say to that, so I nodded before hugging her once more and easing back. She caught my hand, squeezing it. "Take care of my brother."

I nodded again. "I will."

Her eyes clung to mine— fierce, yet outlined in wetness. "I'm a Bennett. First and foremost. If you hurt my brother, I'll come for you."

My mouth almost fell open, but Kai caught my hand and tugged me back. Jonah and Eric had gotten in on the other side. Eric nodded to us through the window. I saw Jonah raise a hand before the vehicle pulled away.

I hadn't known how to process what Brooke said, so I just accepted it. The family loyalty was strong.

Kai's arm had come around my shoulder. "What'd she say to you?"

I repeated it, expecting a laugh, a statement dismissing Brooke.

I got neither. He only stared after them, a somber look in his eyes. We watched as the caravan of SUVs disappeared. Kai moved in front of me, bending down, and picked me up. I faced him, my legs on either side of his waist. I laid my arms over his shoulders, my hands dangling behind him. His eyes found mine, and I rested my forehead to his. I closed my eyes, enjoying the way he carried me back into the warehouse and he laid me down on the bed.

CHAPTER SIXTY

I was pressed against the shower wall, my breasts against the wet glass and my hands pinned above my head as Kai thrust into me from behind. Every inch of him was molded against me, his teeth nipping, kissing the back of my neck and shoulder as he moved deep inside of me.

"Kai," I moaned, gasping for breath as water slid into my mouth.

He groaned in response, his hand moving from my hip to wedge in front of my body. He grabbed one of my breasts, cupping it, his thumb rubbing over my nipple. He continued thrusting in me, moving slowly, so slowly.

I was burning up. The water did nothing to cool me down.

He tugged me back against him, his hands sliding all over me, torturing me. He circled my breasts, caressing them, then trailed his hands down until they rested between my legs. He rubbed over my clit. He'd already given me one orgasm before he began to move inside of me. Now his dick stretched me, filling me completely, and he rotated his hips, getting me in just the right spot.

I gasped, arching my back against him, and his hand moved up to my throat. His thumb stretched up to press against my mouth, and he turned my head back to his, his mouth on mine.

"Oh, God." I whimpered. "Kai."

He growled, nipping my bottom lip. His hips drove against mine, pushing one last time and lifting my entire body from the force. He caught me again, holding me in place, his fingers clamping down on my hip before he dropped his hold on my wrists. Grabbing my waist, he bent over me, sucking the back of my shoulder, and he began moving more forcefully.

I reached back, grabbing his neck. My back arched, and my breasts grazed the glass wall.

I was building, building. Coming. Closer. Higher.

"*Come.*" His command was savage, and my body responded.

With breakneck speed, he pushed me over the edge, and I collapsed in his arms. He waited as my body trembled, and then he turned me around. His cock was still hard. He wasn't done.

Sometimes he would lay me on the bed. Sometimes he would bend me over the bed. Sometimes he would place me on the bathroom counter, slide in, and finish. I never knew for sure where he would take me.

This time, he merely hoisted me up, his arms under my ass. My legs wound around his waist, and he moved back inside of me.

Reaching up, I held on to the shower head and arched my back again. He caught my breast in his mouth, and then he pushed deep, deeper, farther inside. It was these moments—after I had come the second time and right before he climaxed— when he would pause and I would feel him so much inside of me that we were one person.

I breathed that in again, one hand leaving the shower head and trailing down his back. My hips moved with his until he roared, coming, shooting inside of me.

We'd been like this for the last four days.

There was an insatiable need inside of Kai. He never spoke of it, but it was there. We hadn't left the warehouse, not once.

He carried me out of the shower, placing me on the counter and moving away. Silent. This was the pattern.

Now he would dry off, change. He would towel me dry, bring me clothes. Sometimes he would help me put them on, as if I were precious and delicate. Sometimes he'd stand back and watch, a darkness swirling in his depths, his eyes growing heated. When I was dressed, he'd take my hand and lead me back to the main room. We would either eat, curl up on the couch, watch a movie, spend quiet time on our computers, or relax in bed. A few hours later, he would reach for me again, and we'd start the routine all over.

He barely said a word.

I barely asked a question.

This was hedging on day five now. It was four in the morning, and I let out a sigh. I would need to press the issue.

"Kai."

He paused, pulling a shirt over his head. He glanced at me, but said nothing.

"What's wrong?"

He shook his head, his eyes shuttering, closing me out from whatever was going on inside of him. He pulled on some pants and padded over to me. He cupped the back of my head and leaned in for a soft kiss. It was too soft. Tantalizing. I went with him as he started to pull away, unable to keep a moan from escaping.

God. He tasted so good.

His forehead rested against mine. "We can't leave until you've seen your father." Then he pulled away, leaving me in the bathroom. For the first time over the last few days, I walked out alone, with a towel wrapped around me, dripping water onto the floor. Some of me had begun to air dry, but my hair was soaked. Kai was in the closet.

I went to the dresser where my clothes were and finished drying off. I pulled on black leggings and an oversized V-neck tunic that draped at my thighs. When I was done, Kai had moved to the kitchen, so I went after him. I watched him start the coffee machine, still patting my hair dry, and I curled up on one of the kitchen chairs.

"You're waiting for me? Is that what you're saying?" There was more to it. There had to be. I now watched him pull out a pan, a loaf of bread, as the coffee machine brewed.

I waited for him to answer my question. When he didn't, I said, "Kai."

He sighed, pausing to look up at me. "No. I'm waiting for myself."

"For yourself? What do you mean?"

This was it. I felt it then. This was the day we would face whatever was going to happen in the future. A fear pricked me, making me wonder if he had plans for me I didn't know about. My mouth dried. "You're not—you're not going to leave me?"

His eyes widened. He was out of the kitchen in a flash.

I expected him to say something, anything, to ease my sudden paranoia. He said nothing, but he picked me up, so easily and swiftly. I knew he was strong. I had felt it so many times, but I still marveled.

He hugged me to him, smoothing a hand down my hair and back. "I don't think I'll ever be able to let you go, to be honest."

He pressed a kiss to my forehead, and I heard his words like a whisper carried away on a sudden breeze. I wondered if he'd actually said them.

But then I heard, "Not fully."

I smoothed my hands down his front and tried to smile. "You sure? Because you just scared me a bit."

"Hmmm." He hugged me tighter before depositing me on the counter next to where he had the bread. Kissing me briefly, he stepped back, but kept a hand on my leg, pulling more bread slices out, then grabbing a bowl from the cupboard behind me.

"What are you making?"

"French toast." He pulled eggs, milk, vanilla, sugar, and cinnamon from the fridge and cupboards. He began whisking the batter, moving back to stand between my legs and reaching over to turn the burner on.

"You're cooking?"

He had never cooked. This was completely new.

He smirked at me, putting oil into the pan. "Brooke's not the only one who has some culinary tendencies."

I liked this look on him. I liked it a lot.

I remained there, content, never moving more than a step or two away from me. He began piling the French toast he made onto a large plate. He was making more than enough, but then I realized he wasn't cooking just for us. He was cooking for the guards, and with a lost and distracted look in his eyes.

He was cooking to distract himself.

I slid my fingers through his hair, enjoying how he closed his eyes and moved his head like a cat, savoring the caress from me.

"You mentioned my father before."

He grimaced, stiffening. "Can we not talk about him?"

We hadn't been talking about him for four days. I frowned.

"I think we should."

He was so tense now.

"Kai," I said gently.

I touched his side just before he ripped away from me. Flicking the stove off, he took the platter of toast and carried it to the door. He opened it and offered the French toast to the two guards outside. "Here. Take these downstairs to the break room."

I didn't hear what the response was, but Kai grabbed a bottle of maple syrup and passed it to them. He closed the door again and turned to regard me. His tortured expression was back, hitting a nerve in me and stirring me up.

I hated whatever was bothering him.

He raked a tired hand through his hair, reaching behind him to lock the door. He moved to the living room.

I followed him, sitting on one end of the couch and pulling one of the blankets folded over the back to my lap.

I waited. That's all I could do.

He started reluctantly. "Yes, I'm waiting for you to deal with your father. Yes, it's the last thing I want to do here, but we have to. I just, haven't been able to force it to happen."

A lump sat in the back of my throat. "You said you wanted to replace me at my father's company. Do you need him alive to do that?"

He stared at me a full long minute, his tortured look never wavering. "I've already started that process."

He didn't answer my question.

"Do you need him alive to do that?"

He wrenched his gaze away, sitting in the chair next to me, but angling his body away. As he rested his arms on his legs, his back and shoulders grew rigid. "No. Your father is free to die whenever you want him killed."

I hadn't expected that.

"Hey." I sat forward. "What's going on here? What are you scared about?"

He whipped his head to mine, his gaze searing me. "You hating me one more goddamn time."

"What?" I couldn't have heard him correctly. I blinked, confused. "What are you talking about?"

"Your father has to die." He was cold now. "His body will be found. He'll be declared dead. His company will call an emergency board meeting. In the interim, you'll be declared alive. At that board meeting, you'll share with them the news of your resurrection." His tone was biting. "After that, we'll declare a hostile takeover of your father's company."

"Kai."

He kept on. "There will be resistance from four members on the board. The other three have already been turned. They will feign surprise, but joy at your appearance, and one of them will bring a motion to appoint you in your father's place."

He looked away, his head down, his eyes closed. "I have everything in place, ready to move, but after this, after what you'll have to do—there's no going back." His words were soft, making me ache. "You can't go back in the shadows after this."

Oh.

Understanding dawned.

"And you're worried about me?"

"I'm worried you'll hate it. I'm worried you'll resent me because I fucking yanked you out of where you were content, and I'm not allowing you to go back there." He shoved to his feet. "Me. I am destroying the safe world you had erected, and you're letting me do it." He stopped, breathing harshly. "I am fucking terrified that you will hate me at the end of all this."

I moved in a flash, going to him.

He flinched, moving away.

"Kai." Pain wracked through me. I reached for him again.

"No!" He moved farther away, glaring at me. "Stop it. Stop acting like you're okay with all this. I am yanking you into this prison I live in. You're letting me! Stop accepting everything I'm doing to you."

He paused, bit out a curse, and in a second was in front of me. His hands cupped my head, his fingers sliding through my hair, and he tilted me back to look at him as he gazed down. He closed his eyes for a moment, seeming to gather strength, and then he began to speak.

"As soon as Brooke went to you, I started planning. I knew I would kill your father. I knew I would replace him with you. I knew I would wipe out half the council. I knew I would kill Barnes. I have moved on his family. This morning, the FBI will arrest half of his family. My men will kill the other half. In the chaos and sudden absence of the Barnes family, my men will move in and take hold of their assets. There is another mafia family in Milwaukee, and they will receive a bribe from the Bennett family. Tanner is here, heading everything up. Tanner will inform this other family that we've moved in, that we have holdings in the Bello Company—a company they have wanted to push in on for the last thirty years. They'll also be offered a guest sitting position at the next council meeting. Do you know what that means?"

His nostrils flared on the last question.

I could barely process everything he was telling me.

I shook my head. "No."

"That means they'll have a chance at tripling their financial assets. I am creating one entire hold over Canada and over half the Midwest in the States, and I will keep expanding, because that's how my mind works. In seven years, I will eliminate three of those council members and replace them with my siblings, giving us almost an entire monopoly over the council. I know my enemies. I know my obstacles, and I am already making moves to take on or move with the families in Chicago, then Pittsburgh, Boston, and New York. Once I have a firm hold on the East Coast, I will begin looking to the West Coast. Are you understanding what I'm telling you?"

"Yes," I grated out, feeling an inordinate amount of pressure building in my head and chest. My heartbeat was pounding. "You're a calculating bastard. That's nothing new to me."

"My plan was always to seduce you."

I—what?

He said those words so softly and suddenly. Then he waited, stepping back, watching for my reaction.

I...

A second.

Another.

Five more.

"What?" I choked out. He couldn't have said those words.

But he had, and he repeated them, a wall over his face. "My plan was to seduce you. Make you fall in love with me. Use you to insert my position in your father's company. And it worked perfectly."

"What?!"

I couldn't process that. He was saying— "This was all a lie?"

But no. It couldn't have been.

Was it?

No, no, no. Panic rose up in me.

How he'd been kind to me. How he held me. How he touched me.

How he'd seduced me.

But...

I couldn't breathe.

My chest constricted inside of me.

My heart squeezed. I was having a heart attack.

I crumbled, bending over and pressing my forehead to my knees. Breathe in. Breathe out. I kept trying to repeat to myself, but it wasn't working. Everything swirled into a mess in my head. Pain laced through me, all the way to my fingertips and toes.

"You can't do this. I—was it all a lie?!"

Fuck it. I shoved to my feet, advancing on him.

He watched me come, not moving, not saying a word.

"Tell me!"

His jaw clenched. "You should hate me."

"That's for me to decide. And anyway, I can change my mind. I can go back. I can hide, you fucking asshole!"

"You can't, actually."

"What?"

"I've already sent paperwork and proof of life to the courts. In two hours, you will be declared alive. If you leave and try to hide again, I'll declare an international manhunt for you. I will find you, no matter where you go."

He would. He could. He was the only one.

A new feeling of helplessness and powerlessness flooded in, making the room spin around me.

"I have to be there. I have to go to court for that..." Right?

"You don't. I have your double going to court in your place—the one we used when Blade tried to get you back. She'll have an imprint of your prints on her fingers, and I've already had blood tests done." A small hesitation. "I'm sorry for that. If you'd like, I can have her attend the Bello emergency board meeting, if you decide to fight me on this."

"Why?" I shook my head. "Why are you doing this? Saying this? Being like this?"

He was so fucking cold. A stranger. He was the Kai he'd been when I first met him.

He didn't answer. I saw a flicker in his eyes, but it was gone. He hardened again. "Because it's time this charade ends."

God.

"I don't want you anymore," he added, finishing me.

I couldn't breathe.

Sliding to the ground, I gasped for air. My lungs had closed in on themselves, like my whole world.

"You are free to leave here, but you cannot leave Milwaukee," Kai said, his voice coming from farther away. "A car will be downstairs for you. It'll take you to your father's estate. There's staff there waiting for you, a Claude, if memory serves me correctly."

The door opened. "If you try to defy me and disappear or return to the 411 Network, I will kill your previous two roommates. If you wish to speak to your father before he dies, you have the next hour to do that. The guards will show you the way."

And with that, the door shut, and I was left alone. Destroyed.

CHAPTER SIXTY-ONE

I don't know how I got here.

Thinking back, I don't know how I did a lot of things after what Kai said to me. But somehow, I found myself in a room. My father was tied to a chair, waiting for me to come to him. He had a bandage wrapped around his waist, duct tape over his mouth. If his ass itched, he couldn't have scratched it.

Five days ago, I might've been scared of him. I could feel the loathing coming off him in waves. If he could've killed me, he would've. I knew that without a doubt. Tough luck for him, though, because he couldn't touch me, scare me, or hurt me now. Kai had done all of that for him.

I had a brief thought to turn and leave. He would die regardless. Kai had taken a spoon to my insides, gutting everything out of me until I was hollow. The experience had left me with nothing to say to my father, who was my biological father, despite what he said.

Maybe it was that. Maybe that's why I propelled myself across the room to pull the tape off of him. I grabbed the end and whipped it off. The faster the better. I wanted to get this over with, so I could leave.

"AHHHH!" he screamed as I yanked it away, his mouth and surrounding skin reddening. He spat at me. "You fucking bitch."

I acted without thought. I wrapped my hand around his neck and squeezed.

He started to make gargling sounds, rasping, wheezing.

I kept squeezing, an ironclad grip.

He began flailing around, as much as he could, bouncing the chair.

When he began to shake like he was having a seizure, I let go.

He gasped for breath, coughing frantically. He couldn't stop coughing, and all the while, I stood immobile. I just watched the handprint I'd left on his neck, the way the color seemed to take forever to return to normal. When the whiteness was gone, I flicked my eyes back to his.

Finally.

A small satisfaction bloomed in my chest. The first flicker of life post Kai's devastation.

My father seemed cautious now, watching me warily.

I smiled. "I get it. I get why you love being cruel and a monster." I turned away from his eyes. "I see why you wanted to kill me."

The power. It was dark and addictive.

Then my stomach rolled over on itself, threatening to spew. I felt sick. That part of me was from him. I did have his darkness in me, and as I stood there, I felt it pooling, moving inside of me, growing.

My father. My mother. Kai. Having a front-row seat to this world. It had probably even started when I was seeing it through the lens of a Hider operative. I was changed. No, that wasn't right. I was broken. There was a part of me beyond repair now. I could never have a normal life again. Kai had cemented what had been happening to me since Brooke found me.

This darkness wasn't going anywhere. It slithered in me, like a snake, and I knew then that I'd never be able to get it out of me. It was there because of my father, Kai had brought the flame to life, and then it had burst into a bonfire at his betrayal.

And now here I was, standing in front of the man I used to fantasize about hurting, and it all clicked into place.

This was the moment all of it had been leading to, this moment when I decided my fate. Because I was the only one who could, no one else. Me. My decision.

He was frothing at the bit again, wanting to scare me.

I sighed. "You can't intimidate me. You should give up. It's time, don't you think?"

His eyes widened. Surprise fluttered there before it settled into reluctant resignation.

"You thought my mother cheated on you, because that's what you did to her. It's how you make sense of the world. You cheat so you think everyone cheats. That's how you think, but you're wrong. She never cheated. It wasn't in her. Not once."

He scoffed in disbelief.

"She was too broken by you to even try."

Not like Kai's mother. I winced at the thought of her. Brooke's mom. She cheated on their father. She must have done it to rebel. She had to. Why would the wife of a murderer cheat on that man? It couldn't have been a careless mistake, a decision made out of passion. Not if it'd produced two sons—or three with Tanner. Maybe she fell in love after all, but to start? Perhaps it was loneliness? Misery?

She couldn't physically leave him, so she did the next thing she could. She sexually escaped him, emotionally gave herself to others.

"Just kill me. That's why you're here, isn't it?" A hard glint returned to my father's gaze. A small spark of impatience. "I know I'm a dead man. So just do it. Why are you drawing this out?"

My phone buzzed in my pocket. Pulling it out, I didn't recognize the number, but I knew Kai sent it. If not him directly, at his order.

Sender: Hit play on the projector behind him.

Projector?

I looked, and there it was, sitting on a table. I moved around my father and did as Kai instructed, unsure if I wanted to see what he had lined up.

As soon as the screen lit up, silent tears began rolling down my cheeks.

It was my mother. She was at a beach, and as the video kept rolling, a dog ran into focus. My mother reached back and clasped hands with the man who was now her husband, who joined her on screen. They were talking, laughing, smiling. Then, my chest held suspended as my two half-siblings darted around them. They were kicking up sand in their bathing suits.

They looked nine and ten in the video, so this was a few years old.

Still. My heart ached. This wasn't real-time or recent, but it didn't matter.

I knew what Kai was trying to tell me, though if he was *done with me*, as he'd said he was, I didn't know why he'd bothered. Even if he was an asshole, he was giving me the chance to say the one thing I'd always wanted to say to this man. I would've forgotten otherwise, and later I would've wished I had done it.

I turned to my father. "You messed up. Did you know that?"

He swore, his voice cracking. "Why are you torturing me? Just fucking pull the trigger. There's a gun in here, isn't there? Where is it?" He tried looking, making the chair jump around as he did. His voice rose. "Are you sure your man isn't feeding you a pile of bullshit? You're pathetic. You're weak. You're soft. You ain't no kid of mine. You're not—"

I grabbed the side of his chair and moved, yanking it with me so he was pivoted around. I stopped, and his eyes were glued to the screen on the wall.

Blood drained from his face.

His mouth fell open.

He was speechless. For once.

His eyes almost bulged out of their sockets.

I waited, expecting curses, or for him to say it was a lie, but he didn't.

For a full minute, I watched him as he watched her, and a tear formed at the corner of his eye. He swallowed, his Adam's apple bobbing up and down.

"Damn," he breathed.

I didn't want to hear whatever he had to say, so I said my piece instead.

"You failed. In all your miserable, piece-of-shit life, you failed the best thing that happened to you. Her. Me. You didn't kill either of us, and to further give you the middle finger, she's happy. Those kids are older now, thirteen and fourteen. That man is everything you never were. He's kind, loving, supportive, and you might look at him as weak, but he is three times the man you ever could've been."

I leaned down and whispered one last time in his ear, "She beat you. She won."

I was done.

I was done with all of it.

There was nothing more to say.

I turned and caught sight of a gun on the table, beside the projector.

Another gift from Kai, I had no doubt.

I choked up, knowing he had left it in case I wanted to do the deed, but I didn't have it in me. Ironically, I think I would've if Kai hadn't taken everything in me that worked and left it in pieces. I might've even enjoyed pulling the trigger, then feeling sick about it.

I glanced at my father. He was still frozen. Not a sound left him as he continued to watch my mother with her new family. I had a thought... I shouldn't, but... What did I have to lose?

I cut a slit in the rope by his hand. It was small, but enough to give him slack where he could pull it free, if he wanted. Then, I moved the gun closer to him on the table, and I left.

"What the—"

I paused, my back tensing before pushing through the door again. Guards waited for me on the other side. They began to go in, but I stopped them. "No. Wait."

"For what?"

For... I didn't know. I wasn't sure until: *BANG!*

For that.

CHAPTER SIXTY-TWO

A month later

I'd returned to my childhood home.

Claude had been there, welcoming me home with tears in his eyes. He'd hugged me for a full five minutes. A few of the maids were still employed, and they were all happy to see me, but I was different. They saw it. They'd expressed well-wishes to me, then lied as they expressed their condolences after my father's body was found.

Everything had happened as Kai said it would. Every. Single. Thing.

I'd been declared alive and welcomed back into Milwaukee's high society. They'd thrown me a party. All the while, I was on automatic pilot. I barely remembered what happened day to day.

I knew my father's old management team had all been fired. Not by me. Kai likely sent the orders down—a new accountant, a new business manager. Every person I would need to help me manage my father's empire had been replaced. It was an all-new regime.

At home, I kept Claude and the staff I enjoyed and remembered.

On week three, Claude came to the office I'd set up. "A Mr. Bennett is here to see you, mistress."

Mistress. I flicked my eyes up, standing, and trying to ignore the pit in my stomach. "My name is Riley, Claude. Riley."

"Shall I show him into the first parlor?"

The first parlor? I wasn't even sure where that was, but I nodded. "Yes, thank you."

"As you wish, mistress."

"Claude!" I yelled after him, but if I could have smiled, it would've been then. I hadn't smiled since Kai had broken me.

I didn't know if I could get through this meeting, or why Kai was even here, but I forced myself to go. Once I got to the hallway, I stopped. I couldn't. My feet refused to move. Would he come in search of me if I refused this meeting? Could I do this? Could I see him after what we had shared?

I'd have to leave.

He would look for me in the house, so that meant I'd have to physically remove myself. But I wouldn't be able to hide. Those were the stipulations. Kai owned me in every way except sexually now, and I couldn't leave. He would kill Blade and Carol. He was the monster I'd always known he was; I'd just gotten used to his disguise.

I was turning, ready to ask Claude to bring a car around, when the door opened behind me.

"Riley."

I sucked in my breath, relief flooding me. It wasn't Kai.

Turning, I saw Tanner in the doorway.

Kai had sent Tanner down to help with running the company, but after only a few days in the office, I let him take over.

Why had I thought it was Kai here tonight?

My stomach dropped—because I had wanted him to come. I wanted him to try, for me.

I was so stupid.

"Yes." My voice shook. "Hello, Tanner. Hello."

He gave me a knowing look. "He won't come unless he absolutely has to."

I folded my head down. "Of course."

He was still in me. I felt him. I loathed him now, though. The hatred I'd long harbored for my father had a new target.

Shoving all that down, I cleared my throat, my head rising. I moved past Tanner, extending a hand to one of the couches. "Would you like something to drink?"

His gaze followed me everywhere. He shook his head. "Your butler already offered. I'm not here for a social call."

Of course. They'd gotten what they wanted from me. Now I was dispensable.

I drew in a pain-laced breath and asked, almost not even realizing it until the words were out, "Once I sign the company over, will you kill me?"

I wasn't looking at Tanner, but I heard his soft intake of air. "No. Why would you think that?"

I looked, feeling the robot that had inhabited my body take over. "Because you'll no longer need me, of course."

He frowned, his eyes narrowing. "Is this because you and Kai broke up?"

Broke up. I almost laughed at that.

"We didn't break up. Kai had no more use for me, or desire. He ended things."

"What? He did?"

I waved my hand in the air. I felt a hole opening inside of me, and if possible, I could feel my rotting insides starting to spill out. I didn't want that, for my own pride. Embarrassing myself, letting his brother see my weakness, I couldn't do that.

I had to have *something* he couldn't take from me. Some amount of pride, at least.

"Riley, that doesn't make sense—" Tanner moved forward, shaking his head.

"It doesn't matter." I raised my voice, wincing at the shrill note at the end. "You said this wasn't a social visit. Why'd you come?"

"I..." He eyed me, confused. Then he blinked, and it was gone. His hands went into his pockets. "I wanted to tell you Brooke's asked to come stay with you."

"What?"

"Would you like her to come?"

Did I want to see Brooke? She'd been demolished by her brother as well. We could commiserate together, but she was Kai's sister. She was a part of him. She even looked like him. Having

Tanner here, even knowing he was in the same city as me was painful enough. Feeling Kai's presence hanging over everything in my life, literally everything, was starting to wear thin. So did I want another appendage of him inside my home? Or more than whoever was reporting to him from the staff, because I knew someone was.

"I'd rather have Blade and Carol come, to be honest."

His eyebrows shot up. "Really?"

I nodded. "Or if I could visit them?"

"Kai doesn't want you to leave, you know that."

Of course.

"I'm getting sick of your brother's hold over my life." Resentment was filling me up, and fast.

"I know," he admitted, turning away. Grabbing the back of his neck, he let out a sigh. "You've lost weight."

"I've been sick."

"Do you want Jonah to come?"

I scoffed, shaking my head. "Your family is unbelievable."

I wanted to wake up from this nightmare. I wanted to be free of Kai's hold over me. I wanted to live my life in freedom, actual true freedom. I wanted to decide where I went, how I went, who I went with. But I knew my prison was here. I was to be used, after all. I had literally stepped into my father's shoes, except it hadn't been greed that put me there. It had been love.

"I know, and for what it's worth, I am sorry. Whatever happened between you and Kai, I know he's hurting too. If that helps at all—"

"It doesn't," I snapped.

How dare he? How dare Tanner? Kai wasn't allowed to hurt. He'd seduced me. He'd done what he intended to do, then tossed me like a piece of trash.

"What can we do, Riley? How can I help you?" He motioned to me. "It's obvious you're hurting too."

I snorted. "How can you help me? You can release me from this gilded prison your brother's put me in. You can buy me out. Take the entire company. I don't care. I want out! I don't want anything to do with this place. I want to see my friends. I want my old life back."

I wanted to hide.

I wanted to nurse my wounds alone, out of his spying eyes.

I wanted to survive him. That's what I wanted.

Tanner's mouth turned down. "You want out? For real?"

"Yes!"

He paused, studying me, then he nodded. "Okay. It's been a month, but the other board members aren't resisting me speaking for you. I'll talk to Kai. We'll buy out your share, give you a good price for everything."

I was shocked.

My mouth thinned. "Are you serious? I can't—I can't take being jerked around, Tanner. Don't jerk me around, not about this."

"You really do want out?"

"Yes. Please."

"Then we'll buy you out."

"Out of everything?" My father had other businesses he had invested in. I didn't want to be connected to anything he had.

"Everything. We'll take care of it. I'll make sure. I'll have Eduardo make a list of all your father's holdings. Is there...is there anything else you'd like from me?"

"I already told you."

"I can help with the business and investments, but I don't think Kai will allow your old roommates to come down. We'd have to work it for them to request a transfer. They won't come on their own. They can't, but even if they did or we did..." He hesitated, and I knew why.

It would give me a stronger hold on my old self. I would be getting support from someone who wasn't on Kai's payroll.

My heart tore in half, having this small thread of hope taken away from me all over again. I turned, not wanting Tanner to see my tears. My back to him, I crossed my arms over my chest. My eyes closed, though I could feel the tears sliding down. I made a move to wipe them clean. I made sure my voice was clear of emotion. "Fine. That's fine."

"Riley?" I heard him move for me.

"The businesses then." My voice rose, sharp. I didn't want him to see me hurting. "The businesses will be fine then. I'll make do."

"Okay." The floor creaked under his weight. When he spoke again, his voice a little farther away. "What about the homes your father owns? There's a good list of them."

God.

The homes too. Did I want to give him everything?

I could handle the homes. I could talk to a realtor, have them sell everything, unless there was one I wanted to keep.

"No. I'll handle the homes."

"Okay." I still heard his hesitation, but then I heard his footsteps on the floor, down the hallway. I could hear a slight murmur from the distance as Claude met him at the door, and a moment later, Claude was speaking behind me.

"Is there anything you wish of me, mistress? A nightcap, perhaps?"

My stomach rumbled at the mere mention, and I pressed on it. "No, thank you, Claude."

"As you wish."

He was leaving when I rounded. "Claude?"

He paused, and to his credit, he didn't flinch when he saw the tears on my face. "Yes?"

"Can you put a list together of the household staff?"

"Of course, mistress." He started to leave.

"And list their family dependents?"

"Ma'am?" His eyebrows pinched together.

I almost smiled. Almost. I'd never seen Claude confused. And to hell with it. I spoke clearly. "I need to know how many families depend on my father's money to get by. I'd like to know, if you can add this to the list, even though it might be an invasion of privacy, how much in need everyone is?"

"Ma'am?"

He still didn't understand.

"Just make the list, Claude. Please."

"As you wish, mistress."

This time, I didn't correct him. It wouldn't matter soon anyway.

CHAPTER SIXTY-THREE

Two months later

Everything was nearly done.

Tanner was back to conclude our business, and he had been right. Kai gave me a decent price for everything. I was shocked at the number when I saw it.

"I told you he'd give you a good price."

"Yes," I said faintly.

He could've cheated me. He knew it. I wouldn't have been allowed to sell to anyone other than him, but this number, it was at least double what I could've gotten from someone else.

"Just sign here." Tanner showed me all the places.

There was a lot of paper, a lot of different holdings Kai was taking over. I began signing.

"Are you sure you don't want a lawyer to look everything over?" he asked.

I paused, shooting him a look.

"Right." He laughed. "I got it." He nodded, stepping back. "Sign away. Do you want coffee? I was going to grab a cup while you're doing all that."

I shook my head. "No, thank you." I hadn't had coffee for three months, at least.

"I'll be back."

I was nearly done signing when a soft knock sounded at the door. My realtor came in, flashing me a smile. "Hi! I called your butler, and he said you were in here for the day. Hope it's okay I came? I wanted to tell you in person."

"Yes. Of course." I sat back, surprised. "What are you doing here?"

Shannon Caldriss, mid-thirties. She was someone Claude said he trusted, so I'd been working with her over the last couple months to methodically price and sell every house my father owned. I wanted all of them gone quickly, and to her credit, most of them were. There were three left to go: the main home, a cabin my father owned in Colorado, and a lake cabin north of Duluth. I hadn't traveled to either of the last two, mainly because of Kai's no-leaving-Milwaukee clause, but she had. She walked me through them on her phone, so I felt familiar enough to know that I didn't want to stay in either place. There'd been talk that maybe I would keep one for myself. It was looking more like I would sell all three, though.

She shut the door, folding into one of the chairs, her eyes lit up. "So." A bright wide smile. "I have good news. No." She held her hands out, shaking them in excitement. "I have great news, actually! Phenomenal news. A buyer approached us and offered on both homes."

"Both?"

"The Colorado one and the Minnesota one."

"What is it?"

"I've talked it over with both other realtors, and we all feel it's a really good deal. They want to offer ten million, so basically five for each home. There might be some back and forth with the agencies because the Colorado team is already vying, saying it's fifty-fifty, so that means more of a commission to them than they normally would get, but that's between us. We'll figure it out. It's not something for you to worry about."

Her eyes darted down to where I was sitting in the chair before looking back up. She folded her hands together, her elbows on the table, and almost danced in her seat. "That's a great price, especially for both of them. The Colorado one was priced at 3.8 and the North Shore was at 6.4. This is just under our asking, which doesn't happen all the time. We *all* recommend you take it."

"What are the stipulations? How quick to close?"

"Oh yes! I forgot that. Thirty-day close, cash offer, and you leave all the furniture behind. That's it. This is a dream offer. Dream, Riley."

I was in a daze.

I agreed and Shannon left, promising to send over the paperwork. That left me one more home to sell—the hardest one yet because when this house was sold, all the employees were without a job. Initially I'd had it in the paperwork that the new homebuyer needed to take on the staff, but after the first home was purchased and the staff was fired about a week after closing, I knew I was foolish to keep that in. I'd never met the staff for the other homes anyway, but in the main house, I had grown up with some of those people.

They had fed me, raised me, cared for me when my mother hadn't been able to.

They were family to me, in a small way.

"You almost done?" Tanner had returned, coffee in hand. He took Shannon's chair. Putting his coffee on the table, he yawned, stretching. "Man, I'm tired. Lot of traveling over the last few months."

I eyed him, returning to my signing. "Really?"

I didn't want to hear.

I didn't want to hear how Kai had him going everywhere.

I didn't want to hear about Kai at all.

The burn was less than it had been two months ago, mostly because I was distracted, but it was there. I tried not to think about him, about anything really, but I knew all those emotions were still locked up inside of me. They were still churning away, just waiting for me to lift the floodgates and let them spread.

I was determined not to do that. I didn't think I could handle it if they did. I had other things going on, other people who were depending on me.

Tanner nodded, finishing his yawn and pressing a closed fist to his mouth. "I have to head to Vancouver after this. I'll probably sleep the whole way."

A noncommittal "hmmm" from me.

I had five more sheets to go.

"So."

I tensed, feeling him starting to focus on me. He'd been distracted before, but I heard in the way he spoke that word that he was zooming in. I realized then, feeling a shiver go down my back, that he was the same as his brother. I could sense their shifts in a single word.

I hated that I knew that.

I shouldn't know that. I didn't want to carry that knowledge.

"How've you been, Riley?" Softly worded. Almost like he cared.

I knew better. "I'm fine." I felt tense all over, just wanting this to be done.

Four sheets.

He lifted the cup. I heard him take a sip, placing it back down. "You look...like you've lost more weight."

I heard his disapproval.

Fuck his disapproval.

"I'm fine."

"Bullshit."

I looked up, knowing my eyes were heated. "I said I'm fine." I gritted my teeth.

He bit the inside of his cheek. "He still cares about you, you kno—"

"Stop!"

I had enough.

A storm was stirring in me, and I shot Tanner a glare. "What do you think I'm doing here, Tanner? Huh?" I motioned to the pile of papers. "I am trying to get my life back. I am trying to get out from under your brother's hold. I am trying to be myself, just myself. Not Riley Bello. Not a 411 Operative. Not Kai Bennett's lover. And definitely not a Bennett's asset, because that's what I am to your family right now. An asset. A thing, place, or person of value that you can use. I want out. So stop trying to tell me he gives a shit, because he doesn't. I might've been stupid enough to fall for his trick, but I'm not anymore. He doesn't give one shit about me, so do us both a favor and shut the fuck up while I'm finishing here."

I scrawled my name with an extra flourish on the third sheet. Two more to go.

Tanner was quiet. For a second. "I get that you want out. But he does care."

One more.

I ignored him. I ignored how I wanted to throw up. Again.

"I know he wouldn't want me to tell you that, but I don't care. He loves you."

I finished the last one just as he said that, and I locked my emotions down.

Shoving back my chair, my arms shook with my need to get out of here.

I was opening the door when he stopped me.

"You can sell all your homes. You can sell all your father's holdings, but you'll never be free of him."

I paused, my heart filling my throat.

I heard Tanner stand up, the chair being moved back. "He loves you, Riley. That means he's always going to know where you are, and he's always going to make sure you're safe. It's what he does for the rest of us."

My hand formed into a fist, pressing over my stomach.

I was tempted to tell him he was wrong, that Kai didn't love me, that Kai didn't love anyone. He only loved power. But then all the planning I'd done over the last few months would be in vain. Because no matter what, Tanner was still enslaved to his family name and to Kai.

So without responding, I left. One chapter of my life was officially closed.

• • •

Two weeks later, I was on the phone with Blade.

"Are you ready?" I asked.

"Yeah. We're ready to go. Are you?"

I looked at everything before me.

I'd sold the main house two days ago. The papers were signed. The new owners were excited. Every member of my father's house staff was unemployed, but they would get a surprise in the mail in a few days. The car was packed. Every item I wanted to take with me was in there, which wasn't a lot. I should've wept. I should've had more than that to show for a lifetime of memories, but I didn't. I looked at this as finally getting the clean break I should've had when I was fifteen.

I was ready. I was beyond ready.

My hand fell to my stomach, and picking up my last bag, I said into the phone, "I'm ready. I'll see you there."

"Will do. Official lockdown commencing: now."

He hung up. The dial tone rang through, and I left the phone behind. It didn't matter. I had bags of burners ready to go, and in thirty-two hours, I would meet up with Blade and Carol. It was a decision we'd all made. I had to trust they were genuinely okay doing all this. If not, it'd be all for nothing.

I drove to my attorney's office. I had another matter to finish. One last errand before I disappeared forever.

• • •

"Are you sure you want to do this?" My lawyer laid his hand over the last sheet for me to sign.

I was having déjà vu, but not from the second-guessing, from the paperwork. I had to sign a piece of paper for every single person my father had employed in his homes. I wasn't too worried about the company. Those employees would still have jobs. I knew Kai needed the trucking line to keep trucking. That was the whole point, and the other holdings were investments. They would remain active.

I nodded. "I'm sure."

"This is a lot of money you're giving away."

It didn't matter. Not to me. From my father's holdings and homes, I had acquired two hundred and seventy-three million dollars. I was giving it all away, except five million. Five was for me, just in case.

Each of those household staff members would receive five million. And I had divided the rest. Every domestic abuse shelter in Canada and the United States would receive a hundred thousand. After that, whatever was left, five percent would go to homeless shelters. Another five percent would go to any nonprofit fighting sex trafficking. And I left a percentage for lobbyists fighting sex trafficking at the legislative level. There were other stipulations and a good fund for my lawyers to take from for their own bills, but I wanted to do good.

This was my way of doing *some* good.

And signing my last piece of paperwork, I was officially done.

I had nothing hanging over me—not anymore. All the businesses and investments were gone. Every one of my father's houses had been sold. I'd taken care of his employees. Blade and Carol were safe. The last step was for me to disappear.

It was time.

I shook my lawyer's hand and slipped out. I had asked to keep this last meeting discreet, though he had wanted his entire law firm there to "send me off." I wouldn't allow it.

When I left his office, I was no one important. I was merely a client leaving, with a car full of memories and a full tank of gas, ready for a cross-country trip.

The girls at the front desk said their usual goodbyes, and I ducked my head as I waved. Pushing through the glass door, I stepped onto the street, and I was free. I felt it in every step I took, and I embraced it. I loved it. I lived it. It was going to keep me alive for the next decade.

And then I heard, "Riley."

CHAPTER SIXTY-FOUR

No. No. No.

I started shaking my head even before I turned to look. Then I had to laugh. He'd sent Jonah. Not Tanner. Seriously.

"Are you kidding me?" I flung a hand in his direction. "He sends you now? Tanner not enough for me? Or what? I need a secret genius to handle me? Is that why you're here? How's the girlfriend, Jonah? Kai know about her yet? Huh? Or…" I was going out on a limb. "About Tanner's gay lover?"

Yeah. I registered the shock on Jonah's face.

"Does Kai know about that too? Does the 'family'?" I gave him some air quotes and let my arms swing wide. Because I was done. Done. Done! Having Jonah show up on this day, at this moment, took the cake. The whole fucking cake.

I'd been so close to freedom.

Jonah straightened from the building's side where he'd been leaning as he waited for me. He cleared his throat, looking up and down the street and stepping closer. "Kai knows about Tanner's sexual preference. So do I." He stared at me. Hard. Not the way I'd known him to do so before. He resembled Kai now, at least in that moment. "We don't give a shit."

My soul was shriveling up.

He had no idea.

Freedom. I was so close and letting out a choking sound, I started to go around him.

He moved in a flash, grabbing onto my arm. "Kai wants to talk to you."

Three months.

He was three months too late.

I tried to keep my motivation going as I glared back at Jonah.

I didn't care if he was a future doctor. I didn't care how many times he had looked over me, made sure I was okay. I didn't think about Tanner or how I was scared how the rest of the council might feel about who he loved. I didn't consider Brooke, how she was as shattered as I had been, and how I was starting to miss her, just like I missed—NO!

I was not going there.

He didn't deserve it.

I swallowed down a lump. "No." *God.* I hung my head in anguish. "Let me go, Jonah." Falling forward, my forehead found his shoulder, and I stayed there.

Everything.

It was all for nothing.

He had found me. It was Jonah, for God's sake.

I'd wanted them to be my family at one point.

"Please." I whispered that over and over again, and he seemed surprised at first, stiffening.

Then he relaxed and just held me. He smoothed a hand down my hair and back, comforting me.

"Please let me go. You don't understand."

"Shhh." He bent his head down, his cheek resting against my forehead. He held me closer. "Shhhh. It's okay, Riley. It's going to be okay."

But it wasn't. And he didn't see it. He didn't know it.

Nothing would be okay.

He lived in the mafia world. I was trying to break free. He was choking off my last run at it, at actually and finally being free. He had no clue what he was stopping. Swallowing my own tears, I pulled back, shaking my head.

"You don't know." I pressed my fist to my mouth, only able to gasp at the pain. It was too overwhelming, flooding every inch of me.

I couldn't handle this.

I couldn't bear it.

"No, Jonah. You couldn't know."

The street sounds began to blur together.

The sidewalk started going in circles around me.

Desolation. Destruction. Decimation. The same word. The same effect, but I needed all of them to describe how I was feeling, because it was all done. It was all over.

I was starting to show. They would know. Kai would know, and there'd be no going back after this.

Dazed. Confused. I stepped away from Jonah. I didn't know where I was going, but I had to get away. I had to. One last attempt, even if it was a pathetic one.

I started up the sidewalk, and someone shoved me in the shoulder.

"Hey!" came Jonah's voice.

The guy cursed next to me, "Watch it!"

A second shove.

I cried out.

I lost my footing. The world was tipping upside down.

I tripped, trying to catch myself. I went farther than I'd wanted. I felt the brush of a car behind me, a parked car. I reached out for it, trying to steady myself.

My insides were on alert. Red. I was going nuts. I had to get a handle on this, or my worst nightmare would come true.

Gritting my teeth from the sheer force, I righted myself against my own dizziness. I clung to that car and waited for everything to settle around me. And then, still holding on, knowing I wasn't out of danger, but perilously close to it, I felt one last shove against me.

"Fuck! Sorry! Hey—He—"

A horn sounded.

I fell back, my hand flailing in the air, reaching for a stronghold, and then...

Pain.

CHAPTER
SIXTY-FIVE

I woke to a light beeping sound, my mouth parched, and a splitting headache.

"Ow." Lifting my head, I winced. Pain shot through me, and I almost doubled over. That hurt worse.

"Don't move."

No...

I kept my eyes closed, but I knew he was there. I'd felt him even before he spoke. I didn't want him here. If he was here, it wasn't good. There was only one thing that would bring him to my bedside.

God, no.

Please. Please.

I prayed silently, but then Kai spoke. "The baby's gone."

I didn't want to hear those words. My hands moved to my stomach. There'd been the slightest bump starting. It felt flat again.

"No," I choked out, curling in on myself. "No, no, no."

"Riley—" The bed dipped under his weight, and I whirled around.

"NO!" I shoved him. "Get out! Get away from me."

"Riley."

I turned away again. I didn't want to see his pain. I didn't want to see that he'd lost weight, how haggard he looked. Gaunt. I didn't want to see his obvious suffering, because no matter what, none of it mattered. He'd torn out my insides, unknowingly leaving behind a part of him. And now that small blessing was gone.

"No." I started to sob, hugging my pillow. "No."

He sighed from behind me, his voice cracking. "Riley."

"Go away!"

"No!"

The bed shifted even more. The sheet lifted, and I felt his hand on my back. He just placed it there a moment, his fingers trembling, and then he began to smooth it up and down. He grew more confident when I didn't yell or shrink away.

"I can't. I can't—not anymore. Not after this." He sounded so broken.

A tear leaked from my eye, and I hugged that pillow even tighter.

"By the time Jonah called and told me what happened, I was already coming. You have to know that. God. Do you even want to hear all of this?"

His hand paused, but began to move again after a moment. It glided up and down from my neck to my hip. Over and over.

"I thought I could keep you. I was too selfish to give you up, but watching you through my meeting with the council, then knowing how you were going to deal with your father, I got a glimpse into the future. I saw myself. I saw my mother. I saw you being stuck in this world. Me. Tanner. Brooke. Jonah. We were born into this world. We can't get out, even if we wanted to, but the level of ugliness this world thrives on, I don't want that for you."

I didn't want to hear this, but I couldn't move away. I was trying. I wanted to tell him to save it all, stow it, and I wanted to call for a nurse to make him leave.

But I did none of that.

I listened.

"It took me four days to let you go. I thought about it over and over. Every time I thought I could walk away from you, I'd end up reaching for you again, and then that last day—God." He expelled a ragged sound. His hand pressed harder against me, shaking. "You have to know I ripped my own heart out when I said those words. And they were lies. I just needed you to go, be free of this life as much as you could."

A sob caught in his voice. "I don't deserve you, Riley. The reasons you fought against me were the reasons I had to let you go. I had to. You might not think you deserve a normal life, but you do. You deserve that and more. You deserve the goddamn moon and stars and all the cheesy lines in the world, because it's true. You are my goodness. My redemption. My lifeline. Jesus, you woke something good in me that I never knew was there, and I realized every time I held you that I was destroying you. Little by little. The more goodness you gave to me, the more darkness I gave back. I was changing you. I *have* changed you, and now this."

His hand jerked, but then began rubbing in a slow circle. "I knew you wanted out. I knew about the houses, but I didn't realize you were intending to disappear until the Network called."

I tensed. "What?"

My chest squeezed again. If the Network called him, then...

"Your friends tried to leave. They caught 'em and alerted me. Jonah was already down here for another matter, so I sent him to stop you. He tried to tell you I was coming back, that I had things to tell you, but he said some homeless guys started fighting right next to you, and you got pushed."

He stopped for a moment, then spoke again in a raspy voice. "I was on the plane when he called and said you were in the hospital. The doctor told me about the baby, and holy fuck, Riley." His hand paused, trembling again. "Holy fuck, Riles. If I had lost you and the baby? Both of you?"

Every word tore at my soul.

The baby. He or she—I never found out which one.

The baby was gone.

I sobbed again; I couldn't stop. Kai lifted me and cradled me in his arms.

A part of me wanted to resist him. He had hurt me so much, but feeling his tears on my skin, I gave in. I didn't have the strength to pull away. I just folded, pressed my head into his chest and cried.

He wrapped his arms around me, moving to rest against the headboard. He held me as if I were our lost child.

· · ·

Eventually I cried myself out.

The nurse found us and went for the doctor. After a moment he came in, casting Kai a wary look as he moved to look out the window. His head bent, his hands in his pockets, he might've looked like he wasn't listening, but I knew he was. He took in every question the doctor asked me, every vital they checked. All of it.

A car had hit my hip, not enough to crush me, but it sent my body flying in the air. As I landed, my stomach had hit another car parked along the street, which cushioned my fall, and then my head hit the side panel as I slid to a heap beside it.

I had bruises everywhere, a concussion. The impact with the second car had caused me to miscarry. They'd been concerned about internal bleeding, but after surgery, everything was patched up. Except the baby. Except the reason I had tried to leave everything behind.

That was the real reason behind getting out of my father's business holdings, the reason I wanted to sell all the homes. The baby was why I needed to disappear.

Because my child would've grown up as a Bennett. He or she would've lived in the Bennett shadows, and I didn't want that. It was the reason Kai had tried to let me go, and it was why I'd been trying to vanish.

I'd been close, but no. Thinking about it, I'd been sloppy.

If I'd truly wanted to disappear, I would've packed a bag, taken as much cash as possible, and left in the middle of the night. I knew how to leave, but instead, I'd been leaving a trail as wide as the ocean for Kai to find me.

Had I even wanted to go? Or had I wanted him to come for me?

I hurt from so much thinking. Hell. It hurt just to breathe.

My child. I ached at the loss.

Hearing another choking sob slip out, Kai turned from the window.

"Doctor, can we have a moment."

It was no request. It was a command, and I heard one of the nurses sigh before footsteps shuffled over the floor, and the door closed behind them all.

"Riley," Kai whispered.

I shrank back against the bed, shaking my head.

He ignored me, sliding his arms under the covers and lifting me, blankets and all, into his lap. He cradled me again, holding me through the night.

• • •

"The first moment I knew I loved you was when I saw you fighting against my guards and Tanner—that first day I told them to kidnap you."

Kai was curled up behind me the next night as we lay on our sides on the bed. One of his legs rested between mine and his arm snaked around me, holding my hand just under my breasts. His breath warmed the back of my neck, teasing my hair.

He laughed softly. "There you were, in those nurse scrubs. Tanner got into the car, and you exploded out within two seconds. Man, you were fast. I've seen people fight, but you had such life, determination. You were going to take them down with you. That was the only way they were taking you."

My heart ached, right under where our hands were entwined, but I couldn't stop a small smile. "I didn't know you were there."

"I was. I got called away for a crisis, so that's why we ended up meeting later, but I was there. I was supposed to stay in our vehicle, watch it all go down, but when I saw you fighting..." He tensed. His voice dropped. "There was no one else I wanted touching you. I didn't want you hurt."

The shadow. Someone had been coming from the side, and fast.

"That was you? You put me out?"

"Yeah." Regret tinged his voice. He squeezed my hand. "I didn't want to hurt you, but I needed you, and I didn't want anyone else hurting you, or even touching you. That was me."

"Brooke said she stopped asking for updates on me after I went into the 411. She said you were the one who kept watching me, not for her."

His arms tightened, hugging me before relaxing again. "Yeah. You, you affected me the day we came to tell Brooke about Cord. I saw something in you as you held her when we drove up. It was the same the day we kidnapped you. There was such fight in you. It amazed me. I had seen so many wither in this lifestyle, crumble from the weight—and I'm not just talking mafia. I'm talking heartache in general. I knew your past. We'd researched you because of your dad's connection to us. That's why you were put with Brooke. My dad did that. If Bruce Bello did something out of line, he could threaten his little girl's life.

"After a while I realized how much your dad didn't give a shit about you, and that pissed me off. Parents are supposed to love and protect their kids. Your dad didn't do that. Maybe I felt like you were already a part of us, just knowing that about you. Most other mafia families love their kids like anyone else does. Some don't, but some do. It's a shit part of life, but that's how it is. Some get unlucky with parents like I did, and you did.

"Anyway, I don't know what I was expecting when we drove up that day. Nothing, I guess. Just thought you'd be like all the other girls Brooke befriended, but you weren't. There was a sadness in you, but there was more. So much more. Fight. Survival. A fuck-you look that I knew you gave to everyone, even if you didn't know it. Hell, it might've been why your mom shipped you off. She knew you'd give it to your dad one day, and she couldn't protect you against him."

I shook my head, amazed. "I hated you after that day."

He laughed again, a deep baritone coming from his chest. "I know. That made me like you even more. I liked that you weren't scared of us. When you gave me that 'fuck you' look, I was proud. I thought, *Good. Finally someone who's strong enough to help*

Brooke. I knew you'd be there for her after that, no matter what, even if my sister didn't deserve it."

He shifted, sitting up as I rolled to my back. He loomed over me, tucking his elbow on the bed and resting his head on his hand. He met my gaze before trailing down to my lips. He traced a line with his finger over my lips, my chin, my throat, and between my breasts, encircling one of them, cupping it and running over my nipple. His eyes darkened. Dipping his head, I closed my eyes as he pushed up my hospital gown. I felt his mouth cover me there. His tongue circled my nipple, right where his thumb had been, and as he kept kissing me, his hand smoothed down my stomach.

My body warmed, reacting to his touch. He pushed some of the pain aside.

"God, Riley." He raised his head again, meeting my eyes. "I love you. I think a part of me actually fell in love with you on the steps of your school. Another part fell when I saw you fighting my brother and our guards. And I kept falling for you every time you resisted me, until I was gone. I was completely in love with you when you fought me in the elevator." He grinned. "Stop fucking fighting. You remember that?"

I did, and I might've laughed at the memory, but I ached.

I wanted his touch. I didn't know how I was even feeling anything because of the drugs, but his touch was healing. I just wanted more of him, as if he could still make it all right again.

That was wishful thinking, or wishful feeling.

Tears blinded me, and I gasped. "Kai."

He cursed under his breath, moving to hold me. Curling around me, spooning me, he pressed a kiss to my nape.

I reached for his hand on my waist, feeling...feeling... I felt the beginning of something right. I didn't want that to go away.

I'd begun to fall back asleep when I heard him say again, "I love you."

I couldn't answer him, not yet. Even though he was making me feel better, there was still too much hurt. So instead, I entwined our fingers, sliding mine against his.

He squeezed my hand. I settled back against him, and I fell asleep.

CHAPTER SIXTY-SIX

There were whispers from the nurses as I was bundled up in a wheelchair, getting ready to leave. They'd been whispering for the last few days. Kai never left my side, and his guards never left him, so it was a nice circus because of that. I knew the doctor was slightly scared of Kai, but who wouldn't be?

I hadn't thought anyone knew who he was—I mean, he wasn't a celebrity—until I heard one nurse telling another outside in the hallway, "That's him. I'm telling you."

"What?" Her friend had laughed, scoffing. "No way. Get real."

"I'm telling you. It's him. It was his sister who was missing a while back. You remember, the mafia princess. They showed his picture on the news. He's in the mafia."

"Come on," her friend had murmured, sounding slightly less incredulous. "What are the chances?"

"Chances are good, Silvia. I'm telling you, it's him." A pause. "Look! There it is."

"Oh my God." Her friend had sucked in some air. "Holy shit. Holy shit!"

A hiss back. "I know!"

"Holy—"

Kai had been curled up behind me that night, but he'd moved swiftly and silently. Easing out of bed, he walked to the door. "I'm aware that rumors and gossip are unavoidable, but move it along so you're not disturbing my woman's sleep."

They had both gasped.

And I guess they hadn't moved quickly enough, because he'd snapped out, quietly, "Now."

I'd heard them hurrying along as he crawled back under the covers, his arms wrapping around me. "Sleep, Riles. We leave soon."

Riles.

The first time he called me that, I hadn't processed it. I did now, and I liked it. A lot.

After that, the looks of intrigue, fear, lust, and desperation had been more prominent among the nursing staff. The only person who didn't seem to care was a nurse aid. She always had a cheerful wave as she refilled the medical supplies and brought back new nightgowns for me, though I didn't use them. It didn't matter to her. She took out the ones left behind, replaced them with the new ones, and repeated the process the next day.

For some reason, I knew I'd miss her the most, though she barely spoke a word to us.

Kai was conferring with the doctor outside in the hallway, and a large number of nurses were in the room, all watching as he came back in after shaking the doctor's hand.

I noticed the look of relief on the doctor's face as he poked his head in and smiled at me. "You're in good hands, Riley. I've conferred with Dr. Bennett, and he'll be keeping me updated with your progress." That was news to me. "You're going to be fine. Have a safe trip back to Vancouver."

He darted down the hallway after that.

I looked at Kai. "Vancouver?"

"You cut all your ties here." He frowned a little. "I thought you'd want to go back?"

We hadn't talked about the after—my life since he'd destroyed me. We hadn't even fully talked about what had happened between us. I'd listened to his proclamations, but I hadn't had time to digest any of it. The loss of her—that's what the doctor told us when I asked—hadn't fully set in either.

Kai waited once we had left the hospital and were safe in the back of the SUV before he brought it up again.

"Did you not want to go to Vancouver?"

Did I?

I frowned. "I don't know, actually."

He rested his head back, watching me. "We can go wherever you want. Just... I'm going with you. That's the only stipulation." His eyes darkened. They were fierce. "I tried walking from you once. It nearly killed me. I won't be doing it again, so that's out of the question."

His words warmed me.

He took my hand, and I gazed down at our joined fingers on my lap. I felt a tear falling.

"I was going to Montana." I told him everything. "It wasn't too far over the border. Blade and Carol were going to meet me there, and after the fireworks settled, they were going to reach back out to the Network. They were going to try to work with them again, just from where we were. That was a few years down the road. We all thought it'd take that long. There was a cabin on a lake. I had enough cash with me to buy it, and we had the papers all ready. I was never going to let you know about her."

His hand spasmed against mine, but unlike the last few days, I held him tight. He tried to withdraw, but I clamped down and made sure he was meeting my gaze. I wanted him to see inside of me.

"I love you too."

His eyes turned sad.

I knew why.

"I started that first night when you slept with me in the same bed, even though you knew I wanted to kill you. Then I did try, and you caught my knife, but you did nothing. I fell a little more. Then you called me 'slicer.' Then I found out you won't let your family fly because you love them that much, and how you know it's ridiculous, but you don't care..."

I went down the list. It was long, but I told him every moment he'd taken a piece of my wall away.

"You gave me the bigger room at the hotel. You let me run from you at the warehouse, but I knew I was safe, even if you caught me. Part of me wanted you to catch me. When you let Blade go. How I knew, no matter what, that you would protect me."

My voice dropped to a whisper. "You made me feel special, and loved, and beautiful, and you did all of it without saying a word. There were no proclamations. I just knew. I felt it. It was everything I never felt growing up. You knew me before I realized it. Coming into my life, shattering my walls, taking me, and making me a different woman—you challenged me. You still challenge me. Your life, what you do, you're as captive to it as your siblings are. You're a prisoner to your own last name."

My heart started to beat harder. It hurt. There was something I needed to know. It hurt to say it, but I had to know.

I held his hand tight and never looked away, the importance of this question pressing heavily against my chest. "If you'd found out about her, would you have let me stay away? Or would you have come to get us?"

He didn't answer, just held my gaze.

A wall slid away from him. I hadn't even known it was there. He had been letting me see him this whole time, but that wall, it was his last one. I saw the love shining back. It was overwhelming, and I was stunned by it.

I had known, but I hadn't known how much.

Then a shadow crossed his face, and I ached.

He ran his thumb over over my knuckles. "I know the romantic answer here is that I would've come for you no matter what, but that's not the truth. You were leaving to give our child a life away from this world, so no, I would've let you live your life there."

I turned away, a bittersweetness filling me.

He shifted, his hand catching my chin and turning me to him again.

"But I would've watched you," he said fiercely. "You're right. I am a prisoner to this life so I would've watched you from the other side. And I would've loved you from afar. I would've done anything in my power to make sure you and our daughter had the life you wanted. It hurt so much when I found out about the baby, but I understand why. I do."

He stopped, still so stricken. His thumb rubbed over my bottom lip, and he gripped my hand with other. "But I can't let you go. The first time I tried, it nearly killed me. Please don't ask me to do it. I love you too much. I need you too much."

My hand rose to cover his as he cupped my face. "No." I reached for him, cradling his cheek. "I love you too much to walk away."

He nodded, his forehead resting against mine. There were tears in his eyes. "I wish I had known about her from the beginning. I would've loved her so much. I do love her so much."

"I know. Me too."

Tears slid down my face, but I reached for him, and he was there.

Meeting me halfway.

EPILOGUE

Looking down the bank of the Mississippi River, I met the eyes of a boat captain I'd met five years earlier. This time, instead of ferrying the ex-guard Kai had decided to hide and not execute, he had a woman and two children—another thwarted mafia hit. When Kai had received the news of their planned hit, he'd opted to save them instead, hiding them and sending them up through the Mississippi, taking them the entire way to where I was waiting.

I waited, cloaked in darkness along with Blade and Carol, for the survivors. I stepped forward to see it was a shallow-bottom boat. They must've changed to this one when the river started narrowing. It was just sturdy enough to glide over the top of the water. It had no engine, and I eyed the captain's arms. He set aside the paddles, giving me a nod in greeting as I caught the end of the boat and pulled them to the bank. I got it as close as I could, but we still weren't quite there. Large boulders blocked the way, but this was the closest point we could find to get them to a waiting vehicle.

The bottom of the boat scraped over the rocks, but it was cold. Even a small amount of water on someone's shoes could end in disaster on a winter day in Itasca State Park. The temperature had dropped dramatically. By tomorrow this end of the river would be frozen over.

"Any problems I should know about?" I asked.

I wore thigh-high waders and a sturdy coat, and we had a caravan of SUVs just down the trail that would blast the heat on high as soon as we got in.

He shook his head. "No. We were searched by a game warden, but that was farther south around St. Cloud." He jumped out of the boat, but without the waders. Ignoring my look, he picked up one of the kids, carrying her to the bank. He did that with each of them, helping the woman last as I continued emptying the boat of their bags.

These days my help with the 411 Network was completely off the books.

No one knew about it—and by no one, I meant literally this boat captain, the few guards Kai trusted to me, and Kai himself. Blade and Carol weren't even here officially on behalf of 411, though they did still work for them. When they got back to work, those two would purposely mislabel files and shuffle their paperwork into the system. So after this, they would have new names and an entire Network behind them to help. The Network just didn't know about it.

Kai insisted it had to be this way. He had enough people inside the 411 Network to not trust them, but this was my way of helping—Kai's too. The boat captain was the only one Kai trusted, and Blade and Carol were the only ones I trusted, so meeting in areas like Itasca State Park after it was closed had become a part of the business.

Once everyone was wrapped up in the waiting blankets, I eyed the captain's wet pants and boots. "You can't boat back like that." I grabbed one of the blankets and held it out to him. "Here. Take that. Press the button, and it'll heat you."

He took it, then waved me on. "You get going." He was already splashing back to the boat. Gripping the edge, he pulled himself in. He bent down, and I heard a few thuds as he seemed to be changing boots and socks, putting on dry ones instead. I could hear crinkling sounds before he straightened, reaching for the paddle again. "I got warmers in there now. It'll tide me over. I got a buddy's fishing cabin not far from here. Just a few miles back."

"You sure?"

"I'm sure. Once I get enough depth, I'll put on the small motor and make it go faster. I'm good. Trust me." He was already starting to row away. He held up a hand. "Tell the boss I'll be ready for the next shipment. You be safe too, missus."

Safe.

I loved one of the fiercest mafia bosses there was. I helped hide victims he knew his rivals had targeted. Safe had gone out the window the day I chose to remain beside Kai Bennett. Then again, I had no choice. I loved him, no matter what. Enemies would come and go—the woman who aligned herself with Blade once upon a time, the man who had taken Kai's plane hostage for a brief moment. Those were only two enemies that had been a blip in our life together so far. I'd been hiding from my father before that. Kai had murdered his.

Safe was a word that didn't exist for me anymore. *Smart. Cunning. Cautious.* Those were words I now lived by. Or I had—my hand touched on my stomach—until this little one came into the world. This was my last *errand*, the term I'd used when I worked for the 411 Network. *Hiding*—maybe that was a better term. But helping people like this live, that was my job.

"We're ready to go."

Blade nodded, but stayed back as Carol led the family down the path. He grinned. Even in the moonlight, I could see the fondness.

"I'm surprised Kai let you come out," he said. "You're what? Eight months?"

I grunted, slipping off the waders and folding them into a watertight bag. Grabbing two warmers from my pocket, I crumpled them up before slipping them into my sneakers. If I had to run, my feet would be extra toasty this way. Blade took the bag of waders and slung it over his shoulder.

We headed down the path in darkness, keeping our flashlights in hand in case we needed them. Until then, we'd use the little bit of moon that filtered through the trees to light the way. It wasn't a long trek.

"I feel like I'm ten months." I laughed. "I'm about ready to pop, and no, he didn't want me to come." I had insisted. The little girl was the same age our daughter would've been.

"Well…" Blade said as we drew close to the two SUVS and a van he and Carol were using. Carol was just closing the sliding door. "Looks like we're ready to go."

She headed back to us, raising her arms.

I stepped in for a hug.

She patted my back, holding me tight and rocking us back and forth. "I miss you. I wish we were doing more of this with you."

I smiled, stepping back. "I know. We'll do another. Time will go fast. It'll be before you know it, and you're welcome for Thanksgiving."

"You'll be back in Vancouver?"

I nodded. "We're heading back in the morning. Brooke and Eric got married the other week, so we're in transition from there to back home."

"Really? Brooke got married?"

I laughed. "It was the social event of Toronto. She's happy."

"That's good." Carol smiled, exchanging a look with Blade.

I knew that look. After another round of hugs, it was time to go. Before letting me go, Blade whispered in my ear, "Carol gave me the go-ahead to tell you…" He paused, leaning back, his smile so wide. "We're together."

"What?!"

"Officially."

My mouth dropped, but then I was hugging him again, and I squealed louder than I should have. "Oh my God! That's amazing. Carol!"

She blushed, grinning over her shoulder as she got behind the steering wheel. She waved to me, but she wouldn't get out to talk to me again. They had to go. Waiting around with survivors was just never a smart idea.

Blade cast a glance at the SUVs waiting for me. "I know you're in safe hands."

"You're happy?" I asked him.

He nodded. "I'm happy. Truly happy." He smoothed back some of my hair and pressed a kiss to my forehead. "I know you're a Bennett now, but you're always a member of our family too. Don't forget. We both love you."

I blinked back tears, feeling warmth all over.

I grabbed for his hand, holding it a second. "Take care of her. Take care of them." One last squeeze. "Take care of yourself too."

"I know." His gaze went to my stomach. "And take care of my future nephew."

He stepped back. I let go, my hands going to my stomach. "I will." And as if he'd heard us, my little guy gave me a swift kick inside.

Blade got in with a final wave, and the van headed out. They'd turn left onto a back road out of the park, and our SUVs would go right. I didn't know where they were going after that, but that was the whole purpose of the Network. I would never see that family again. And that was a good thing.

I headed to one of our SUVs, and as I stepped to the door, the guard opened it for me.

There he was, waiting for me.

Kai was in the back seat, and he grinned, pushing aside his laptop. "Hey."

"Hey." I smiled in greeting, sliding in. The door closed behind me. I knew the guard would get inside, that the SUVs would all start to leave, but I wasn't paying attention. I didn't stop moving as soon as I got inside. I went right in, sliding all the way until I was in Kai's arms and his mouth was on mine.

I was with my family.

Word of mouth and reviews go a long way,
so if you enjoyed *Bennett Mafia,* please leave a review!
I truly appreciate them so much.

For more books and more mafia stories, go to
www.tijansbooks.com

ACKNOWLEDGEMENTS

Man. This book. Guys, this book came out of nowhere to me. It started from just a scene that occurred in my head. I don't even think that scene got put in the book. It was where Kai wanted Jonah to do something for him and Jonah looked at him and said, "I'm a doctor." Then Kai returned with, "You're a Bennett." And that was it. That started the spark for this book. Then came along an idea I had of a network where their sole purpose was to help hide those in situations where the law can't help them. I actually wrote another short story titled 411 that was referenced in this book. It's super short and I'll probably put it up for free reading on my website or I'll load it for a shorter read later on. I haven't decided, but here we are.

I genuinely hope you guys loved Riley and Kai's story. As of right now, this is a stand-alone, just because I'm reluctant to commit to a series when I have so many other projects waiting for me to tackle them.

I tried to stay true to the characters. They did some seriously shitty things that I don't personally condone, and yeah, that's the first time I've really felt like I needed to put that disclaimer there. Lol!

Thank you to my entire team of beta readers, admins, proofreaders, Jessica! Thank you to my agent. Thank you to the readers in Tijan's Crew. You guys give me inspiration on days when I'm exhausted and need a little pep in my step. Thank you!

Tijan

CPSIA information can be obtained
at www.ICGtesting.com
Printed in the USA
LVHW091809191221
706641LV00032B/188